Slanted Light

Also by Teddy Jones

Jackson's Pond, Texas

Well Tended

Nowhere Near: Stories

Slanted Light

a novel

By

Teddy Jones

NEW YORK, NEW YORK

Publisher's Cataloging-in-Publication Data
Names: Jones, Teddy, author
Title: *Slanted Light* : a novel / Teddy Jones
Description: New York, NY: Midtown Publishing, 2020
Identifiers: LCCN: 2020940455| ISBN 978-1-62677-025-6 (hardback)| ISBN 978-1-62677-022-5 (pbk)|ISBN-978-1-62677-023-2 (e-book).
Subjects: LCSH Marriage—Fiction.| Man-woman relationships—Fiction. |Family—Fiction.|Texas—Fiction. | Women—Fiction. | BISAC FICTION/ Small Town & Rural-Fiction. FICTION/Women. FICTION/Family Life/General.
Classification: LCC: PS3610.0632 553 2020 |DDC 813.6-dc23

"*The artist must learn that it's not light itself—its intensity, its quality, its direction—that elevates art above mediocrity. Rather it's how the light touches the subject, what it reveals and what remains hidden.*"   Professor Barker, Studio Art 3328

Class notes, Willa Lofland
University of Texas
Fall Semester, 1951

Praise for *Slanted Light*

"Reading *Slanted Light* is like falling into some beguiling, if unsettling, dream that you don't ever want to wake up from. Teddy Jones loves her characters and makes us love them, too. And she knows that every story is many stories, and at the heart of every story is a secret waiting to be revealed. Claire and J. D. Havlicek's marriage is in turmoil, their children are in pain, and their very way of life in Jackson's Pond is threatened. When Claire embraces her vulnerability, circumstances begin to change. This is what we talk about when we talk about hope. And this is the heartfelt, redemptive, and irresistible novel you've been waiting for. So find yourself a comfy chair, send the kids to the sitters', and call in sick to work because once you start reading *Slanted Light*, you won't want to stop." John Dufresne author of *No Regrets, Coyote*.

"*Slanted Light* does exactly what readers love in a novel: swoops us into situations that involve our hearts and imaginations and leaves us highly satisfied. These wonderful characters, vividly drawn against the small-town and Texas ranch life setting, come to life with the perfect combination of tension, humor and affection. A fine read to be savored." Anne Hillerman, *New York Times* best-selling author of *Rock With Wings* and other Leaphorn, Chee, and Manuelito novels

"In *Slanted Light*, Teddy Jones has crafted a lyrical continuation of her Jackson's Pond series centering on the Jackson/Banks/Havlicek ranching family in the rugged panhandle of modern-day Texas. Economic pressures and competing crises contribute to complicated family dynamics. Secrets, pride, temptations, and misunderstandings spring from these stressors and pull at the very fabric of their relationships. Thanks to the author's astute insight into the psychology of human behavior, her knowledge of medicine and the corporate-driven system of healthcare delivery, along with the essential details of running a cattle operation during a four-year drought, *Slanted Light* is a compelling and authentic tale sure to whet your appetite to hear more from the resilient and inspiring folks who reside in Jackson's Pond, Texas." Sue Boggio, author, with Mare Pearl, of *A Growing Season* and *Long Night Moon*

Acknowledgments

Writing colleagues who offer candid critique and enthusiastic encouragement are treasures indeed. I am fortunate to have found my tribe of such good writers. "Thank you" seems hardly adequate, and public recognition on this page is a meager expression of my gratitude. Until you are better paid, please know I value you each and all above measure.

Martha Burns, my steadfast first reader, labored through each page, every paragraph, in each iteration of this work. The members of the 2015 Master Class in Novel conducted by John Dufresne at the UNM Taos Summer Writers' Conference: Richard Hillman, Cully Perlman, Maura Rae, Frances Burke, and David Norman steered me toward improvement.

Since the time that the UNM Conference was disbanded, the group that has continued with John Dufresne's guidance in annual Master Classes in Taos has included Jill Coupe, Peter Stravlo, and Karen Kravit, in addition to Cully Perlman, David Norman, and Scott Archer Jones. We have stuck together, and I am a better writer for their contributions to my work. Elizabeth Trupin-Pulli, literary agent, has become a vital factor in my continued development. And after eight years of his guidance in workshops, I now think of John Dufresne as the mentor most vital to my writing.

Supportive family, friends, and acquaintances will not be named here for fear of omitting someone. But I hope that the thanks I heap on them for attending readings, for buying my books, and for cheering me on help them know that I truly appreciate them.

Thanks also to the team at MidTown Publishing for continuing to believe in my work.

Finally, and daily, I give thanks for my husband, Jim Bob Jones. His encouragement and good humor make every day a party.

Teddy Jones
Friona, Texas
2020

Slanted Light

CHAPTER 1
Downhill

No one else could have heard what Willa said to him. He'd loaded the last suitcase in the Suburban and situated the drink cooler on the back seat between Amy and Jay Frank. Claire had already said her goodbyes, fit a pillow between her head and the passenger window, and closed her eyes. Willa, his grandmother-in-law, and more importantly, his partner and mentor, beckoned him with a twitch of her left index finger.

He moved to where she stood, a bit apart from the rest of the family waiting there to see them off. "Yes, ma'am?"

She said, "There's something I want you to keep in mind. I know things aren't easy now. When there were hard times, Frank would say, 'Don't be surprised if things get worse before they get better. But eventually, one way or another, things will get better.' That's what Frank believed and you know how wise he was."

J.D. said, "I'll keep that in mind."

She said, "It's important." She focused on him, holding him in a long, steady gaze. "He would be so proud of what you've done with the ranch, for the family."

J.D. wanted to tell her something, but all that came out was. "Thank you." And that was sort of mumbled. Then he hugged her, got the vehicle started, and headed downhill toward home.

At the time, he thought she'd given him that little pep talk to keep his spirits up going into this fourth year of drought. Here it was the beginning of September, 2013 and no sign of it letting up. But you never could tell, with Willa. She didn't waste words. He'd always thought she had some direct line, that she knew the future when others only saw the small details right in front of them. Maybe she had seen that some things were unraveling in the Havlicek household.

"Daddy, I need to go to the bathroom." It was Amy, from the back seat. When had she started calling him Daddy again? He hadn't heard that word, that little girl sound, in at least a year.

J. D. looked at Claire, crumpled in the passenger seat

pretending she was asleep. He knew she wasn't. She usually dealt with such things, anticipating and seeing that their kids took care of those matters before bathroom stops or starvation turned urgent. She'd gone off duty, it looked like.

"It's not far to Las Vegas. We'll stop there."

"How far? I don't know if I can wait." Amy's tone, belonging to a six-year-old, not a young teenager, made every word an accusation. They'd left Taos early, hurried the kids right after breakfast. His choice. And they'd made good time until now, all the way down through Angel Fire and the Mora Valley. If he stopped, he could make up the time when they hit I 40.

"Not far."

Her sigh mocked a groan. Sounded like a prisoner chained in the back seat. But she'd been on her best behavior all weekend, not a single slammed door or argument about clothes or food. He'd give her that. Straightened up her act for her great-grandmother's eighty-third birthday party.

Claire told him, every time he threatened to ground their daughter for a door slamming episode or backtalk, that the start of puberty was difficult for girls, that moodiness was part of it. "She'll grow out of it. We just have to set limits and stick with them. And live over it."

Claire always managed to sound like she knew what she was talking about. She'd usually been the one to deal with their daughter's Jekyll and Hyde days until the last few months. But he'd seen her grit her teeth quite a few times, too. And then she turned too busy with her two clinics and whatever else she had on her mind. It seemed as if she'd signed off, and not just about Amy.

Las Vegas, New Mexico, took its time waking up on Labor Day. As he slowed to match the posted speed limit, J.D. watched for a convenience store. The sun gouged at his left eye from over the tops of low buildings along the road—a dentist's office, a motel wearing a neon No Vacancy sign with the y missing, a fortune teller's storefront, a pet grooming place. "There's a gas station, Daddy. Stop there. I have to go, now!"

He felt in the between-seat console for his sunglasses and

passed the seedy looking, no-brand station. Amy reached over the seat and shook Claire's shoulder. "Mother, wake up. Make Daddy stop."

The Allsup's he intended to stop at was another block south. Set limits, stick to them, live over it. Apparently that meant turning deaf—Claire barely stirred. She didn't say a word.

Jay Frank, plugged into earbuds, holding his phone ever since they'd left Taos, occupied the other half of the back seat, probably playing a game. Phone reception was spotty out here. He seldom complained about anything but watched everything. J.D. thought of him as his ten-year-old shadow.

He made a turn into the Allsup's parking lot. Before he switched off the ignition, Amy was out and fast-walking toward the store's front door. Claire sat up straight. He saw her shake her head, like she disagreed. She said, "Before you ask, no, I don't know what that's all about." Still staring straight ahead, she said, "Do we need gas?"

"I filled up yesterday evening. Are you getting out?"

Claire opened her door. J.D. turned toward Jay Frank, now unplugged from his phone, caught him staring at Claire, thought again about a shadow. "Come on, son, let's all use the bathroom here. Maybe we won't have to stop again before we get home."

Amy passed them on her way out, wiping at her face with a paper towel, her head down. She didn't answer when he asked if she needed anything else.

Back in the Suburban, J.D. took a sip of the coffee he'd bought and waited, watching Claire through the windshield. Standing in line at the checkout counter holding a soft drink and a package of peanut butter crackers, her profile looked unfamiliar—her body thin, face planed sharp, all of the soft curves whetted away. Maybe it was a trick of the fluorescent lights or the horizontal crack that bisected the windshield.

He checked the rearview mirror and saw Jay Frank keeping an eye on Amy. She busied herself creating a nest of two pillows, one between her and the cooler between her and her brother and the other against the door. Hemming herself in. Claire shut the passenger side door and J.D. pulled out and drove south again.

Used to be, long drives across pasture land or farming areas pleased him, particularly when the whole family rode along. He'd felt sure and sort of important, maybe the way a pioneer man taking his family west had felt, like he was bound to and able to protect them. He'd even sometimes imagined them all in peril from harsh weather or renegade bands roaming the plains. He always warded off danger and delivered them safely to their new homestead, driving a team of eight mules, the front wagon in a long train. Too many John Ford movies.

The turn east onto I 40 outside Santa Rosa didn't bring a comment from anyone in the vehicle; reminded him he wasn't the head of a hopeful band of westward bound homesteaders. Just as well. He'd probably have been happier as the scout, riding alone ahead of the green settlers from the east. He'd have grown up knowing the ways of the rugged country, living alone, just he and his horse.

A cattle truck blew by on his left, running empty, the driver hurrying back for another load or rushing to get home, probably talking on his cell phone. When he let himself think about it, he'd get depressed at the number of loads of cows and calves he'd seen hauled off the Panhandle as the drought worsened in the past three years. Only the fact that he'd thinned his cow herd, keeping the healthiest and best, and had a good looking group of young bulls to sell off this month had kept him from having to liquidate like some folks had. They would be years building back up their herds, if they ever did. Some of them would convert to feeder and stocker operations and never get the chance again to breed selectively and see the results all through gestation to the day the calf dropped, and then to watch that calf grow into a prize bull or heifer, or a steer destined to be prime beef.

Willa's advice, to stick with older equipment as long as it could be maintained and not to be tempted to invest in big irrigation, had seemed old-fashioned when everyone else went with new and bigger. But now he was thankful he'd followed her lead. Even if it had been necessary to spend the reserve down below what they had planned, they had done better than break even every year. She had trusted him enough to bring him into the ranch when he wasn't much more than a kid. He wasn't going to disappoint her.

Damn, this part of New Mexico looked dryer than West Texas,

if that was possible. He accelerated to seventy-six and set the cruise control. Another four hours to go, if nobody whined for another stop. Lots needed doing at home.

Just after he made it to Amarillo and turned south again, Claire stirred and sat up straight in the seat. She ran her fingers through her hair, rubbed at her eyes. "I guess I needed that nap."

"More like a full night's sleep."

"I'll drive if you want me to. If you want to take a nap."

"Not necessary. I've got plenty to think about. I need to stay awake."

She probably didn't hear what he'd said, digging around in that tote bag of work she carried with her everywhere. With her stethoscope sticking out the top. Still pulling papers out, stacking them on her lap, she said, "There's no other way. I'm going to have to start working Saturday mornings every week."

Maybe she was talking to herself. She never asked his opinion about anything to do with the clinics. Seldom told him anything about them unless he asked. And he'd quit that about the third time she told him she "couldn't ethically discuss patients." It wasn't like he'd asked about patients' personal information. He'd mostly just been trying to make conversation. People at the coffee shop passed along more about other people's health in one morning than she'd ever let him in on at home. Except that one time, early on, before she opened the first clinic. She wanted to know how he felt about the risk, her having more responsibility, the legal set up the lawyer had recommended to separate the clinic from their personal property for liability purposes. At the time, he'd been impressed by her knowledge. He recalled her asking if he had any objections they needed to discuss. He couldn't think of any; he wanted her to have the opportunity to accomplish what she dreamed of.

It was only fair. Willa had given him that same chance when she made him her manager, raw and young as he was. Then later, she made him manager and full partner in charge of and profiting from the Jackson family's years of building the ranch.

He concentrated, half on driving, the other half thinking about plans for the bull sale. This would be the first one, an old-fashioned "invite buyers onto the ranch and show them a good time" kind of sale. A few of the other ranches, bigger ones, had been doing them forever. Now was a good time for the Jackson Ranch to start. Some of the people in the Cattle Association had been talking to him about running for some office in the organization. Couldn't hurt to get noticed for a nice sale, even if it would be a small one.

Claire said something. He hadn't heard anything until she said, "What do you think?"

"I didn't hear you."

"You must be losing your hearing."

"Maybe. What did you say?"

"Never mind." She shook her head like he was some sort of hopeless case. Hell of an attitude for someone who'd work herself into the ground for other people.

The exit for Plainview snuck up on him. He had to slow from seventy to forty in a stretch about a block long. Claire stomped the floorboard with her right foot like she had a brake. Never uttered a word, just gave him a look that said, "You fool. You're supposed to take care of us, not kill us."

"Stop it, Jay Frank!" J.D. saw in the rearview that Jay Frank and the cooler had both fallen into Amy's pillow-protected territory.

"I couldn't help it. Dad was going too fast."

J.D. said, "Amy, settle down. It wasn't his fault. You'll live."

Now that they were both awake, J. D. knew the chances were the kids would want to use the bathroom or eat, even if they were only fifty miles from home. "I can stop at the Dairy Queen. Anyone want to?"

Both of the kids said no. Claire shook her head, then said, "I need to get home. Lots to do. I have to go to the clinic this afternoon."

"Why? They're both closed."

"It's more than you'd want to listen to. Take my word. It's necessary."

"How long? I need to talk to you about the sale."

"Can't it wait?"

"Until when?" Without looking, he knew Jay Frank was watching them. He accelerated past the prison outside Plainview. He said, "We'll talk when you get in. Try to make it before midnight."

Papers flurried, the tote bag thumped to the floor like a statement of some harsh fact. Then she said, "I'll do what needs to be done when we get home—feed you and the kids, unpack, start the laundry, talk about the sale. I'll go to the clinic after."

He glanced at her, imagined he heard her grit her teeth. It wouldn't hurt her to pay attention to something at home for a change. "Thanks. I'll try not to take too much of your time."

He'd barely stopped in the driveway before Amy and Claire were out, carrying a bag each, Amy with a pillow under one arm, hauling up to the porch. Jay Frank didn't open his door until after J. D. did. He said to his son, "Looks like we're in charge of getting the rest of this inside, buddy."

Claire was an old hand at making fast meals. Before they'd taken the rest of the bags to the bedrooms and emptied the cooler, she'd set the kitchen table and put out potato chips, dill pickles, and a plate of sliced carrots. As she reached for glasses in the cabinet, she said, "Do you want one grilled cheese sandwich or two?"

She must be talking to him. He was the only other person in the kitchen. Before he could answer, Amy walked in. She said, not whining for once, "I'm not hungry."

"I'll make you a sandwich and you can eat it later. You'll still need to come to the table with us."

As far as J. D. was concerned, they'd all been together enough for the past several hours. Maybe this was part of the "setting limits" plan. He didn't say anything.

"One or two?"

"One."

"I'll leave a chicken spaghetti casserole thawing. You can heat it for supper."

She sliced cheese, fast as a short-order cook, and set the griddle on the stove top.

It couldn't have been more than fifteen minutes later, she called them to come and eat. Amy pulled out her chair, which complained as she scraped it across the floor. No one spoke as three of them began eating their sandwiches. Amy poked at the carrots with her right index finger and eventually chose one. It snapped loudly when she bit into it.

About halfway into his meal, J.D. smiled in the direction of the kids and said, "I'm glad to be back, but I had a really good time in Taos. What about y'all?"

Jay Frank paused before taking another bite of his sandwich. He said, "Did you mean that about going back sometime and taking the horses?"

J.D. wanted to hug the boy for looking so cute biting the sandwich, his eyes wide. "Can't see why not. Would you like that?"

Jay Frank nodded. He knew better than to talk with his mouth full.

After a long silence, when no one else spoke up, J.D. said, "Well, son, it's a deal then."

The boy said, "Just you and me, maybe?"

J.D. didn't bother trying to make any more conversation. The meal was over in no time. Jay Frank took his plate to the sink and Amy slid off her chair and left the room just after he did.

After Claire cleared the table, she stood at the sink, leaning against it, facing him, holding a dish towel. She said, "Okay, what is it?"

He couldn't read her face anymore. Sometime over the past couple of years, it stopped telling him all he needed to know. What he saw there these days was either coiled and ready to strike, like now, or neutral, distant, which was most of the time. He could describe that expression, but he could never get behind it.

He hauled in a deep breath, thinking he sounded like his dad had when he was old and tired. "You know the sale's scheduled for the twenty-seventh." He waved the newspaper he'd gotten from the mailbox. "The people who bought the motel won't have it open until October first. There's at least two, maybe three couples coming from Central Texas who'll expect to have a place to stay. You'll need to make arrangements for them here—have the kids stay with your parents."

She held up her right hand, looked like a traffic cop. "Whoa! You said you'd take care of everything—a tent and a caterer, the auction. Now you're saying I have to entertain people here before and maybe after the sale. You just heard me say I'm going to have to work six days a week for who knows how long."

"I don't expect you to entertain them full time. Just make arrangements. Get the one couple that will fly from Austin at the Lubbock airport. Others will drive. Have rooms ready. Plan something for dinner Thursday night, and breakfast Saturday, then something for Sunday morning. I've got Friday and Saturday evening covered, the caterer. Seems like the least you could do is act interested."

"You don't hear me telling you to entertain people when I have clinic business. I handle it all without interfering with your work."

"The other wives help when there's a sale on their ranch."

"I'm not all the other wives. And what about that woman you're friendly with, the one who runs her own ranch—does her husband take care of all the smiling and cooking?

"She's not married."

"Well, I'll bet that's tough."

"I'm asking you to take some time out of your busy schedule and act like you give a shit, for once. The sale's not for three more weeks."

"You don't need a wife, you need a secretary. I suggest you hire one. Maybe a maid and a housekeeper, too."

"You're right. If I did, I wouldn't need a wife."

She wadded the dishtowel and threw it in the sink. "I'll take care of getting the kids out of the way that weekend. But don't count on me to be here. I have some hiring to do myself. Sandra, the new NP quit the day before we left."

"Why didn't you say anything?" That explained the six days a week.

"I didn't want to spoil the vacation." She walked, stiff-legged and straight-backed, to the dining room door. Without turning around, she said, "I'm going to the clinic. Make sure the kids are in bed by nine. Instructions for heating supper are on top of the casserole."

"Which clinic? Jackson's Pond or Calverton?"

"Here, Jackson's Pond." He heard her say that as she walked away.

They never used to leave an argument unfinished. They'd settle things and mend what needed to be. Until the last couple of years, he'd known he could always count on her, known that even when she was involved in work or with the kids, if he needed her, he'd come first. He knew, even with the way they left everything ripped and unsettled today, she'd do her duty, take care of everything the way she always did or die trying. Now it felt like she'd do it in spite of him, not because she cared.

Around seven his stomach reminded him he was supposed to heat the casserole. Soon it spread the aroma of green chiles past the kitchen into the dining room where he'd laid out his sale files.

As they all they ate large helpings of the casserole, Amy talked about the fun she'd had in Taos. Jay Frank offered to put the dishes in the dishwasher. Both of them said they had everything ready for school in the morning. Then they disappeared into their bedrooms. Afterward, J.D. stood on the front porch, looking toward town, thinking about taking Jay Frank to the high country, just the two of them, next summer. A sound in the distance, maybe a diesel pickup motor, interrupted his high altitude fantasy. No headlights showed on the county road and the sound faded, replaced by coyotes' yipping, which soon went silent and left him alone in the dark.

He'd been in bed, thinking about the sale and about how a family ought to be when he heard the front door open, then close. The bedside clock showed 11:30. There was nothing else he wanted to say to his wife tonight. He rolled to his side and closed his eyes. She didn't need to know he'd waited up for her.

Floyd County Tribune
Thursday, August 29, 2013
Jackson's Pond Motel To Open Soon

Mr. V. R. Patel, new owner of the former Hayes Haven in Jackson's Pond, announced today that the establishment will open for guests on October 1, 2013.

Patel said, "Although we had hoped to open sooner, we chose this date in order to be ready for hunters who come to the area for the opening of deer season."

Half of the motel's rooms will be designated pet friendly and all rooms are non-smoking. There will be an outdoor area for barbecuing for those who wish for a bit of "roughing it" along with the comforts of the twenty-five newly renovated guest rooms.

"The motel had been closed since 1975, so there was much upgrading to be done. We believe our guests will be pleasantly surprised to find our facilities modern and comfortable, and the outdoor recreation facilities enjoyable."

Patel previously operated a motel in Ft. Stockton and currently owns two others in West Texas. The Patel family lives in the owner's quarters at the Jackson's Pond motel where they have been on site since early summer, supervising the renovation. They have two children, ages 11 and 13, who are newly enrolled in the local school system.

The motel owner said, "We have come to stay. Our family hopes to become a part of efforts to revitalize Jackson's Pond."

CHAPTER 2
Violated

Even though she loved being in the mountains in Taos, and seeing Gran and Chris and Andrew, Claire had slept restlessly and woke early while they were there. Tonight, if things worked out, she could take care of some work so she could devote time to replacing Sandra. If things went her way, she'd be back home before the kids went to bed.

She drove the one-block-long alley behind the clinic. Even though it wasn't quite dark, the sun's rays sliced low across the building, casting a long shadow. Without leaving her vehicle, she saw the back door was closed. At the end of the block, she turned right and then right again onto Jackson's Pond's main street, passing the empty corner storefront where a faded sign, "Hardware," hovered above its awning. Next, her clinic waited, in the middle of the block.

She parked head-in against the curb, and noticed the white door and the long windows that usually added a bit of sparkle to the line of fading storefronts. But this evening, shadows emphasized the empty sidewalk. No sparkle anywhere. And here she was, alone in an empty town with a single stoplight two blocks away. She watched its steady blink in her side mirror.

Seeing the clinic's bright sign—red and black letters on white—Jackson's Pond Wellness Clinic—always prompted her to smile, as if a patient might be watching from inside. Not tonight. She had too much to do. Finding a replacement for Sandra wouldn't be a simple chore. Recruiting to a small town, for the salary they could pay was tough. Finding Sandra had taken months. At the time she had hired Sandra, Claire had wondered if she and Susan, the other nurse practitioner who staffed Calverton, had settled because they were feeling desperate. But she'd plunged ahead, and now Sandra had quit. That gave Claire two weeks, beginning tomorrow morning, to find a way to keep both clinics running. Tonight she'd take care of all the catching up—review charts of patients seen while she'd been in Taos, identify any billing problems, inventory medication supplies. She told herself to stop thinking about J.D. and his bull sale, and to get inside and take care of her own business.

But she didn't move. As if it happened yesterday, the night she'd decided, definitely, she'd open the second clinic pushed aside her already jumbled thoughts. Two years ago last July, wiping the kitchen counter after supper, she'd said to J.D. "I'm thinking of opening another clinic. The two docs in Calverton have closed their practices to new Medicare and Medicaid patients. People end up in Emergency because they can't pay. There's a real need."

He shook his head and said, "I don't see how you can do any more. You always take on too much, plus there's the kids and all you do here at home."

She'd wanted to tell him that if he helped at all, the kids and things at home wouldn't be a problem. But she knew what he'd say—that it didn't have to be all or none. He'd say that and then they'd be off the subject again. Instead, she said, "I'm just going to be supervising. I'll hire another NP."

His only response was a long silent stare.

Not waiting for him to speak, she said, "You know I can handle it. Remember I managed graduate school and being pregnant with Jay Frank and Amy a toddler and I've never failed to do everything both of them need and take care of you, not then or since I started the Jackson's Pond Clinic."

He interrupted, "Yes, and you won't let me or anyone help with any of it, even if I offer. You don't have to prove a thing to me. And just so you know, I'd be happy if you hired a housekeeper, or if you never took care of another patient again." Turning to leave the room, he said, "I'll say it again, you take on too much. But you're going to do whatever you want to, so I might as well save my breath."

After he left the room, she scrubbed at a cast iron skillet, muttering, "I'll be damned if I hire a housekeeper." The next day she started searching for a clinic site in Calverton.

She'd felt then as if she'd made an important beginning. Tonight she wondered . . . but she didn't have time for wondering. There was work to do.

She got out, pulled her tote bag across the seat and hoisted it on her shoulder, closed her door, and pressed the lock button on her key fob, focusing on each action as if it were critical. It was the way she'd taught herself to avoid making dosage errors prescribing meds for children. Now the step-at-a-time sharp focus had become habit.

Three years ago when she and her dad renovated the building, he had wired switches, one just inside the front door and another inside the back, to operate all the lights at once. He'd said, "Anyone who comes in here when it's dark should be able to light the entire place, for safety."

She had agreed just to please him. Since then there had been several nights and early mornings she'd been glad he'd thought of the precaution. Not that anyone had ever bothered her when she was here alone.

"Is anyone here?" she shouted into the dim space, knowing it would do about as much good as whistling in the dark.

Locking the front door behind her, she left the reception area and quickly checked each of the four exam rooms, the restrooms, and the storage room, then opened the door wide on the other office and hers. Everything looked right, like Friday had ended in a rush. On the counter in reception, billing sheets and charts in neat stacks showed there had been several patients that day.

She pulled on the handle of the cash drawer. It slid open; it shouldn't have. Claire pushed aside the reception desk chair and pulled the drawer out its full length—no metal organizing tray, nothing. She shot a look toward the front door. Still locked. She sat, not sure her legs would hold her, dizzy, her heart rate rapid. A deep breath, held for twenty seconds, then exhaled slowly settled the tachycardia. It didn't stop the question that thundered in her mind—what else might be missing?

Most patients wrote checks for their co-pays, but occasionally one paid cash. Clinic procedure stated there would be one hundred dollars in small bills for change placed in the drawer each morning. At closing time, any excess would be taken to the after-hours deposit near the bank's ATM, and the hundred would stay locked in Claire's office in her desk drawer. Anyone planning to steal, who might have watched Laverne working, would see the empty organizer and presume there was no money left in the building overnight. At least that was their thinking when they came up with the procedure.

Laverne, the receptionist, had taken care of that money as if it were her own, each day since the clinic opened. And she *never* took out the drawer organizer. She called it "our decoy." And she never left that drawer in reception unlocked, not even after she put away the change in Claire's desk at night.

They had posted a small sign on the front window, **No Narcotics Kept In This Clinic**. But anyone who'd ever been handed a packet of samples knew there were other drugs.

She had to focus. Slumped, head in hands, Claire tried to form a list. The first thought—call the Sheriff—made her shake her head. No, first get more information. She had been gone. Friday had been the only day clinic had been open without her. Surely Laverne could explain, or had left a note.

The med room and her office were the only places Claire hadn't checked closely. She stood and pushed the drawer closed with her knee, realizing as she did she'd already smeared any fingerprints. Whatever made her want to operate a clinic, much less two? She hurried toward the back to her office.

On her desk, in the center, lay an envelope with her name on the front. Unable to find the letter opener that belonged next to the telephone, Claire ripped an end off the envelope and shook out the single sheet of paper. She scanned the page. It said the change was locked in her desk. After reading the second of the two brief paragraphs, she dropped the paper and exhaled, air rushing through her nostrils with the hiss of a tire deflating. The nurse practitioner who'd turned in her resignation had left and said she would not return. Said she had a family emergency and had to leave town, couldn't work out her two weeks' notice. A male, Laverne didn't know who he was, hung around inside the clinic and outside in an old pickup, from noon until Sandra left with him at a quarter of four.

On the back of the envelope, Claire started a list, each item headed by a heavy dot of the pen, inserting equally heavy, dark question marks for missing information:

- Cash organizer missing or out of place.
- Sandra Berry, NP left without working out her notice
- Berry left clinic before close of business. A patient arrived after she left and was turned away due to her absence. Not an emergency patient.
- ? Charts completed for patients seen

- ? If charts complete, any errors in care/charting
- ? Took only her own possessions when leaving?

Claire's ballpoint ground a hole in the envelope as she made the last question mark. She stopped writing and fit the key into her desk drawer's lock. She turned and pulled on the handle. It wouldn't open. She rotated the key and the drawer slid open. It had been unlocked. There lay the one hundred dollars in small bills, wrapped in a wide red rubber band. She exhaled and sat back.

Because the volume of patients at the Jackson's Pond location was low, but steady, averaging around fourteen daily, only two people were on duty each day. The nurse practitioner was with the patients from the time they left the reception area until they returned there to check out. Laverne did reception, record keeping, and insurance billing—and everything else. The practitioner cleaned the exam table and equipment after each patient. A woman from town came in each morning at 7:30 and did all other cleaning, supervised by Laverne, who worked from 7:30 until 5:30. The day's last appointment or walk-in patient was taken no later than 4:45. Laverne locked up after Claire or the other NP left, no later than 5:30.

At least that's what their written procedure said. Claire sometimes stayed after the door was locked, to audit charts from the days the other practitioner was on duty, or to finish up her own charting. Sometimes, recently, she'd just sat in her office, waiting for the whirling in her head to stop.

In the med room, the samples left by pharmaceutical reps, plus stock drugs were organized by category—antihistamines, cough remedies, bronchodilators, SSRIs, antibiotics, statins, drugs for hypertension, for diabetes, miscellaneous—in locked cabinets above the counter that occupied all of one side of the eight by ten foot room. Vaccines and some other injectables were refrigerated. The sign in the front window told the truth. Anyone in pain acute enough to require an injectable pain med, even something non-narcotic like Tramadol, they sent to Emergency at the hospital in Calverton.

A ring binder on the cabinet top held an inventory sheet for each drug, stock or sample, with spaces for each item dispensed, patient name, and stock remaining, plus initials of the nurse completing the entry.

Reminding herself, again, to breathe, Claire inhaled. An odor of sweat and grease gouged at her as she rifled through the categorized, alphabetized pages. She lifted the notebook near her face and sniffed—definitely something there. Thinking of fingerprints, she pulled on exam gloves and turned to the first page of antihistamine/decongestants—Allegra D.

Purchases of pseudoephedrine, either alone or in combination meds, such as Allegra D, were documented in pharmacies. Anyone stupid enough to try cooking methamphetamine from those drugs would also probably be dumb enough to steal them to avoid the control process in a pharmacy. Cooking the meth required only a secluded spot, some rudimentary knowledge of the process, equipment scavenged or stolen from junk piles, and a view of right and wrong Claire couldn't comprehend. She leaned toward the pages and sniffed again. Grease and something else, she couldn't quite place.

According to the Allegra D page, there should be twelve boxes of samples containing four tablets each. Her initials showed on the last entry, five days ago, dispensing two boxes to Amos Gutierrez—14-2=12 in stock. As soon as she unlocked and opened the cabinet, she saw too many empty spaces. Every speck of pseudoephedrine, no matter what brand or combination, was gone. She slammed the cabinet door, locked it. This wouldn't keep until tomorrow morning.

Laverne's husband answered the phone. "She's already in bed. Said Friday wiped her out. That and other things."

Claire apologized for bothering them, but said she had to speak to Laverne tonight. She'd hold on. About three minutes later, when Laverne answered, her voice came out deeper than usual, and thick.

"I'm sorry to wake you. I'm at the clinic. Got your note. Things have been stolen. The drug samples."

"A break in?" Laverne sounded alert now.

"No. Both doors were locked when I got here. Tell me about Sandra leaving. What did she say?"

"Remember, I told you I never liked her. Looking down her nose at old people like they moved too slow to suit her. Always on her phone. Telling me to clean instruments, like she was too good to."

"Yes, I remember. I talked to her about that." Claire had

accepted Sandra's explanation about adjusting to the slower clinic pace after working emergency. She'd bowed up a little about the cleaning, saying she was accustomed to better staffing. "Your note mentioned her leaving with a man. Can you describe him?"

"Dirty—clothes, hands, and all. Maybe a mechanic."

"Age?"

"Young, like her. Hard to tell. He kept coming in and going back outside, leaning on his pickup, smoking."

"What kind of pickup?"

"Old, white, dirty. I couldn't tell you the year. I had work to do."

"Were you in the clinic the whole day?"

"Up front, except when I went to the bathroom." She hesitated. Her voice near a whisper, she said, "You do remember my little problem."

When Claire had noticed her frequent, almost hourly, trips to the bathroom, Laverne had admitted she'd embarrassed herself with a spell of incontinence last year. She had said, "If I go once an hour, it's not a problem. It doesn't interfere with my work, I swear."

Claire asked, "What about lunch?"

"Just called in an order at the café and picked it up. I was back before the next patient came."

"Did anything out of the ordinary happen Friday, other than Sandra's leaving early and saying she wouldn't be back?"

Laverne didn't answer for several seconds. "I'm thinking," she said. "Nothing other than what's in the note. I had to send that patient away. Like I said, I never did trust that girl." She hesitated, then said, "There is one other thing. I got to the grocery store after work, and when I went to pay out, I noticed a hundred dollar bill I had in my purse, not in my billfold, but stashed in that little zipper compartment, was missing. I know it was there because I got it at the bank on Thursday. Friday morning, I made sure it was there because I intended to go grocery shopping that afternoon. Then when I got there I had to write a check instead. When I told my husband he said he hadn't borrowed out of my purse; someone must have taken it."

Claire said, "I'm going to have to call the sheriff because of the drugs and I'll tell him about your money. Do you think someone could have gotten in your purse when you were in the bathroom?"

"I suppose so. I don't take it with me for such a short trip. Oh, Claire, I'm so sorry."

"It's not your fault. I'm sorry to have had to wake you. The sheriff will probably have to ask you all this again, tomorrow."

"Do you want me to come down there now?"

"I know you wouldn't steal."

"I don't mind. I probably won't be able to sleep anyway."

"No sense both of us being awake all night. See you in the morning."

"I'm so sorry. You don't need one more thing to worry about, honey. You have too much as it is."

Claire stared at the phone after hanging up. She didn't know it showed. Jaw clinched, she added to her list:

• Absent from front for brief periods in clinic restroom, once to pick up food at café.

•Old white pickup.

•Dirty man, grease under fingernails. Stranger.

•Decongestant drugs missing from inventory. Any other drugs? How many units?

She'd been able to handle any of the problems that naturally cropped up in developing the two clinics on her own. Her father had worked closely with her, but she was the boss. Every hitch, she'd managed to find a solution. And so far, they'd never missed paying salaries, even a little for her, or had a month in the red after the first six months. Seeing the financials each month, seeing her clinics breaking even, always made her do a little silent cheer alone in her office.

The idea that someone stole, probably a person she'd employed, and had trusted because she was a nurse, a colleague—Claire closed her eyes and tried locate the word for how she felt right then. Angry, violated—those words came to her quickly, but neither one said it all. Sick.

The whole town would know before long, and they'd talk—she was too young, thought she was so smart. And worse would be explaining to J. D. and her mother. Neither one of them said it, but she knew they expected her to fail.

She paced to the door of her office and then back to her desk. No sense spending time inventorying the rest of the cabinets or auditing the charts. That would come later, after she called Sheriff Clark. She stared at her list, at the holes in the back of the envelope. Then she added another item, then others.

- Audit Friday's patient charts
- ? Report to Board of Nursing?
- Finish drug and equipment inventory

She left her office and walked through each room, stopped at the front door. Not a soul on the street. No wind, the only sound a dog barking, three high-pitched complaints, then going quiet. The red light blinked a pale, intermittent glow from its perch down the street. She took her time returning to her office, preserving that lonely, calm scene as long as she could.

Further delay wouldn't improve the situation. She had to call her dad. If she bypassed him, the clinic manager, he'd be hurt. Otherwise, she'd handle it herself. Even though she could get him with a press of one fingertip next to his name, tonight she punched in each of the ten numbers, one at a time.

He and her mother had gotten back from Taos around six, after taking a side trip through Mosquero; he said for old time's sake. She didn't ask what that meant, just gave him a brief version of the situation. The only other thing she said was, "Don't bring Mother with you. We'll call the sheriff when you get here."

When her dad arrived ten minutes later, she showed him the envelope, holes and all. No need to explain things twice; she let him call the law while she inventoried the drug cabinets. In short order Sheriff Clark knocked once on the front door and walked right in. When the tall lawman, wearing his cowboy hat and gun, stepped into the med room, already crowded with her and her dad, Claire knew how an asthmatic must feel. "We can sit in the waiting room to talk," she said as she pushed past them toward the doorway.

Before he had time to ask, she told Sheriff Clark the events since she arrived. He listened without interrupting. She noticed him raise an eyebrow at her dad. She stopped to consult her list, and Clark asked her dad what he thought. Before her father could answer, Claire said, "I wasn't quite finished, Sheriff." She took her time going over the rest of the notes, telling him all the details. Then she sat back and waited.

His first question hit her like a fist. "What about prescriptions pads, particularly the triplicates?"

She hadn't thought of that. Except the pad in use, carried in the practitioner's lab coat pocket, all the other pads were supposed to be locked in her desk. The two men followed as she hurried back to her office. She heard the sheriff ask her dad if Sandra's references had suggested any problems at her previous job. Although he didn't say it directly, his answer made it clear—Claire had made the decision to hire her and had only told him after the fact. She couldn't fault him for telling the truth. She was the one to blame for this whole mess.

Opening her locking desk drawer confirmed it. The drawer was entirely empty. No prescription pads, neither the plain ones nor the triplicates for narcotics. She hadn't even noticed when she checked the drawer earlier—other than the money, the drawer was empty.

Sheriff Clark said, "I'll have to call Drug Enforcement. Whoever took those probably planned to paper area pharmacies with them. They had Friday evening, Saturday, and today. Lots of drugstores were open, even if it was a holiday. Don't plan on writing any prescriptions until we get this taken care of."

He was stating facts, but the sound of his voice made Claire feel like she was some ignorant rube. She said, "I'll close the clinic here until further notice, and send patients over to Calverton."

By 10:30, the sheriff had made calls—DEA, then his dispatcher to have deputies start efforts to apprehend Sandra and the unknown man, starting with her address in Calverton—had taken fingerprints from several spots and Claire's for comparison, and said he'd be back at 7:30 in the morning to talk to Laverne.

Claire watched his Suburban disappear beyond the blinking light.

Her dad, leaning against the reception counter, said, "You okay?"

"Not really. But I guess I will be eventually." She sighed and shook her head. "No one's bleeding, nobody died."

"I'll take care of things in Calverton in the morning." He turned at the front door. "You're going home now, too, aren't you?"

She nodded—it was all she could muster. After he left, she moved slowly through each of the clinic's room, stopping to clean up fingerprint dust, positioning chairs, doing things that didn't need doing. Finally, she dragged her tote bag from behind her desk, locked the door, and left.

When she got home, without turning on any lights in the house, she locked the front door, undressed, put on her pajamas, and slid into bed. J. D. never moved.

Jackson's Pond Wellness Clinic
Policy and Procedure Manual

Policy—Collaborating   Physician   Agreement   for   Delegated
Prescriptive Authority

An agreement for any nurse practitioner practicing in this clinic to have delegated prescriptive authority must be in place, per the requirements of rules promulgated by the Texas Board of Nursing and the Texas Medical Board, most recent version. (See Texas Administrative code Rule 222 and the Texas Occupations Code section 157.0512) All requirements of the delegation agreement meeting those legal requirements must be met at all times as an expectation of the Nurse Practitioner's professional responsibility.

Procedure:

1. Each nurse practitioner will enter into a collaboration agreement which shall be dated and signed by both parties to the agreement.

2. All requirements for face-to-face meetings between the nurse practitioner and the collaborating physician must be met and documented per the abovementioned requirements. That documentation will be retained in a locked file in the clinic.

3. Any nurse under investigation by the Board of Nursing must cooperate fully with investigator(s) and must immediately report the investigation to the collaborating physician.

Date of most recent review 1/14/13
Signature of reviewer: *Claire Havlicek, APRN*

CHAPTER 3

Negligence

Amy's voice, from the direction of the kids' bathroom, slapped Claire awake. "You can just wait your turn, you little turd!" Claire closed her eyes, clenched her jaw and inhaled slowly through her nose, then exhaled without a sound. Then she opened her eyes, telling herself it was time to wade in.

Seconds later, she stood beside Jay Frank at the bathroom door. "Go ahead and use ours. Then eat your breakfast."

"I already ate. She's mad she has to ride the bus. She's always mad."

Claire turned him toward his room. "Give her a few minutes." As he ambled away, a ten-year-old version of his dad's way of walking, Claire knocked once on the bathroom door. "I heard that, Missy! Watch your language unless you want to lose privileges."

She headed toward the kitchen, but stopped when she heard Amy, from the bathroom, parroting the warning she'd just issued. Rather than going back to push open the door and scream at her, Claire waited a few seconds until their daughter opened it. Without raising her voice, practicing the restraint she knew she'd need all day, Claire said, "March right into your room. We're going to talk right now."

In her room, Amy turned away from Claire and jerked her backpack from under the edge of her bed. She said, "I have to be at the bus stop in ten minutes." Then she whirled to face her Mother. "Dad said *you* were too busy to take me to school. What a surprise."

Claire didn't bite. She had a rule: never debate with a drunk or a teenager. "This won't take a minute. It's simple—speak respectfully or don't speak at all. Otherwise, there will be consequences. Got it?"

At the doorway, she turned back and said, "I'm not going to clinic in Calverton today." She didn't wait for a response from her daughter. Then Claire smiled, knowing that doing it would soften her tone. She said, "That shirt you got in Taos looks really nice. Turquoise is a good color on you."

The backpack seemed to have Amy's full attention. Her tugging on its zipper made the only sound in the room.

Coffee might make the day tolerable. In the kitchen, Claire's insulated cup waited next to the pot. Without looking up from the newspaper he'd spread on the kitchen table, her husband said, "Your dad called. Said he'd meet you at the clinic at 7:30." He lifted the paper and pointed to her phone. "I dug that out of your bag. You were dead asleep. Guess you were late getting in last night."

She picked up the phone. He said, "You going to tell me?"

"It's seven. I need to get dressed. If anyone asks, tell them it's under investigation." She poured coffee into her cup, her back to her husband.

He said, "I'm not just anyone."

"I'll tell you this evening. The sheriff's going to be there this morning. I need to get to town." She faced her husband. "I'll get Jay Frank to school and pick him up in the afternoon and keep him at the clinic until I finish."

J. D. had his eyes on the paper again.

As she left the kitchen, coffee cup in hand, she said, "Will you pick up Amy at the bus stop?"

"Can't she walk? I've got quite a few things going on, myself."

"She needs to be supervised." Claire didn't wait for a response.

Washing her face, brushing her teeth, and climbing into slacks and a shirt took only about ten minutes, three of which she spent finding a scarf to brighten the outfit. She'd be damned if she'd let everyone see how grim she felt. Attacking her hair with the stiff-bristled brush tamed it a little, the best she could do. She scooped her earrings off the vanity and dropped them in her pants pocket, then hurried outside, tote bag slung over her shoulder. The sound she heard might have been J.D. saying goodbye.

Jay Frank waited in her Suburban, earbuds in place. He smiled and rolled his eyes her direction when she opened the door. Claire couldn't help smiling in return. Ten was such a sweet age—hormones haven't struck, parents are still sources of useful information and important rewards. And best of all, fifth graders still attended elementary school. After this year, he'd be on the bus to Calverton like his sister on the days Claire worked the Jackson's Pond clinic. His being at the elementary just down the street gave her a warmth in her chest that made her think of a mother cow watching her calf roaming a pasture on its own, but near enough to protect.

After the turn from the dirt road onto the pavement, she felt in her pocket, then drove one-handed while putting on her earrings. She noticed Jay Frank watching. He said, "Momma, you look nice."

She thanked him and wished she could keep on driving, not stopping or letting him out of her sight until he was grown. Minutes later, when she stopped at the elementary school, he handed her his game and earbuds. No electronics allowed in school. Her boy followed the rules.

Her father and the sheriff each pulled up at the clinic just as she fit the key in the front door lock. Claire worked to hold a confident smile as she greeted them. The sheriff nodded, not disturbing his frown. He said to her father, "Ray, have you had any other trouble here?"

Claire stepped toward the sheriff, near enough that he couldn't avoid looking at her. "Dad deals with the business side of things, Sheriff Clark. Daily operations and clinical issues are part of my duties. We've never had a theft at either clinic." She pushed the door open and held it for the men. As she relocked it from the inside, she said, "Let's go back to my office. Patients will want to come in if they know I'm here."

As she passed the reception desk, she grabbed the stack of charts and the billing sheets from Friday. Clinic procedure required peer review of all patient records. Those had to be audited immediately. A sign, never before used, was somewhere in that desk. She squatted to open the cabinet doors below the counter. The fifteen by twelve inch sign lay face up on the bottom shelf. Large letters across the top read, **Clinic Closed Today Due to an Emergency**. Smaller letters encouraged calling the Calverton Wellness Clinic for an appointment or, if necessary, going to the Calverton Hospital Emergency Department, and listed phone numbers. "I'm right behind you," she said to the men's backs. "This sign has to go in the window, now."

Laverne opened the back door just as Claire neared her office. She whispered to Laverne to cancel the cleaning woman for today, then pointed to her office door and said, "I'll be in here with the sheriff for a while. He'll want to interview you." She stepped near the office door, then turned back, and whispered again, "Don't worry. We'll get this all resolved."

Laverne's usually happy expression had been replaced by something that belonged at a relative's funeral—pained, sad, tense. Claire didn't have time to hold her hand.

"That girl no more had a sick relative than nothin'. She's probably been planning this ever since she got here."

"I have to get in here. Check the exam rooms and the supply pantry to see if anything else is missing. Make a list. And if you get that finished, take care of the billing and filing."

"I know what needs to be done. Count on me."

Claire's dad and Sheriff Clark sat in the two office chairs. She faced them from hers behind the desk. "Sorry, I had to get Laverne started on a few things. She'll be ready whenever you want to interview her."

Sheriff Clark started in talking immediately. "We can't find a trace of Sandra Berry, but did confirm she had an apartment in Calverton. We got a warrant to open it and it looks as if no one has been there in a while. Spoiled milk in the refrigerator, no clothes in the closet. Apartment manager said he hadn't seen her in a week, at least. According to him, some man stayed there, but hers was the only name on the lease."

"Have any forged prescriptions turned up anywhere?" Claire had stayed awake for hours imagining losing her license. She wasn't certain what the charge would be; stupidity, maybe. She'd also spent time in the dark rehearsing a call to Dr. Habib whose name, as collaborating physician, was on the prescription pads along with hers. Even though she dreaded talking with her, that call had to be first, as soon as the sheriff left.

"We contacted the chain stores first—CVS, Walgreens, Wal-Mart—they alerted all their stores in the Panhandle and South Plains. I've got someone calling all the independents in the area. DEA said that was the procedure. Lab will start working on fingerprints this morning."

Claire asked, "What do you need from us now?"

Sheriff Clark stood. "These are all criminal charges we're working on. You'll want to see if there's anything with Berry's patient care that could be the basis for other charges by the nurse licensing board."

And then they'll begin to wonder about me. Negligent supervision, failing to protect patients. She said, "I have these charts to audit from Friday. For the two months she's been here, either I or Susan, the other practitioner, have reviewed her charts and haven't found mistakes."

What she said was accurate. No actual mistakes in histories, physical exams, or medications prescribed, but Sandra's charting had been minimal, had only met the basic requirements. A question had nagged at Claire several times, a feeling that what was charted might not be true or at least not accurate. Nothing she could point to specifically, just a feeling.

One particular day, she'd even questioned Sandra about a line she'd charted—"chief complaint: patient here for follow-up on blood pressure and blood glucose. States she feels well and exercises daily." That was plausible, considering the normal blood pressure recorded, the spot glucose of 100 mg/deciliter, and a weight ten pounds less than the previous visit three months before. But Claire had been in clinic that day and seen the patient in the waiting room. Seventy-five year-old Mrs. Martinez had been diaphoretic, had used a walker to move to the exam room, and if she'd lost any weight, it certainly wasn't apparent. The woman packed 250 pounds on her five-foot-three frame if she weighed an ounce. It hadn't varied from that in any of the three prior visits. And never in any of the numerous visits in her record had she ever failed to report some sort of misery—joint pain of arthritis, headache, a vaginal itch, something each time.

Claire had said, "What do you think accounts for Mrs. Martinez's improvement?"

Sandra said, "It's in the chart, exactly what she said and all the physical exam findings. I don't know her from before, but that's how she was today." Then she'd rushed off to see the next patient.

Sheriff Clark said, "I'm going to interview Laverne and then get back to my office. I'll be in touch later in the day."

Claire nodded as he left. What was there to say?

Her dad said, "You okay?"

Claire stared at the charts in her lap.

Negligent supervision. That day, or any other time she had wondered, she should have gone in the room with Sandra, supervised her the way she did when she'd precepted students. That would have meant watching her with the patient, then having her explain each step she had taken during the visit, her differential diagnosis, her rationale for the plan of care, and each item recorded in the chart.

But Sandra wasn't a student. She was a certified nurse practitioner with nearly four years of experience and good references. None of that meant a thing—Claire hired her and should have observed her with patients at least when she first started in the clinic. Reviewing her charts hadn't been enough. Claire knew that if she were on the licensing board, that's what she'd say.

She looked up from the charts. Her dad's expression told her she'd missed something. He must have asked a question. She said, "Sorry, what?"

"I asked if you're okay. I'm going on to Calverton. Need to get the day started over there. Call me if you need me." He put a hand on her shoulder. "This will work out. Try not to let it get you down."

She opened one of the charts. "First, I have to call Dr. Habib. Then I've got to audit these. I'll let you know. "

Dr. Habib, who practiced in Plainview, always answered if Claire called her cell phone. Today was no exception. Her soft voice and calm manner suggested that gray-haired lady might be a pushover. From having worked with the expert family practitioner as a student, Claire knew otherwise. She had asked Dr. Habib to be her delegating physician for that reason. She was exacting and thoroughly professional. And she'd been willing to accept the fee for her consultation that Claire's new clinic would be able to afford.

When the doctor answered, Claire recited the important facts first, including that the Sheriff and the DEA and Department of Public Safety had all been notified and the Board of Nursing would be this morning. Silence from the other end clutched at Claire. Then Dr. Habib said, "I know you are entirely conscientious. Let the law do what is required. This will change nothing between us."

If she could have reached her, Claire would have hugged her. "Thank you for understanding. All our documentation regarding your supervision is in order. There's no fault that could be attributed to you. I'll keep you informed."

Alone in her office, she spread the charts and then restacked them in order of the time of their appointments, according to the billing sheets. She opened the first chart and found nothing. Mrs. Carson's last visit recorded was in April. Yet, on the billing sheet, the diagnosis and billing code for essential hypertension was circled. By the time she'd opened each chart and matched it to its billing sheet, the only thing that kept her from throwing everything across the room was knowing she'd have to pick it up.

Fourteen patients and not a single visit had been charted. If those visits were billed, and the charts were ever audited by Medicare or another insurer, the clinic could be cited for fraud. The old rule, ingrained in her from her first day in nursing school, "If it isn't charted, it didn't happen," had never made more sense.

Laverne sat alone at the reception desk, holding a blank sheet of paper torn from a yellow legal pad. "I told Sheriff Clark all I could remember. He told me I did fine and not to worry. And to keep my purse locked up from now on."

Claire patted Laverne's shoulder. Laverne didn't have to work. The only reason she was there was because Claire had told her she trusted her more than anyone in the whole town and that she needed her. All of that was true. If anyone could keep a secret, it was Laverne. And there was always plenty that went on in a small town clinic that should be kept in confidence.

Claire knew that Laverne, a high school classmate of her mother's, had lived through her own hard times with an abusive first husband, and no one in town even had a hint. Years back, he'd dropped dead at work. Laverne said they told her a horse kicked him as he was trying to saddle it, ruptured his abdominal aorta. She had told Claire, "He'd probably beat that horse one too many times."

At nine o'clock, Claire left the clinic, headed seven miles east to the home of Joy Harmon. She had decided to deal with the patients, rather than wait around dithering. When she called the Board of Nursing she'd need all the particulars. Mrs. Harmon, age eighty-two, lived alone. Even though her daughter tried to get her to move off the farm, live with her, Joy had confided to Claire she intended to die where she'd lived her life.

Of the patients who'd been in clinic Friday, ten had been under fifty and of those, six were under twelve. Sandra had circled pharyngitis as the diagnosis on each of those six billing sheets. Two also had charges for strep tests. That made sense. Sore throats made the rounds as soon as kids returned to school every year.

Claire reasoned that the four older patients required her first concern; most suffered one or more chronic illnesses and needed several medications. Plus—Claire's greatest concern—Joy and one other needed, but didn't accept, some assistance with their activities of daily living. A fall and a hip fracture for either of them could begin a downward spiral—hospital, to a skilled care facility, to a death in a place other than home.

A telephone call might alarm the patients, require an explanation she preferred to make in person. Even though a trip would be wasted if one of them wasn't at home, she intended to see each of them before she finished the day.

Joy took a while getting to the door, but when she did, she stood upright to her full height, just over five feet, and said, "Why Claire, I can't think of a nicer surprise than a visit from you. Come in and I'll make a new pot of coffee." She pointed to a chair in the large living room. Claire put her tote bag on the floor near the chair. She'd be there for a bit. Joy's gait was steady as she walked to the kitchen. A low coffee table in front of the couch held fifteen, Claire counted, photographs in frames of different sizes and shapes. At least three generations of children in situations ranging from sports events to Santaland visits to formal family group poses covered the surface. No dust. Pine cleanser and a hint of lemon oil tinged the air. She relaxed into the wing-backed chair, considered putting her feet on the ottoman next to it, but didn't.

Freshly brewed coffee joined the aromas in the room. Joy handed her a mug and said, "I doubt if you were just in the neighborhood, although you'd be welcome any time."

"I came to check on you because you were in clinic last Friday."

Joy cocked her head. "You weren't sure about that other nurse, were you?"

Claire couldn't help but smile. "I'll just say I was concerned. What makes you think I might not be sure about Sandra?"

"I wasn't sure about her and I'm a pretty good judge." She sat back on the couch and sipped her coffee. Claire waited. Joy said, "She moved too fast; didn't listen, hurried me out. If I'd been there for anything besides refill prescriptions for my medicines, I'd have just walked out and waited for you to get back. But since I felt fine and nothing had changed, I let her finish."

"Did she examine you, ask you any questions?"

"That's the other thing. She never even listened to my heart. Barely even touched me when she took my blood pressure. I doubt the reading was correct because she slapped that cuff on over my sweater."

"That's all she did?" Keeping her tone neutral taxed Claire's patience.

"Wrote out refill prescriptions and hustled me out of there. Laverne can tell you, I was in and out in less than ten minutes."

Claire told her about Sandra's sudden departure and the empty charts, not mentioning the money or the drugs. She told her the sheriff was investigating, so she couldn't say any more, but that her first concern was her patients.

"Well, I'm just fine. So you just enjoy that coffee and let's visit a little before you go."

They chatted a few minutes about the weather, Joy's memory of the drought of the fifties, Claire's kids, and her grandmother, whom Joy counted as a friend since childhood. She asked, "When do you think Willa's going to move on back over here where she belongs?"

Claire told her about the family's birthday celebration for Willa in Taos. "I'd love to have her here. But more than anything, I want her to do exactly what she wants. I feel the same about you, Mrs. Harmon. I want you to stay as healthy as possible and live where and how you want to."

Joy rewarded her with a smile. Claire finished her coffee, told herself she had to get out of the chair or she'd nod off to sleep in this comfortable room. "Would you mind if I check your blood pressure and listen to your heart and lungs before I go?"

Satisfying herself Joy's condition was stable took several more minutes—a few questions, a brief exam, all the things Sandra should have done—and confirming that Sandra had refilled but not changed her prescriptions.

The coffee kept Claire moving through her next three stops, and the total of forty-five miles in between. So far, so good. None of the four had suffered any harm; all told essentially the same story. No one trusted Sandra, but it was because she seemed not to care enough to do a thorough job, not because she did anything suspicious.

Driving back into town after the last visit, Claire remembered how she had loved home health care—seeing people in their homes, where real life is conducted, not in the controlled circumstance of the clinic. She'd always worked to find a way to add value to the visit, bring something more to the patient than a dressing change or medication administration, something that could help them regain life as they preferred to live it, whatever their condition. The patients doted on her. But she'd wanted to be able to do more, so the next step was becoming a nurse practitioner, and then the clinics. Today, she allowed herself to wonder if she'd lost what she'd loved the most about being a nurse the day she opened the clinics. *No sense dealing in regret.* She turned on the radio.

Back at the clinic, she explained to Laverne why there would be no billing for Friday's patients, and they agreed to open clinic the next morning as usual. Laverne came up with a brief, factual reassurance she would repeat to anyone who might question the rumors that were certain to spread. She said, "I'll bet we'll do a rushing business for the next few days. Lots of people using an ache or pain as an excuse to come in here and give me the third degree. Count on me to disappoint them."

There'd been no word from the sheriff and nothing from her dad. Claire resisted an urge to call J.D. She'd tell him everything tonight. A breakfast bar, an apple, and a pint carton of milk, consumed at her desk, quieted her growling stomach. Breakfast and lunch all in one, efficient if nothing else. By twelve o'clock, she'd charted the home visits and set out to see the other ten patients.

By four, a serious energy ebb in progress, Claire told herself she'd done what she could for that day. She had contacted the Board of Nursing and, after an interminable wait through the automated phone system, learned an investigator would be assigned and should contact her tomorrow; all her patients were safe; she'd repeated her no-information explanation a dozen times; and she picked Jay Frank up at school on time.

At home, Claire carried her tote bag and Jay Frank hauled his backpack as they trudged from the Suburban to the back door. She thought they looked like a pair of weary peddlers. As they walked into the kitchen, she heard J.D. talking. "I don't know, Jan. I'm not certain how I'll swing it. There are complications I can't talk about right now. I'll explain when I see you."

He walked in from the dining room, replacing his phone in the carrier attached to his belt. "Oh, I didn't expect you until later." He frowned, then quickly changed to a smile toward Jay Frank. "Good day at school, buddy?" The boy moved the milk carton he was drinking from away from his face and nodded. With a look, Claire reminded him to drink from a glass. Without a word, he closed the refrigerator door and busied himself at the cabinet, pulling out a glass, then opening the cookie jar.

J.D. said, "Amy's in her room. Probably on her phone. Everything okay?"

"I can talk about it now, if you have time."

"Sorry, I don't. Phone calls to make. You can tell me later."

Spread out on their bed, wearing sweats, Claire turned to her side to stop staring at the ceiling. The day rolled past in her thoughts, freighted like a long train loaded with questions and threats. And there at the end trailed that conversation she overheard minutes before—J. D. talking about *explaining, complications, may not be able to swing it now, explain when I see you*—he'd clearly said *Jan*, not *and*.

Jackson's Pond Wellness Clinic
Policy and Procedure Manual

Policy—Patient Record Review

Review of patient records will be conducted on a regular schedule to assure compliance with Board of Nursing, Board of Medicine, and Board of Pharmacy regulations and as a measure of quality of patient care.

Procedure:

1. At least one time monthly the collaborating/delegating physician will conduct a review of selected patient records to determine that patient care, including prescription of medication and other delegated medical acts meet agreed to standards of care.

2. At least weekly, peer review of all patient records will be conducted on the records of all patients seen in the clinic.

3. Any deviations from agreed standards of care, including content of records, will be discussed and documented. If errors in care or recording are noted, those will be documented in personnel records and remedial action taken immediately, including any reporting to licensure boards required by regulations and/or follow up care of patients.

4. Each record reviewed shall bear an indication of the date and the person conducting the review. A record (documented in a designated notebook) shall be made and retained in the clinic of all reviews conducted, citing the reviewer's name, patient clinic number, and dates of entries reviewed, and any subsequent actions taken based on those reviews.

Date of policy/procedure review: 1/14/13
Signature of reviewer: *Claire Havlicek APRN*

CHAPTER 4
Still Missing

"If you're a burglar, please come in the front door so I don't have to get out of my chair!" Laverne yelled as she heard Claire at the back door. The cleaning woman had just left through the front, so it was safe to joke a little. Maybe Claire would even smile. Until all this mess, coming to work had been the biggest joy of Laverne's life. But the last week had turned Claire grim and Laverne couldn't help feeling sad for her. Maybe today the sheriff would bring some good news. So far, he'd been tight-lipped every time he turned up.

Claire sat down in the chair next to Laverne's and dropped her bag on the floor between them. "I'm going to decide which one of those computerized record systems to buy. And soon. Carrying these charts home to review convinced me." She pointed to her bag, which fell on its side. Two charts slid to the floor. "They must weigh twenty pounds. I reviewed them all, every chart Sandra wrote in while she was here. Nothing. Only the charts from her last day show bad practice."

"That's a good thing, isn't it?" Laverne gave up on smiling. Claire looked like she hadn't eaten in a week—her face drawn, pale except for the blue shadows under her eyes. "I brought us a couple of those burritos you like. They're on your desk." She'd also made chocolate chip cookies. Claire never refused one of those.

"Thanks. I forgot breakfast. Everyone at the house moved in slow motion this morning."

She emptied the charts from her bag, stacked them on the desk. "When you have time, these can be filed. I'll be in the back."

"First patient's not till nine. Why don't you go ahead and eat?"

She watched Claire walk toward Exam Room 1, treading like she was wading upstream against rushing water.

Nancy Reese, always heavy but even more so in the last year, pushed open the front door. A gust chased a measure of dust in as she struggled getting in. When she finally did, she stopped and fussed with her hair, then said, "Wind's already up; I'd say we're in for a blow today."

From where she sat, Laverne could see Nancy didn't have to worry about finding an anchor if it did. They'd been to high school together. Along with Claire's mother, Nancy had been one of Laverne's friends. Maybe that was using the term loosely; they'd spent quite a bit of time together. Even before she married Junior, Nancy was one to look down her nose at people. Laverne always wondered what made her think she had the right. Her people didn't get to Jackson's Pond until she was in eighth grade, so it wasn't as if they were old money or, for that matter, any money. Her dad had worked at Proctor's filling station as a mechanic.

"How've you been, Nancy? I haven't seen you in town in a while."

"I've been in the mountains in New Mexico all summer, Red River. Junior got over when he could."

Laverne gave her a nod, trying to hint she believed it. She knew Junior hadn't missed many days at the coffee shop down the street. "Have a good time?"

"Just great. Really good." She leaned against the counter, directly in front of Laverne. "I loved every minute." Her voice trailed off on the last two words, down close to a whisper.

Laverne rolled her chair back a few inches, looked up at Nancy. "Mmmm. You here for a follow up this morning or something new?" She didn't expect an answer. She only asked so she could see Nancy's face. That stricken expression—the silent movie virgin in peril—always made Laverne's mouth twitch, hiding a laugh.

"Lots of pain in my limbs. Excruciating."

"Claire'll be with you in just a few minutes. Till then, you probably ought to sit down, get off your feet."

Ducking her head, Laverne stared at a stain on her desk until the urge to roll her eyes passed. Well, maybe Nancy really was sick. She hadn't even asked about the burglary. Laverne abandoned studying the desktop and said, "Can I bring you a glass of water or something while you wait?"

By noon, Claire had taken care of seven patients and Laverne had filled all eight afternoon appointment spaces. It amazed her how Claire could keep smiling, convincing every person who walked in they were her one and only concern. Always brought them to the front when they left, the way you would a departing guest. Laverne knew her well enough to tell she was running on fumes.

Laverne locked the front door just after twelve. "I brought lunch enough for both of us. Let's sit and not talk at all for a few minutes, just eat."

She heard Claire's sigh all the way across the waiting room. "Do I look that bad, Laverne?"

"I brought tuna sandwiches and carrots. Healthy food. Energy food."

Another sigh, then Claire walked to her office. Laverne followed, lunch bags in hand, shaking her head at the sight of Claire's slumped shoulders. "And don't forget we have cookies, too."

She spread the food on Claire's desk and sat in the chair facing. "I know I promised not to talk, but I just need to ask. Is something else going on besides this thing with Sandra?"

Claire shook her head, then picked up a half sandwich and took a bite, chewed for a long time. Laverne held her breath, waiting for her to swallow. She said, "I'll get us something to drink. Milk, Diet Coke, water?"

When Laverne returned from the break room with a bottle of water and a carton of milk, she said, "Well if there is, you know you can tell me. It won't go anywhere."

Claire nodded. One more bite of the sandwich and she rewrapped it in the foil and zipped it into the plastic bag. Laverne edged the bag of cookies across the desk toward Claire's right hand. "Fresh. Made 'em last night."

Again, with the nod. Laverne had to give it to her, anyone who didn't know, people who didn't see her this way, would think everything was just dandy. The girl could gut it up when she needed to.

Laverne knew about pasting on a happy face and getting on with things. All year long, since her daughter left town last New Year's day, she'd been doing everything she could, short of calling the law, to try and find her. Meanwhile, working her hardest not to let on to anyone.

Her second husband had always been the one the girl thought

of as Dad, so when she left, Laverne spent a lot of time thinking he knew where she'd gone. He swore he didn't. "We could get the law on it, but if they brought her back, she'd leave again," he'd said. Laverne agreed because she knew he was right, but she hadn't liked it.

Since then, except that note she left behind saying she had to learn to be on her own, nothing gave them a clue. That and one phone call back in July—offering nothing except another "I'm fine. Don't worry about me."

Claire stood and looked out the window. Without turning around, she said, "I blame myself. Whatever Sandra did, if I'd supervised her properly, this might have been prevented."

Laverne said, "I'll put that sandwich in the refrigerator. Maybe you'll want it later." She cleared the food away, replaced everything except the cookies in the two brown paper lunch bags. "It's easy to look for a cause, hard to find one."

She knew that at twenty-three, her daughter probably should be on her own. They'd babied her all her life. They'd about given up; how many thirty-six year-old women get pregnant after trying for seventeen years? The girl had every reason to be rotten.

But until she took up with that cowboy from one of those ranches close to Matador, she never gave them a minute's trouble. Dated a few boys in high school, nothing serious. Had lots of girl friends, most of them married and left town by now. Commuted to junior college and right after she graduated, took a job as a teacher's aide at the elementary. Then up and left in the night.

Laverne returned from the break room, sat down again. She watched Claire until she turned from the window. After a long silence, Claire said, "When the nursing board asks, I'm going to have to admit I didn't ever actually watch her with a patient. I mean in the room, every step. I assumed since she never asked for help, her charting was right, patients didn't complain, I could trust her. A person ought to be able to trust another professional."

"Ought to." Laverne gave Claire a chance to keep talking. After a long silence, while Claire stared back toward the window, Laverne said, "You were full-time busy filling in at Calverton, and Susan had her vacation."

"I could make a thousand excuses. None of them justifies what I didn't do." Claire crumpled into her chair again, leaned back and closed her eyes. After too short a rest, she sat forward and took one of the cookies and bit into it. "Maybe they were right. I don't know how to run this or anything else."

"Who?"

"Everybody who expected these clinics to fail. Me to fail."

"Anyone in particular?"

"My mother, for one."

"Want another one of those cookies for later? I'm going to make a bathroom stop before the afternoon starts."

Claire took a cookie, placed it on the desk pad. "I'm sorry to whine. You're kind to listen to me." She ran her fingers through her hair. "Do I need lipstick?"

"Yeah, you're kind of pale."

"Shows, huh?"

Laverne nodded, then drew a deep breath. "It's not my place to say this, but I will. I know you're wrong about your mother. She's proud of you. Always has been."

Claire was standing at the window again, staring out.

Looking at herself in the bathroom mirror, Laverne teased her hair up a little in the back, wondering again if she ought to color it instead of letting the gray show. Mother had kept hers dark until the day she died. Although she often missed her mother, last January Laverne had been glad she had already passed on. The woman would have been on her like a gnat when Wendy left, like she had been when Laverne first got pregnant. She never missed a day all nine months, telling Laverne she was too old to have a baby in the first place.

The first person who showed up after lunch was Carl Hofer, one of the last patients Sandra had rushed through that Friday. He said he didn't need an appointment, not really, but that when Claire stopped by his house to check on him after that other nurse left, she convinced him he should monitor his blood pressure more often than once a year. "So I made her a promise," he said. "I'm going to have it checked once a week, startin' today. Wrote it on the calendar, too."

"You just have a seat, Mr. Hofer. She'll be glad to hear

you're doing that."

He chose the chair nearest the door, eased himself down into it. He said, loud enough for Laverne to hear, "I told her I'd keep takin' that medicine for the pressure, too."

"You'll win the prize for best patient, if you keep that up. Good for you!" Some people need a lot of encouragement to take care of themselves, Laverne was convinced. She always did all she could.

The mailman waltzed in around three, back in town after finishing his rural route. He wagged a handful of envelopes in one hand and a box about twelve inches square under his other arm. He was another one who knew how to convince folks everything was dandy. Always smiling and clowning a little, like he had an audience. Never failed to make Laverne smile. "I come bearing mail!" he said.

"Aside from drug company ads and the circular from the furniture store, what did you bring?"

He said, "This box looks interesting." If she gave him half a chance, he'd hang around until she opened it.

"Samples, I imagine." She put the envelopes on the desk and the box under the counter. "Thanks. See you tomorrow." She looked over his shoulder at Carlene Lewis coming in the door, toting her two year-old on her right hip.

"Off on my appointed rounds, spreading cheer all over the county. Till tomorrow!" He delivered his parting line, the same one every day, and added a little salute.

Claire came from the back and invited Carlene and her daughter, LaTosha, to come with her. She had taken off her white lab coat, like she always did. It seemed to work; hardly any of the kids started screaming as soon as they saw her.

Laverne knew it didn't make a bit of sense, but the stack of envelopes gave her a tiny bit of hope. Any mail did. One day there'd be a letter from Wendy. Not here, probably, more likely at home. One by one, she read the address and the return on each of today's items—all to Claire or to the clinic. Laverne's hope seldom vanished entirely in the absence of encouragement; it only receded a bit. There would still be possibilities waiting in the box at home.

The rest of the afternoon patients were in and out, and then the waiting room stood empty by four-fifteen. Five minutes later, Sheriff

Clark parked out front. Laverne watched him glance up in his rearview mirror and adjust his hat before marching in the front door.

By the time he got to the reception desk, he'd worked up a big smile. "Is Claire here?" You'd have thought he was Claire's uncle, not the law from Calverton.

Laverne looked him square in the eye. She had voted for the other candidate in the last election. She said, "Yes, Sheriff Clark, Mrs. Havlicek just finished with the last patient of the day. Would you like to speak with her?"

"Yes." Then he added, "Thank you."

Claire was staring out her office window again when Laverne rapped on the doorsill. "Sheriff Clark would like to see you. Looks like he's happy about something."

"I'll come up there so you can hear what he has to say, too."

Claire offered the man a chair in the waiting area. He preferred to stand, he said, lots to do. "I wanted to bring you up to date on our progress. First, the man we identified from fingerprints here . . ." He stopped talking and consulted a piece of paper he pulled out of his pocket. "Hardy Bowden was apprehended this morning by officers near Grady, New Mexico. A pharmacist in Tucumcari called the local police because Bowden tried to buy a several packages of Sudafed. The pharmacist refused to sell him more than one. Bowden got upset and left the store. A while later the pharmacist remembered an alert." He put the paper he'd been reading from back in his pocket. "Guess he was on his way back to Texas." He checked his watch. "I need to go. I'll be in touch when we know more."

He got as far as the front door, then turned around, holding it open. "Oh, the nurse. We found her mother living down near San Saba. Father's dead. Says she hasn't seen her in four years, since the girl finished her Master's degree in Austin. Gets a money order in the mail every so often. No letter, no return address. Said she'd tried to find her lots of times. Got to wonder, though."

Laverne watched him drive away. She said, "You can bet her mother did everything she could."

She felt Claire's hand on her shoulder and then heard her walk away toward her office.

Lubbock Journal
Monday, September 9, 2013
Area Crime Reports

Arrest in Jackson's Pond Clinic Theft

Hardy Bowden, age 28, was arrested in Grady, NM September 8 and charged with possession of illegal drugs and related offenses. He remains in custody in Clovis, NM awaiting extradition to Texas where he is accused of multiple felony charges stemming from thefts last week at the Jackson's Pond Wellness Clinic.

A second suspect, Sandra Berry, age 31, a practitioner who worked at the clinic, is also sought in conjunction with the thefts.

Would-Be Rustlers Apprehended Near Dickens.

Two males and a female were arrested near Dickens September 7 on charges stemming from what Special Ranger Marty Broadus described as an unsuccessful rustling attempt. Names of those arrested are being withheld because the three are all minors.

Broadus said, "There has been an increase in reports of thefts of equipment from area ranches in the past three months. This is the first definite attempt to also steal animals. They had two stock trailers, one loaded with 8 yearling steers and the other with two horses, all carrying the brand of the ranch where we arrested them. An air compressor and a Craftsman tool tower, full of tools, were also recovered from the bed of the suspects' pickups.

CHAPTER 5
Decision

When he heard Claire's voice, J.D. looked up from the work he'd laid out on the dining room table. She'd come home just after five, early for her. After saying to him, "We need to talk before supper," she'd gone straight to Amy's room. Next thing he knew, now she was in the kitchen.

He moved the stack of breeding records he'd just finished entering into his database to the only clear spot on the table. Jan had said he was smart to have started digitizing all that before the sale. It would be good to have printed copies of the entire record available on all the young bulls he was selling. He walked to the kitchen doorway and said, "What? I didn't understand you."

She hustled to the kitchen table, four supper plates in one hand and a fistful of silverware in the other. "If you have time now, I'll tell you about the problems at the clinic while I fix supper."

He sat down on the stool at the kitchen counter. "I wondered when you'd get around to it. Heard some things in town when I went in this morning."

"I'm sure," she said. Back at the kitchen counter, she laid out four pork chops on a sheet of waxed paper. "You said you were too busy when I tried to tell you earlier."

Before he could answer, she'd turned around, bent down to the drawer under the oven, rattled skillets around. He watched her from the back, waited to see her face when or if she got around to telling what had had her twitching in her sleep every night that whole week since they got back. Like she was running.

Cast iron skillet in her hand, she faced him. "I won't bore you with all the details. I doubt you're interested. The main thing is that Sandra, the NP I told you quit, took off with some guy, along with all the drug samples of everything that contained pseudoephedrine, all the prescription pads, including the ones for narcotics, and some money from Laverne's purse."

"Has the sheriff done anything? Or just looked at himself

in the mirror?"

"They caught the man over in New Mexico. He's been arrested and charged with felony theft, attempting to pass a forged prescription, possession of illegal drugs, and manufacturing meth. They haven't found her yet."

"Well, as long as they've got it under control, I guess that settles it, right?" He leaned back and tried smiling as he said it. Maybe now she could pay attention to her family.

"Did you not hear me say they haven't caught her yet?" She turned, reached in the cabinet above the stove. He heard her mutter, "What she did is as bad or worse than him. I don't know why I even bother trying to tell you anything." After slamming a bottle of canola oil down on the counter, she spun around, reached into the flour canister, and flung a handful of flour on the pork chops, slapped them around in it until they were white, not pink. "It's far from over. I'd explain it, but it's clear you have absolutely no interest in knowing."

He stood and pushed back the stool. "And you don't have a clue what I'm interested in. Haven't had in about three years."

"You might be surprised about what I know about your *interests*."

"That so? Tell me this, when was the last time you rode with me to check the cattle?"

"You've made it clear, the ranch is *your* business. And if you hadn't noticed, I've been busy."

"Too busy, as far as I'm concerned."

"Not too busy to notice Amy's turning into a bulimic." She dug in the trash under the sink and pulled out an Oreo bag, empty except for a lone cookie; three Snickers wrappers; and a small box labeled Ex-lax. "All hidden in her bedroom under a pile of dirty clothes. But I guess you already knew that, right? Being the super family man that you are."

The back door opened and Jay Frank stepped into the room. "When's supper?"

Using a different tone, a gentle one J. D. hadn't heard lately, she said, "I'll call you, honey." She pointed toward the table. "If you're hungry, there are some sliced apples there."

Jay Frank grabbed a handful of the fruit and started toward the bedrooms. J.D. saw him sneak a quick look at both of them. The boy barely got out of the kitchen, then he turned back and said, "The goats are all fine. I'll be doing homework."

J.D. clamped his jaw until Jay Frank was gone. Then he said, "I suppose you've diagnosed him with something too, doctor?"

The look she threw at him said he'd gouged too deeply. Tough. If she wanted to be independent, she'd have to learn to take it.

She said, low, but he heard it, "When did you turn into such an asshole?"

"Probably happened when I got fed up with you being too busy to be a wife."

"Is that why you've been spending all your time on the phone with *Jan?*"

"That's business."

"*Right.*"

He paced to the kitchen table and back to the bar twice, then pulled the stool out again, but didn't sit, just held onto it. He hardly recognized her face. Light from her green eyes had always invited, encouraged him. Now, with them narrowed down, he only saw a glint reflected off a hard gemstone. "I've got work to do. When you calm down, you let me know."

Taking care not to stomp, he returned to his laptop at the dining room table. He yelled back toward the kitchen, "Just leave me a plate on top of the stove. I'll eat later."

She didn't answer.

After she and the kids ate, he heard Claire cleaning up from supper, pots and pans clanging loudly enough to let him know she hadn't cooled off. Then the kitchen went dark, and Claire walked past him without a word. She left the front door open. The screen slammed behind her.

There hadn't been a sound from the kids' rooms since they left the table after supper. They knew when to take cover.

It would have been easy to walk out on the porch and look for Claire. Two hours had passed and she still wasn't in. Instead, he moved aside a drape on the living room window. Her Suburban hadn't moved, and she wasn't sitting in one of the porch chairs.

Their bedroom windows faced east, overlooked the corral and barn. He pulled the blinds to the side about an inch. On her horse, bareback, Claire was riding a circuit around the corral, like she might be cooling the horse down. Gus stopped and she leaned down with her face on his mane, her arms around his neck. Riding off alone, a stupid thing to do in the dark. He didn't bother to walk quietly as he returned to his work, aiming to enter all the information before stopping for the night.

J.D. kept his eyes on the computer screen, checking the data as he went. Slow and steady worked best for him. He heard the front door close, and looked up briefly. Claire in the hall, he could barely see her there. She said, "We have to talk about Amy."

He looked at the spreadsheet displayed on his laptop. "It'll have to wait until morning. This has to be finished." He worked hard to sound natural.

She didn't answer. Her footsteps told him she'd gone to the bedroom.

Amy wasn't going anywhere tonight. And besides, Claire had predicted the worst before for what turned out to be small problems. Like that time she'd insisted they take Jay Frank, when he was just fifteen months old, to a specialist to have his hearing checked. She'd thought that's why he wasn't talking much. Turned out he started talking in sentences a couple months later. Now, Amy. Hell, lots of kids like Oreos.

He checked the pile of breeding records. Down to the last three. His phone vibrated, not ringing because he'd set it that way just in case. Jan had told him to call if she could help. "*Anything* at all," she'd said.

He glanced at the phone. Debating whether to answer, he felt the phone's jittery thrill twice more, checked the time—10:23. Surely Claire was asleep by now.

Jan started talking before he had a chance to say hello. "I haven't heard from you in a couple of days. Is everything okay?" Her voice sounded shaky, different from the other times they'd talked.

He glanced toward the bedroom, shifted in the chair to turn

his back toward the hallway. He said, "Yeah, moving along, just working on the breeding records. How about you?"

"Oh, I'm fine. I guess." There was a long pause. Then she said, "Sometimes I need someone to talk to." Another long pause.

J.D. didn't say anything. Nothing that came to mind sounded like something he ought to say to another cattle rancher, one who happened to be a woman. He finally came up with, "Problems on the ranch?"

"Not the ranch. My foreman handles most things anyway." He heard her breathing. "I'm in Dallas, shopping, visiting. My sister lives here."

That was the first he'd heard about her trusting her foreman to run things. "You're staying with her?"

"No, I'm at the Stoneleigh. Alone."

"Uh huh," he said, like he knew where that was. A question came to mind, something he *had* intended to ask her. "Have you ever had a video sale instead of one on the ranch?"

"No, always on the ranch." Then after a stretching out a long tale she'd heard about a South Texas ranch that had a bad experience with some video outfit, she got around to asking, "Are you thinking of changing to a video sale?"

"It's good to have as much information as possible. Just in case."

"I was looking forward to coming to your place. Seeing people at home helps me understand them."

"No mystery here. I'm just another cowboy." He made it sound like a joke, added a little laugh. A beer would be nice about now, but he stayed put, didn't head for the refrigerator.

"Not in my books, you're not."

He said, "Well, we'll see. I've just thought about switching. Wanted to be sure before I send out invitations and so forth."

"Don't forget. I'll do anything I can to help."

"I won't. I appreciate that." He stood, about to go to the kitchen for that beer. When he turned, he saw Claire's back, walking slowly toward the bedroom. "Guess I'd better get finished with this computer work, now."

"Thanks for keeping me company tonight. It helped."

He sat down, facing the computer. "Okay, thanks for calling." He waited, watching the phone's screen go dark. Not a sound from their bedroom.

He hadn't done anything to feel guilty about. Claire wouldn't have any reason to flare up about him talking to Jan. But he expected she would.

In the kitchen, a beer in one hand, pork chop in the other, J. D. stared out the back window, watching the nearest turbine make its ceaseless, dutiful circuit. They always made him think of a bird tethered, wanting to fly but restrained, frustrated. Slaves to the wind.

If Claire's grandmother hadn't signed that contract, none of these troubles would have started. He turned away from the window. Shit, who was he kidding? Claire would have figured out a way to start those clinics, whether she had that turbine money or not, come hell or high water. He poured the last of the beer down the sink. As he passed the computer, he closed its lid. He made a decision. He'd sell the bulls on video auction. Then he turned out the dining room light, checked the front door lock.

Without turning on the bedroom light, he saw Claire lying on her left side, facing the wall, breathing like a sleeper. He undressed in the dark and moved the cover as little as possible getting in bed. Even though he wanted one, he didn't get up to get a blanket.

Floyd County Tribune
Thursday, September 12,
2013 Jackson Ranch Bull Sale Plans Change

J.D. Havlicek, Managing Partner of the Jackson Ranch of Jackson's Pond, Texas, announced today a change of schedule for the ranch's first on-site bull sale, originally planned for Friday, September 27, 2013, with related activities on September 26 and 28.

Havlicek said, "Due to some problems with accommodations and logistics for visitor comfort, we have chosen to conduct this first sale by video rather than onsite at the ranch."

"We regret not being able to have all our friends present for the sale, but next year, with more opportunity to plan, we hope it will be a weekend to remember. Meanwhile, we offer these excellent bulls this year by means of Internet auction services of Carson and Gillman Livestock Auctions."

Interested parties can register for the sale, which will be held on Thursday, September 26, 2013, at www.carsongillman.com.

Rural Health and Wellness Clinics Hours Change

Hours of operation for the Rural Health and Wellness Clinics in Calverton and Jackson's Pond have been changed.

Beginning Monday, September 23, 2013, both sites will operate on the schedule below, until further notice.

Monday—9 a.m. to 5 p.m.
Tuesday—9 a.m. to 5 p.m.
Wednesday—10 a.m.to 5 p.m.
Thursday—9 a.m. to 5 p.m.
Friday—9 a.m. to 4 p.m.
Saturday—9 a.m. to noon
Sunday—Closed All Day.

CHAPTER 6
Rumbling

Phone in hand, Amy cracked her bedroom door open. She'd heard a timid knock. Jay Frank had learned not to burst in, finally, after she yelled at him about a hundred times. "What?"

"I need to ask you a question."

His face was so pitiful, she opened the door. He looked over his shoulder like a spy, then slid inside and shut the door behind him. "Just a minute." She held up the phone, pointed to it and mouthed, "Chelsea."

Turning her back, she said, "Chels, my twerp brother wants something. I'll call back in a few minutes." He hadn't moved, was standing there looking like he was ready to cry. "What's wrong?"

"Are they going to get a divorce?"

"Who?"

"Mom and Dad."

"Why, what did you hear?" Even when he acted like he wasn't, he was watching and listening to everything.

"Nothing tonight, not yet. But they talk loud in their room, when they think I'm asleep. Mom yelled once. About the bull sale, the Sheriff, you, Jan."

Me? What about me?"

"She thinks you're bul—something."

"Tell me exactly what she said, what he said."

"I don't remember. That was last week." He pressed his right side with both hands. "My stomach hurts."

"Who's Jan?" She sat on the bed, patted it as an invitation.

He shrugged. "Business, Dad says." He came over to her bed, didn't sit, paced back to the door. He looked like an old man, all humped over, his right hand clamped to his stomach. "Who would we live with?"

She'd bet anything he'd start crying next. "Try to remember what she said about me."

"I covered my ears with a pillow. I didn't hear any more."

"You're lying." Now he *was* crying, shaking his head, blubbering that he wasn't lying.

With him all panicky, she'd never get anything out of him, even if he knew. "Settle down. We'd probably get to choose who we'd live with or maybe trade back and forth."

Shaking his head again, he said, "No, I couldn't choose."

The sniveling stopped. After a while, she said, "I'd go with Dad." Nodding as if that settled it, she said, "I've got to call Chelsea back." He stood there looking like such a little kid, in his pajamas with snot drying underneath his nose and tears on his chin. She hugged him. "Quit worrying. Nobody's getting a divorce." She picked up a towel she'd left on the floor. "Here, wipe your nose and dry your face and go get in bed."

He got to the door and then turned around, shaking his head no. "You didn't hear them."

Amy sat with the phone in her hand, staring at the mountains on the screensaver, trying to feel the way she'd felt those days just two weeks ago when they were all in Taos. Ten, the phone said. She remembered the second day, that late afternoon coming back to Taos from Questa, passing through that little valley where the road rolled down the mountain into a tiny town. The way the sunlight in the late afternoon painted everything there and showed her more shades of green than she knew existed.

That day, the whole weekend really, everyone seemed happy, the way families are supposed to be. Uncle Chris and Andrew had treated her as if she were a princess, taking her around town, showing her the gallery and their house. And that night, her mother hadn't even gotten upset when she asked why they never visited the ranch. She had said, "Uncle Chris has some bad memories of Jackson's Pond."

Amy asked, "Because he's gay?"

Speaking to her like she was an adult, for once, her mother surprised her, not asking how she knew what gay was. She only said, "When he was growing up, it wasn't easy being different in Jackson's Pond."

"I hope he'll come sometime. Chelsea and Jennifer and Rick, everyone at school would be so impressed to meet a famous artist.

Well, maybe not everyone. Some people pick on Rick and call him queer."

Her dad had spoken up from the other side of the room. "I hope you don't keep friends who treat people that way. It's cruel." Then he went back to staring out the window at Taos Mountain, probably daydreaming about being at the top.

That's the way she wished her family was, always. But that had been like watching a video of people acting, not her real family. Jay Frank was right. She could feel it when they were both in the house, even if she hadn't heard the word, divorce.

Amy punched the first name in Favorites. Chelsea picked up right where she stopped, in the middle of telling what Tiffany had told her. How she explained that vomiting after every meal, no matter how much you ate, would keep you from gaining weight *and* would stop you from having periods. Amy half-listened until Chelsea asked, "Have you tried vomiting?"

"Never, I won't because it ruins the enamel on your teeth." Never wasn't exactly true. She learned that laxative cramps weren't near as bad as vomit burning a track from her stomach up into her nose that time she stuck her finger down her throat after eating a bunch of candy.

Chelsea started up again, going on about how she was never going to let herself weigh more than ninety pounds, no matter what. And would do *anything* to keep from having periods.

Amy made a sound she thought passed for agreement and said, "Yeah, ninety, max." That morning, she'd weighed 108. And then, she told Chelsea she was pretty sure she'd already stopped her periods because there hadn't been a sign of one in several weeks. Before she knew it, as if she couldn't stop talking after she'd started, she blurted out about her mother finding the Ex-lax box and the food wrappers. As soon as she said it, she knew Chelsea would spread that around before the night was over. That girl couldn't keep her mouth shut.

Hoping she could turn time back, picturing herself with super powers, Amy said, "That's what I'm afraid of, that she'll find something. I mean she *hasn't*, but she watches me all the time, snoops in my room, even though she swears she doesn't."

"You said she *did* find the Ex-lax. I heard you."

"What I *meant* was, it's what I'm afraid will happen."

"Liar. I can tell when you're lying."

"You're the liar if you repeat that."

Neither one of them said anything for a few seconds. Amy's stomach grumbled. "I have to go. I'll call you in the morning before school."

Chelsea said, "Yeah, sure. I need to go, too. Tiffany's supposed to call."

Amy opened her bedroom door, checked the darkened hall, then tiptoed into the bathroom. Her dad, in the dining room—she could only see his back—had his phone to his ear. She'd heard her mother go to their bedroom earlier.

Pulling down her leggings and underwear, she checked the light-days pad, just in case. It had been thirty-two days. Her mother had explained, in more detail than Amy wanted to hear, about periods, back when she turned ten, even brought home "supplies" as she called them—tampons and three different types of pads. Then four months ago, the first time she found her underwear spotted dark reddish-brown, Amy had tolerated one more session on the subject, and once again nodded when her mother reminded her to use the proper terms for body parts.

Twice since, for about three days each time, bloody evidence she was female appeared, and she hated it. Worse than that, all she wanted to do was eat or cry all the time, period or not. If her mother knew that, she'd have her seeing some kind of specialist. She sat on the commode and waited to see if the noise in her stomach meant anything, and tried to think of someplace she could hide the box of laxatives Tiffany had given her today at school. Bought them at the Convenience Mart, she said. "My mother never pays attention to what I do. I'll get them for you anytime. That or anything else." Her mother was divorced.

Hunger, that must be the reason. She needed something to eat. Nothing hidden in her room, not since having to lie to her mother about those Oreos and Snickers—she'd told her Tiffany stuffed them in her backpack. "Tiffany likes getting people in trouble," she'd added.

Her stomach cramped and she passed gas, the odor of something that belonged behind a cow.

Tiptoeing again, she made it to the kitchen without her dad seeing her, grabbed an unopened bag of Cheetos and a jar of peanut butter from the pantry, decided against crackers because getting them out of the storage tin would make noise, crept back to her bedroom, and then allowed herself to exhale. Using her right index finger as a scoop, she extracted a glob of Jif, put the finger and its contents into her mouth, and without chewing (what was there to chew?), swallowed it down. Three more bites, same size, followed. Seconds later, a spasm of coughing made her reach for the last of a Diet Dr Pepper that had sat on her bedside table all afternoon. Nothing nastier tasting—flat, tinny. RE-pulsive. Seconds later, her stomach roared, causing her to reach for a pillow to hold against it. The grumbling stopped and the Cheetos beckoned. Something made her hold off on opening them. She stowed them, the peanut butter, and the laxatives in her bottom dresser drawer, under her outgrown ballet leotards and leg warmers.

Propped with a pillow against her headboard, she checked her phone, again. No messages. Nothing new on Facebook. If her parents loved her, they'd let her have TV in her room. Her homework already finished on the bus on the way from school, not sleepy, still hungry, she stuck in her earbuds and clicked on her favorite playlist, One Direction, Taylor Swift, and Bruno Mars.

With her luck—she was not a lucky person, ask anyone—if they divorced, they'd argue a lot about the two of them, both wanting Jay Frank. Then, they'd decide to send her to boarding school somewhere. She flipped back to her screensaver and closed her eyes to imagine herself there in those mountains. Maybe Gran would let her come and live with her in Taos. That would be for the best, for lots of reasons. Or maybe Uncle Chris would build her a little casita of her own, like Gran's, right out behind their house. And she could learn to paint, or maybe, if she didn't grow any taller, she could be a dancer the way she'd always planned.

A Taylor Swift song she didn't remember the name of came on, one of the sad ones. Next thing she knew, she had tears on her chin, probably looking the same as Jay Frank had, like some pitiful little kid. She jerked out the earbuds, and heard her mother's voice from down the hall, every word loud and clear. "It's not my fault you're embarrassed. It was your decision to change the sale. Besides, I'm sure your *business associate* is more than glad to help make it all work out and keep your reputation spotless."

Her dad wasn't loud, but he sounded old and mean, a person she didn't know and didn't want to, when he said, "If you weren't too damn busy . . . reputation matters . . ." Then something else lower she couldn't hear. Amy covered her head with her pillow and tried to see those shades of green.

Sometime later, she'd been asleep until a pain grabbed her below her belly button, wrenching and cramping. She sat up, pulled her knees to her chest and wrapped her arms around them, rocking to ease the pain. Another pain cramping and twisting pushed her up, toward the bathroom. Something ran down her leg. Oh God, was this a period starting? She grabbed at the top sheet, pulled it around her and between her legs, trailing it behind as she hurried to the bathroom. Barely to the commode, she untangled the sheet, jerked off her leggings and underwear, and lowered herself to the seat, just before her bowels emptied. Hot and explosive, wave after wave, until dizziness made her think she'd fall face first to the floor. Then it all stopped. She flushed, hoping to make the smell go, not choke her. Trying to stand, she reached for the wall to steady herself, took a deep breath, sat back down. Another cramping wave rolled across her lower belly. And it started again. Nothing but liquid, and the threat of vomiting.

"Momma, help me." It came out so weak, she barely heard it herself. Eyes closed, head in her hands, her elbows on her knees, she waited. They'd find her in the morning, on the floor, if she didn't get up. She breathed deeply again, and managed to stand. Bits of undigested food, things she didn't remember eating, floated in the toilet bowl. No blood. The brown-stained sheet lay on the floor.

Shuffling, bent forward, she reached her room, but pushed herself farther down the hall. Without knocking, she opened her parents' door. A few more steps and she held onto the mattress and knelt next to the bed, her mother's side. Whispering, she said, "Momma, I'm sick."

As if she'd been waiting, her mother sat up. "What's wrong, honey?"

"I'm sick."

"Oh, hon, let's go in your room so I can see what's wrong."

From the other side, her dad asked, "What ?"

"It's Amy. I'll take care of her."

Her mother reached behind Amy, grasped her arm on the far side just below the elbow. She said, "Lean on me."

In her room, on her own bed, Amy rolled to her side and gave weak-sounding one-word answers to the questions her mother asked. "Where's the pain? When did it start? How many times?" Plus lots of others. Then she turned to her back and let her mother examine her belly. To the last question, "Is there anything else you can tell me?" she shook her head no and because she couldn't help it, she closed her eyes.

"It could be a virus, or something you ate. You don't feel feverish. There's no rebound tenderness, so I doubt it's your appendix. I'm going to get you some ginger ale. I'll be right back."

Usually, her mother's way of speaking, using medical words and precise descriptions made Amy want a different, normal mother. Tonight, hearing her calm statement, "no rebound," gave her comfort, even if she wasn't sure what it meant.

As promised, her mom soon sat again on the bed beside her watching as she sipped some of the liquid. "In a minute, I'll get you cleaned up and you can go back to sleep. We'll see how you feel in the morning. Keep drinking that while I get a washcloth."

Amy wiped at the tears leaking down both her cheeks. "I'm sorry, Momma."

"It's okay, honey. I was awake anyway. I heard a truck or something on the road."

Her mother returned with a wet cloth, a towel, the soiled sheet, wadded, and a clean one she flapped out, then tucked in at the foot of the bed. Feeling like a baby, not resisting, Amy let her wash her face and hands, and turned over to let her clean her behind. "Here, slip on these p j bottoms," her mother said. "Feel better?"

Amy nodded, "A little." She couldn't help how her voice came out, small, like a four-year-old. As her mother turned out the bedside lamp, Amy pulled the cover to her chin and rolled to her side again. She said, "I'm scared."

"I think you'll be okay.' Her mother sat on the bed. "I'll rub your back, help you relax."

After a few minutes, her mother said, "How's that?"

Amy nodded. Near a whisper, she said, "Please don't leave."

She felt the mattress shift and then her mother's arm over her, holding her. "I won't. I'll sleep right here, baby." Then she kissed the back of her head.

CARSON AND GILLMAN CATTLE AUCTIONS
SAN ANGELO, TEXAS
www.carsongillman.com
1-866-423-1506

****

Home	About Us	Auctions

OUR FIRST EVER SALE FROM A RANCH SPECIALIZING IN GRASS-FED NATURAL ANGUS BEEF—PRIME BREEDING STOCK

Jackson Ranch Bull Sale from Jackson's Pond, Texas Register for a Buyer's Number Midnight, September, 18—Midnight, September 25, 2013

Auction at 11:30 a.m. Central Time Thursday, September 26, 2013. Open to Internet and telephone bidders holding buyer's numbers issued for this sale.

Fifteen bulls, all three and four-year-olds, from premium lines will be offered. Video of these bulls will be posted at this site tomorrow, September 19, 2013, beginning at 8 a.m. Central Time.

Link to videos and to request a buyer number
www.carsongillman.com/jacksonranchbulls

Partner/Ranch Manager J. D. Havlicek will respond promptly by email to all questions about the bulls submitted via this site until the day of the sale.

See terms of sale link for payment and delivery conditions.

CHAPTER 7
Rustling

J.D. stood in the barn brushing his horse, Dobie, in long, smooth strokes, talking to him, telling him he was going to be having his picture taken and needed to look especially nice. The horse rolled his eyes and twitched his left ear, probably thinking he might refuse to smile. From behind him, J.D. heard Claire saying, "I need to talk to you."

Without planning to, he said the first thing that occurred to him. "Will it wait?"

"No, it won't." There was that same don't mess with me tone. "Amy was up last night, sick. She insisted on going to school this morning, said she felt fine. I'm almost certain she took a laxative, a large dose, that gave her stomach pain and diarrhea. That's what I was *trying* to tell you before. Binging and purging. An eating disorder. I'm going to get her an appointment with Dr. Habib. You have to back me up, make her go."

As little as she'd been civil to him lately, he thought about balking. But he didn't have time to get into another argument. It wouldn't stop at Amy's eating. Arguments never did. Before he knew it, they'd both be dragging up any and everything they'd been pissed about for months, the way they had the other night. And then she'd bring up Jan. He brushed the horse from neck to tail in one stroke, then patted him on the rump.

"Okay. If she gives you any trouble, I'll step in. Otherwise…" He moved to the saddle rack. His favorite saddle could use cleaning. Peering in the box where he kept the brushes, for a can of saddle soap, he said, "That it?"

"Yes. *Thank you.*"

He nodded, and she left the barn. After he heard the kitchen door slam, he hurled the can of saddle soap. It slammed against the barn wall. He had to apologize to the horse. He waited until his better humor caught up with him, then walked Dobie to the horse pasture gate. Before he could get the latch closed, Dobie loped to the far fence where the other five horses stood clustered. He proceeded to fling himself down and roll, covering himself with dust. J. D. shook his head, remembering his dad saying, "Count on it. Anytime you need a tiny bit of cooperation, nothing and nobody's willing."

That wasn't the end of it. While she loaded dishes in the dishwasher, after supper, during which the only sounds had come from forks against plates, Claire said, "Just so you know, they caught Sandra Berry, the nurse practitioner, yesterday down at Round Rock. Sheriff Clark says she's charged in the thefts at the clinic and the guy she was with on possession and other drug charges. I may have to testify whenever they try them, unless their lawyers make a bargain."

"I guess that settles all your problems, right?"

"It'll be hard finding a replacement. It was hard enough to find her, for the salary I offer. So, no, everything's not settled. I'm afraid Susan's not going to stay when I tell her she'll have to work Calverton alone every day. But it's either that or close…"

"Closing one of them's a good idea anyway. You might have time for your family now and then."

The look she focused on him just after that could have drilled hard rock. She said, "Forget it. Let me know if there's something the *ranch owner* wants me to do. Otherwise, I won't take up any more of his time."

In case the tone of her voice left any doubt, she slammed the door on the dishwasher and left the room. Later, when he finished reviewing the breeding records one last time and walked past the family room, he saw her asleep on the couch.

The next morning, he woke up before dawn. First he worked at the computer. He checked the auction website as soon as he got online. The announcement blinked near the top of the company's website. Everything was there except the video the auction people would be out to shoot today. They'd promised to be there by 7:30. He'd told them the cattle would photograph best just after the sun came up.

Now he stood on the porch, hoping the wind didn't pick up too much and push dust into the air. He hadn't wanted to make too much of it to men he didn't know, but over the years, he'd paid attention. Wheat, grass, cattle, even the fences, all took on a special quality when early morning and late afternoon sunlight brought out colors that noon's direct, short rays washed out. If anyone asked, he'd have to admit that's why he was out here on the porch, watching for the crew to arrive. Five till seven and no sign yet. That and he hadn't slept much last night after that set to with Claire.

Day before yesterday, he and his only full-time help, Tag Butler, and one of Butler's sons brought the four bulls from the Havlicek place in a trailer. Then they gathered the other eleven bulls from their usual pastures to put them all in the large one down near Jackson's Pond. Not that there was much of a pond left, but the grass on that piece of ground had stayed greener through the drought than any place on the ranch and he'd left it ungrazed since mid-June. Of course, a lot of the green was weeds, not native or improved grass. Still, it looked pretty good, considering it had rained only once this year.

The three of them had worked from horseback, taking care to ease the other bulls over, not to get them stirred up. After they got them in the pasture, Tag went on to check the cattle on the rest of the ranch, and J.D. rode the fence line around the whole pasture, once more, to be certain nothing needed mending. While tending the fence, he watched for any sign the young bulls might be itching to start some territorial disputes. But they seemed more interested in the pond and the novelty of something green to eat. He took that as a positive sign.

The map he'd faxed to the auction company should have been clear, but maybe they got lost. He poured the rest of his coffee on the patch of grass next to the front porch step, set the cup on the rail, and yelled into the house, "I'm going to the pasture to meet the video people." That was just in case anyone in there gave a shit where he was.

Driving to the cutoff near the pond, he admitted to himself what he wouldn't to anyone else. If this sale worked out, it would be far simpler than it would have been having a lot of visitors and potential buyers out here poking around, expecting entertainment and beer. He'd figure out another way to get people in the association to know his name, later, after this was taken care of and things settled down.

He stopped the pickup on the road and walked the quarter mile to the gate near the pond. He'd enlarged that pasture to include the pond a few years back. And he'd paid attention to cutting back any new mesquite growth that tried starting up around the rim that had originally marked the edge. He'd spent lots of days, from the time he was a kid, sitting on that low bank, thinking. Now the only wet spot left of a pond that used to be ninety feet long and seventy feet wide was about twelve feet across.

According to the almanac, the sun would rise at 7:36. Seven o'clock and they still weren't here. Walking, looking at the glimmer of pale coral along the eastern horizon, wishing for a cloud or two for background interest, J.D. stumbled. He looked down to see what his foot had struck and saw a low spot and a shallow tire track. Unless Tag had been back here, no one drove on this road. Looking ahead, then back toward his pickup, he saw two sets of tracks, overlaid, showing in the dust. A trailer had been pulled down here sometime recently.

Doubting he'd have overlooked the tracks two days ago, he pushed the speed dial number for Tag. Two rings and Tag answered. "Yeah, boss?"

"You on your way?"

"Sure am. Just about to turn off the county road. I think that was the video guys I passed about ten miles back. Driving like they're from out of town, slow. Reminds me of a joke. Want to hear it?"

"Not now. Get to the cutoff to the pond. I need you to look at something."

Tag's voice changed, all business, no early morning b.s. now. "A problem?"

"Maybe. When you get here, don't drive to the fence. Stop on the road."

As soon as Tag stopped and hauled out of his pickup, J.D. waved him over to the single lane leading to the pond. "Follow me."

He walked in front of Tag beside the tracks from the road to the fence, pointing to several places that showed two separate impressions. "Does that look to you like a trailer and a pickup?"

"Whatever it is, it wasn't here two days ago."

J.D. agreed and pointed toward the southwest corner of the pasture. He said, "I see six bulls from here."

Tag climbed on the gate, stood on the four-inch drill stem frame, holding on to the support pole. "Six, eight, ten," he counted, using his right index and middle fingers like a pointer, ticking off the bulls as he added to the tally. "Twelve, fourteen…For the life of me, I can't see number fifteen."

J.D. didn't want to drive into the pasture. It'd make the animals restless. But damn, he needed an accurate count. "Trade places. Let me count." He clambered to the top of the gate, counted silently, using the same method, and came up with the same result.

Tag said, "Don't that beat all? Who rustles one bull and leaves fourteen behind?"

"Probably whoever had that pickup I heard late one night not long ago. I should have gotten out and looked right then. Shit!"

He jumped down from the top of the gate, grunting when he landed. One of the closest two bulls, about 200 feet away, looked up, but never moved. J. D. pointed to the lock on the loop of heavy chain holding the gate. "Look here. Still locked." Shaking his head, he said, "I'll be damned. Whoever it was knew how to pick a lock."

"Or cut it off and left a new one in its place."

"Hadn't thought of that." J.D. pulled a toothpick from his shirt pocket, stuck it in his mouth. After chewing it a bit, he said, "Okay, when the video guys get here, I'm telling them we decided to hold one back because he was too rowdy. Then I'll give the auction manager the same story. Never mind about us being in the picture on horseback. I didn't think much of that idea anyway."

"What about the law?"

"Soon as we're rid of the guys with the cameras, I'll call Sheriff Clark, then the Cattle Association. They'll send one of their Special Rangers. Clark couldn't find Dallas with a GPS, but those guys know their business."

"I reckon we need to preserve these tracks. Want me to head the video guys off, take them to the other side?"

"I'll meet you over there." J.D. pointed toward a column of dust moving toward them on the county road. "Hurry."

Skirting the tracks on the way to his pickup, he looked back toward the pasture. Three black bulls dallied near the pond, outlined by the rising sun's oblique light against the grass it colored a vivid green. He couldn't help admiring the whole scene. Trouble or not, there wasn't another place he'd rather be right then.

By 8:45, he'd glad-handed the video crew off the place, thankful they'd brought long lenses and hadn't needed to get in the pasture at all. Before they called their work complete, they showed him a preview which, just as promised, showed the animals' best features. Then he held his phone, waiting to be connected to the sheriff.

He gave his location and used the word rustling. Right away, Clark said he'd be out within the hour. He tried to give J.D. the phone number for the Cattle Association's Special Rangers. J.D. said, "Thanks, I have it. Broadus is a friend of mine. I'll call him soon as you give us a case number."

The sheriff didn't have anything else to offer.

J.D. and Tag spent a few minutes using binoculars to check the numbers on the fourteen bulls' ear tags. The missing one wore number 3355.

"Let's wait up at the house for the sheriff. He promised to be here within the hour."

Tag said, "Did you ask which hour? I've never seen him in a hurry unless it was close to dinner time."

The house stood empty, the front door locked. Claire was good about doing that any time she left. Once they got inside, J. D. made a pot of coffee, and he and Tag drank a cup and speculated about who might have taken the bull, how much the theft cost him, and when it might rain again, among other subjects. Then he checked the record on number 3355 so he could provide all the particulars for the lawmen.

He went to the kitchen to get more coffee, checked his watch again on the way. A note stuck under a magnet on the refrigerator stopped him. "I'll leave clinic and pick up Jay Frank at school and Amy at the bus. Dr. Habib is coming here to see her." She signed it, "Claire." Nothing else. Leaving notes wasn't her way. She might not talk to him much if she was mad, but she always talked, never treated him like a correspondent, a distant acquaintance. Back before they married, she'd told him she thought it was important to always talk problems out. Said when she was young, her parents didn't. She thought that's why they divorced.

When he pulled the note from under the magnet, another sheet of paper fell to the floor. The cell phone bill. Each call on his number, to or from Jan's number, stood out like a headline, highlighted in bright yellow. Jan's number. Had to give his wife credit—she didn't miss a thing. No doubt she'd called the number or used that reverse lookup website. Replacing the phone bill under the magnet, he drew a deep breath. Claire's note, he wadded to the size of fifty cent piece. The wad went into his front pants pocket, next to the loose change.

From the dining room, Tag yelled, "They's a cloud of dust coming this way. Must be the high sheriff."

They both went to the front porch. As far as J.D. was concerned, there was no sense making the man comfortable. All he needed from him was a case number.

Clark strolled from his vehicle to the porch. He shook hands with J. D., then Tag. He said, "Spell of bad luck for the Havliceks, it sounds like. First your wife's business and now yours."

Before Clark could pontificate further, J.D. said, "I wouldn't call this bad luck. I'd call it cattle rustling. Do you want to follow us down to the pasture to see the tracks or let the ranger take care of all that?"

The sheriff didn't move. "I'll need to fill out a case report. Why don't you tell me what happened and then we can go see tracks."

J.D. made it short, took about three minutes to tell it all, including the part about hearing a motor sound on the road several nights back.

"Uh huh." Clark wrote it all down, laboring as if he might get graded on penmanship. After asking a couple of useless questions, he allowed as how he'd follow them to the pond, since it was on his way back to town.

On the way to the pasture, Tag, riding shotgun in J.D.'s pickup, hitched a thumb back toward Clark, driving along in no hurry behind them. "He puts me in mind of something my daddy used to say. Soon as election time came around and guys started puttin' up posters, givin' away emery boards, and vote-for-me handbills. He'd say, 'There's another guy with a sore ass.' One day I asked what he meant. He said, 'Son, you see a man running for office, he's got a sore ass, and lookin' for a soft seat.' Now that I'm older, I see I should have give up on cowboying a long time ago, run for sheriff or county commissioner. A soft seat."

J.D. had to smile. He could always count on Tag.

Clark stood over the tire tracks, bending a bit from the waist. "See what you mean about double tracks." He pulled his notes out and frowned at the page. "And you say the gate's locked, chain not cut." He stared toward the gate. "Okay, well, I'll get on this and once I assign a case number, I'll call you."

As soon as the sheriff's vehicle turned toward the county road, J. D. called Marty Broadus, who said he'd be out just after lunch. Tag took off to make his usual rounds.

To keep himself occupied, J.D. checked on Jay Frank's goats. The four of them had been fed and watered, and were lounging in their pen. They clambered up and clustered at the fence, fixing him with gazes their slit-pupiled eyes made into questions. If Jay Frank kept exercising them and practicing the show routines, his animals could do well at his first County Junior Livestock Show in January. Working up from goats to sheep to cattle preparing for that same show, from the time he was a youngster, set J.D. toward becoming a man dedicated to raising animals. Maybe it would do the same for his son.

He stood on the back porch, debating whether to eat, even though he had no appetite, or to get on the computer. Fact was, he'd done all he could do about the auction. Starting tomorrow, it was up to the potential buyers to bid, if they did. He'd have to sit at the computer alone, and wait.

For all the advantages of the Internet auction, it couldn't match the excitement of seeing cattle enter a sale ring, hearing a live auctioneer's patter, and watching bidders make the sly signals they used to tell spotters they'd up the ante a notch—an index finger to a hat brim, a bid number card twitched once, a simple nod—all as mysterious to the uninitiated as the rituals of a secret society. Somehow imagining a lone rancher bidding from a computer just couldn't match what J.D. still thought of as a real cattle sale. Something missing, maybe the smell—a mixture of manure, ammonia, and dust—and the way it made your eyes water.

A smart guy would eat while he had time, a sandwich, at least. He stared in the pantry and chose Fritos, ate a handful, decided against bothering with a sandwich. From the refrigerator door across the room, the highlighted phone numbers glared at him. He grabbed another handful of corn chips and slammed his way back outside.

He drove six miles north to the house he grew up in, the only piece of ground he could actually call his. It stood just off the county road on the east side. Once in a while, late in the evening he drove up there and sat on the porch and thought about his life so far.

His dad's legacy included a quarter section that J. D. had planted back to grass, which was where he kept four of the young bulls. A barn, a corral, and a small five-room house completed his folks' home place. It took some effort that sometimes seemed wasted, but he kept it up—utilities connected, commode flushed, furniture in place, appliances working, doors and gates locked, new paint last year—even though no one had lived there for nearly eight years. He felt sure Jacob Havlicek would have called himself lucky; he'd died there in his sleep one night, spared by a heart attack from ever growing frail and feeble.

J.D. pulled into the driveway at his home place a few feet and stopped. Tire tracks all over the place. He hadn't seen them when they got the bulls out of the pasture because the pasture gate was a quarter mile south. He reversed and sped back toward the big house.

Just before he reached the turn from the road toward the house, his phone vibrated against his hip. He saw the number, then answered. "Hi, Jan. I can't talk right now, got something going on."

He took the turn too fast, sped up to correct the drift, and hit the driveway at about forty.

She said, "Just tell me you're okay." He'd heard that shakiness in her voice once before.

"Sure, I'm fine. Just busy. I'll call you later and explain." He clicked the connection off.

Broadus, driving a Dodge diesel pickup, roared in right behind, seconds later, and Tag pulled in behind him. They gathered by the ranger's truck, didn't bother sitting down to visit. Tag said, "Y'all raised so much dust, I thought I might be late for a stampede or something."

Broadus, short and barrel-chested, with a steer wrestler's shoulders and biceps, said, "I was just keeping up. He was the one speeding."

Any other time, J.D. would have been inclined to joke along with them, but he couldn't even summon up a smile.

The ranger eased a ballpoint and a skinny notepad from his shirt pocket. "After you called, I talked with Collins, the Special Ranger for the Amarillo district. No reports of stolen cattle in his area recently. And I posted a short item on the Cattle Association website. I'll fill in details there later. I'll need a copy of your brand." He stopped talking and gave J.D. a long glance. "This bull was branded, right? Not just tagged."

"Of course." J.D. didn't mean to sound quite as offended as what came out.

"And there's one other detail I have to ask. So don't take it personally. This bull yours or yours and the bank?"

J.D. shook his head. "Yeah, I heard about those sharp pencil guys selling what wasn't entirely theirs. No loans. All our cattle are paid for."

Broadus flipped the notebook closed. He said, "Now all that's out of the way, how 'bout we go to the pasture where this thing started?"

They loaded into Tag's pickup, all three crowded in front and Broadus' equipment bag stuffed behind the seat. As they rode, Broadus told about the procedures he'd use to find the bull. That's how he put it, like finding the animal alive and in good shape was his biggest concern. It was four thousand dollars' worth of J.D.'s, for sure. Losing that bull would take a bite out of his profit, even if all the others sold well.

At the pasture, J.D. and Tag recited what they recalled and Broadus asked a few questions. Then he unpacked a fancy camera outfit with attachments and some rulers and took a lot of shots of the tire tracks. "Sure be nice if we had some mud. It'd help a lot," he mumbled as he set the rulers beside the tracks at different angles and moved around trying for good shadows to bring out detail.

He walked to the gate, and studied the lock and chain. Moving fast, talking as he returned, he asked, "That lock wasn't cut off, or none of the links?"

J.D. said, "That lock on there could be a new one." He tried the key that should open the lock. It didn't. "I'll be damned."

Broadus said, "Came prepared."

J.D. nodded. He picked up a stick and drew the brand in the dust. Every time he saw it he thought about the day Willa signed the papers making him a full partner when she'd told him to figure out a way to add an H to the J and P of the original. She'd said, "Half of this operation is yours. The brand should show it." He hated to have to tell her about number 3355.

"Okay," Broadus said, "let's go see those other tracks." Then he mumbled some more as he packed his gear. Something about, "Good the wind hasn't blown much in the last couple of days."

At the Havlicek home place, after going through the same procedure, the ranger stood and dusted his hands on his Wranglers. While packing his gear, he asked some more questions, without waiting for answers between them. "Seen anyone unfamiliar out here or in town lately? Any teenagers live nearby? Anybody stop by asking for day work?" J.D. and Tag both answered with head shakes.

Tag said, "What I'm wonderin' is who'd steal one bull out of a pasture full?"

Broadus said, "Rather than all of them?"

"Yeah. Why not make it worth the trouble?"

"Somebody with a small stock trailer. And more guts than brains. That's why I asked about teenagers. I don't think this was an organized rustling operation."

Back at the house, they clustered around Broadus' pickup. He said he'd be in touch in the morning with an update, and throttled his way back to the county road.

After Tag left, J.D. went straight to his computer and opened the auction website. They already had the video posted. At least something was going his way. Bidding wouldn't begin until the twenty-seventh. His job was to stand by for questions from prospective buyers. Check in once or twice a day, the auctioneer told him, when he gave him the procedure for responding.

He had his phone in his hand about to call Claire, then didn't. Busy as she was, the rushed way she'd answer, the professional-woman tone she used talking from the clinic would leave him feeling the way it always did.

An hour later, J. D. sat parked in the lot at the Walmart close to downtown Lubbock. It took his pocket knife and some determination to open the package on the no-contract, prepaid cell phone. With a wad of change left from the hundred dollar bill he'd thrown down at the checkout counter, he expected to feel better about the deal he'd found. Fifteen minutes later, he'd read the instructions and stared at the newly activated, entirely anonymous, disposable device in his hand. Moving only as fast as his idling truck took him, he circled the lot to the back, where he threw that package and receipt in a Dumpster.

Outside of Crosbyton, taking the downhill turns just over the speed limit, he told himself he probably couldn't get a cell signal here, so don't bother, just enjoy the ride. At the Silver Falls rest stop, the one with trees and the nearly dry creek they called a river, he pulled into the empty parking area. He punched in the number. After one ring, Jan answered, sounding businesslike but pleasant. He said, "Now I can talk a minute or two. Do you have time?"

"Sure, since it's you."

He gave her an abbreviated version of the cattle rustling story.

"Are you okay? That had to be upsetting."

He shrugged it off, said he was fine, all a part of doing business. "One other thing. If you need to call, use this number from now on. If I miss it, I'll call you back." He didn't give her time to ask any questions. "Need to go now. Talk to you later."

He made good time getting back to Jackson's Pond and on out to the house. No vehicles waited in the driveway, so he took his time locking the phone in the glove compartment.

http:cdc.gov
Centers for Disease Control and Prevention
Healthy Weight - it's not a diet, it's a lifestyle!
CDC Healthy Weight Assessing Your Weight

BMI Percentile Calculator for Child and Teen: Results   Print

Information Entered

- **Age:** 13 years 3 months

- **Birth Date:** Friday, June 02, 2000

- **Date of Measurement:** Wednesday, September 18, 2013

- **Sex:** girl

- **Height:** 5 feet 5 inch(es)

- **Weight:** 108 pounds

Results
Based on the height and weight entered, the **BMI is 18.0**, placing the BMI-for-age **at the 36th percentile** for girls aged 13 years 3 months. This child has a **healthy weight**.
What does this mean?
What should you do?

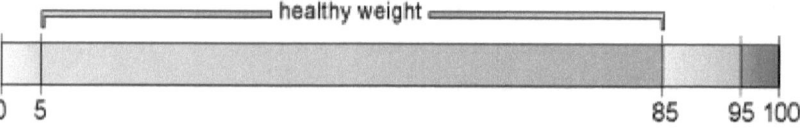

- underweight, less than the 5th percentile

- healthy weight, 5th percentile up to the 85th percentile

- overweight, 85th to less than the 95th percentile

- obese, equal to or greater than the 95th percentile

You can also view these results on a BMI-for-age Percentile Growth Chart .

BMI is calculated using your child's weight and height and is then used to find the corresponding BMI-for-age percentile for your child's age and sex.
BMI-for-age percentile shows how your child's weight compares to that of other children of the same age and sex. For example, a BMI-for-age percentile of 65% means that the child's weight is greater than that of 65% of other children of the same age and sex.
Based on the height and weight entered, the **BMI is 18.0**, placing the BMI-for-age **at the 36th percentile** for girls aged 13 years 3 months. This child has a **healthy weight**.

CHAPTER 8
Shouts and Whispers

After her mother dragged her into the clinic to see Dr. Habib, Amy had expected to get the third degree on the way home. But instead, when Claire Havlicek, Nurse Practitioner, finished with her patients, they left on time—*amazing!*—and with Jay Frank in the back seat pretending he wasn't paying attention, she only asked if they minded having the radio on. "Amy, you choose the station," she'd said. Not another word.

Amy hit the first auto select button and half listened. The things the doctor said occupied her thoughts.

When her mother picked her up from the bus, she explained that the doctor came once a month to review records and consult, so it was lucky this was her day and it worked out. Before she could stop herself, Amy had said, "Yeah, lucky."

Mother didn't even raise her eyebrow. Amy didn't say another word, but by the time they got to the clinic, an urge to run away, slamming every door she passed, nearly overpowered her.

The first thing Dr. Habib said, "I would prefer to see Amy alone, unless you object," gave her a chance to relax for the first time all day. At school, she'd walked humped over like her backpack weighed a ton. She couldn't help it. Coming up with a story her mother would believe, leaving out any mention of how food seemed to taunt her, and so did the laxatives, and why she needed to lose down to ninety pounds, made walking from class to class a chore. Even while she worked out the details, not listening at all in history class, she couldn't make it seem anything but lame. She didn't tell Chelsea, who was at her all day. And she didn't say *anything* to Tiffany, not even hello.

Dr. Habib told her to get undressed, and handed her a gown and a sheet for cover. To begin with, she asked Amy about her periods and if she had mood swings and had she had sex, and a lot of other questions. Some of them surprised her so much, she just told the truth, knowing she probably sounded like a six-year-old without a clue. Answered everything including about feeling ugly and fat. All except the questions about secret eating and had she ever taken laxatives or made herself vomit. To those, she'd only shrugged and pulled the sheet covering her lap up closer to her waist.

After the doctor examined her, she said to get dressed. Then she came back in and sat in a chair next to Amy, the way a friend would, and said it was likely the stomach problem was resolved. And she handed Amy a printout with her weight and height and stuff on it that said her current weight was healthy, and told her when she had time, to check the website it came from. "The site contains much information about how your body is growing and changing. For example, based on your parents' heights, you are likely to grow another couple of inches in the next three or four years. That's only one change. There will be many more as you become a woman." Amy felt the doctor watching her. "You may often feel that everything is out of control." Amy nodded because talking would have been a chore right then. The doctor put a hand on her shoulder and said, "I need to see you again next month when I am here."

Even though she knew better than to really trust the woman, for some reason, Amy agreed. Maybe Dr. Habib's soft voice and accented English, which sounded like she was singing, had something to do with it.

Then the doctor said, "I want you to promise me that between now and then you will not weigh yourself more than once a week and you will not take any medicine without checking with your mother."

Amy was tempted to shrug again, but instead, didn't answer at all. Dr. Habib said, "Do your friends encourage you to diet and take medicines, laxatives perhaps?"

Without hesitating, Amy said, "No." She looked toward the closed door. "Anyway, why do I have to promise you anything?"

"Only because I want to help you stay healthy and happy."

Amy did shrug then. "Okay. I'll try."

Even if her mother had let her choose the radio station and never asked question one about what the doctor said, Amy knew that wasn't going to be the end of it. She was sure that Dr. Habib told her everything they talked about. But even after they got home, the only thing mentioned was that Dr. Habib would save time to see her next month when she made her regular trip to the clinic. And Amy had said, "She told me."

At supper that night, Dad ate and said nothing and tapped a foot like maybe he was listening to music only he heard. Jay Frank picked at his food, darting his eyes from one parent to another. Mother broke the silence about the time everyone's plates were nearly empty. She said, "I think we should have a family meeting tomorrow night. Some things need to be discussed."

Shit! Here it comes. Me as the topic of a family meeting.

Jay Frank sat up quick as a lizard at the words "some things need to be discussed." She kept her eyes on the enchiladas she was making sure to eat, and concentrated on not running out of the room.

Dad's private playlist must have stopped. He got a wrinkle above his eyebrows and said, "We're all here. If we have to do this, let's do it now."

Using the voice she did at the clinic, calm and professional, her mother said, "We all need time to think about the things we'll need to discuss."

Her dad cut a bite of enchilada, ate it, keeping his eyes on her mother. He said, "Like what?"

"I think a few changes need to be made in what we do as a family to make certain we work together. It's mainly to see that you two," she nodded toward Amy and Jay Frank, "do well in school and stay healthy."

The more her mother talked, the more Amy felt like she'd been put under a microscope. She cut a small bite, mostly tortilla.

As he reached for the bean bowl, her dad said, "I have to get on the auction website after supper every night for the next week, starting tomorrow, until the sale. This meeting will have to be short."

"I'll have supper ready early, by six-fifteen." Amy saw her mother's left cheek twitch, as if a muscle escaped her control. She would bet Jay Frank didn't miss that either.

Sure enough, he jumped in with his bid. "I can take care of my goats early, too."

With a nod to him, and a smile that disappeared before it finished forming, her mom said, "Thanks everyone. Amy, do you need more salad?"

The only sound in the room was Jay Frank's fork against his plate, spearing his pinto beans, one at a time. Before long, her dad finished off his rice, which he rounded up with a buttered tortilla, and pushed his chair away from the table. When he stood and walked out, everyone else moved, looking like a movie played fast forward—Jay Frank took his dishes to the sink, Amy ate everything on her plate and asked if she could be excused, and Mother followed Dad to his computer in the dining room. Neither of them looked up when Amy passed, going to her room.

Chelsea probably had tried to text or call, but Amy hadn't turned her phone on when she left school. She pulled the phone from her backpack and looked at it, then stuffed it back. *Let her wonder. If she wants someone to talk to, she can call Tiffany. She always answers.*

A soft knock on her door. Jay Frank, as always. She let him in. Maybe he knew something else. She asked, "What now?"

"This may be when they tell us. About the divorce. You heard her, make some changes, she said."

He paced from the door to the window and back, his boot heels dragging each step.

"I don't think so. Are they talking now?"

He nodded. "She's standing behind him and he's staring at his computer screen."

"Crack open the door."

Their mother spoke like he was deaf. Even down the hall they heard every word. "Sheriff Clark says Sandra's denying everything. Claims I never kept records, she got no supervision, the guy only gave her a ride home. The Nursing Board investigator who was here several days ago said those charts and billing sheets showed her negligent practice, possible fraud. But now, with her making those claims, they may investigate me."

Then Dad said something she couldn't get all of, about "always risky being in business." She heard, "Don't make a big deal out of it." Then more that sounded like mumbling. "This *meeting*. You should have talked to me first. Got my own problems. I'm sure you've heard."

"Not from you."

Amy pushed Jay Frank away and shut the door. "She's coming this way."

He went red in the face, ready to burst. She put an arm around him and pulled him over to sit on her bed. He said, "We can tell them we won't choose either one of them."

After she got him calmed down, talking about his goats, and promised to help him work them every afternoon, he slumped out of the room.

With no one to text or talk to and no television in her room, the only thing left to do was listen to music. She dug in her dresser for her MP3 player and, for a second, thought about the stash of food and laxatives in the bottom drawer.

Lying on her bed, listening to Bruno Mars, she remembered Dr. Habib asking what she enjoyed for recreation, could almost mimic her accent, maybe from England, very proper. The answer she'd given was what she *used* to do before she outgrew her ballet clothes—practice dancing and dream of being on stage. She didn't tell her what she did now—homework, music, text, talk on the phone, same as all her friends. The things everyone did.

Later, when Amy woke, the house was quiet. On her way to the bathroom, she saw the glow of her dad's computer screen, but he wasn't anywhere in sight. She thought again about the food in her dresser. She tiptoed back to her room, picked up the jar of peanut butter, but left the Cheetos in place, in case of an emergency. Before she could talk herself out of it, she'd replaced the p b in the pantry. Less chance of hearing it calling to her from there. Feeling crafty as a burglar, she made it back to her room without a sound.

The next afternoon, reading the printout Dr. Habib gave her, Amy focused on the words, "This is a healthy weight." She'd checked the website and proved it to herself, and even though she hadn't intended to, had spent time reading about body changes in puberty. All that about body hair and breast buds made her want to throw up, but there it was, fact. Happens to everyone. She experimented putting in weights up to 136 and saw that she could weigh a lot more and still be "healthy." Nothing said she'd be pretty. Bookmarking the page, she closed down the computer.

The next day, Mother made it home on time. When she called them to eat, Amy saw they were having her favorite, chicken strips and mashed potatoes. Without any conversation other than the usual "please pass" and "thank yous," the four of them finished most of the food, including the beet salad.

Dad said, "Let's get started with this meeting. I have things to do."

Mother said, "Amy, Jay Frank, help me clear these dishes off the table."

Amy saw that twitch in her mom's cheek again, even though she really did smile. About two minutes later, they sat at the table, three of them looking toward the woman who called the meeting.

"I believe that all of us have developed some habits that aren't healthy and aren't helpful for Amy and Jay Frank as they try to do well in school. There are lots of reasons, and I don't think blaming anyone is helpful, but I hope we can discuss what we can each do to change. Does anyone else think there are habits some of us need to change?"

Jay Frank, quick as a shot, said, "I play video games all the time. My teacher says we shouldn't have more than two hours a day of screen time besides what we do in school."

Amy said, "Yeah, our teacher, too."

Dad had been sitting tipped back in his chair. He leaned forward and put his arms on the table. "What does screen time include? Television and all that stuff on your iPad?"

Jay Frank nodded like his head was loose. "Yeah, Dad, all that. Laptops, big computers. And smart phones too if they're connected to the Internet."

Smart little twerp!

Mother spoke, looking down at the table, like she was reading what she said. "I let work come home with me, and stay at work late more than I should."

The room was quiet for a while. Then Mother said, "If everyone agrees that too much screen time for Amy and Jay Frank and too much work time for me are habits to change, we can talk about what we can do to improve."

She waited before she said any more, but no one else spoke.

Amy saw her give Dad a look. He looked right back at her. As she watched her parents' staredown, thinking this meeting could go on all night, Amy wished for dessert.

Jay Frank squirmed in his chair and said, "I have an idea. I can bring my iPad in here and leave it after supper."

She had to give it to her brother, he got things moving again. By seven o'clock, three of them had promised to put all screens, turned off, in the kitchen after supper, not to use them until the next day. And their mother added that she'd be certain not to bring home any work and unless there was a patient emergency, she would leave the clinic at or before closing time every day. Dad said he'd have to think about what habit he wanted to change. Said he'd let them know.

"It will help me if we post these plans somewhere we can see them," her mother said. "Amy, you have the best handwriting of all of us. Would you make a list and put it on the pantry door?"

Standing on a chair in front of her closet, Amy pulled the sketchpad from the shelf where she'd put it many months ago. An eye-catching poster would make the rules more noticeable. It took a bit of searching in her desk drawers to locate the colored pencils. Around the edges, she'd draw different screens, then color in…. She heard her mother's voice, loud enough to drown out Taylor Swift coming through her earbuds. "The least you could do is make a small effort. Sitting there above it all." Her dad's words were muffled. Then her mother's voice again—"These kids need two parents." Amy turned up the volume.

She walked from her room to her brother's and knocked on his door. "Come help me make this poster." He scuffed along behind her like a scolded puppy.

He said, "I had some more ideas. But I was afraid to bring them up."

"Like what?"

"Our teacher said we should make sure to get outside every day. Get some exercise."

She sketched in an iPad with a game showing on it. He pointed to the lower corner, the fingernail on his index finger chewed down, ragged and bloody. "Put a laptop down here."

The first item, she wrote in large red letters, **Screens off after supper.**

He said, "They're arguing again."

Mom doesn't bring work home.

Mom leaves clinic at closing time unless a patient emergency.

"I said I'd help you with your goats. Let's add that." She wrote it in. Then she said, "I could practice dancing, but I'd need you to help me with my dance music—make a playlist."

His eyes widened. "You'd let me?"

"Sure. But I have to have some new tights and stuff. Mine are too small." After adding the last two items and sketching in a telephone with its screen glowing, she turned the list so he could see it. Her mother's voice rose again. Jay Frank's smile disappeared.

"Come on," Amy said. Carrying the sketchpad, her brother trailing, she went toward the sound of voices. The argument stopped when she knocked on their bedroom door. "Mom, Dad, we're hungry for dessert."

Mother opened the door. Jay Frank said, "Come see the poster Amy made. Do we have any ice cream?"

She and her brother had vanilla; Mother ate an Oreo; Dad made himself some coffee. Mother taped the poster on the pantry door and stood back to read it. "I see you made some additions. That's great."

Her dad carried his coffee to the dining room.

Jay Frank disappeared, then returned and placed his iPad on the kitchen counter.

In her room again, Amy started another sketch, a ballerina, the star, with three others together behind her, en pointe. The star stood tall, far taller than the others. Peeking from behind the stage curtain, a crown-wearing prince made a disgusted face at the principal dancer.

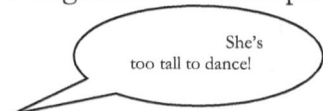

Amy drew in a cartoon "thought balloon" above the prince's head.

She tore out the page, wadded it, threw it toward her wastebasket, missed. On a fresh page, she drew a bag of Cheetos, orange and red, then told herself she'd needed a model, the bag she'd hidden. In a few minutes, after eating every single squiggle, leaving her fingers covered with the powdery orange dust, she brushed the crumbs from the sketch paper and flattened the empty bag, checking her drawing for accuracy against the real thing. Every detail matched. She folded the bag into a small rectangle and stuffed it in the bottom of her backpack.

In the bathroom, she scrubbed at the Cheeto residue on her fingertips, avoiding looking at herself in the mirror. Then slowly, she thrust her clean right index finger past her tongue into her throat. At first, she only retched and nothing came up. On the next try, she vomited, a lumpy orange mass, and without trying, a second wave emptied only yellow liquid. She rinsed her mouth and brushed her teeth. She heard no sound from her parents' room. Now she would sleep.

Floyd County Tribune
Thursday, September 26, 2013
Letters to the Editor
Dear Sir:

I am writing this letter in hope you will publish it as a warning to all parents of children in the Consolidated School District Middle and High Schools. <u>Someone is supplying our children with over-the-counter medications that can harm their health.</u>

My daughter brought home a large box of laxatives hidden in her backpack. I found the box when I was looking for dirty clothes on laundry day. None of the medication was missing from the box. She said that someone, she refused to say who, told her if she overeats, she could take that medicine and she wouldn't gain weight. (She worries constantly about being obese even though she is not.) That same "friend" gave her the medicine.

I am not a health professional, so I consulted our doctor. He told me that large doses of laxative can cause electrolyte imbalance leading to fainting in addition to massive and repeated bowel movement with painful cramping.

My daughter did not admit taking any other medicines or any illegal drugs, and I have not found any in her room or her possessions. I will be on guard because next time, it could be something more harmful or illegal that a "friend" supplies.

I have spoken to the school authorities, but there is little they can do.

A concerned parent

Editor's note: Our policy of not publishing anonymous letters has been waived in this one instance. We invite comment in response and request that you sign your letters.

CHAPTER 9

Hypocrisy

The last patient of the morning sat on the examining table. The fact she came from Idalou prompted Claire to ask what brought her to Jackson's Pond. After a three breath hesitation, the patient said, "I usually go to my family doctor in Lubbock. But I don't want him to know about this." Another long pause followed, and Claire waited. "I heard about you from my cousin in Calverton. She said I could trust you."

Claire scanned the patient questionnaire the woman completed when she arrived for her appointment. She didn't assume that the facts—forty-one year-old, divorced female, church secretary, gravida II, para II, no surgeries, no chronic illnesses—told the whole story. She expected that something more than "painful menstrual periods" written in neat script in the "current illness" blank accounted for this woman's obvious distress. Claire sat on the low stool facing the exam table where Deborah, that was her name, sat. Claire said, "Tell me what I can help you with today."

It took the patient a several long seconds to force out the answer. "I think I have a sexually transmitted disease. I can hardly sit, I itch…down there, and I have a discharge."

Claire asked all the questions protocol demanded—onset, how many sex partners, previous STDs, difficulty urinating, burning, description of discharge, and the one that made the patient look up, surprised—had she looked at her vaginal area with a mirror. Deborah closed her eyes and said, "I was afraid of what I'd see. You must think I'm such a fool."

"Not at all. You're human and you're alarmed. I'll need to examine you." She confirmed that the patient's last menstrual period had been two weeks before with no sexual contact since then, and that she was taking no medications and had no medication allergies, then handed her a gown and a cover sheet. "I'll do a complete exam, not just the pelvic. And while I'm doing that, you can tell me the things that are worrying you the most about this. I'll knock before I come in."

When she returned, the woman hunched on the table, gripping the cover sheet over her lap, alternately wadding and flattening it. As Claire quickly checked her ears, nose, throat, heart and lung sounds, her patient squeezed out her story in short bits—three years since her divorce, working two jobs to take care of herself and two children, bitterness toward her ex who had left her for someone younger and more fun, avoided men, never dating until six months ago. "I met him at church." After she said that, she made a noise that sounded like a laugh, but wasn't. "Like that's a recommendation."

Claire asked her to lie down while she palpated her abdomen. "Everything seems fine so far. Your temperature is normal, heart rate's a little rapid, and your blood pressure is one thirty-six over eighty-eight, slightly up, probably related to this situation." She knew she wouldn't have to ask, eventually it would come out.

Sure enough, Deborah said she'd only ever had sex with her husband. "In my whole life, no one else. So I was wary of starting anything with another man. But after six months and we'd been talking about marriage, well . . ." She began crying. "I thought I could trust him. He said his wife had died six years ago, and I was the first woman he'd even been interested in. How stupid was I? I believed every word."

Claire waited until Deborah stopped crying before asking her to scoot to the end of the table and put her feet in the stirrups. "I'll tell you each thing, step by step, before I do it. First, I'll touch the inside of your knees, to position your legs where I can do the best job. Breathe slowly and deeply—it helps you relax."

With gloved hands, she gently spread Deborah's legs. She looked up over the sheet stretched across her patient's knees and saw that Deborah had placed her hands on her chest. Her breathing no longer carried the ragged sound of suppressed sobs. Claire positioned a light over her left shoulder and lifted the sheet. A raging case of genital warts greeted her. She quickly collected specimens to test for other STDs, explaining as she worked.

After labeling the specimens, Claire stood, removed her gloves. "You can sit up now. You're correct. This is an STD, genital warts. It can be treated. You go ahead and dress. I'll be back with your prescription."

Claire told Laverne she could lock the front and go to lunch. She would see the patient out when they finished. After she handed Deborah the prescription for imiquimod cream and explained its use, and took care of other details about lab reports and a follow-up appointment, she showed her to the office, where she could sit in a chair, not on an exam table.

Printed handouts, filed alphabetically by topic, filled a file drawer in Claire's desk. Some health care providers didn't take the time, assuming patients could look up anything they wanted to know on the Internet. She offered patients the printed information for two reasons. First, they were something tangible, therefore as valuable as the medication prescriptions she wrote; and second, after receiving this other sort of "prescription," patients often began to talk more openly about their concerns, things that needed to be aired, but seldom were uttered in a brief exam room encounter.

She handed Deborah the sheet about genital warts. "You might want to look over that while you're here to see if you have questions."

When Deborah looked up from reading, she said, "This part about a healthy immune system can often fight off the virus—I've been under stress for so long, I doubt my immune system works at all."

Claire nodded. Deborah said, "Since way before my divorce. And now look at me. A grown woman with a sexually transmitted disease."

Then, with no prompting, she talked. Disjointed rambling thoughts poured out. For the next twenty minutes, Claire listened to Deborah berate herself for poor judgment, stupidity, and bad character. When there was a pause, Claire said, "You were lonely. We all want to be loved. Want to believe and trust. That doesn't make you a bad person."

Deborah shook her head, and said, "I'm so embarrassed." Then she sagged forward, hiding her face in her hands, sobbing. "This is punishment. A sign. No one will ever love me."

Claire said nothing until the crying changed to sniffling. "That's your feeling now. It will change."

Deborah sat up straight, wiped her eyes. "I doubt it." She spent several seconds folding the information sheet, pressing down each fold. "How long?"

"As long as it takes to forgive yourself." Claire watched her stow the prescription and the folded sheet in her purse. "Tell me what you plan to do the rest of today."

Deborah said she just wanted to go to bed and hide under the covers. Claire agreed that resting would help. As she walked her to the door, Claire asked Deborah to promise she would come back before the return appointment if symptoms didn't improve or if she needed to talk.

After the patient left, Claire sat in her office, leaning back in her chair, eyes closed. She wondered if Deborah knew what a fraud her understanding nurse practitioner was, preaching forgiveness, prescribing rest. What a hypocrite. Forgiveness? The truth was that for Claire Havlicek, slights or disrespect from others stayed unforgiven in a secret part of her heart. Rest? When anxiety loomed or disappointment bore down on her, Claire struck back by pushing herself with work and physical motion. And forgiving herself? She knew of her flaws, but knowing hadn't changed her, at least not enough.

When Laverne returned from lunch, Claire put on her sunglasses and walked to the front door. "I'll be back before the 1:30 patient comes. Just taking a walk." What she wanted to do was run.

Traveling fast toward the blinking light, she made a full circuit of the four block downtown area. If she kept walking, how far would she get before someone came looking for her? Instead of retracing her steps, she walked the ten residential blocks south of Main, never slowing her pace. After yelling, "Go home!" to a small pack of Chihuahuas that growled along behind her for two blocks, she crossed Main and paced along the streets to the north.

The first street held the line of churches—Church of Christ, no steeple; Methodist, stained glass windows, her mother in the choir each Sunday; Presbyterian, steeple and broken concrete steps, services the second and fourth Sundays of the month conducted by a minister shared with the church in Dougherty; Baptist, largest sanctuary, largest congregation. Next in line squatted an empty building once owned by an Assembly of God congregation, and at the end, Saint Margaret Catholic Church, the newest in town, masses conducted en Español. Doctrine and parking lots separated them all.

Banks Preschool, housed in a metal building with an attached playground, filled half of the next short block. She sped up, intending to turn right at the corner and return to clinic.

Melanie Banks' preschool operated mornings, Monday through Friday. She worked with one assistant and enrolled only fourteen children. Although the Consolidated School District provided free preschool, every space at her mother's school had been filled each of the four years it had been open. Some parents paid and others' children attended through a Federal grant to the Migrant Center. When her mother was planning the school, the two of them had a conversation Claire remembered, mainly because it made her realize how little she really knew of her mother's beliefs. She had said, "Children aren't born full of prejudice. This is a tiny bit I can do to delay their learning it."

From the time her mother opened the school, actually from the time her parents had remarried, Claire had heard something different in her mother's voice, more musical, gentler. Melanie Banks now favored more people with the smile she'd until then reserved for her grandchildren. The advice she'd always been quick to issue had been replaced by phrases like, "What do you think?" or "I'm so sorry you're having a hard time." Yet, Claire expected that "but" or "should" lurked, just waiting to remind her of the mother who had always known best, who managed like a superwoman, and who never failed at anything she attempted. The two of them seldom chatted on the phone, but saw one another at least once a week, unless Claire was too busy with work.

Her mother stepped outside just as Claire approached. She said, "Beautiful day for a walk. I was going to call you this afternoon. Do you have time to come in?"

Claire joined her at the door. "I won't stay long. Patients."

Inside, the space held the odor of small children, recognizable to any mother—sweet, faintly yeasty. They walked together to a pair of child-sized chairs next to a low table. Her mother said, "I know there's lots on your mind these days."

Claire shook her head. "It'll be okay. Eventually."

"No advice. I promise." Her mother added a smile that looked genuine. "Kids okay? J.D.?"

"Busy, as always." The chaotic array of toys and books and children's art that covered every surface made her want to pick things up, neaten. Twenty years ago, her mother would not have stepped out the door until every item rested in its assigned space. Claire leaned back in the small chair. "Dad probably told you Sandra's denying all charges, and she's out on bail until her trial. The prosecuting attorney said I should expect to testify. I don't know what will happen with the Nursing Board—haven't heard from them again."

"Does that bother you?"

"I don't know how I feel about it." She shrugged. "I haven't had much time to think."

"What about letting the kids spend the weekend with us. Give you and J.D. a break? We could take them to Lubbock, go shopping, do kid stuff."

"Amy's not much fun to have around these days."

"Kids always act better away from home. Besides, I'm good at ignoring tantrums."

Claire unfolded from the chair, stood. "Let me think about it and let you know tomorrow morning. I've got to get back to clinic."

A quick frown, immediately replaced by a smile, crossed her mother's face. She rested a hand on Claire's back. "Have you lost weight? Your face is thinner."

Claire pushed her sunglasses up the bridge of her nose a fraction, and fussed with a stray curl. She edged toward the door. "Probably just because my hair's pulled back."

"If you want, they can stay longer than the weekend. Just let me know. Your dad would be tickled to have them."

"I'll call." At the door, she turned and said, "Thanks." As she passed the corner, she turned back and waved. Her mother hadn't moved from the doorway.

After turning the corner, she slowed to trudge along the block that would take her back to Main Street. Exercise usually helped, increased her energy, calmed her. Today, after a brisk thirty minute walk, all she felt was thirty minutes older.

At the end of its last block north, Main Street abruptly became Farm-to-Market 2282, like a divorcee taking back her maiden name. She turned right, stopped in front of an empty store that once had been June's Apparel. In the display window, a female mannequin stood upright, wearing a faded, flower-print dress and a vacant smile. Left behind, she'd stared out on Main for as long as Claire could remember.

Her own reflection, interrupted by oblique shadow obscuring half her face showed what her mother had seen. That face looked weary, shopworn. Some lipstick might help. As she pushed herself toward the clinic, she remembered something else from that day her mother had told about her vision for the school. She'd said, "I know how it feels to want to succeed. I had to lose a lot to learn what would really mean success to me." Then she'd changed the subject. She hadn't explained and Claire hadn't asked.

When she got home that evening, Claire stopped in the dining room where J.D. sat at his laptop. "Is pizza okay with you for supper?" Cooking a full meal sounded like a chore she couldn't complete. She'd seen twenty patients by the time Laverne locked the door. She didn't care if she ate at all.

He looked up, like he was surprised to find her standing there. He said, "I don't have time to talk. This auction." Then he returned his attention to the computer.

If she had the energy, she'd have repeated her question. She didn't and she wouldn't. In the kitchen, she sliced an apple and an orange, put six pecan sandies on a plate, and set two glasses and the milk carton on the counter. She yelled toward the bedroom, "Jay Frank, Amy. I put a snack on the counter. We'll eat in an hour." No one answered or appeared in the kitchen. She walked quietly to her bedroom where she changed into her Levi's.

When she approached the corral, Pegasus greeted her with a shake of his head and a nuzzle to her hand. He expected an apple. She didn't disappoint him. A screen door slammed. In seconds, Jay Frank stood next to her, his arm around her waist. She said, "Did you find the cookies?"

"Amy tried to take all of them, but I got two."

"Enough?"

"Uh huh. We having pizza tonight?"

"We are."

The door slammed again. Amy, wearing old jeans and boots trotted toward the corral. J.D.'s voice followed her, "Quit slamming that door. I'm trying to work."

Later, when Claire called everyone to the table, J.D. stopped in the doorway and said, "I'll eat later." He squatted to reach the bottom refrigerator shelf and pulled out a beer, then went back to his computer.

Amy pointed to her phone, which she had put in the basket on the counter on top of Claire's and Jay Frank's. She said, "I guess the rules don't apply to Dad."

After the kids each polished off two slices of pizza, Jay Frank reported, "I finished all my homework. Way easy math."

Amy pushed her plate away, empty. "I'm done, too."

Claire complimented them and said, "And you worked the goats." A knot spread across her shoulders and a dull ache lodged at the back of her head. "I saw Memaw today. She asked if you wanted to come to her house this weekend. She and Granddad will take you to Lubbock, if you want to."

Jay Frank didn't hesitate saying yes. Amy frowned, then said, "Could we go shopping?"

"Is there something in particular?"

"Ballet clothes."

"I'll let her know to pick you up after school."

Amy said to Jay Frank, "You promised to help with music. Let's go do that now."

Claire wrapped the pizza in foil, and put the salad in the refrigerator. J.D. didn't look up when she stood behind him and told him where she'd left his supper. She watched as he closed down an e-mail and opened the auction site. He said, "What?"

She repeated what she'd said, not making the effort to sound reasonable. A good wife would ask how the sale was going. That would take effort she didn't have the strength for.

"Okay. Hand me a beer, would you?"

Later, she woke when he dropped a boot as he undressed for bed. She kept her eyes closed. In minutes, she turned to her side, away from the beery smell of his deep sleep breathing. Then sometime later, another sound woke her—the toilet in the kids bathroom flushing, then flushing a second time.

Floyd County Tribune
Thursday, September 26, 2013
Area Crime Reports

Investigation of Bull Rustling Continues

Special Ranger Marty Broadus reports that he and local law enforcement colleagues continue collecting evidence and following leads on the theft of a registered Angus bull from the Jackson Ranch near Jackson's Pond. Estimated value of the bull is between $5000 and $7500.

"We've identified three persons of interest in this felony and expect to make arrests soon. However, we will proceed only after developing firm evidence to assure swift conviction of those involved."

In response to a question of whether a rustling gang was working the area, Broadus said, "We've had no other reports from ranchers in our district or the contiguous districts of similar thefts recently. There have been several equipment thefts, but all of those cases have been investigated and are now cleared. This theft is the only livestock theft reported in the past month."

CHAPTER 10
Alone and Lonely

Thursday morning, the only light in the dining room came from J.D.'s laptop. He'd been up since 4:30, first checking the sale site again, then drinking coffee and trying to decide. He hadn't put on his boots yet, telling himself that was being considerate to Claire and the kids.

He thought about riding Dobie down to the bull pasture. Seeing sunrise from horseback, watching the day spread over the grass and onto the cattle, made getting up seem worthwhile. Even if everything was so dry that any little breeze raised dust, the wind didn't usually pick up in earnest until the sun sliced its long rays above the horizon. Those fourteen bulls got along so well in the pond pasture, he'd left them there. Plus, after 3355 went missing, having them all in one place made keeping an eye on them lots easier.

After the auction today, he'd still be responsible for those bulls until the new owners claimed them. Terms of sale required they take possession no later than October fifteenth. It'd be nice if one person bought the whole lot and hauled them all away in one trip. But since grass fed, natural beef was a specialty market, the auction people told him not to be surprised if buyers from as far away as the West Coast, maybe even Canada got in on the sale looking to buy into a good bloodline. That meant one bull at a time.

He'd know in about six hours. The catalog listed the Jackson Ranch sale at 11:30 Central Time. Probably over with by noon. He'd told Tag yesterday to come watch with him if he wanted to. Tell the truth, he'd like a little company.

Marty Broadus had been out last Thursday and the two of them had gone back to J.D.'s home place, walked the whole area where they'd found the tracks. Broadus told him he had a feeling there was something he'd missed, evidence. And he said that best he could tell on initial analysis, the tracks were the same as at the pond pasture.

Feeling like someone on CSI, J.D. followed the ranger's instruction and walked in a deliberate pattern on one side of the drive while Broadus did the same on the opposite side. He'd said, "If you find anything, just stop, don't pick it up. I'll take care of that."

Neither one of them said anything, just walked the pattern. About five minutes after they began, Broadus held up a leather work glove and yelled, "This yours?"

J.D. hollered back, "Check inside. All mine have my initials in them. Tag seldom wears gloves." He watched as the ranger dropped the glove into a plastic evidence bag.

A minute or two later, J.D. came across a cigarette butt. He and Tag didn't smoke and neither did Tag's two boys. Everybody chewed or dipped, if they felt a need for nicotine.

Broadus put on a latex glove to bag the snipe, which he said was one of those cheap generic brands, said maybe they could recover DNA. Then the ranger turned up the best clue, a receipt dated September fifteenth from a convenience store in Matador. And he'd called yesterday to let J.D. know that receipt produced a solid lead.

Six o'clock. The kids would be up making noise soon. Claire, too, busy being a responsible parent, professional woman. He poured coffee into a large insulated cup and stuck a package of peanut butter crackers in his shirt pocket. Pulling on his boots, he decided to use the pickup instead of Dobie this morning.

As he opened the front screen, he heard Jay Frank's barely awake voice say, "Bye, Dad." He didn't take time to answer, but told himself he'd take the boy out riding as soon as he came in from school. Right now he had some things on his mind.

After driving by the bull pasture, counting to confirm they were all there, J.D. sped past the house where he and Claire lived when they first married, where Willa and Frank Jackson lived before that, and on north the few miles to his home place. When he pulled off the county road, he drove to the barn, out behind the house. It wasn't likely anyone would come looking for him. There was plenty for Tag to do, and he got more done when he worked alone, when he didn't have an audience for his b.s. He'd be the only one who might need J.D.

He parked and unlocked the glove box. It had been two days since he'd checked the phone. Three missed calls showed on the log, all from Jan, yesterday. Last time they talked he'd told her he'd let her know today if he was coming to the association meeting. It would start at eight Saturday morning. He'd have to leave tomorrow if he was going to make it. The committee she chaired, where she said she really needed his help, was charged with a project called "Rebranding the Association." He'd mentioned, just in passing, that some guys wanted him to run for an office. When she heard that, she told him that being on the committee would increase his visibility. He'd wanted to laugh, but she was serious. She told him she'd worked for some state senator before she quit to ranch full-time, said visibility was important.

Maybe so, but the main reason he might go to the meeting would be to help her out. Besides, he liked talking to her. From all he could tell, listening to other people, watching her at meetings, her natural beef operation was succeeding. She could teach him some things.

After swallowing some coffee, J.D. cleared his throat and pressed the call button. It rang five times and then went to voice mail. He closed the phone.

Whoever made the tracks in the yard hadn't bothered the house. He and Broadus had checked and found both the front and back doors locked and all the screens intact on the windows. In the barn, his first saddle, some ancient hand tools that qualified as antiques, assorted junk, and the old pickup his dad had kept after J.D. bought him a new one were all in place.

He unlocked the back door to the house, went in and made his usual circuit—turn on faucets, flush commode, turn on the stove, check the refrigerator, listen to his footsteps echo in the five small, empty rooms, wish his dad were there to give him advice, even if he seldom took it.

He sat in his dad's recliner, the only piece of furniture J.D. had left in the house. Once before, he'd thought about making this his headquarters for the ranch, getting a desk and desk chair, a decent file cabinet. He'd even checked on whether he could connect to the Internet on the phone line or if he'd need satellite service. They'd been lucky to get fiber optic as far as the big house. Now, since someone invented smart phones and air cards, he could probably do without any kind of wires.

But those were details. If he wanted to work here instead of at home, he could. If he didn't mind a lot of questions. Well hell, this was his *business*. A business shouldn't be run out of a man's hip pocket and off the dining room table. He took out the pad he carried in his shirt pocket and made a note. Desk, chair, file cabinet.

This time when he called, Jan answered. "J.D., I'm so glad you called." He'd learned to count on hearing that from her. It made him smile. She said, "I see your sale is on at 11:30. I'll be watching. It'll be the second best thing to being there to help make the bidders more competitive." She hesitated, drinking coffee, he thought. "I guess you'll have to decide after the sale about the meeting this weekend."

"I've decided. Unless the wheels fall off, I'll be in Fort Worth tomorrow evening."

"You have no idea how happy that makes me. The two of us can get this committee moving. I'll be at the Worthington. Will you?"

"I haven't made a reservation yet."

"I can get you a special rate. At least one of the others on the committee will be in tomorrow evening. I'll make dinner reservations." He'd heard that brisk professional-woman-gets-it-done sound before, but not from her.

"Can't say when I'll get in. Don't wait on me."

"J.D., one more thing. Thanks for listening when I called that time feeling so low. It helped."

"Sure." He flipped open the pad and added couch to the list.

"It was my birthday and a sad one." She hesitated, like she expected a question, then went on. "I might as well tell you. My husband died on my birthday five years ago. It's never a good day for me."

"I'm sorry. I didn't know." He'd heard talk she inherited that ranch. "Well, glad it helped."

"It did. More than you know."

"Well. Um, I got a lot to see to today. Talk to you later."

He walked through his home place again, slowly, then wrote coffee pot on the list.

Back at the big house, silence met him. Two pieces of toast

waited on a plate along with a slice of ham. Another note from Claire said she'd be in on time and "We need to talk."

He cracked two eggs to fry, but had to scramble them when he busted a yolk. When they were cooked, he took his plate to the dining room. The auction website showed they were running on time. Still two and a half hours until the Jackson Ranch bulls came up.

He opened Bing and typed "Jan Taylor and Taylor Ranch and Rotan, Texas" into the search query. After seeing several photographs of Jan at political receptions, at fund raising events, and at a Cattle Association convention, he turned up an obituary of Paul Taylor. He'd died at home, it said, September 2008. Age sixty-eight. Survived by wife Jan and one daughter, Lisa Boardman of Cambridge, Massachusetts. Then it went on for three paragraphs about his career in the field of banking and petroleum, along with a string of charities he supported. An all around good guy, if you believe obituaries, and a lot older than Jan. She was nowhere near sixty. If he had to guess, he'd say somewhere in her early forties, closer to his age.

In the kitchen, he washed his dish and silverware, then took a slow walk out to the corral and eventually into the barn. He thought some more about the trip to Fort Worth. Staying home and fixing whatever was wrong between him and Claire crossed his mind. But maybe it was something he couldn't fix. Far as he knew, he hadn't done anything to end up the target of her bad attitude. Sure, she laid it off to worrying about Amy and stuff at her clinics. Still, it felt like she'd taken aim at him.

Used to be the only thing he ever had to worry about was her wearing herself out. Then after the kids were born, there'd be spells where she got all stiff and determined. But even then, all he had to do was put his arms around her and tell her he was concerned and she'd slow down. Or he'd take the kids somewhere and drop her off to see Willa. There was something about being with her grandmother that always made things better for her. She'd been younger then. Maybe that was it. Now she called herself grown. Didn't need him.

Tag yelled from the barn door, "You in here, J.D.?"

"Back here." He'd spent some time checking Jay Frank's goats and then got involved in cleaning up a pile of old tack. The smell of saddle soap acted like a drug on him, relaxed his muscles and made him look out toward the horizon.

"You serving lunch at this sale? I came early in case you needed help with the barbecue."

J.D. checked the time. "Guess we better get on up to the house. It's baloney sandwiches for this one. Have to make 'em ourselves. Caterers refused."

When he opened the auction company's site, it showed a sale running in South Texas, selling Santa Gertrudis heifers and steers. The heifers, a truckload sized lot of them, showed first. The auctioneer's voice, talking up the good points of the cattle, played as the video switched back and forth between the cattle and eight men in cowboy hats at a table taking bids as they were phoned in and two who kept up with computer bids. Every time one of them got a bid, he pointed a finger toward the camera and shouted it out. J. D. figured that action was intended to liven things up, make it interesting for those watching but not bidding.

Tag said, "That old boy knows how to work the bidding up. Good auctioneer."

J.D. nodded. A crawler inched across the bottom of the screen, showing the real-time change in the top bid. The rhythm of the auctioneer's voice and the steady movement of the numbers going right to left could hypnotize a person. He said, "It's twenty more minutes till ours. Let's make a sandwich."

Standing at the kitchen counter, smearing mustard on two slices of bread, Tag said, "Have any idea what those big boys might fetch?"

J.D. shrugged. "What I'd like and what they'll bring may be two different things." He focused on covering his bread with mayonnaise. "Pass the baloney over here. Want a Dr Pepper?"

They took their plates and drinks to the dining room. J.D. sat down, then got up again, and returned with a bag of Fritos. "I'd cut us an onion, but I'd be sorry later."

Tag polished off his sandwich in no time flat, no talking between bites. J.D. had only done away with half of his.

He said, "No breakfast? Go get you another one if you're

still hungry."

Tag headed for the kitchen. One bite later, J.D. stopped eating. The South Texas sale finished, the bottom banner switched to showing Jackson Ranch, Jackson's Pond, Texas, all in capital letters. The video showed long shots of the bulls in the pond pasture. The grass looked almost lush. The cameraman had found the best features of the place, for sure. He didn't know when the guy did it, but he also had zoomed in and lingered on the Family Land Heritage marker.

Tag got back to his chair in time to see that. He said, "Makes the place look mighty shiny, don't it?"

Next, each bull had his moment of fame, a lingering closeup. The auctioneer had told J.D. he intended to run each bull separately. He'd start the bidding pretty high, the company rep had told J.D., so the auction for each bull would move pretty fast. The whole thing should be over in thirty or forty minutes. J.D. turned the speaker volume up, pulled the pen and pad from his shirt pocket.

As soon as the auctioneer called the first bull, the animal's picture came up, showing his ear tag and below, his weight. "All the bulls in this lot are from a grass fed, natural beef operation. Each one has been fertility tested and complete breeding records were available from the owner prior to this sale by private message. Bull number 3351 …"

J.D. had sold plenty of cattle before, and it was a matter of pride, his own secret, that he'd never once lost money, even taking into account all the factors like transportation; pen fees at the auctions barn; the downward adjustments, like for shrinkage or overweight; and so on. Willa never mentioned it to him, but her records told him she'd paid attention when she was in charge, the same as he did.

The bidding started and in less than five minutes, climbed higher than he'd even hoped. He heard the auctioneer declare, "Sold." It was then he realized he'd been holding his breath. He wrote on his pad the price per hundred and the bull's weight. After that, the auction moved efficiently through all fourteen and then it was all over but the shouting.

Tag jumped up and slapped him a high five. "I think that calls for a beer! Got any?"

J.D. allowed himself to smile as he walked to the kitchen and came back with two Buds. He knew Tag would have to talk, rerun every bit of the action. J. D. half-listened and nodded a couple of times and drank his beer. When there was just a little left in the can, he said, "Well, I got work to do and you do, too. We better get on it."

He stood and as he did, his phone rang. The Carson Gillman representative had the details for him. J.D. said, "Hold on a second." Then he said to Tag, "Thanks for the company. I'll see you later on, down at the pasture."

Later, back at his home place—his office, he'd now decided—he parked near the barn and got the phone from the glove box. Just as he expected, there had been a call. Jan answered and didn't even say hello, just started talking fast, her voice reminding him of a high school cheerleader. "Congratulations! I don't know what you had in those bulls, but they definitely sold above the market. I'm as excited as if they were mine. Why, I'd hug you if I could reach you!"

"Well yeah, we did all right."

"Always modest. There will be a celebration in Fort Worth, I promise. Drinks are on me."

"I'll let you know when I get there. Can't say right now what time it'll be."

"I'm looking forward to seeing you. And I'm glad you called."

Nothing he could see out on the horizon gave him an answer about what to do next. The glow of the sale's success had him itching to accomplish something. After a few minutes, he backed out and drove to the county road and when he came to the highway, he turned right and drove to Lubbock. In town, after only two stops, he'd bought a desk, a chair, a couch and a coffee pot. With the load tied in place, he turned back toward Jackson's Pond. On the way, he called Tag and told him where to meet him and to bring one of his boys.

By four o'clock, they had it all unloaded and set in place in the dining room of the house where he grew up.

Somehow Tag managed not to ask any questions. J.D. wondered if the man was sick. He locked the house and they went to see about a heifer in the north pasture that had separated from the rest of the herd.

They found her near the back fence, far away from the water tank. She'd died sometime since yesterday. Neither of them could see any obvious reason. But she'd only been weaned a while back, and had always been small. They drove the lane around the pasture edge. All the rest were up and eating. Tag asked, "Want me to come back and get her?"

"No need for an extra trip. Let's do it now. There's a come-along in the tool box."

Claire had supper on the table and a grim expression on her face when he showed up at the house after dark. She said, "I didn't know you were planning to be late. It's stew and cornbread. Yours is in the oven. Coleslaw in the refrigerator."

He washed his hands at the kitchen sink. "Had a heifer to drag out and take to the used animal pit."

Neither of the kids asked a question. He wasn't surprised; they knew cattle sometimes died.

Claire said, "Your sale today, how did it go?" She didn't sound particularly interested, more like someone asking his opinion on when the drought might break.

He opened the oven door and looked in, then shut it. "I'm not real hungry right now. I think I'll wait, maybe make me a sandwich later." He leaned against the kitchen counter. "You kids have a good day?"

Amy nodded and pointed to her mouth, full of cornbread. Jay Frank said, "Yeah, school was okay. And we got all four of the goats to walk on the lead."

"'Cause you're doing a good job with them. Taking care of business."

He eased over to the refrigerator. As he opened it, he said, "The sale went fine. All fourteen sold high." A beer in his hand, he headed toward the dining room. "I'll be in here, taking care of some business."

It didn't surprise him when, after she cleared the supper away, Claire came in the dining room. "Did you get my note this morning?"

"I did."

"I don't know what's going on here, but we need to talk."

"About Amy?"

"Yes, among other things."

He pointed at the laptop. "This has to be done and it'll take another hour or two at least."

She sat in the chair opposite him. He exhaled, louder than he intended, then half-closed the top of the computer. He said, "Okay, what about Amy? Didn't she see your doctor?"

Claire nodded and said, "And she'll see her again next month. I thought it helped. And maybe it did."

"I haven't heard her sassing you."

"Not as much. But I have a feeling . . . It seemed too easy. As if she straightened up just enough to keep us from knowing."

"You have a *feeling*?"

"Be sarcastic if you want to, but she spends too much time in the bathroom and up at night."

"This again. So now you're a detective with a *hunch*?"

"If you'd search her room . . ."

"Whoa, I'm not the one with the hunch. Nope, you want to search, you do it."

"Lower your voice. I don't want them to hear."

"You're not whispering either."

Her jaw tight, she leaned toward him. Barely audible, she said, "Can you hear me? We should deal with Amy *together*."

Leaning across, mimicking her voice, he said, "You do what you think needs to be done. I won't stop you. Happy now?"

She sat back against the chair. He'd always thought she looked exactly like Willa, but with her face grim, sitting so rigid, she was her mother made over. She nodded and he heard a sigh. She sounded older and tired when she said, "I'll wait a few days. See if anything changes."

"Let me know." He opened the computer top. The screen glowed. The screensaver's goldfish floated by, flipped his tail and disappeared, only to return from the screen's other side. J.D. glanced toward Claire. She'd stood but hadn't moved from the table. He said, "If that's all you wanted to talk about, I need to answer these buyers, make appointments for them to pick up bulls."

She moved toward the hallway. He said, "Oh, I'll leave

tomorrow around noon. There's a Cattle Association meeting starting Saturday in Fort Worth. I need to be there."

She returned to the table, stood beside his chair. Speaking again in that near whisper, she said, "Anything *else* I should know?"

"I'll be back Monday."

Later, after eating some cornbread and drinking a glass of milk, he walked slowly toward the bedroom. Maybe he'd tell her now about his new office. As he passed the family room, he saw her asleep under a quilt on the couch.

The next morning, he made sure to take time to sit at the table for breakfast with the kids. He told them about his trip and when he'd be back. Jay Frank asked if there were any jobs he needed him to do. Amy said, "Who'll take care of the goats? We're going to Memaw's."

"Mom and Tag will take care of things here. You go have some fun."

Claire came into the kitchen dressed in a bright yellow sweater and dark brown slacks. She made a movement he took for a good morning nod, grabbed a breakfast bar and filled her insulated coffee mug. She smiled at the kids, and said to them, "You two need to move fast to get Amy to the bus on time." The circles under her eyes told him her night on the couch hadn't included much sleep. She stuffed another breakfast bar and an apple in her tote bag.

She turned toward him and said, "Will I see you again before you leave?"

"I'll get out of here around noon." His voice sounded unnatural to him, and so did hers, as if they were both reading to an audience, careful of their diction.

J.D. saw their son watching their faces, then shifting to look at Amy as she put a breakfast bar in her backpack. A child aware of everything could get old too soon, he thought.

He patted Jay Frank's shoulder and hugged Amy as long as she let him, about three seconds. "You two have a good time. See you Monday."

Claire had already left the room. He could see her standing on the porch, holding the front screen open.

In a less than a minute, they were gone, the Suburban's

progress marked by moving puffs of dust rising, then falling, quickly settling without the wind that usually blew, but didn't that morning. He watched until the puffs disappeared.

It didn't take him long to pack. Starched Wranglers and white shirts, underwear, his best boots, and a sport coat, plus the kit with his shaving gear and deodorant were all he needed for three nights. Next, he gave Marty Broadus a call, wasn't surprised he didn't answer. Not long after, the ranger called him back, sounding excited.

"We arrested two guys over in Paducah. All the evidence pointed their direction and sure enough, they'd put your bull in with a bunch of Hereford heifers on a place between there and Matador. Poor man's herd improvement, I reckon, trying to get some black baldy calves. Found bolt cutters in the pickup, so we added that to the rustling charge. We'll get a conviction."

"Great! Can I come pick up the bull?"

"I've got a helper. We're bringing him home right now. We'll be at your place in an hour."

"I'll be waiting down at the pasture. I can't thank you enough."

"It's my job—your Association at work."

True to his word, Broadus showed up before ten o'clock. J.D. and Tag helped unload the bull and they shook hands all around. J.D. asked, "You drink beer?"

"Been known to. Why?"

"So I can buy you a case. You deserve it."

"If you insist. Make it Modelo."

As they watched, the ranger and his helper wheeled the big diesel back onto the county road, Tag said, "This here's what I call a happy ending."

J.D. agreed and told Tag he'd be gone and to call him if any problems came up. As he got in his pickup, Tag said, "You know what'd be a real happy ending? If a guy who bought one of them other bulls decided to take 3355 off your hands, too."

J.D. said, "We can hope."

One worry off his mind, J.D. drove to his new office. Inside, he sat in his new chair. He'd gotten one called Executive, because it had arms. He pulled his pad from his shirt pocket and wrote file folders on it, then added blotter. When he went to the office supply store in Lubbock, he'd also need to look at a new printer. The kids or Claire might need the one at the house. The couch divided the room into two parts, one that looked sort of like a living room and the other side the office. He'd need a desk lamp or a floor model. He had to laugh at himself, all excited about furniture.

On the way back to the main house, he stopped by to check the other house on the ranch, the Jackson tenant house. No one had lived there since he and Claire moved to the big house when Willa left. They kept it in good shape like his home place. He checked his watch and then made a quick tour of the yard and barn and the inside. Everything still worked. Standing there a small slow sadness visited him—he remembered when he and Claire lived there, when everything felt just right. Maybe that was how homesickness felt.

Fort Worth was 300 miles, give or take. If he left by one, he'd be there by six, even with some traffic after he got to Decatur. Back at the big house, he made one last stop on the way in—the goat pen. Jay Frank kept it neat, paid close attention to their water and feed. J.D. told himself he'd done everything he could.

He passed through the kitchen on the way to pick up his bag, stopped in front of the refrigerator. He thought about leaving Claire a note, sticking it up there, but didn't know what to say. Going away used to be different back when he could count on what he'd find when he came home.

He skirted around town, drove directly to the highway and turned east toward Matador. This drive always relaxed him. Dropping down in elevation, steadily from 3100 feet up at their place all the way to Fort Worth at about 790 feet, the land changed from the flat mesa where Jackson's Pond sat, down off the Caprock onto the Rolling Plains. As he drove, he met an occasional pickup or car and passed even fewer. With the cruise control on seventy, he sailed through some curves making them exciting, and zipped along the straightaways.

Lots of the ranches now had ten-foot fences to keep exotic game inside. Instead of making their money from cattle, these ranchers took payment from hunters from Dallas and other cities bent on shooting a big trophy. Not on the Jackson Ranch. Never would be, as far as he was concerned. A select few people were allowed to hunt on the east pastures of the Jackson Ranch, but only the mule deer and quail that nature saw fit to supply. No exotics, no hunters who stayed longer than a day at a time. And none this year. The cattle needed the grass.

In Vernon, J.D. turned right onto 287 and set the cruise again. Lots of trucks used this highway, but nothing like the interstates. He'd make good time. When Claire had come with him, they'd sung along with the radio, acting like teenagers. When things got straightened out between them, he'd make sure they took a trip, just the two of them. They hadn't in a long time. It would just be a matter of planning ahead.

After a lot more miles, he thought he'd figured it out. They both had lots of responsibility for other people and things they'd promised to do that got in the way. And they were taking it out on each other. That was one way to look at it.

But for some reason he had trouble making himself believe that was all there was to it. Whatever was wrong, he couldn't fix it today. He'd promised the Cattle Association people he'd be on this committee and maybe run for office. Now that Broadus had found that rustler, J.D. was more certain than ever he ought to step up and be a real part of the organization, try to make a difference. Even as he thought that, a piece of him said, "Who're you trying to convince? Mostly, you want a reason to get away from home."

When he got to Decatur, he stopped to buy gas. After using the restroom, he bought a bottled Dr Pepper, wondered if it was the old fashioned kind made with cane sugar, then wondered why he cared. While he was at it, he let himself wonder what it was about driving a little over 200 miles that made him feel completely unconnected from home, the way astronauts must feel.

As he saw the Fort Worth skyline to the south, he heard the phone in the glove compartment playing its odd ringtone, five notes repeated, which reminded him of "Born to be Wild." That needed changing if he decided to keep the phone. He pulled onto the roadside and stopped. After pushing some papers and a pair of work gloves out of the way, he got the phone in his hand. "This is J.D."

Jan's cheerful greeting perked him up. Just checking to see

when he'd be in, she said, and to ask if he wanted her to get him a room. He told her he'd be in town around six. According to her, cocktails and dinner were already arranged.

"Call me when you get here. I won't start without you." Then after a pause he didn't try to fill, she said, "There's a little surprise waiting for you."

J. D. parked in the driveway of the Sheraton. No matter how much he'd made on those bulls, he didn't see a need to go the extra expense of staying at the Worthington. That's what he told himself before, when Jan offered to get him a room. You couldn't tell what a special rate would involve. No sense getting obligated.

Even without a reservation, he got a room, and parked in the underground garage. Before he left the pickup, he sent Jan a text saying he'd meet her in the lobby of her hotel at 6:30. He stuck the phone back in the glove box, locked it, lifted out his bag, and headed to the elevator.

He and Claire had stayed there the time she came to an Association meeting with him, about three years ago. Since then, he hadn't asked her to come along because she'd have to make too many arrangements—the kids, the clinics. And besides, to tell the truth, he'd gotten a bit rankled by all the attention. Guys who'd barely given him the time of day during the three meetings he'd been to before made a trip across the room to shake his hand and stare at his wife, close up. One older rancher, an association bigwig, had pulled him aside and said, "Son, a woman like that can be a real asset to you, whether she knows anything about the cattle business or not. I'd keep a short lead on her if I was you."

It wasn't her fault she stood out. That curly black hair, her long legs in those Levi's, those startling emerald eyes turned a lot of heads, even though she stuck close to him the whole time. He didn't understand how he could have been proud of her and wanted to hide her all at the same time.

Walking to the Worthington relaxed him after those hours in the pickup. Jan waved at him across the lobby as soon as he hit the door. Some guy he didn't know stood beside her, looking pleased to be there. She hooked onto J.D.'s arm when he got close, and introduced Ansel Phillips III, from San Saba. A head shorter than J.D. and about fifty pounds heavier, Phillips gave J.D. the once over and a big smile. "Folks call me Trey," he said. He was dressed like a rancher come to town, but his handshake felt like he might be a banker.

Jan said, "Let's not clog up the lobby. The bar's right over there." She led the way. "J.D., I told you we wouldn't start without you."

They sat on high stools at the bar facing a wall-covering mirror where a person couldn't avoid seeing themselves and everyone else. Jan ordered a Cosmpolitan—"I know these aren't the trendy drink now, but I like them." Trey said he needed a Jack neat—make it a double. J.D. asked for a Shiner—bottle. She said, "Want to find a table or sit here?"

Trey said, "I won't be able to stay long. You know, when you have relatives in town they expect to feed you. I have to have supper with my mother and sister."

J.D. didn't see any reason to move, and said so, making sure to smile. The drinks arrived and they raised them in each other's direction. Jan said, "Here's to our committee!"

Without any urging, she told them there were two other members of the committee and there would be a staff person assigned to do follow-up. "I think we should be able to get our work done before the spring meeting, or at least have a report with plenty of progress by then. I'd like us to meet once a month."

J.D. didn't intend to let his concern show, but she could see the mirror, too. She said, "Do you think that's too often?"

He looked directly toward her, not her reflection. "Not too often for a committee, but I might not be able to get away for all the meetings. I'm essential personnel at my place. That's how it is when you run as lean as we do."

Trey swiped at the screen on his phone with his right index finger, frowning. He tuned back in and said, "Whatever you think will work, Jan. Count on me." He downed his drink. "I'm going to have to go. Supposed to pick her up." He pulled a hair-on cowhide billfold from his hip pocket, extracted two twenties and set his empty glass on top of them. "My treat. See y'all in the morning. Meeting room at headquarters? Eight?"

J.D. watched Jan's reflection nod. He stood, shook hands with Trey, said, "Good to meet you. See you in the morning."

Before he could pick up his beer, Jan turned her stool toward his. A pendant, a single large diamond suspended from a thin gold chain, nestled between the tops of her breasts. Her red blouse's heart shaped neckline showed much of her slender neck and shoulders and plenty of the location of the diamond. When she angled back half toward the mirror, the stone caught light from one of the small fixtures above the bar. He could have sworn it winked at him.

She said, "I'll tell you about Trey. He and my husband were college roommates. The Board planted him on this committee, probably to see we don't stray too far."

Returning his attention to the mirror, he said, "I'm no good at politics."

"You don't have to be. I am." She held her glass up, looked through the pale red liquid at the light above the bar, then drained it. "Are you hungry?"

"Yes." Eating might get rid of the gnawing sensation that had started in his stomach. "Steak would suit me. Any other committee members coming?"

She shook her head. "Del Frisco's? It's a short walk."

Friday night, 7:30, and a line had already formed out the door of the expensive steakhouse. As soon as they walked in, the hostess looked toward J.D., raised her eyebrows, and said, "Reservation?"

Jan answered, "Taylor, for two." As they were led to a table, she said, "Hope you don't mind. I like to be prepared."

She ordered wine, a bottle, with the meal. As they ate, she explained the idea of rebranding to him, giving the association a fresh face, bringing its public appearance more in line with the sensibilities of the times, she said. He couldn't resist asking what was wrong with its brand now.

"The modern rancher, livestock owner, is often hands-on and tech-savvy, too, but is also a businessman. Or woman. More like you than Trey. Everything has to convey that."

She went on to tell him about her background in public

relations and advertising, about the Executive Director thinking rebranding was vital to the organization's future, that some of the Board didn't want anything to change—talking so much she didn't spend any time eating, only drinking occasional sips of wine. She'd wasted a perfectly good steak.

J.D. finished his meal and leaned back in the chair, listening. He hadn't drunk wine since college, and then nothing as nice as this.

When the bottle was empty, and the check came, he said, "This one's mine. Celebrating."

She drew a breath like it might be her way of gearing up to argue. But she surprised him just gave a little shrug. "As you wish. Thank you." She didn't say any more.

They took their time walking toward her hotel, both quiet. About a block from the convention center, she said, "Let's take a short detour." She pointed left toward the Water Garden. At the largest of the three pools, she sat on a marble slab, close to the water, patted the space next to her. He sat.

"Notice my new boots?" She pulled her denim skirt up to show the tall boot tops plus her knees and part of her thighs.

He took a long look. White with black filigree cutouts on the toe and the throat, the boots were western, with a riding heel, very fancy, surely expensive. They reminded him of some Willa wore. "Nice."

"Custom made. M. L. Leddy's, San Angelo."

"Not meant for work."

"Depends on the work." She scooted closer to him, dropped her skirt to cover her knees, and then opened her purse, stuck in her right hand. Then both hands. "Everything falls to the bottom of these big ones."

He watched without commenting. Finally, she pulled out a small, flat, charcoal gray box the size of a deck of cards. She held it in her palm and said, "I told you I had a surprise. Here it is. Congratulations on your sale!"

His mouth wouldn't seem to close, but no words came out. He turned the box over, but didn't open it. There was probably a better thing to say, but he couldn't explain what ran through his mind just then, so he took a deep breath and said, "Thanks."

She sort of giggled, then said, "Are you going to open it?"

Inside the box lay a money clip—plain, smooth, silver, about an inch and a half wide. On the top side of the clip, a silver medallion the size of a fifty-cent piece, thick sterling, carried the brand ⅃Ⴒ. This time when "Thanks!" came out, it sounded different. "How'd you know?"

"Checked my copy of the brand register."

He handed her the box, then spent some time arranging the cash from his front pocket in the clip and thinking about what he wanted to say. All that came out was, "Perfect, just perfect."

During a silence while he fiddled some more with reorganizing the money, all the bills facing the same way, folded exactly to fit, he felt her watching him. Heat rose up his neck. Maybe it was dark enough. Grown men don't blush. He said, "It's too nice. I don't know how to thank you."

She said in a husky voice, "You could have a nightcap with me. Maybe we'll come up with a way you can."

He nodded. Now he was staring at her boots. "Okay, sure. Why not? Where?"

"Back at the hotel would be handy."

All the way to her hotel, she held onto his arm like she belonged there. They seemed to take a long time getting to the Worthington. By the last block, he might have been dragging his feet.

They ended up in the lobby, near the elevators. She showed him her room key. He wondered where she'd carried it—not in that big deep purse. Her arm still linked to his, she moved closer to the elevators. She said, "I'm on eight. We won't have to use the mini-bar. I brought my own bourbon."

In the elevator, J.D. caught a glance at their profiles in the mirrors on both sides of the compartment. Jan, small and blond, standing close to him. With his luck, one of the other committee members would have a room on the same floor, see them get off the elevator. But the doors whispered open onto a completely empty hallway on eight after an express trip from the lobby. He felt in his pocket for the money clip. Besides, if someone had seen them, what harm would there be? Two adults, members of the same committee had business to discuss and were finishing the evening with a friendly drink. Just winding down after a busy day.

Jan slid her key card in and out and the door to 807 opened. Jan had called it her room, but it was a suite. She made a sweep with her right arm, reminding him of a game show host revealing what was behind door number one. J.D. half-expected a maid to greet them. He said, "Nice. Very nice."

"Make yourself comfortable."

Large windows, drapes open, offered downtown Ft. Worth for their approval. J. D. ambled past the sofa and coffee table and stood looking out at Cowtown's lights.

Jan had stopped at the built-in bar area. She said, "I told you I had bourbon, but I also brought wine. What's your pleasure?"

He turned away from the windows and watched her remove her boots. "I think I'll stick with wine, if that's okay with you."

"Coming right up." She lifted a bottle from the granite bar top. The label said Llano Signature Red. "What do you think?"

"Looks good to me."

She glided across the carpet barefoot, bottle in one hand and corkscrew in the other. "Will you help?"

He twisted the corkscrew and removed the cork with a slight pop, handed the bottle to her. She smiled up at him, and hesitated. He waited for whatever she was about to say. But she eased back to the bar and returned with two glasses and the bottle. She said, "Let's sit on the couch. Would you pour, please?"

He half-filled each glass, his hands steadier than he expected. He promised himself that one glass would be all and then he'd head to the Sheraton where he belonged.

Jan leaned against the soft leather back of the sofa, took a long sip of wine and angled her knees onto the seat, so she faced him. She raised her glass in his direction.

It had been a long time since he'd been alone in a hotel room with a woman who wasn't his wife. Conversation didn't come easily, not at all for that matter. So J.D. took a long sip from his glass.

The bottle sat where she'd left it on the coffee table. She pointed and said, "We'll have to finish that, now that it's open."

He smiled, gave a little laugh. "If we must, we must." Sounded like a line from a bad movie. So he refilled his glass.

When he looked her way again, she said, "You remind me a lot of my husband, the way he was when he was younger." She nodded as if she agreed with herself. "No one knows this..." She stopped talking and filled her glass and his. ". . . but I had been seeing him since I was nineteen. He was in his forties then, a friend of my father's. Married, like you. Had a daughter. Neither one of us intended it, but we fell in love. It was wonderful and it was awful. Before long, I left, transferred to Arizona to finish college. I wasn't going to be a home wrecker."

J.D. took a drink and then another which drained his glass. He said, "University of Arizona? What did you study there?"

She shook her head and put on a sad smile. "You're right, I'm feeling sorry for myself again. You're sweet to listen to me. These past five years have been hell. His daughter has always hated me, and she's been contesting the will since probate began." She drank more wine, then reached for the bottle. "We'll finish this off and I promise I won't open another one. Please."

"Does that tie up your ranching business? The will, I mean."

Jan shook her head. "He'd taken care of that years before. The ranch is in my name. But not his other businesses." She waited until he looked her way, then said almost in a whisper, "Would you do me one favor, just between us?"

"If I can. What is it?"

"Would you please just hold me for a few minutes? I am so damn lonely. Five years is a long time." Then he saw a rush of tears start down her face, even though she never made a sound.

He sighed and moved over next to her. "Come here." He put his left arm around her shoulders, telling himself it was like hugging his sister if some guy had stood her up, if he'd had a sister. She sagged against him and buried her head on his chest, her breathing ragged, streaming tears wetting his shirt. He shifted, and she wrapped herself around him, glove tight. He pulled her close and held her with both arms until she relaxed. Next thing he knew she pulled him into a kiss, a long, hungry kiss that he didn't resist. Another one, and another followed. By then neither one of them would have been able to blame the other.

Her arms tightened around his chest again. He moved and her grasp loosened. He said, "Wait, we have to stop."

She pulled away. The sound she made was somewhere between a sob and a laugh. She sat up and sniffled. "You're right. For now."

Getting to his feet, he shook his head and said, "I'm sorry. I shouldn't have done that."

"Don't apologize. You were being kind. It's not wrong for friends to be kind to one another."

"I'm going to go on, now. Thanks for the wine."

She shrugged one shoulder and her blouse slipped lower and the diamond winked at him, again. She said, "I really should get my notes organized for tomorrow. I'll walk you out."

He edged toward the door. "There's no need."

"Thank you for a lovely dinner."

At the door, he said. "Thank *you* for the money clip. See you in the morning."

She linked her arm in his and walked with him to the elevator. When she let go, he felt a weight lift.

Out on the sidewalk, he blamed the wine for putting him off balance, unsteady the whole three blocks to the Sheraton.

Abilene Courier Online Edition
Lifestyles
Sunday, August 18, 2013
Abilene Dances With Heart

The third annual Abilene Dances with Heart event, benefitting heart and cardiovascular research through the Heart Association, brought out a record crowd of more than 250 Saturday night August, 17.

Local stars, all seasoned ballroom dancers, plus two winners from last season's nationally televised show *Dancing With the Stars* provided the entertainment for the gala. Barry Carson and Tanya Underwood, from Los Angeles, complimented their local partners, Jan Taylor and Wes Turner. Carson said, "Either one of them could be a winner on our show." Winners of the local competition were Andrea and Buck Baldwin.

Afterward, the Abilene Symphony's Dance Band provided music for the non-competitors in the crowd to practice their steps. A silent auction featuring fine art and collectible firearms made intermission lively. At evening's end, Event Chair Jan Taylor (photos below) and Event Committee members Kathy Dalrymple, Evelyn Martin, Terry Ainsley, Barbara Cox, and Karen Reiger announced that even with auction results still not tallied, the event had raised more than $35,000. All proceeds go to heart research, as the event was underwritten by Ms. Taylor, in memory of her late husband, Paul Taylor, local rancher and banker.

CHAPTER 11
A Cry for Help

Claire heard and then dismissed the sound, some vehicle, probably on the county road. She needed a nap, a coma would be better, before she moved from the couch. Thirty minutes, she'd promised herself that as a reward for making it through the week, and for smiling and assuring her parents she'd lock all the doors, as if she'd never stayed alone on the ranch. A better mother wouldn't have been as relieved as she had been when she dropped the kids with her parents. But both Amy and Jay Frank had hurried inside their house as soon as she stopped the Suburban. Why not? Claire knew she wasn't much fun these days.

The kids had followed their granddad to his garage workshop. When she extracted herself from the living room and her mother's concerned scrutiny, they had yelled, "Bye, Mom," from the garage door. A hard week finished, she deserved this nap.

Now she could tell the sound came from a pickup, and it had just stopped in the driveway. She hauled herself off the couch and worked on a smile as she walked to the front door. Tag. She stepped out onto the front porch. He started talking as soon as he shut the pickup door. Never at a loss for words. "I promised J.D. I'd keep an eye on the place while he's gone. Thought I'd be sure you have my number."

"Same one as always?"

He nodded. "Just got through checking on the bulls. Now that 3355's back home, they're all settled. Guess J.D. told you."

"We were lucky to get him back." No need for him to hear how little she knew.

"I'll say. And I'll take care of them goats in the morning, case you want to sleep late."

"I'd like that. I seldom get the chance."

Tag stood with one foot on the bottom porch step. If she encouraged him at all, he'd settle on one of the porch chairs and stay to visit. Claire stepped back toward the screen door. "I promised everyone I'll lock the doors, so don't worry about me. Thanks for stopping."

Any other time she wouldn't have hurried him off, but the weariness she'd held off for days threatened to ambush her any minute. She knew better than to let herself get too tired. Forget napping, think early to bed. First, she'd eat whatever she found in the refrigerator, then she'd settle herself in the middle of all the pillows, occupy the entire bed, and read until she fell asleep. Having a plan always pushed her worst thoughts into the background and kept her moving until she allowed herself to stop.

As planned, her next stop would be the refrigerator. But she went toward the bedrooms instead. In Amy's room, she did what she'd warned herself not to, snoop. The first thing she noticed, Amy's sketch pad and colored pencils strewn on the top of the small desk, told her to relax, her daughter was a normal teenager. She smiled at the phrase; normal and teenager formed an oxymoron. She should have left the room then, because her next steps took her to the dresser where she opened, then closed, each of the top three drawers, and found only underwear and t-shirts. But the bottom drawer held another box of Ex-lax, partially empty, and ten large Snickers, plus wadded wrappers from three packages of Twinkies. She sat on the bed and thought how stupid and naive she'd been to believe one visit with the doctor had helped Amy. She unloaded the stash from the drawer and stowed it in a paper bag. In the kitchen, she put the bag on the top pantry shelf.

Keep moving, stick to your plan. Following her own advice, she stared into the refrigerator. An apple and a chunk of cheese in her hand, she wandered to the kitchen counter and sat on a stool. The first bite of apple seemed to expand as she chewed it, until she had to spit it into her hand. The cheese smelled moldy. She'd eat later, after she rested.

Skirting through the dining room, aiming for the bedroom, she stopped at the table, the computer. *Bulimia might not be the problem. A dietary deficiency might explain.* She sat and lifted the screen on the sleeping computer. It woke. She opened the browser, which offered to return to the previous session which "had closed unexpectedly." When she accepted, the list of sites that showed all included the name Jan Taylor.

Her hands shook as she opened one, then the next, scrolling through several news releases about Jan Taylor's charity activities and appointments in the cattle association, and then several photographs of her, always surrounded by men, always dressed fit to kill.

She pulled the power cord from the back of the computer, and jerked the plug out of the wall socket. Standing posed a problem. Her legs shook as badly as her hands had. She sat back down. When he called—he always called when he was out of town—she wouldn't say a word about what she'd found. But this was going to be settled as soon as he got back. All the rest of the problems could wait.

Coming to that conclusion helped stop the trembling. A few minutes later, she left the table. After a long shower, she put on pajamas and her robe. She would stay awake until he called, then she'd sleep as late as she wanted in the morning. That was her new plan.

After the ten o'clock news, she debated calling him. Instead, with each minute that passed, images of him alongside Jan Taylor flashed in her mind, one after the other, fast as a slide show, whether she closed her eyes or opened them. In every scene, J.D. looked proud and happy. Each one featured Jan Taylor, with her perfect blond hair, smiling up at him as if they belonged together.

Claire couldn't help herself, she reconsidered the last three years, how she had changed. As she did, sadness damped the anger down to an ember. Then just as quickly, the flame grew again. She wasn't the only one; he'd changed, too.

Tears she hated to waste streamed down her face. They weren't her usual tears, the ones that rose slowly, announced themselves with a sigh, filled her chest and eventually dribbled in sluggish streams, then in mucous lubricated paths past her nose, and if she lay supine, welled in her ears. Like an intermittent creek in dry country, her typical tears, shed seldom and always in secret, flowed briefly. The tracks they followed dried and hardened in the sun.

She didn't recognize these tears tonight. They rose like a seizure, involuntary, sudden, wrenching. She couldn't breathe. Then the sensation of falling, the one she feared the most, edged into her body and hovered, waiting to take her mind, also.

I will not let it happen.

Exercise and movement always made things better. She wiped her face, stood, stepped slowly up the stairs to the second floor, then made the circuit from one floor to the other and back again and again. All it did was make her muscles quiver. The darkness she feared came closer. She climbed the stairs once more.

The big room that covered the upper floor of the house, the room some remembered as the Jackson's ballroom, hadn't seen a party or a dance band in forty years. Claire opened the French doors onto one of the small balconies outside. Jay Frank's toy box, forgotten now that he followed his dad's every step on the ranch, sat in a far corner where partygoers might have once taken a break to observe fun in progress. Until recently, when puberty struck, Amy called the room her ballet studio, practicing hours before the mirrors installed on the wall opposite the balconies. Tonight, a glimpse of her own reflection assured Claire she was alone, a woman too worn for dancing.

As Friday became Saturday and the half moon rose directly in front of her, a pack of coyotes yipped in the distance. She pulled the sash of her robe tighter and stepped onto the balcony barefooted. The wind had laid at sundown, after gusting all afternoon, dropping the temperature near forty, announcing colder weather would soon follow. The telephone weighted her robe pocket and bumped against her leg as she moved left to gaze at the wind turbines. Two miles and more away, atop 200 foot towers, their red lights blinked a predictable pulse, their three-bladed heads rotated steadily, even on the calmest night. Standing at attention like a squadron of sentries, they usually gave her peace. Not tonight.

Claire cradled her phone in her right hand. Pressing Chris' name on contacts should be simple, would keep her promise, and could connect her to one of the two people who might understand. But the phone she pulled from her pocket might as well have been a rock—heavy, dumb, useless. She shivered and closed her eyes against the watching moon, then opened them when her horse whinnied from the corral near the barn. Her usual impulse to protect him didn't stir. She was absent as a sleepwalker.

She pressed the phone's button. Chris answered on the third ring. He would still be up. In Taos, he was on Mountain Time, only a little after eleven o'clock. "Claire? Are you there?"

She moved the phone away from her ear, the only voice she could summon was the one in her head.

"Claire, answer me!"

The energy she needed to push out the words rose on a sigh. "I need you to come." After what seemed like a full minute, listening to her brother's breathing, she said, "I need help."

"Are you hurt? Where's J.D.?"

"Gone. Ft. Worth. A meeting, he said." She hated that tiny, weary voice. It couldn't be hers.

"The kids?"

"At Mother's."

"Call her. She'll come out if you're afraid." His next words sounded muffled, probably explaining the call to Andrew.

"I need you. And Gran." Her throat clutched so tightly no other words could pass. Now that she'd allowed herself to cry once, she knew tears might come again too easily.

"Where are you?"

"Ballroom."

"On the balcony?"

She didn't answer, her attention remained focused on the nearest wind tower.

"Listen to me. Go downstairs, now, to the front door and lock it. Stay on the phone."

She obeyed his voice, moving from the balcony, but leaving the doors open and the moon waiting for her. It seemed to take hours, not seconds, to get down the staircase to the front door. "It's locked."

"Now go to the back and lock the kitchen door. Don't hang up."

She didn't bother turning on lights. She'd roamed these rooms all her life, from the time she was a child and Gran had lived here. When the worst had come before, when she was sixteen, she'd stayed here weeks, not talking, barely moving from the bed. Gran had understood she needed time and rest. Her mother hadn't.

"Is it locked?"

"Yes."

"Can you tell me what's wrong?"

"What isn't? I don't know. I..." She sat down on the floor near the back door, leaning against it, too tired to move farther.

"Are all the guns locked up?"

She laid the phone on the floor, without strength to hold it to her ear. Chris, from far away, said something she couldn't understand. She leaned forward, then curled on her right side near the phone. "You still there?" His voice pushed her to pick up the phone. Loud, stern, he said, "Answer me. What are you going to do next?"

"Go to sleep?"

"Yes, good. You go to bed and I'll be there by seven in the morning at the latest."

She looked at the blue-lit screensaver on the phone—mountains and a lake. Twelve forty-five. She said, "Tell Gran."

"I will. Now you get to bed. See you soon."

Sometime later, she pushed back her hair, and her fingers touched a crease across the right side of her face. Apparently she hadn't moved for hours, had fallen asleep on the floor inside the back door. Now she heard Chris' voice calling her name. Eyes still closed, she breathed in and held it, then exhaled, trying to rid herself of the fog isolating her in a place without structure or landmark.

Eyes open now, she stared at the phone, gone mute. His voice hadn't come from the phone. She rolled to her knees, then stood, rising with the unsteady effort of someone concussed. She cinched her robe tight at the waist. "I'm coming."

Crossing the kitchen, she stepped on a goathead that had made it into the house, probably on J.D.'s boot. Stopping to pull it from her left heel, she balanced against the dining room door frame. "I hear you." She tried to make her voice sound less like it belonged to an invalid. "I'll be right there."

As soon as she opened the door, Chris pulled her against his chest and held her tight. "What's wrong with your face? Did someone hit you?"

Claire shook her head. "Slept on the floor." A shrug was the only other explanation she could muster. "I shouldn't have called. You have work."

"That doesn't matter."

He steered her inside, his arm around her shoulders. She tried to keep her head up, not to watch her feet. She couldn't; moving forward took all she had. "I need to go to bed."

Chris said, "I need coffee. I'll make some. Did you eat last night?"

She answered with a shake of her head, leaning against him as he paced her to the bedroom. He pointed to the bed. "Rest. We'll talk when you're able."

The questions that crowded her mind wouldn't form themselves into sentences. J.D., how to explain. Clinic coverage, inspection. Jan. Stealing, forging prescription. Sell out. Mistakes. Malpractice. Give up. Never wake up.

She surrendered to the bed and rolled to her left side, eyes closed.

Chris' warm hand touched her brow. He said, "You don't have fever. Any vomiting or pain?"

She shook her head and sank back toward the safest place she knew.

She and her horse under the full moon, determined to fly, consequences irrelevant, they speed across ground made unfamiliar by shadows. Sheer elation; as close to flight as anyone without wings. The world smells like cinnamon and chocolate, all meant to be consumed.

Then she's flying, arcing from the horse's back, catapulting up and forward as he suddenly halts. She tries to soar, clutched by dread, knowing that the crash will come.

Under the comforter, she thrashed, flailing the cover away, struggling, but unable to sit up. Pinned flat on her back by gravity and pain, she gasped, a sound that woke her. Holding her painful right wrist, she made another sound, then two words, doubting anyone would answer. "My horse?"

"He's in the corral." Claire looked toward the voice, and found Chris sitting in the armchair across the room. "You're safe. He's safe. It's a bad dream."

He came and sat on the side of the bed, and patted her back as if she were an infant. His hand left a circle of warmth each place it rested. He said, "Take deep breaths."

An "oh" escaped when she pushed against the pillow. He pointed to her right wrist. "Does that hurt?"

"Old sprain." Every word forced her further from the sleep she wanted to grasp again. She closed her eyes. He didn't ask more questions, but minutes passed before the edge of the bed rose as Chris stood. And then she found her way back to sleep.

Flying alone, from high above, she sees mountains and a wide, turbulent river. No people clutter the banks or clutch for her as they had when she ran headlong into the wind, fast and far enough to gain altitude, then catch an updraft that set her free of the crowd. She circles, without effort, gliding eventually westward. Passing over the river, she lofts upward through a pass between two peaks. Nothing familiar beckons. Adrift, alone, she peers below for a spot to rest.

Claire pushed back the sheets and comforter. A slim column of morning light slid between the curtains and painted a path from the window to the bed. She sat on the edge of the bed with her feet on the floor, just as she'd shown elderly patients to do, waiting before standing. Not physically infirm and only thirty-four, she shouldn't need such precautions. But as she woke, wondering how many hours she'd slept and what hadn't been done that should have, she felt as fragile as a good reputation.

Five steps to the bathroom, taken slowly, accompanied one clear thought. *Until that one night recently, I haven't been on horseback in months, only flew in that dream, not the way I did when I was sixteen. This is not like before.* And then she remembered the psychologist's words. She'd seen the woman when she was in nursing school. Her mental health course had made her wonder if the amazing feeling of power that preceded her sense of flight and the fall from her horse that struck her silent signaled mental illness. After a thorough physical exam and extensive discussions, Dr. Hamer had said, "None of us learns all the lessons at once. We revisit important things again and again. Live long and learn much."

What she had learned about herself in the years since was that even when she felt tremendous energy, as if she could fly, she needed to guard against fatigue. Taking measures to cope with stress was essential. Those were understandable. The hardest lesson, the one she resisted, was that she couldn't do everything. Back in bed with the cover over her head, she heard another thought she knew she wouldn't yet be able to explain aloud. *You should have seen it coming.*

The next time she woke, bright sunlight elbowed in through the parted curtains. The only sound came from outside, gusts intermittently rattling the wooden chairs on the front porch. Rocked by the wind, the chairs sounded impatient, as if they yearned to be anywhere other than on that long porch staring directly ahead at drought-brown grass and a single field of hopeful green shoots of new winter wheat.

Instead of sinking back into the shelter of sleep, Claire told herself she should get up. But if she did, she'd have to explain to Chris. The thought of getting up, dressing, explaining, exposing her weak self, even to Chris, overcame her, siphoned away her spirit. She turned her back to the sun, covered her head, and closed her eyes.

Chris knocked on the door, then came in the room without waiting. He set a cup on the bedside table. "There's coffee. I cooked eggs and toast. It's five o'clock."

Claire stared at her brother, who always understood and never pushed. But here he was, pushing, just like her mother would. And his voice sounded stern and humorless.

"I mean it. You've slept ten hours plus the time between midnight and when I got here. Now you either get up and tell me what's going on or I'm taking you to Emergency." He pointed to the cup. "Drink some."

Anything to keep from talking; she drank the coffee, tiny sips. She stared at the cup for what seemed like a long time, then put it on the table. She heard herself sigh, wished she hadn't.

"Dammit, Claire, I mean it. Something was wrong when you were in Taos on Labor Day. Some people might buy your act, but not me. You've lost weight and you look awful."

Her voice came out as loud as his. "Stop yelling at me. I'm not a child.

"Quit behaving like one."

"I shouldn't have called you. You're no better than J.D."

Now he was standing over her; she wouldn't look up. He said, "Not if you won't let me help."

"I'm not sick." She sucked back a sob, turned her head to wipe a tear that could betray her. "I did blood work. CBC, Chem panel, TSH, T3, all normal. Pregnancy test negative."

"A fool treats herself. You know that."

"I'm sorry I wasted your time. Go back to Taos." Even as she said it, she knew if he tried to leave, she'd beg him not to. The bed invited her to give up again.

Her brother, who always took her side, grabbed her left arm and pulled her to standing. "Listen to me. I'm giving you three minutes to get to the kitchen table. You'll either tell me what's wrong and let me help or I swear I'm out of here. Your choice."

Chris let go of her arm and turned toward the door. "Three minutes. Starting now."

"Is Gran coming?"

He turned around. "That's one reason you have to get up. I can't hold everyone off much longer."

"What did you. . ." She stopped talking. He'd already left the room.

In the bathroom, her hands shook as she washed her face. She avoided the mirror. Back in the bedroom, she wanted to fall on the bed again. Instead, she pulled on Levi's thrown on the floor one day last week and a t-shirt that declared **Nurses Care All the Time**. Barefooted, she headed toward the kitchen, wishing she knew where to start.

Floyd County Tribune
Thursday, September 26, 2013

Drought Prediction
   Current West Texas drought conditions may last another 15 years, if climate experts' predictions are accurate.
   Jack Harkins, professor of meteorology at Texas A&M, says that although some parts of Texas are in fair shape as far a rainfall goes, much of the state is still 10-15 inches below normal for rainfall and has been since 2011, the worst one-year drought in state history.
   "If an El Nino pattern arrives in the next few months, that could bring the jet stream south and increase chances of rainfall. But it's too soon to know when or if that will happen," Harkins said. "This is not yet the worst drought period recorded in the state. That was 1950 to 1957."
   Another expert, Miles Woodall of Texas Water Board, said that even if normal rainfall levels occur, West Texas reservoirs won't fill to pre-2011 levels. "They're too far behind. It will take several years of normal rainfalls to just catch up."

Water District Board to Discuss Metering
   Average depth to water level changes in Floyd County observation wells of -3.62 feet in the past year make the topic of metering irrigation wells a top priority of the local committee of the Water District. A meeting scheduled November 2 at Water District headquarters lists "Development of Draft Criteria for Metering" as the only topic. All interested members of the public are invited to attend the meeting at 7 p.m.

CHAPTER 12
Returned Home

Chris waited in the kitchen for Claire. Earlier, after drinking an entire pot of coffee and consuming three scrambled eggs and two tortillas, he'd looked in on her. She didn't appear to have moved since he covered her. After that, he'd accomplished a couple of things during the waiting. Somehow they left him more unsettled than when he arrived. Mid-morning, he'd called J.D. After six rings and no answer, he left a voice message asking for a call back as soon as possible. Then later, when he made one of his hourly checks on Claire, he'd heard her mumble something about a horse. After her breathing returned to a normal rate, he closed her bedroom door soundlessly and went to the corral.

The horse, a tall buckskin, ambled up to the corral fence and nosed at Chris' fingers on the top rail. He rubbed his hand the length of the horse's neck and said, "What's your name? I'll bet you're hungry."

The horse shook his blond mane and nosed at him again. Chris eased along beside the corral fence to the barn door where a mixture of hay, horse urine, diesel, tractor grease, and about ten other unnamed scents all went together to smell like his granddad after a day's work. He'd said he'd never come back to Jackson's Pond, and all those years away, he'd never wanted to. But there in that barn, a message—that he'd returned home—came to his mind as clearly as if it had been spoken.

The horse had followed him at a distance and stood at the gate end of the corral, next to the barn, watching. He whinnied, just once. Chris said, "Give me a break. I have to find the oats. I've been gone a while."

As the horse ate, Chris checked to see the water tank float was up and the spigot worked. On his way out of the pen, he stopped and rubbed along the horse's neck again, slowly, gently.

The horse stood still, then leaned against Chris' shoulder, like an old friend he hadn't seen in years. Chris shook his head. He'd never seen this horse and now they were buds. "You're easy. A bucket of oats and I'm your pal."

The horse backed away at the sound of Chris' phone ringing. J.D said, "Chris? What's up?"

He heard that much and didn't understand the next words because of noise wherever J.D. was calling from. Chris said, "Are you in a crowd there? Can you hear me?"

"Barely."

Chris raised his voice and in two sentences told J.D. Claire had called him, said she needed help, and he'd come although he still didn't know why. While he talked, the horse backed away into a shadow cast by the barn.

"You? In Jackson's Pond? Is she sick?"

"She looks awful, but won't go see a doc. All she's done since I got here is sleep."

A long silence, punctuated by a woman's laughter in the background, filled several seconds. J.D. said, "Do I need to come back now?"

"I don't know what's going on. Maybe you have an idea."

Another silence hovered. Chris watched the horse move slowly toward him again, half in shadow, half in long-beamed, slanted sunlight.

"No, I don't. She was okay when I left. Listen, break's over, I have to get back to this meeting. It's important. Can you call me back at five o'clock?"

Chris said, "You're busy. I'll make it 5:30." He didn't wait for a response.

As a newspaper photographer in Austin, assignment or not, Chris had taken his camera everywhere he went. Last night, when he finished packing, he'd turned back and pulled his camera gear bag from a box in the closet. At the time, he'd told himself it was an impulse prompted by heading toward Texas.

In seconds, his camera in his right hand, the bag of lenses slung over his left shoulder, he closed his car door. The horse stood watching Chris. With his neck arched, ears erect and twitching occasionally, he seemed expectant, as if he were vital to and ready for whatever Chris might have planned.

Maybe this horse, waiting to pose for a dramatic chiaroscuro portrait, was something he'd been assigned to record. He'd seldom shot portraits. His subjects had been people in action, accident and crime scenes, landscapes and landmarks, and for his own enjoyment, photo essays. But to Chris, this horse deserved the same treatment as a high-ranking elected official—the photographer's job would be to capture his essence. As with human subjects, Chris chose to ease into the shoot, aiming and clicking, not directly at the horse, but with each frame letting the horse see and hear the equipment in operation, all the while talking softly to him.

If he'd known the horse's name, he would have made his words even more personal. As it was, Chris told him he was handsome and strong, that he knew they'd be friends. All that might have been unnecessary; he had a willing subject. The horse stood unmoving while the September light cast a glow across his left cheek and flank and gave a sheen to his mane and blond tail. That same light colored the slender leaves of recently emerged winter wheat beyond the corral a shade of green seen only at this time of year. After he shot enough frames to satisfy himself he would find at least one good one, Chris thanked the horse as seriously as he would a senator. "I'll be back tomorrow. Maybe we'll go for a ride."

He'd set out a fresh pot of coffee. Scrambled eggs, crackers, peanut butter, and jelly clustered together in the center of the kitchen table. He almost regretted being rough on her, but here she was, barefoot, in Levi's, sitting head down at her table.

He said, "Let's hear it."

She drew a deep breath and raised her eyes. Exhaling, she said, "I'm not able to make anything right."

"That's how you feel. What's behind it? We can't fix it if we can't name it."

He wondered where that bit of wisdom came from. But he didn't back up. "Choose one thing that's wrong. Tell me so I can help."

"An employee of mine was arrested for stealing drugs and prescription pads from the clinic, passing prescriptions at pharmacies. She's denying it all and accusing me of negligent practice. I'll end up in court. The nursing board may investigate me. Everyone will know."

He waited. For a long time, she didn't say anything else.

She picked up a spoon and dug a large blob of peanut butter from the jar. Staring at it, she said, "I could lose everything. My clinics. My license. My reputation."

She licked a tiny amount of the thick brown substance, and then a second one. "Would you mind getting me some milk?"

He got up, poured a half a glassful and handed it to her. "Is that it? The only thing?"

"Isn't that enough?"

"You never run from problems. But here you are hiding under the covers, looking like a skeleton. I'm not buying it. What else?"

She put the spoon down on a napkin and drank a sip of the milk. It left a rim around her upper lip. "Amy's developing an eating disorder."

"Anything else?"

"That same practitioner left without notice. So I have to see patients all day, every day and then supervise everyone in both clinics except Dad."

She sat up straighter in the chair and reached for the apricot jelly. It took her a full minute to assemble a cracker, jelly, and peanut butter sandwich. "Maybe I didn't supervise her enough. This all may be my fault." The cracker crumbled as she bit into it. She dropped the spoon, making a helpless gesture, a signal of surrender. "See, I can't even feed myself."

"You're pitiful." He hated to say it.

A tear spurted from her right eye and dribbled past her nose. She wiped the tears and sniffed. "You're right." After another sigh, she said, "I don't have the energy to do anything about any of it. And before you say it, yes, I'm exhausted. But that's not necessarily the same as clinically depressed."

"Who said anything about depression?"

"You're not mad at me?"

"Only enough to get you out of bed."

She finished eating the broken cracker sandwich and assembled another one. "I'll eat now."

He watched without saying anything. She'd held something back. Damn her pride. She'd always been intent on handling things on her own, never would admit trouble until after she'd overcome it.

"So far, you've told me about a problem with Amy, a clinic employee gone rogue, and short staffing that has run you ragged. Is that all? More milk?"

She shook her head. "Coffee."

"What's your horse's name?"

"Pegasus. Gus for short." She drank a long sip of coffee. "Why?"

"We're friends now. I fed him."

"See, I can't even take proper care of my horse."

"Well, that tops it. You *are* pitiful." That got a half smile from her that lasted about ten seconds.

"I shouldn't have called and bothered you." Her voice was smaller when she said, "But I was so empty and alone. I was afraid."

"Of what?"

"Losing hold, the way I did before."

He frowned. "You mean when you were sixteen?"

She nodded, not looking at him. Shoulders slumped, she pushed her hair away from her face, then dropped both hands to her lap, as if the effort had spent her. "Thank you for coming."

After waiting a couple of silent minutes, as if she were waiting for some strength to arrive, she worked her way through two more peanut butter and cracker sandwiches and the rest of the milk. When she finished, she asked, "What about Gran?"

"She'll be here. Andrew's bringing her. I'm not sure when, exactly." He followed her as she left the kitchen. "We'll start working on these problems, put them on paper, this evening. I'll stay as long as you need me to help."

Claire leaned against him as they walked to the front porch, his left arm around her shoulder. They each took one of the rockers. He said, "You know you have to tell me the rest of it."

"I know. Just give me a little time."

"Hours or days?"

"Maybe an hour."

His phone rang. Chris showed her the name on the screen before he answered, J.D. She shook her head.

"Yeah? I know it's after 5:30. Got busy. Yeah, she got up and ate and now she's resting again. I don't really know. I'm going to ask her about mono. Remember that time you had it? Yeah, you call me tomorrow when you're not in a meeting. Yeah, I'll tell her."

Chris didn't have to ask. Watching her face, he knew at least one other problem was between her and her husband, the person who'd always been his best friend, at least until now. He said, "When you're ready, we'll talk. I'll clean up in the kitchen."

After she went inside, moving like one of the walking wounded, toward her bedroom, Chris paced a ten-foot trail across the east side of the front porch, then retraced his path, waiting for Gran to answer. On the ninth ring—he'd counted—she answered. "I'm sorry, Chris. I'd buried the phone under my luggage, packing, and couldn't locate it."

Maybe it was age, or all she'd lived through and seen; somehow Gran always sounded and appeared composed, as if nothing that happened could shake her so deeply that she couldn't continue. Chris had wondered if it was that quality that gave her art a luminous peacefulness that drew viewers hoping to bathe in the glow. It had made her famous. He'd painted enough to know that an artist's soul shows in her work. The dark undercurrent in his own recent canvases carried some message about his soul that he wasn't willing to think about.

Gran asked, "How's Claire?"

"Sleeping. Not injured, no fever or pain. Looks haunted."

"Can you handle things until tomorrow afternoon?"

"Why? You're not coming today?"

"I'll explain when I get there. Here's Andrew. He'll know best how you can help Claire."

"What's your assessment?" The Andrew speaking now was all concern and clinical questions, the psych nurse.

Chris repeated what he'd told Gran. Then he said, "Depressed is the only thing I can guess. Or exhaustion."

"There are other conditions to rule out."

"She holds everything in, always in control."

"Do you know if she takes any kind of meds? Has she ever been treated for clinical depression?"

"I need you here. A brother's no good at this."

Andrew didn't say anything. Chris imagined him concentrating, his left eyebrow drawn down, shoulders hunched. Chris said, "I'd swear she's lost ten pounds since we saw her the first of the month." He'd had to turn away when he held her against him walking to the bedroom. His beautiful sister had lost something of herself with those pounds. "Should I worry about her sleeping so much?"

"Worrying won't help. Your being there is as good as medicine."

"When will you be here?"

"As soon as Willa says. I'm making arrangements while she packs. I'll tell you…" He stopped speaking. Chris heard Willa's voice in the background. Andrew said, "Chris, everything will work out just the way it's supposed to. Do what you think is right."

"I love you."

"Love you, too."

The past few months, questions arising from the surprising changes in his paintings had nagged at Chris. He'd had other work, all the things it took to run the gallery, and managed to focus his energy there when the questions threatened to become major concerns. Now, here at this house where he'd spent the happiest moments of his young years, those questions joined others and left him pacing and weary.

Why had Andrew gone silent when Chris asked when they'd arrive? Why did Gran delay coming? What had J.D done that had laid Claire low? Why did that camera in his hands feel so right after so many years?

He knew Gran would tell him to be still and listen, the answers would come. Smiling at the thought, he returned to the porch chair. Andrew's advice, if he asked him, would be the same. With Claire too worn to deal with the problems that had brought him here, he felt himself surrender to their guidance. There was nothing he could do. The answers would come.

After a few minutes of rocking, the only answer that came was simple. He needed sleep. Tomorrow would bring more information.

September 28, 2013

Mr. Elmo Tanner, Chair
Board of Directors
Holy Cross Hospital
Taos, NM 87571

Dear Mr. Tanner:

Please accept my resignation from the hospital's Board of Directors, effective this date. A family emergency requires my departure from Taos, and therefore I must relinquish my position as Board member.

I have gained much, both knowledge and colleagueship, from my association with members of the Board and staff. For that reason, I regret I will no longer be able to participate as a member. Please convey to the other board members and to the administrative staff my gratitude for welcoming me and for allowing me to serve the community as a member of the board.

My best wishes to you and the other members of the Board as you continue to work for high quality health care in Taos.

Sincerely,

Ms. Willa Jackson

CC: Mr. Gary Traylor, Interim CEO

CHAPTER 13
Time To Go

Sunday morning, Willa sealed the final box, then showered and dressed in jeans, a blue chambray shirt, and purple sweater. Her squash blossom necklace and turquoise earrings were stowed in her shoulder bag for later. She carried her boots as she left her bedroom. No need to rush. Andrew had said they would leave at seven; her clock showed five a.m. He would come at 6:30 to load her things. It wouldn't take long.

As she perched on the edge of the couch, and then stood again, she thought of a raven searching for the best branch. Then, as if the trip might reassure her, she toured the four rooms of the casita, opening drawers, the closets, looking under the bed. The furnishings would stay. Her clothes fit into two suitcases and five boxes stacked in the bedroom. Sketchpads, watercolor supplies, and two easels, one a portable, fit in three other boxes. Yesterday, she and Andrew had taken the seven paintings from the walls to the gallery. Her collection of walking sticks would travel with them.

In the living room again, she ran her hand around the base of a pot in one nicho and lifted a vase displayed in the other. Finding a one hundred dollar bill folded and tucked under the vase brought a smile. *Never leave without your throw down money!* She could hear Frank's voice saying those words he'd always said anytime she traveled. She nodded and dropped the bill in the boot in her left hand.

After a few seconds she knelt, then lay supine on the Navajo rug in front of the couch. Several stretch positions later, her muscles moving more smoothly than when she woke, she closed her eyes and inhaled deeply. She never called these exercises yoga—somehow that seemed a bit trendier than she liked—she preferred thinking of this continuing effort to remain mobile and agile as one of the benefits of her ballet training. That's where she'd learned that body and mind were one. Inhaling again, she caught a scent of piñon from the fireplace ashes. Someone else would need to clean that out.

Her eyes still closed, she watched scenes and hues of Taos and northern New Mexico parade before her. She would never forget the seasons of the past eight years in this high desert. The mountains, the light, the busy water of the Rio Grande, and enough more to have filled twice as many canvases as she had already used to capture what she saw and felt. None of it would be forgotten, because this place, like Jackson's Pond, had become part of her, mind and body. Leaving meant changing, not discarding, as far as she was concerned.

Thankful she was still able to, Willa rolled to her left side, rose to sitting, then to standing, slowly but steadily.

At precisely 6:30, Andrew knocked on the door. When she opened it, his first words were, "Are you still certain?"

"I am. It's time."

She'd been considering moving back to Texas for several months. The family's visit earlier in September and completing what she had decided was the final painting in her Taos series had made it clear to her. When Claire called Chris asking for help, Willa knew she'd go and would stay on in Jackson's Pond after this crisis passed. She'd explained all that to Andrew.

He said, "Well then, let's get loaded and go to Texas."

Willa followed as he walked through the casita, counting suitcases and boxes. With a suitcase in each hand, headed toward the door, he said, "You're taking back less than you came with."

"It's a good idea to travel light." She hoped he'd smile at that. It hurt her to see sadness in the eyes of the man she thought of as her other grandson.

Andrew loaded her pickup quickly. And they left, heading south down Pueblo del Sur. After a stop to drop off mail at the post office, they turned east on Kit Carson and into the Taos Canyon.

Willa sipped the coffee Andrew had brought, and watched the first rays of sunshine burst over the mountains. She said, "That was my resignation from the hospital board I put in the mail. Comes at a good time. The new administrator treats the board as if we are decorative rather than functional. But ornament or not, I still heard things—dissatisfaction among the nurses." She saw Andrew raise his eyebrows. "Did you have any problem taking time off from work?"

"Not really." He nodded in her direction. "But you're correct, there's unrest in the ranks. I haven't mentioned it to you, but I've told Chris, I'm about finished there."

"Tired of nursing, or this job in particular?"

"This job, definitely. Maybe both." He drove with both hands on the wheel, staying just at or slightly above the speed limit. "I'll be forty my next birthday and it's been nothing but sick people and hospitals for me for more than twenty years, counting school. I'm happy to be away to have time to think about that."

Willa reached into the bottom of her handbag and extracted her sunglasses. The day promised to be clear and bright. She said, "Forty's a time for taking stock." After situating the glasses, she turned toward him. "Actually, anytime's good. Maybe every morning."

After finishing her coffee, she asked, "Is there anything you've always wanted to do, but couldn't?"

"Not exactly."

Down the road a few miles, Andrew said, "According to my father's plan, I was supposed to be a vet. Go to A&M and come back to Ozona to practice. You can imagine how it went over when I transferred to UT after my first year. And to nursing school! Up till then he'd convinced himself I wasn't actually gay. But that's when he changed his mind. His version of things was that women are nurses. Not a job for a real man."

"Did you hear lots of that when you were growing up?"

"Not cool to be gay in Ozona back then. I think because I fought everyone who ever called me queer or tried to bully me, from junior high on, and won, and played basketball and ran track, he thought I was, underneath, not really gay. Wanted to think that till he died."

"Did you ever want to be a vet?"

"Actually, yes." He chuckled, shook his head. "But since he wanted me to—well, you know about adolescents."

"Proving him wrong?"

"Cutting off my nose, is more like it."

"What about your mother?"

"Her only child was perfect, as far as she was concerned. But she didn't argue with my father."

They passed through Angel Fire and into the Mora Valley. Willa appreciated Andrew's long silences as much as she did his conversation. Both seemed, to her, evidence of careful thought.

Farther on, as they passed a large meadow, Andrew pointed to the right—a herd of alpacas grazed. One lifted its head, favoring them with its long, wise gaze. He said, "I'd love to raise animals, maybe horses."

"Or alpacas?"

"Or unicorns. About as likely."

In all the years they'd known each other, he'd never told her the things he'd just said. She hoped he'd heard the message in his words. He'd helped Chris live his dream; it was time he attended to his own.

Later, they stopped in Las Vegas at the Spic & Span on the town square for a quick breakfast. Before walking from the parking lot, Willa stretched in every direction, using the pickup tailgate to steady herself. Resting an hour each afternoon had stopped the worst of the clumsiness. Before adding the daily rest, she'd concluded her final long, slow decline had begun. All the while, she avoided thinking the words "idiopathic cerebellar degeneration."

Afterward, as they left the cafe, she said, "That's one thing I'll miss."

"The Spic & Span?"

"Northern New Mexican food. I may have to start cooking again. You two have spoiled me, delivering so many home-cooked meals."

"That's another reason not to leave for good."

They rode, neither speaking until the turn east onto I 40 near Santa Rosa. Willa noticed Andrew's frown, just before he spoke. "I don't understand why Claire called for you and Chris to come."

"Instead of her mother?"

He nodded.

"Let's say Claire and Melanie are more alike than either one admits." Willa hesitated, then said, "Both of them believe their mother will never really understand them." She'd never put it exactly that way before, but saying it, she knew it to be true. She took off her sunglasses and rubbed the bridge of her nose. "And both of them have a hard time admitting to themselves they make mistakes."

"You think Claire's made some mistake she can't admit?"

"She expects a great deal of herself."

"Do you think she's self-destructive?"

"I doubt she'd harm herself, if that's what you mean."

She shook her head, then replaced her sunglasses and closed her eyes.

Willa woke just before they passed the ten cars buried nose down in a field just west of Amarillo. "Cadillac Ranch," she muttered. "Some call that art." She waited until Andrew made the turn south out of Amarillo before she asked the question that had been on her mind. "Before Claire called, had Chris mentioned anything about her having problems or not feeling well? I know they usually talk every week or so."

"I think Chris was concerned before because he hadn't heard from her in about two weeks. Then when he got there and called me, he seemed pretty worried about her. I had told him to get her to talk if he could. Otherwise, the main thing was to be there. That might be the most important thing."

"Maybe she needed him there, since J.D.'s gone."

"I wonder…" He concentrated on the exit sign for Plainview. "Is this the one?"

"Yes. Nearly home."

"How does it feel?"

"Awfully dry." As they passed the prison, surrounded by its farm and razor wire, she said, "No cotton crop there this year." She turned toward Andrew. "A while ago, you started to say you wondered something. Was it why Claire didn't call J.D.?"

"Well, yeah."

"A good guess. The answer is, I don't know why." A few silent miles farther on, she pointed toward a field of milo where an irrigation pivot sprayed a fine mist over the stalks as it marched ahead, slowly. She pointed toward the pivot and said, "They're wasting what they're pumping. Those heads aren't going to fill out."

Andrew said, "I suppose we'll find out what's wrong soon enough."

"What's wrong is seldom one thing; it's one *more* thing."

Willa knew she sounded more certain than she was about Claire, although she believed that a crisis was sometimes necessary. She said, "Setting things right may take some time."

Just before three o'clock, when Andrew made the turn off the highway onto the county road outside Jackson's Pond, he phoned Chris. When they stepped out of the pickup at the house, Chris hurried from the porch and embraced them both. He said, "I'm relieved not to be doing this alone now."

Willa said, "Claire?"

"Asleep again." Chris pointed to the boxes in the pickup bed. "What's all this?"

"I'm moving back. This saved a trip."

"Now?"

"It's time. And this is as good a time as any."

Chris shook his head and said, "Where do you want these things?"

She looked at the sky, cloudless and almost blindingly bright. "Leave them there for now. It's not going to rain on them."

She leaned against his arm as they walked up the porch steps. The three of them sat in the porch chairs. Chris said, "It's good you're here. As far as I can tell, all I've accomplished is getting everyone I've talked to so far pissed at me."

"Who all?" Andrew asked, sounding as if he might enjoy hearing the list.

"First, I got Dad when I called to ask about Amy and Jay Frank staying another night, getting them to school tomorrow. Before he could get my point, he handed the phone to Mother, who tried to grill me. 'Why did Claire call you, not me? Flu? Does she need to see a doctor?' and such. I had to be firm telling her not to come out today, which was when she got huffy. Then Dad got back on and asked a bunch of questions about whether there was a problem between me and Andrew, basically, asking if I was running away from home, and then he was p.o.'d when I laughed at him being protective."

Willa patted his arm. "There's an old saying about people getting mad at you—they can get happy in the same clothes. Who else?"

"This is the odd one. J.D. hardly asked any questions at all when I first got him on the phone, right after I arrived. I told him what I knew at the time, which was she felt too bad to do anything but sleep." Chris talked fast, leaning forward. "It was as if we were strangers, and I'd interrupted him in a meeting. He called back later and asked if he needed to be here, like I had a clue. Then yesterday he called again and said he'd be here tomorrow afternoon."

He sat back in his chair and stared toward the corral. He told them the few details of what Claire had said when she was awake that one time, and that she'd gone back to bed. He hadn't had the heart to wake her since then. "So unless I want to be drummed out of the family, we need a plan."

Willa said, "*Claire* needs a plan. She's grown. *She* has to decide how to deal with these problems. Unless she's not able to." She rocked the chair a few times, leaning her head against the high back of the old chair, then stopped and rocked forward. "Andrew, do you have any suggestions?"

"Not without seeing her."

Willa stood, lifted her arms above her head and stretched side to side, then forward. She said, "Let's wake her."

Floyd County Tribune
Thursday, September 26, 2013

Home School Cooperative Informational Meeting
Scheduled

Dolores Montoya, of Jackson's Pond, notified the Tribune this week of an upcoming meeting, October 15, 2013 at 7 p.m. at the Methodist Church Fellowship Hall. All parents interested in home schooling or currently home schooling their children are encouraged to attend.

"Many in the area have expressed interest in forming a cooperative of home school parents. Organizing can increase the benefits of home-based education by bringing special skills of individual parents into the educational process of many children, in addition to their own," said Montoya.

A home school veteran, Mrs. Montoya has guided the learning of three of her four children from early childhood through to grade nine. A fourth child is now working through the eighth grade curriculum and hopes to complete all grades through high school in the home-based program. She explained, "My husband was career Air Force. I chose to home school our children because our frequent base changes would have meant disrupting their learning."

"The curriculum materials from American Home School Resources furnish guidance and basic lesson outlines. Each week we invent specific lessons using resources from the Internet, libraries, museums, and a variety of other sources. As their teacher, I have the opportunity to continue my own education every day."

CHAPTER 14

Mothers and Daughters

Late Sunday afternoon, as soon as Willa stopped her pickup in the driveway, Melanie opened her front door. She watched her mother walk to the porch, moving steadily without her walking stick. She'd used it most of the time when they saw her in Taos earlier that month. When they hugged, Melanie held Willa tight, feeling like a nearly-lost child. Before they could get into the living room, Jay Frank also wrapped himself around his great-grandmother.

Amy followed, wearing her new leotard and tights with a turquoise t-shirt long enough to be a tunic. She twirled once, finished with an arabesque, and said, "See, I haven't forgotten what you taught me. I've been practicing. Do you like my new tights? Will you be here long enough to teach me more?"

Willa held Amy's hands. She said, "You're full of questions. I'm staying. So we'll be certain you get dance lessons."

Melanie said, "Staying! Wonderful!"

"It seemed to be a good time and I had a driver. So here I am."

The kids disappeared toward the kitchen. Melanie stared after them. So it had taken Claire's illness to bring her mother back. She said, "They're having a snack. Would you like something?"

"Not right now. I stopped by to let you know I'll stay with Claire until she's feeling better. Then I'll get settled."

"You can stay here." She watched her mother's face, but saw no hint of her thoughts. "Permanently. Or stay until you find a place."

"I'll figure all that out later, after Claire's better."

Melanie nodded. She said, "How is she?" Melanie told herself to let go of the dish towel she had twisted in her hands, relax her fists. "I wish she'd talk to me, really talk. Do you think she ever will?"

She saw her mother's smile, and knew what she'd say. "It may take time, but I think she'll understand some day how much you love her. Time and experience."

"She came by my school the other day, out walking at lunch. I could tell then something was wrong."

"She needs rest."

"Is that all?"

"Probably not, but it'll help."

Melanie sighed, then said, "I'm not the one to tell her she does too much."

Ray stopped in the doorway from the kitchen. From the couch, Willa said, "Come over here and kiss your mother-in-law on the cheek."

He did as told, then sat beside her. "The kids said you came home to stay. If that's right, well good for you."

"You know how it is with people from Texas. We all eventually come home. One way or another." She sat forward, holding her keys and sunglasses. "Oh, she wanted me to tell you she's canceling clinic here tomorrow, in case some extra patients may come to Calverton. I had to be firm, but I think it's best. She assures me she's already done labs on herself." She shook her head, held up a hand. "Before you say it, I know, not smart. And she did admit she might have tried to do too much, for a long time."

"J.D. home yet?" Ray frowned. "I don't have a reason to say it, but I wonder if they're having trouble."

Willa shrugged. "He'll be back tomorrow."

They sat without saying more for a minute or two. Then Jay Frank stuck his head around the door frame. "Can we stay here again tonight?"

Melanie said, "We'd love to have them stay all week."

Willa said, "It's fine, maybe until Wednesday. We'll see."

Jay Frank said, "When's Dad coming home?" Then before he got an answer, he asked, "What about my goats?"

"Chris and Andrew can take care of them."

Amy stood behind her brother. "When can we start lessons?"

"Do you have slippers, too?"

"They're still in the box. I didn't want to get them dirty." She bourréed her way across the room, ending in a plié in front of Willa. "My friends will be so jealous."

Melanie said, "Maybe you don't want to tell them."

"No, I want them to be. I don't like them anymore."

Amy danced out of the room

Willa said, "I didn't know she remembered so much. It's been years."

"Claire used to work with her. Before things got so busy. Before Amy turned thirteen."

Melanie watched her mother, watching Amy. She said, "Did you notice the new businesses when you came through town?"

"I did. Do you think they'll survive?"

"Hard to say, but it's nice that a couple of the storefronts are filled. So many are still empty."

"I noticed the motel's been renovated, too."

Melanie nodded. "It's supposed to open soon."

"Are any new people moving into town?"

Ray said, "A few, and some of the children returning. For one, Junior Reese's grandson moved back here from Austin. He's farming part of their land."

Melanie, frowning, said, "There's also something less positive. I heard a rumor there's talk among the Consolidated School District Board of shutting down the elementary."

After a long pause, Willa said, "It would be hard to attract young people if there's no school in town." She shook her head. "I don't suppose any of these new people are Democrats." She had to laugh at her own joke.

Ray laughed, too. He said, "I seriously doubt it. Probably unaffiliated survivalists. I heard the Reese kid's building a bunker. Don't know who he thinks will want to steal a piece of land that's going dry."

"Something I read in the paper this week has me wondering," Melanie said. "An announcement of an informational meeting to form a home school co-op."

Ray said, "What do you think?"

"It depends on the parents, usually the mother." Melanie heard herself sounding like the always certain-school administrator she had been. In a softer tone, she said, "Perhaps a co-op could help. With concerns about drugs, kids as early as middle school, I can see why some would choose that route."

Willa said, "Drugs, at Amy's age? Here? Seems it's harder every generation to be a parent." She checked her watch, then stood. Melanie noticed she used the couch arm for leverage. "I'll go, now. Things to do at the house."

After Willa left, Melanie wandered out to the backyard, wondering what her return meant. It wouldn't surprise her if Claire had sworn her to secrecy about some problem. Or maybe she knew without being told.

Ray called from the back door. "What's my girl doing out here alone?"

"Just enjoying the afternoon, thinking. Come sit with me."

He pulled up a lawn chair beside her. "Thinking about what?"

"Claire, Mother. Did I ever tell you that all my life I thought my mother had some special power, that she knew things without being told. And I was certain I would never be able to be as smart as she is. Or as pretty."

"When did you figure out your daughter would probably feel the same about you?"

"Today." She laughed. "I mean it. Just this minute, I finally put it together exactly that way, particularly the part about Claire. And here you are telling me you knew that all along?"

"Not really. But sometimes I do know what you're thinking."

"How?"

He shrugged. "It can happen when people are in love."

Melanie rested back in her chair, enjoying the late afternoon warmth. Hearing the kids in the house, talking and laughing, made her smile. With their solemn faces when she picked them up on Friday, they'd been less like children than like a pair of too-burdened young adults, putting on brave faces for their grandparents.

The day before, on the way to Lubbock, she'd been concerned about Amy's being quieter than usual, not even picking at her brother for sitting too near or some other infraction of her rules. But at the dance clothing store, she'd dashed from one counter to the next and lingered over choosing between a black leotard and pink. The sales person, a slim, dark-haired girl who could have been Amy's sister, convinced the thirteen-year-old she *didn't* need the larger size. The magic words had been, "When I was your age, I looked just like you. I wore a medium then and I still do."

Melanie had added the pink leotard to the black one Amy

chose. Since yesterday, the ballerina had changed outfits several times, pink, the black, different tops, and had danced into every room she entered.

Jay Frank stuck with his granddad, asking only for a giant pretzel, with mustard. But he broke into a big smile when they steered him to the western wear store and told him he should choose something for himself. Such deliberation. He finally pointed to a red and black plaid shirt. "Texas Tech colors," he'd said.

Ray showed him a belt buckle in the glass case at the checkout counter and told him Uncle Chris got one like it to wear at his first stock show. Sold!

Melanie could have drifted into a nap among those thoughts, in her comfortable lawn chair, and might have, but she heard Ray's voice.

He said, "There's something I didn't tell you on Friday. Actually two things."

She sat up, "Secrets?"

"No, and one may be nothing but gossip. But it started me thinking. The first thing is Jackson's Pond's illustrious mayor called and asked me to consider being appointed for Tuff Johnson's unexpired term on City Council."

"What did you say?"

"I'd think about it. You and I need to discuss it. But not today. I'm off duty and happy to be here with my wife next to me and the grandkids inside."

Melanie heard Jay Frank's voice from the house. "Memaw?"

Rather than shout, she went to the back door to answer. She returned to the lawn chairs seconds later. "They were just checking on us. Wanted to use their iPads. Two things, you said. What's the second?"

"I had lunch with a couple of clinic administrators, one from Idalou and the other from Hale Center. Complaints were the usual, slow pays from some insurance companies, increasing frequency of payment denials, recredentialing nightmares. Then the guy from Idalou asks if either of us has been approached about selling out. We both immediately grilled him. He'd heard from someone in Lubbock that some company had an eye on buying up rural clinics, forcing buyouts, setting up competing operations to force you out."

"Do you think that threat's real?"

Ray shrugged. "Never know. Usually it's hospital systems aiming to broaden their customer base. Not some distant company. They'd have to have lots of money and not care much about making money off the clinics they buy."

"Sounds bad for the clinics. Do you think they would target Claire's?"

"Depends on what their real business is. Buyouts are a good way for the large systems to almost guarantee losing money. Lots of us rural places don't make any profit, don't expect to, just meet overhead, provide a needed service. But acquiring them gains profits for the corporations in the end by capturing established patients in places where there's no competition."

"Did you tell Claire?"

He shook his head. "Maybe I should have, but I told myself until it's more than a rumor, there's no sense. Not right now, anyway. She's got enough to deal with. But maybe she heard a rumor."

"About Claire and J. D. . . . do you suspect something?"

"No." He looked toward the back fence, on past to the western horizon. "Just that they're both awfully busy. When he left, she got sick."

Tiffany J
Guess what Chelsea said about U.
No I'll tell u. said u r gaining wt in
butt. Evry1 talks about it

Tiffany J
Didn mean 2 hurt ur feelings. Chlc
a bitch!
Weighed 2day 89
New pills work!!!

Tiffany J

Ansr or I'm telling evry1 what C
said.
Amy H
She lies.
Get me some.
Got2 go. Gmothr watching.

CHAPTER 15
Uphill

J.D. woke Monday morning with a headache, a dull presence more than a pain, in the back of his head and neck. He was getting familiar with it. Even with Tylenol, the headache had stayed with him like an unwelcome companion since it drove him from sleep around five Saturday morning. Then, he'd laid it off on lack of sleep and the wine he'd drunk the night before. The last time he drank more than a couple of beers at a time had been college; he'd graduated seventeen years ago.

Last night, when Trey suggested the two of them get together for some dinner away from the hotel, J.D. had admitted he was off his feed, had been since Saturday morning. Trey had winked. "Yeah, Friday nights away from home will do that to a man."

J.D. shrugged and concentrated on rounding up the papers he'd made notes on during the meeting. He said, "It's probably something I ate. But I can't seem to shake it."

Trey moved in too close to suit J.D. "Where did you and Jan eat . . . and drink? Maybe you got hold of something that disagreed with you."

J.D. stood and moved toward the door. He said, "Del Frisco's. Remember? She already had the reservation."

"You were a big help in the meeting, even if you didn't feel good. I hope you'll be here for the next one." With that, Trey broke off to talk to another committee member.

J.D. had done his best in the meetings and he'd watched Jan, but not so anyone would notice. If she was upset with him, she never let on. She made sure everyone on the committee got equal time from her and smiled through the whole thing. He had to give her credit; she knew how to handle a meeting, and by the time it was over, they'd accomplished a lot.

He'd thought about leaving last night, right after the meeting was over at six. But he didn't. He told himself even though Claire was sick, she was in good hands and they didn't expect him until today. Besides, he didn't feel so good himself. Then he thought about calling home, but didn't do that either. The conversation with Chris on Saturday was enough to tell him he had things to smooth over and that had to be face to face. Trouble was he didn't know what those things were. Dammit, he hadn't done anything wrong.

He said to Jan, "I have to get on the road. It's six hours back." J.D. didn't let on about a sick wife and everyone else who expected him, all probably wondering why he wasn't already there.

She urged him to have one more cup of coffee before leaving. He'd already sat there in the hotel dining room longer than he'd intended, but two of the other committee members had stopped by the table to talk, mainly to Jan, he was sure. He could have left directly from the Sheraton, gone on earlier. But Jan had made a point to encourage everyone to stop by for coffee. He didn't want to be rude.

Now it was just the two of them and her telling him what a help he'd been in the meeting. "I don't think I could have gotten Trey to agree to our committee's proposing the new website and a Net-based campaign to the under-forty demographic if you hadn't offered all those examples." She reached across the table, hand outstretched. "We make a good team. Let's shake on our partnership."

A man could take that a lot of different ways. But she didn't seem the least put out with him about Friday night. So he shook her hand, then stood. "I'm happy to help when I can. Let me know soon as you know the next meeting date. I'll try to be here."

He'd already checked out over at the Sheraton before breakfast. So all that was left to do was walk to his pickup in the underground garage, then head west. In the lobby, he stopped at the valet stand. He handed over his tag and said, "I'll get it myself. Just need my keys." Then he pulled the money clip from his pocket, and peeled out a five. A man ought to tip well, especially if he planned on coming back. The valet returned his keys along with a big smile. Next thing he knew, Jan stood beside him.

"I'll walk out with you. Mine's in the garage, too."

He thought about saying he'd forgotten his sunglasses or something, but didn't. All the way down to the first parking level, she didn't say anything, just strolled along smiling. Maybe she was humming a little, under her breath, too. He pointed to his pickup.

"That's me."

"I'm down on two." She touched his arm, then backed away. "Careful on the way home." She started off, and gave a little wave with her back to him.

Jan made her way down the incline of the ramp, more like dancing than walking. Sashaying. He turned away. She didn't need to catch him watching.

Getting out of the garage didn't take long and getting out of town didn't either. J.D. managed to put off thinking about Jackson's Pond until about 170 miles later, when he passed through Vernon, turned due west, and started the steady, uphill miles toward home. Back in Fort Worth, he'd been a different person, part of an organization, no need to take charge, just work with the group. In a way, he'd itched to speak up a lot more, but held back, left the leading to Jan. He'd shifted gears, moved into low, and focused on being a good committee member.

But thinking about what waited at home got complicated. He remembered how, when Willa first hired him, before he and Claire married, he'd taken on managing. Each year, he'd gotten a better hold, seeing a future as partner in a thriving operation, the result of his own hard work. In some ways, back then he'd been making it up as he went along, playing a role he'd never really auditioned for, let alone fully understood. Straight out of school, no real management experience. He'd given it his best, hit his marks.

Then he and Claire married and everything enlarged, colors all seemed brighter, and each year brought something new. He became partner in the ranch, parent—one of the men, no longer Jacob's son or Willa's manager. Grown into being those things. Mastered them. Everything he wanted, he worked until he got. Then one day, forty stared him in the face. And when he looked around, nothing seemed right, starting with Claire. She'd turned into someone he didn't know.

In Paducah, sixty miles from home, he stopped at a no-name convenience store with a single gas pump. Paying inside, because the old pump didn't take credit cards, he stared at the bags of chips, peanuts, Slim Jims, cookies. Even though his stomach growled, he guessed he'd left his appetite somewhere back down the road.

"Got any maps?" he asked the clerk.

Something on her phone had most of her attention, but she managed to nod toward a nearly-empty metal rack holding one map each of Texas, New Mexico, and Oklahoma.

He knew the way home, but had half a notion to find that place where the rustlers took #3355. Broadus had told him it was on County Road 20 fifteen miles south of Paducah. The faded red on the title flap told him the map had been there a while. Most county roads had, too. So he put two dollars on the counter, nodded to the clerk, and strolled back to his pickup.

One block down the highway from the convenience store, a boarded-up Dairy Queen offered him a place to park and look at the map. Without any trouble, he found CR 20, a West Texas style road, straight as a string, east-west off the highway south out of Paducah. The map resisted his effort to refold it just long enough to make him cuss, which for some reason made him feel good for a second. Not much longer, though. The emptiness in his stomach couldn't entirely account for his mood, but he couldn't name any other reason for the uneasiness he felt.

After starting over with the map, using the creases for a guide, he managed to return it to its original shape and size. He reversed direction, then headed south out of town. When he came to the intersection with CR 20, a wide dirt road, he turned east and drove about five miles, then slowed and stopped when the phone in the glove compartment rang. He waited out ten rings, staring toward its hiding place the whole time.

Opening the glove box, he pushed aside several old weigh tickets from the elevator and the service record on the pickup, and pulled out the secret phone. With his pocket knife, he popped off the phone's cover and lifted out the battery. All three pieces fit in the palm of his hand. He started the pickup and rolled forward about twenty feet, hurled the empty back cover as far left as he could. Another quarter mile farther, he disposed of the battery with an overhand toss that landed it in the ditch on the right. A group of six scrawny heifers watched from near the fence. He wondered if they were pregnant.

In two moves, he turned the pickup around, and then drove

slowly back to the paved highway, aimed toward town. A few miles farther on, he stopped again and walked to the front of the pickup. As if the move required precision, he placed the guts of the phone under the left front tire. When he rolled forward, a crunch told him he'd finished it off.

When he was a kid, and some of his friends thought riding bulls would be the coolest thing, he'd chosen steer wrestling instead. It was possible to get hurt jumping off a horse, grabbing a steer around the neck, and throwing him down, but not certain. As far has he'd been concerned, getting hurt, bad, was guaranteed with riding bucking bulls—not a matter of if, only when. Maybe it was a coward's way, but even as a teenager, it made sense to him to avoid fractures. It wasn't that he'd backed away out of fear, as much as from caution. His friends took to avoiding him, calling him a pussy. Chris had been the only one who understood.

One push of a button on the only phone he needed, then after two rings, Chris answered. "Where are you? I thought you'd be here by now."

"Paducah. On my way. How's Claire?"

"Hard to say."

"She can hear you?"

"Right."

"Will you meet me at the pond in forty-five minutes? I need to talk to you."

"I'm in the other room now. What in the hell's going on? What did you do to her?"

"Nothing."

"I doubt that. I'll see you at the pond."

The next thirty miles, moving steadily upward into a stiffening wind, seemed like a hundred. After passing through Matador, nearing the final climb onto the edge of the Panhandle's flat mesa, he punched the accelerator and minutes later pulled off the county road at the turn to the pond. Chris stood outside his SUV, leaning against it, hands in his pockets, back to the west wind. Andrew sat in the passenger seat.

As soon as J.D. stopped, Chris got in the pickup with him.

J.D. said, "Is Claire okay?"

"I have no idea what's happening, not really. She's up, out of bed, has been since noon, pacing around, mostly. She won't tell me, but I know something happened between you two, and it was the thing that broke her. She can handle a lot—the clinic problems, Amy, but whatever's going on with you is the thing that put her down."

J.D. glanced at the glove compartment. "She said that?"

"She didn't have to. And no, she's not the kind to tell. It would probably be better if she did, but she won't. But I'm asking. The thing that would hurt her most. Are you having an affair?"

J.D. shook his head. "She and I are alike about not telling." He stared at his hands, holding the steering wheel, even though the pickup was stopped and the motor off.

Chris' voice belonged to an old man, harsh and grim. "If you hurt her, I swear you'll answer to all of us. And I'll be first. I haven't fought anyone in a long time, but I promise you, I'll personally beat the shit out of you. You know I can."

He'd have rather taken that beating than see the look in Chris' eyes. "You know me, Chris. I wouldn't cross the line. If I had, I'd stand still for whatever you dished out." Telling the fact of the truth wasn't the same as talking about how close to the line he'd stood. "But I'm probably to blame for her thinking that, if that's what she thinks." He watched the jagged wind slicing up topsoil, lifting it into the air already full of dust from the county to the west. "What do you think I ought to do next?"

"We're going to town, to Mom and Dad's. That was our excuse for leaving. Kids are there. Gran's at the house with Claire." Chris' eyes gave nothing away. "Fix it."

At the house, the "WELCOME" on the doormat was already invisible under an inch of grit. Opening the door against the wind took some doing and he had a time holding it, once he got it open, then had to slam it shut. So much for getting in quietly.

Willa met him in the hallway. And when she hugged him, it made him feel worse than he had when he got to the door. She said, "Claire's lying down. I had to make her stop wandering around. She's not asleep, and I know she needs to talk to you." She picked up her walking stick from where it leaned against the wall next to the door.

"Is the door at the little house locked?"

He extracted a key from his ring and handed it to her. "Yeah. The utilities are on." He moved to hold the screen for her. "You don't have to leave on my account."

"I'll be okay. Back later."

"You sure you want to go out in this wind?"

"I've been in worse."

J.D. watched her move steadily and slowly toward her pickup. He hunched, then relaxed his shoulders, trying to shrug the heaviness away. Thank God, he'd left the headache somewhere outside of Fort Worth. When he got to the bedroom, he worked up a pleasant expression before he opened the door. He didn't need the smile. His wife was lying, facing the wall, covered with the spread up to her neck. He set his bag on the floor, shut the door behind him, then sat on the side of the bed, his hand against her back. "Willa said you were awake. Can you tell me what's wrong?"

In a voice frayed and ragged as a torn bed sheet, she said, "Why didn't you call?" Then before he could answer, she said, "No, I don't want to know."

"Didn't think you'd care whether I did or didn't."

She pushed back the cover, and moved to the far side of the bed, stood. Her Levi's hung loose at the hips. She said, "I thought I could always count on you. Shows how wrong I was."

"No, it's not like that. It's just that lately there's been nothing I did that was right." Even to him it sounded like an excuse. "You were sick. You could have called me."

"Would you have come back? And I'm not sick. I'm worn out." She turned toward the window.

"No wonder. You always do too much."

"Someone has to." She faced him again. "It's like you're a visitor here, not part of the family."

J. D. stood and looked directly at her as if she'd called his name. "A visitor. Unwelcome, right? We could've settled this. You didn't have to call Chris."

He watched her clench her jaw, and then straighten the bedspread, fluff a pillow. She said, "I'm up now and I'll be fine. I'll apologize to Chris and Andrew."

"No. We're going to talk about this."

"Not now."

"Yes, now. You've been after me to talk. Well, we aren't leaving this room until we do." To fill the silence, he unzipped his bag, emptied it on the bed, stared at the small pile of clothes and toiletries. What to do next stumped him. He pushed the deodorant and razor aside and sat on the bed again, staring toward the door. "Please, come sit beside me."

Soon, her weight on the bed showed her presence. But she said nothing. Still facing the door, he said, "First, I want to know if you've been to the doctor."

"Now you ask?"

He waited. She had to get it out of her system. He pulled in a deep breath.

She said, "It's not that kind of sick. It's the ready to give up kind."

The sigh that followed told him rest wouldn't be near enough. "If you knew that, why did you call Chris?"

It took a long time for her to answer. "I promised him a long time ago."

"Before me?"

She nodded. "I needed help."

"And I wasn't here."

She had leaned forward, gotten smaller, her back shaking. He knew she'd hate it if he saw her tears. Not raising her head, she asked, "What can we do?"

"I'm not going anywhere. We'll fix this, everything."

"Can we?"

"One thing at a time. Start with one. Name it."

She sat up straighter, sniffed. "Amy."

"Worse?"

"You're always Mr. Nice Guy. Standing back. You make me do all the work, be the bad parent."

Once she started, she spilled out how he'd made her effort to get rules agreed to look foolish, by ignoring them. Every word aimed toward the floor, her lap, anywhere else, she never looked directly at him. After a couple of examples—him walking out when they talked about the rules, his avoiding eating with them—she stopped, stared at her bare feet. Her voice louder, and harsh, she said, "All the things like that make me mad and I can't help showing it. Why should I?"

He shrugged. "Yeah, why should you? I get it. All I can say is I'll do better. I promise."

She made a sound that told him she doubted he'd make the effort. For a second, he wondered if he had a doubt, too. Then he said, "Give me credit. I said I'd do better. What are *you* willing to do?"

"If you paid attention you'd know I'm already trying. I stopped bringing work home. Like I promised. I leave clinic on time. Like I promised."

"And you come home mad and stressed because you've taken on too much. Again."

She stood and walked to the window, her back straight as a rod, head up. "This isn't going to work. Down deep, you want me to fail. So you blame my work for anything that makes you feel bad. You won't help. And now I've proved it. I got sick and fell apart. You should be pleased. "

He thought she must have gathered up all the strength in the room, hers and his too. He shook his head. "We've let this go too long. Should have stopped and talked sooner. Lots of this is my fault. But you need to know you're wrong about one thing. I never want you to fail. I'm proud of you."

His inclination to leave the room evaporated when he tried to stand. He propped his elbows on his knees, and supported his head in his palms.

She might have been whispering when she said, "Thank you."

He patted the bed next to him. "Please."

She sat, rigid, not near enough to touch. He said, "I know we have to work this out."

Neither of them moved for what seemed like a long time. Then she asked, "Where's Gran?"

"Said she was going to the little house, her house. Maybe I should check. The wind's pretty stiff." He said, "Let's both go check.

I have something else to show you, too." All that got was a frown. But she did pull on a sweatshirt and shoes and follow him.

They found Willa inside the house where she'd grown up, where she and Frank had lived when they first married, and where J.D. and Claire had started out. As if she were expecting visitors, Willa had opened the blinds in all the rooms, letting in the sunlight tinted beige by blowing dust. Sitting in the recliner that no one had used in several years, she pointed to the boxes Chris and Andrew had placed in two stacks against the opposite wall.

"Were you concerned about me? I was just thinking about where to put things when I open those boxes. The last time I lived in this house was 1958. I hope you don't mind if I move back in."

J.D. said, "Mind? I'll be happy to have you near for advice. If this drought keeps up, I'll be on your doorstep needing help every day."

She said, "The first thing we have to do, Claire, is find a woman who can clean for both of us. I got smart and gave up housework years ago. You should learn early."

She explained her plan to get cleaning done the very next day and have Chris and Andrew unpack for her before they left to go back to Taos. Claire promised to call a woman who might want the work. J.D. knew Willa's plan involved more than moving in the little house, and that Claire would likely not resist whatever Gran told her she must do. Right that minute, she probably couldn't even if she'd wanted to. Dark circles smudged the skin around her eyes and she had sat soon after they entered the house.

J.D. checked the time—close to 5:30. He asked if they were ready to eat something or if they were up for a little surprise first. They both shrugged and he took that as agreement. Getting everything out in the open seemed important right then. At least most of it.

On the way to the Havlicek place, he explained about needing to separate work and home, wanting an office. He hoped it came out sounding like a good idea, not like a middle-aged man running from, or toward, something. Just as he parked at the house, he finished by saying, "So last week one day, I started getting this together. I have a ways to go."

Once the door was unlocked, he held out a hand, like an usher. "The Jackson Ranch Headquarters, at least the start of it."

Willa said, "What a good idea! I like this desk. And this." She sat in the chair, gave it a small push to test its rocking motion. "What do you think, Claire?"

The expression on his wife's face told him nothing. Not what he'd hoped. But she said, "It could be nice. We have an extra file cabinet at the clinic if you need one."

He told about how this would help him separate the work from home, and as he did, realized he was repeating himself. In fact, the sound of his own voice startled him, told him he was working too hard at heartiness. Maybe so, but some of the weight that had sat on his chest most of the day had lifted.

Back at home, Willa said she'd done nothing all day and planned to earn her keep by cooking scrambled eggs for supper. Claire sat silent for a while and then managed to call around and find a woman to clean—she'd be out early in the morning.

Right after they ate—he and Willa like they hadn't in days, Claire just barely, leaving most of hers on the plate—Claire said she needed to rest. Without another word or a look toward him, she went to the bedroom. He helped Willa clear the dishes, then thanked her for cooking supper. She said, "I imagine you have things to do. I'm going to watch TV a while and go to bed early. See you in the morning."

The sun had set soon after they got back to the house. Not long after, the wind stopped. J.D. stood on the porch in the twilight for a long time, staring at the dry ground, dreading the morning when he'd have to go out to the field where he and Tag planted wheat three weeks ago.

He'd hoped for at least some small amount of moisture to plant the wheat into. But he'd had to dust it in. It'd be a miracle if what had come up stayed up. All they needed was that one half-section, enough to finish up the steers that had been on grass for most of the year. Grazing on new wheat, they could gain the weight needed to make them ready for sale as natural beef. The heifers were left on grass; they could qualify for grass-fed natural. Even if the heifers had to be fed some grass hay, if he could find some to buy, they'd be okay. But the steers might have to be sold to a feed lot instead of going straight to slaughter. It could be a losing proposition. Everything depended on the weather.

Fact was, none of that would matter much if he didn't get himself corralled enough to make things right with Claire. But there she was inside, asleep in the dark, too worn out to talk, or maybe avoiding it the same as he was.

Locking the front door, he heard the television go quiet, and then the light from the family room went out. A bit later, the door to the fourth bedroom closed with a soft click

His phone rang. Chris. He said he and Andrew were going to Lubbock to eat and would find somewhere there to stay overnight, and be back in the morning to help Willa. J. D. might as well have answered a call from a stranger, until right at the end, when he managed to gut it up and say, "Chris, I need to tell you this. Claire and I are talking— were, she's resting now. But I have to know you and I are going to be all right, too."

It took a long time before Chris answered. Finally he said, "Brothers fight each other sometimes. That's how it is in families. We'll see."

After he hung up, J.D. made as little noise as possible in the bathroom, then undressed in the bedroom with the lights off. As he lifted the cover to get in bed, Claire turned toward him. "I'm not asleep. I was, but not now. I have to know. Were you with Jan?"

The only light came in between the slats of the barely open blinds, a pale, indirect moonglow that crept about a foot across the floor before surrendering to the dark inside. He said, "She's in charge of the committee I'm on. We had drinks and dinner and then meetings starting Saturday morning until Sunday afternoon."

She didn't say a word. He knew she was waiting, maybe expecting to have to sort out a lie hidden in facts. She was good at that.

"There are five of us on the committee and a staff person." He hesitated, thinking about TV crime shows and polygraphs, and felt her watching him. "The only time it was just the two of us was that first night at dinner. She'd made reservations for three, but the other guy, Trey, had family in town, so he left after a drink."

"Where did you stay?"

He told her, and waited. He knew she would ask if Jan was in the same hotel. When she did, and he answered, he thanked God he'd had the sense to choose the Sheraton. It was probably the one thing he'd done that made sense.

If she hadn't been sitting up, leaning against the headboard, he'd have thought her silence meant she was asleep. Finally, she said, "I'm going to tell you the truth, what I really think." Another long silence followed. "Even if nothing happened between you two, it's likely to, sometime. You're a handsome man, she's a single woman— yes, I looked her up—and you're unhappy at home and maybe with your whole life. I can't prove it, but I'll bet she's already made it clear she's available."

He moved so he could look at her directly. She brushed a hand across in front of her like swatting a gnat, then pointed an index finger at him. "Don't bother disagreeing. Maybe you can't even see it. Women know. Flatter a man, let him know you need him."

"It's not that way. She's not."

"No? Don't dare defend her to me. You're not responsible for what *she* does."

He focused on the bit of light angling into the room, and felt the bed shift as Claire stood. She hadn't undressed. She said, "But you're responsible for what *you* do. I never wondered before if I could trust you."

"Nothing happened. It won't." He watched her shuffle things in her dresser drawer, pull out a nightgown. He said, "Are we going to be okay?"

She didn't look his way. "I don't know. Maybe you'd be happier if we got a divorce."

"Don't say that."

"Why not? Think how much easier your life would be. No disappointing wife, no teenage daughter. Free to do what you want, when you want? Don't think I've forgotten that time you met that girlfriend from college—just seeing an old friend for coffee, you said— while I was pregnant with Jay Frank. You'd have never told me if I hadn't found out. "

"That was just what I told you, she called and asked and I met her. Nothing else."

"Do you think I'm completely stupid? I have no way of knowing what you do. And when I can't trust you . . . this isn't the way I want to live."

"You're wrong, wrong about all of that."

Neither of them said anything for a while. He thought that "coffee with an old friend" explanation had settled that business a long time ago. Until now Claire never mentioned it. He hoped those words she'd just struck him with came from frustrations and overwork. Most of all he hoped she believed what he'd said about Jan. Finally, he asked, "Do you have to go to work tomorrow?"

"I'm not going until Wednesday."

She passed him on the way to their bathroom. He reached for her hand, held onto it. He said, "We'll talk more. About your work, about the ranch. About Amy. I'll do better with her."

She pulled away. When she came out of the bathroom and got into bed, she turned toward the wall. He waited until her breathing settled. Then he moved close and wrapped an arm around her. She shrugged him off and moved farther away.

Floyd County Tribune
Thursday, October 3, 2013

Jackson's Pond City Council Agenda
　　Next meeting of the Jackson's Pond City Council is scheduled for October 10, 2013 in the Council Room of Jackson's Pond City Hall. The following agenda is as posted in compliance with Texas Open Meetings Act. All citizens are welcome to attend.
　　　　　　　Agenda
　　Jackson's Pond, Texas City Council
　　October 10, 2013 7:00 p.m.
　　Council Room City Hall

　　　　Call to Order
　　　　Minutes of last meeting
　　　　City Manager's Report
　　　　Old Business-none
　　　　New Business
　　　　　　Resignation of member
　　　　　　Nominations to fill unexpired term
　　　　　　Information item-RBJ Data
　　　　　　Solutions
　　　　　　Citizen Input
　　　　　　Adjournment

CHAPTER 16
We'll See

Tuesday morning, Claire heard voices. It sounded like her grandmother and J.D. talking—all she could make out were occasional words. She told herself to go back to sleep. Her bladder urged otherwise. She made her way into the bathroom where she concentrated on the reason she was there, not turning toward the mirror. The bed invited her and she accepted, covered herself, and fell asleep again.

When she woke later and stood, the sun streamed between the blinds and demanded she move. As she fumbled for a shirt and jeans, a sensation of thickness, like wearing an overcoat and mittens, made dressing a chore. Tying on her sneakers, clumsiness taxed her. But she couldn't stay in bed forever.

Gran had left a note on the kitchen counter. "I've gone to meet Chris and Andrew at the little house. Coffee's fresh." Claire poured a large mug full and treated herself to five minutes at the counter, sitting still, not thinking. She lifted the cup and inhaled the aroma, the best part of coffee aside from the caffeine. The strong, brown brew warmed her stomach and encouraged her to eat the cinnamon toast that waited next to the pot. After a few bites, she added half a banana and a glass of milk.

Standing at the sink, rinsing her plate, her woolen cover dropped away and left her edges defined and her fingers nimble. Sunlight, pouring through the kitchen window, warmed her chest and face and welcomed her back.

She jumped at the sound of J.D.'s voice. "We didn't want to wake you. How do you feel this morning?"

"I didn't know anyone was here."

He poured a cup of coffee. "Just came in from the goat pen."

"It must be late. I should go help Gran."

"About ten. Chris and Andrew have everything under control. Told me to leave, get on about my business."

"I'm going to shower."

As she passed him, he touched her shoulder, and said, "I'll be out checking that wheat. Call if you need me."

She nodded and moved away. As she went toward the bedroom, she heard him say, "Try not to overdo."

Even though she could tell the wind wasn't high, she shrugged into her red sweatshirt and slid her phone into her jeans pocket. Other times she would have walked the three miles to Gran's house, telling herself she could use the exercise, but today she chose to drive.

As she parked at the little house, she saw Gran on the porch, sitting in one of the two metal chairs. They needed paint. Willa said, "Come sit with me. Your brother told me to get out of the way until they call me."

As she stepped on the porch and settled into the other chair, Claire said, "Since when do you take orders from Chris?"

"Since he and Andrew and Alicia created such a storm of activity in there. That's some fast cleaning woman. She's already finished dusting and vacuuming and now she's scrubbing the bathroom. The boys moved the furniture and are checking the appliances. Nothing for me to do until I can get into the boxes."

Claire said, "I'll be right back."

In the house, she checked with Chris to get his version. He said, "She's fine. There'll be plenty for her to do later. We need to get a bed for the second bedroom. She's planning for a visitor. Apparently soon."

She couldn't help frowning. "Anyone in particular?"

"Didn't say, but I'd guess Robert Stanley. They talk on the phone almost every day." He opened the cabinet under the kitchen sink, lay on his back on the floor and worked his head and shoulders in below the pipes. "If you'll keep her company, we'll be through in about thirty minutes."

Claire hoped he was right about Robert. She'd watched Gran light up whenever he was around when they were in Taos at Labor Day.

The screen door flapped shut as Claire went back to the porch. "He ran me off, too."

The two of them sat without speaking, rocking the rusty chairs gently. She heard Willa sigh. Her eyes were closed. When she opened them and caught Claire watching, she said, "Did you think

I was napping?"

"Not certain."

"I was remembering how happy your grandfather and I were living here when we first married. Every day was an adventure. We worked together a lot of the time, but he would never let me stop painting and encouraged me to keep dancing. Not many men would have done that."

Claire said, "Chris always wanted to be just like him."

Willa nodded and said, "J. D. reminds me of him in a lot of ways. The other thing I was recalling was how he kept me from losing myself when Little George died. Did I ever tell you?"

"No. I wondered."

"Yes, well I've realized, almost too late, that silence may not be the best policy."

"What do you mean?"

Her grandmother turned toward her. She told about the baby's sudden death and the tornado that followed and how she slipped into a deep depression. "The only thing I knew to do was work. Otherwise, I thought I'd die, and if it hadn't been for Frank, I probably would have. I lived through it, but I know now I'd have been better off not to use work to avoid those dark, frightening emotions. By doing that, I was missing half of life. Then later, I nearly let go again, when your granddad died. I never told anyone."

"Does it make you sad to be here? There's room for you at the big house."

"I came to terms with sadness a long time ago. I don't fear it now. When I feel it, I let it settle with me, then I wait and when it's time, it passes.

Claire turned away. Tears made her vision blurry. Willa had stopped talking, then began again. "I'd probably told myself I was being self-reliant all those years, showing others only the sunny parts."

"You said nearly too late."

"Overstatement, I guess. Maybe everyone has to learn their lessons at their own time, if they ever do. I meant I wish I'd known some of this soon enough to have told or shown your mother. She had some difficult times."

"I think she's happy now."

Willa nodded. After another pause, she said, "You're not."

"I'm so sorry you came back because of me. I'll get myself together."

"I came because of me, not you." She stopped rocking. "False pride kept me away too long."

Claire said she didn't understand.

Willa said, "A full explanation could take a long time. The short version is this. False pride makes a person do all they can to make things appear perfect when they aren't. That leads to being unwilling to ask for or accept help."

"You?"

Chris yelled from inside, "Okay, you two can come in now. All the real work is done."

Willa said, "My grandson, the diplomat." She pushed herself up from the chair, and took Claire's hand.

Claire followed her grandmother inside and tracked behind her from the living room through the larger bedroom, then into the bathroom between it and the other bedroom. If she closed her eyes, she could see small-child versions of Amy and Jay Frank in those rooms, herself and J.D. laughing and making love. She said, "Gran, give me a job."

Chris and Andrew left, saying they'd be back with lunch later. Soon after, Alicia asked if there was anything more she should do. With Gran, the three of them agreed on a schedule for twice weekly cleaning, Wednesdays at Gran's and Mondays at the big house. It would be hard for Claire, letting someone else do part of what she'd always taken as hers to do.

When the two of them were alone again, Gran assigned Claire to open boxes and help put things away. The two of them worked steadily, transforming the long-vacant house. As she followed Willa's instructions about placing the contents of the boxes, Claire kept returning to her grandmother's words—false pride, asking for help.

"Claire?"

She left the remaining two boxes and went to the main bedroom. "Need something?"

"I'm thinking about Amy and Jay Frank. I'd like to be at the big house when they come in from school each day, if that's all right. I want to have an excuse to spend time with them, get to know them again."

"And you know it would help me and J.D., right?"

"I'd be glad if it did. There's another reason, too. The balcony upstairs, looking toward the turbines and the grass pastures, never fails to offer subjects for me to paint. And the view from the front porch is also one I love."

"Only as long as it works for you. Don't feel obligated if you have something else you want to do."

"Just say thank you."

Claire said, "Thank you." She lifted a framed board from a flat box. The frame measured about two by three feet, with ten two-inch wooden pegs angled in at intervals across it. "This holds your walking sticks, doesn't it?"

"Yes, it goes in the living room."

"I'll find a hammer and put it up if you'll say where."

After Claire fixed it on the wall, her grandmother stepped back and nodded. She said, "Thank you."

They were down to the final box when Chris and Andrew pulled into the driveway. Claire heard them laughing as they walked onto the porch. Andrew said, "Ready or not, lunch is here."

He and Chris each carried two bags from the Subway in Jackson's Pond. Chris said, "Looks like someone lives here now. Good work!"

After they ate, sitting around the kitchen table, Willa said, "I have a routine. Each day I rest for at least half an hour after lunch. I find it helps my energy and my balance. So I'm going to my newly arranged bedroom to rest."

Claire noticed Chris and Andrew exchange a look as Gran left the room. She asked, "Is she all right?"

Andrew said, "She's eighty-three."

Claire said, "You'll miss her in Taos. It's selfish of me, but I'm so glad she's here."

Chris said, "You're right. On both counts." He reached in one of the paper sacks. "We baked cookies."

"I doubt that." She grabbed for one and ate it in two bites.

After they cleared away the paper bags and other trash, the three of them stood on the front porch. Chris put an arm around Claire and said, "You look like you might live. How do you feel?"

"Like I might live." She leaned against her brother. "I'm sorry you had to come. Embarrassed. Thank you both. I'll try not to let it happen again."

Andrew said, "How?"

Leave it to a psych nurse to get to the point. She said, "For one, just this minute, I decided, I'm going to close the clinics, both of them, on Saturdays. Another thing, Alicia will clean our house once a week."

Chris had his head down, watching a beetle work its way across the porch. He said, "That should help." After a pause, he said, "What about you and J.D.?"

She'd never been able to keep Chris in the dark for long. She shrugged. "We're working on it. We'll see."

She wished she could have sounded more certain. She stepped away from her brother. "There's one other thing. If you'd stay and cook dinner every day, my life would be close to perfect."

He grabbed for her sweatshirt, but she stepped out of reach. He said, "You might not live after all."

Gran said from the bedroom, "If I hear any more noise from out there, I'm coming with a switch."

Chris said, "It's Claire, Gran. She's the loud one."

Either lunch or laughing with her brother, or both, brought energy Claire had worried would never return. She said, "I need to check on Gus. Want to come?"

As if he'd been waiting for company, Gus deserted Dobie and Britches in the pasture and greeted Andrew, Claire, and Chris at the corral gate with a head shake and nickering. Claire watched Andrew talking to her horse, same as she did, as if he were human, while Chris checked the water trough. She said, "Want to go riding while Gran and I finish up? You could take Gus and Britches." She pointed to the big palomino gelding approaching the corral, slowly. "That's Britches.

Dobie's the one hanging back. He's J.D.'s horse, and he acts up if anyone else gets on his back."

Andrew said he hadn't ridden in years, but after a silent stare from Chris, admitted he'd like to. She told them to be careful, and watch for snakes, then waved as she drove away, back to Gran's house. She wished the two of them would never leave.

By four o'clock, Gran's house looked completely inhabited, other than the space where the bed would go in the second bedroom. She and Gran were discussing when and where to shop for one when Claire's phone rang. Sheriff Clark quickly delivered the news. The prosecutor convinced a Grand Jury Sandra Berry should be charged and tried as accomplice in the clinic thefts. Faced with that, she'd accepted a plea bargain to a lesser felony in exchange for testimony and received five years probation. "We've already reported that to the nursing board. She'll lose her license. I hope this is good news for you."

Relief left her weak. She sat on the footstool near Gran's chair in the living room and told her, as concisely as possible, the story of the clinic theft. When she finished, she said, "What you mentioned about false pride, you're right. Worrying what people would think made the whole thing worse."

Willa said, "It would." She stood and walked to the screen door. "I see someone coming down the road."

The kids piled out of J.D.'s pickup, and he followed, carrying a grocery bag in each hand. He said, "We brought provisions."

Amy and Jay Frank ran to the porch. Jay Frank said, "I was a baby when I lived here."

Gran opened her arms and they both rushed to her. She said, "Yes you were, but you're big now. And here's my dancer. Come inside. School's hard work. You need a snack."

The three of them crowded around the kitchen table, and soon apples, crackers, and cookies were disappearing. J.D. and Claire watched through the screen. He said, "You look like you feel better."

"I have reasons to." She told him about Sheriff Clark's call. A nod was his only comment. Then she said, "Plus, we have Gran all moved in except for a second bed."

"Where's Chris?"

"I left them at the big barn a couple of hours ago. They were going riding. I told them Dobie wouldn't work for anyone but you."

"I'll check on them. Chris said this morning he wanted to talk to me before he left."

"There's something else. I decided to close both of the clinics on Saturdays. I'll have weekends off."

"You okay with doing that?"

She nodded, looking beyond him toward the road. "I am."

He turned, following her gaze, then shrugged, a tiny movement. "I'll go on down to the barn."

He stepped off the porch, then turned toward her and smiled. His eyes seemed sad to her.

Later, Claire was sitting in a porch chair, watching the distant turbines turning, half-listening to the voices from the kitchen, when Amy and Jay Frank hurried out, followed by Willa. The kids chattered at the same time, "Gran's going to help us get music for my ballet lessons. Gran wants to see my goats. Let's go."

As she followed them to her Suburban, Claire wanted to bottle the feeling she had just then, keep it as a liquid treasure, call it Essence of Happiness; it would have the aroma of spice and lemon. She'd open it only on special occasions, to share it with the people she loved.

As soon as she parked in the drive at home, Amy and Jay Frank hopped out. Then, as if by some silent agreement, they both moved more slowly, matching Gran's pace across the uneven trail to the goat pen. The aroma of lemon and spice grew stronger.

Seconds after she went into the house and passed the dining room table, that fragrance she'd thought of bottling disappeared. J.D. had cleared away his papers and the computer. All gone. She didn't have to ask. She knew he'd taken them to his home place, his new office. That was one way to make certain she'd never see his browsing history again. No doubt he'd also changed his e-mail address

Floyd County Tribune
Thursday, November 21, 2013

Home School Co-op Meeting
The second meeting of the Cooperative will explore organizational structure and conduct a skill inventory of interested members on Monday, November 25 at 6:30 p.m. in the Jackson's Pond First United Methodist Church Fellowship Hall.

Mrs. Montoya, who convened the first meeting of the group said, "More than 30 interested parents attended that meeting. This next one will move our organization forward by working on a formal structure and identifying skills of members who are willing to share with other home school parents."

All interested parents are invited to attend, even if they were not at the initial meeting. A written summary of that meeting will be available.

Date Set for County Junior Livestock Show
Glen Robertson, Superintendent for the 57th annual Floyd County Junior Livestock Show, announced the dates for the show. It is scheduled for January 15 and 16, 2014 at the County Events Center. More details will be published in early December

CHAPTER 17
Meeting

J.D. stood at the clinic's front desk, visiting with Laverne. He'd gotten there early, and Claire was seeing the last patient. She'd only scheduled the morning, so they could keep their appointment in Plainview with the counselor.

Laverne said, "I'm so glad everything's back to normal around here. Best of all I won't have to look at the Sheriff's smiling face again for a long time. You know, I didn't vote for him."

"Have to give him credit for trying to get that theft cleared up."

"You're nicer than I am." She cocked her head toward the hallway. "I hear Claire giving the patient his instructions about exercise and diet. That means she'll be finished in just a minute or two."

"I'll wait out in the pickup if you'll tell her I'm here."

In a couple of minutes, he saw Mr. Hofer leave the clinic. Soon after, Claire came out. J.D. said, "Right on time. I brought us a picnic." He pointed to a bag on the console between them.

"Subway?"

"Nope, I made those sandwiches myself."

She opened the large bag. "And did you make these Fritos, too?"

"What's a picnic without Fritos?"

"Want to eat in the park?"

He shook his head. "Might attract a crowd. Let's go to the pond."

Before they got there, he could see it was a good idea. Claire leaned back in the seat and closed her eyes. He said, "It's been a long time."

"It may be too cool to eat outside."

It couldn't be any chillier than their bedroom. In all these weeks, Claire hadn't budged from the far side of the bed. He said, "I'm pretty sure it'll be okay."

He parked and they walked toward what remained of their favorite place. No bulls roamed; no people intruded. All the grass had turned brown after the cold snap at the end of October. But the pasture around the pond calmed him in any season. He'd made important decisions there all his life and watched sunsets that filled him with hope more times than he could count. And he'd proposed to Claire there.

After strolling slowly to the low rocks on the far bank, they sat. He opened the bag and made a show of presenting his wife a turkey breast sandwich he'd wrapped in waxed paper, secured with a frill-topped toothpick he found in the cabinet. Next, he produced two chilled Dr Peppers and a plastic bag full of carrot and celery sticks. Then the Fritos. And finally, he produced a large Snickers from the bottom of the bag.

She said, "You went to a lot of trouble. Thanks."

He nodded and bit into his sandwich, watched her extract the toothpick and open hers. In the bright, flat midday sun, he saw a warm glow had begun to return to her cheeks. More importantly, her eyes shone emerald again, not haunted by the shadow he knew he'd cast there. It had taken six weeks, and some serious work, but things were getting better slowly. He knew about patience.

She faced west, and spoke without turning toward him. "What are you thinking?"

"Lots of things, all at once." He filled his mouth with a big bite of sandwich.

"What's at the top?"

"Wondering what the counselor will tell us about Amy." He reached for his drink. The bread and meat wadded, hung in his throat. Two swallows relieved the pressure. "I think Willa's dance lessons have helped."

"We were part of the problem."

He knew she was right. After another gulp of Dr Pepper, he said, "Have you thought any more about going to Fort Worth with me?"

"I guess I could finish my Christmas shopping there if I go. I won't be able to accomplish anything about recruiting a new nurse practitioner on the weekend anyway."

"Say yes and I'll make hotel reservations."

Claire checked her watch. "We need to leave. We shouldn't keep the counselor waiting."

She gave him directions to the office when they got to Plainview. Immediately after they arrived and pushed the button next to the sign on the wall, the counselor opened the door on the far side of the waiting room and invited them in. No receptionist, no one else waiting. He remembered to take off his hat before he followed Claire inside.

The counselor didn't waste time. As soon as they took the seats she offered, side by side on her office couch with her in a chair facing them, she confirmed that Amy had given permission for her to meet with them. Then she explained that Amy had "flirted," as she put it, with bulimia, but that she felt it was likely a response to the mass of concerns brought on by peer pressure, onset of puberty, and family stresses. After that last item, she sat silent. Maybe she thought they would disagree. Neither of them said a word. He wouldn't have known what to say, if he'd wanted to talk, which he'd just as soon not.

Then she outlined a plan that would require monthly appointments for six months. Her focus would be on helping Amy explore methods of coping with stress-related anxiety and with peer pressure. She said, "What she's perceiving in interactions with some of her friends sounds very much like bullying to me. Two girls in particular, Chelsea and Tiffany." The counselor wrote the names on a sticky note and handed it to him. "She feels tremendous ambivalence toward them. She even spoke of wanting to be home schooled so she'd never have to see them again."

He saw Claire's mouth tighten, and felt her shift and sit forward. If she'd been an animal, she'd have bared her teeth and snarled.

He touched her back gently. Then he said to the counselor, "Anything we can do, other than encourage her to work with you?"

"She told me about her dance lessons. Anything like that makes her feel strong and capable. It can help. Home schooling could be an option you may want to consider." He noticed she shrugged when she mentioned home school, as if she weren't certain.

After encouraging open communication at home and

discussing the difficulty of being a young adolescent in today's world, she ended the meeting on a positive note. "You described her as a bright, happy child before puberty arrived. That's important. It shows she once knew how to feel confident. Together, I think we can help her remember how."

They rode silently until they'd passed through Calverton and turned east toward home. Claire said, "Matador's no farther than Calverton. Maybe we could find out about transferring school districts."

He said, "I'll look into it next week." He reached for her hand, held it. "I was no help when this started."

When they pulled up at the house, Jay Frank waved from the goat pen. Before they were out of the pickup, Amy came out on the porch, wearing her ballet slippers, tights, and leotard. Willa stood in the doorway. Claire said, "Go ahead and make that reservation. We deserve a little vacation."

His mother-in-law had announced a week ago that she was in charge of Thanksgiving dinner, at their house in town. Ray would cook the turkey and she had everything else under control. So he, Claire, and Willa, plus the two kids arrived mid-morning Thursday empty-handed, except for the Scrabble game. Willa had challenged them all to a round-robin tournament. She'd take on all comers, she said.

Claire insisted on setting the table, saying it was the least she could do. When they sat down to eat, they all stuffed themselves. Claire even finished a full plate. They hadn't even gotten to dessert yet. Melanie said, "Before we have dessert, we have an announcement. Ray, you should tell them."

He stood and said, "You are looking at the newly appointed member of the Jackson's Pond, Texas, City Council."

Lots of questions and jokes about bribes and kickbacks followed. Ray took it all with a serious expression, and made a speech about better government and economic development. Willa hooted and said, "Good luck with that."

Ray said, "I'm practicing in case I decide to campaign for the real term. I'm only appointed until May. Interim to fill an unexpired term."

J.D. said, "Seriously. Congratulations. You'll do a good job."

"I don't expect it will take a lot of time. Not much happens here. You may have noticed." He sat down and picked up his fork, both elbows on the table. He said, "Okay, enough of that. I'm ready for pumpkin pie."

The afternoon passed quickly, as Willa, with Claire as her partner, won at Scrabble against every team the other five formed. When Willa declared a bathroom break, Claire followed her mother into the kitchen. She came out a few minutes later and told J.D. the kids would stay with their grandparents the following weekend. Her smile made it easy to accept the beating he and Ray took at Scrabble.

Around four, Willa said she needed a nap after all that winning, so Melanie loaded them up with leftovers and they headed home. The kids kept them all laughing on the way, making jokes about how Willa cheated at Scrabble. She denied it all.

Friday, J.D. left Tag checking the pregnant cows and the steers and heifers and drove to his office. When he fired up his computer, an e-mail from Jan popped up. He hadn't spoken with her since the meeting, but had answered the one email she'd sent, asking how delivery of the bulls had turned out. He'd responded with a two line account of the smooth transfer of ownership, plus the surprise purchase of #3355 by a man who'd bought one of the others. He doubted it was the information she was looking for.

Today's mail was addressed to all committee members and contained the agenda for the meeting on the seventh and eighth. The final line said she'd made reservations at Del Frisco's for cocktails at 6:30 followed by dinner at 7:30, and requested a response. He quickly composed an answer. "Claire and I will be there in time for cocktails. She looks forward to meeting everyone and finishing her Christmas shopping on Saturday while we do our work." He used the "reply to all" button to send it. He sat back and exhaled. Then he deleted Jan's message, her earlier one, and both replies. After a second, he also emptied the entire deleted mail folder, wondering as he did where all that stuff went. Then he locked the office and drove out to help Tag.

Friday at noon, he waited outside the clinic. Claire had arranged to close early, give Laverne an afternoon off. As soon as she finished with the last patient, he pointed the pickup east and they were on the way to Fort Worth. Somewhere near Crowell, Claire said, "I hope I brought the right clothes."

"You'll be the prettiest girl there, no matter what you wear."

He pushed the speed limit all the way from home down to Vernon, slowing only for the few small towns between. He took the fact that they got checked in at the hotel in Fort Worth by six p.m. as a good sign. As soon as they were in their room, Claire moved fast, stuffing things in the drawers and closet. He shucked out of his clothes in the bathroom and changed into a starched white shirt and Wranglers. He heard her drop something and say damn.

Before he could shove his belt through the last three loops, she tried to muscle him out of the bathroom saying she needed to get to the mirror, had to do something with her hair. The fact she was bare except for bra and panties stopped him. He hadn't seen her like that in months. He eased around behind her, wrapped his arms around her, his hands touching each side of her waist. He pushed, gently, to turn her toward him. She didn't resist. He leaned down and kissed her, long and deep. She relaxed toward him, pressed her full length against him. He brushed her hair back and ran his tongue slowly from below her left ear to her collarbone, then kissed the hollow formed there between muscle and bone. She shivered and pulled him back into another long kiss. A soft moan rose from deep in her chest. Her perfume invited him to continue.

She pushed away from him, shaking her head, and turned to face the mirror. Finger-combing her curly black hair, arranging it so the tiny streak of gray at her right temple showed, she glanced at him in the mirror, raised an eyebrow. He said, "We could be late, make an entrance."

"Tell you what, cowboy, you hold that thought. After dinner I'll take you up on what you have in mind."

"What's that?"

"Let's call it dessert." She turned around, gave him a push toward the door. "Now get out so I can finish dressing."

When she stepped into the bedroom, wearing a low cut white blouse with loose puffed sleeves; a calf-length denim skirt that looked made for dance twirls; her waist cinched by a black belt with a huge silver buckle set with turquoise; and black riding-heel boots with tall turquoise tops, he thought about missing dinner altogether. She said, "All I need is my jewelry and I'm ready."

"New boots?"

She busied herself situating inch-diameter turquoise sunburst earrings in place. As she slipped on a silver cuff bracelet, she said, "Gran's. Mine now. She said they were great for dancing. We wear the same size."

"That's why they're familiar. When we went to Austin a long time ago, she wore me and Chris and Andrew out two-stepping that night, in those boots. Us and a bunch of fake cowboys in a bar we went to on 6th Street."

"Help me with this necklace?"

"If you'll save every dance for me." She dropped a larger, matching sunburst medallion in his hand and turned her back to him. The whiff of sandalwood-tinged vanilla he caught as he placed the necklace's single strand of silver beads around her neck made handling the clasp a chore.

She moved arm's length away, turned toward him. The medallion sat just at the point of the blouse's plunge and encouraged him to notice the swell of her breasts. "She gave me this jewelry, too. Early Christmas present, she said. Am I overdressed?"

"You're perfect. Beautiful."

He reached to scoop his change and money clip from the dresser. She clamped her hand atop his just as the first quarter dropped into his other hand. She said, "When did you get that?"

He felt himself blink several times, rapidly, knew that liars did that. He lifted his hand off the clip and coins and said, "Jan gave it to me at the last meeting. She said it was to congratulate me on the bull sale."

A half-smirk passed across Claire's lips, followed closely by a roll of her eyes and a shake of her head. He'd seen that expression before, when she dealt with one of the kids breaking something, like she couldn't prevent what had already happened and knew she'd have to be the one to clean it up.

She said, "See what I mean? Don't ever think I don't know

how some women get what they want."

She held the money clip up and examined it front and back. "Nice."

Then she handed it back to him. He said, "If you want me to, I'll get rid of it. I told you, nothing happened."

"And I told you it's your actions you're responsible for, not hers." She gave him a long look and her smile, the real one, returned. "Do we still have a dinner date tonight?"

She was right. If he didn't understand women by this time, he probably never would.

She slipped a dark blue shawl decorated in red and turquoise Navajo patterns around her shoulders. He put on his black blazer and his best hat. They stepped out of the hotel lobby as the downtown trolley stopped at the curb. Three short stops later, it delivered them to the restaurant.

He saw Trey, the two other committee members, and Jan clustered on two low couches in the bar. The men stood as soon as he and Claire approached. Trey could have been a lifelong friend, the way he greeted him—handshake, back-slap, and big grin, all the while looking Claire over like some prize filly he might bid on. The other two were only slightly less obvious. J.D. introduced her to everyone. Jan stayed seated, greeted Claire, offered a brief handshake, and maintained a wide smile that never reached her eyes. The men continued standing, talking among themselves. J.D. felt Claire move away from him, toward Jan. He thought about holding his breath. Instead, he turned his back and pretended to listen to the three other men's talk about the cattle market.

But he heard every word Claire said, and was sure she intended it that way. "It's so good to meet you. I know you must have wonderful taste so I want to ask you a question, if you don't mind."

He didn't hear all of Jan's reply, then Claire said, "It was so thoughtful of you to have that money clip made for J. D., and such a unique idea. I'd been meaning to get in touch and ask who made it. I'm thinking of having a larger one done on a belt buckle."

He slid a glance toward Jan, saw she had flushed an unflattering shade. She said something about not recalling the name.

Claire said, "That's okay, just let J.D. know when you think of it. I know you have his phone number and e-mail address. He'll tell me. I guess I'd better get back over there. He likes to keep an eye on me."

She sidled up beside him and stood so close he felt her breath on his neck. Trey suggested they all sit down and relax. J.D. wondered if Trey knew he needed to right then. After their drinks came, he leaned back in the soft leather seat and admired the way Claire fielded the men's questions. She managed to respond with little in the way of personal information. Then she'd return a comment or question that allowed each of his fellow committee members to paint a flattering self-portrait the way guys will in front of a pretty woman. No wonder her patients loved her. He called himself a fool for being jealous the other time she came with him. She didn't seek the spotlight, it found her.

He slid a glance toward Jan. The smile she'd greeted them with remained wide, but was now directed toward the red drink in the martini glass she clutched. Before long, she raised her focus toward Claire and the other men. Her smile evaporated, replaced by a thin slash of red lipstick. She shook her head as if dismissing something or someone, and not a strand of her frozen hair moved. She beckoned the waiter and said, "If our table's ready, we are."

The smile reappeared, beamed toward her group. She said, "Follow me." She stepped in behind the waiter. Coy King, a guy about J.D.'s age, hustled along, attentive as a drone bee, and caught up with her. J. D. and Claire, trailed by the other two, lagged behind, all carrying their unfinished drinks. After following the waiter in an unruly parade along a winding walk through the main dining room, they entered a small private area where a rectangular table for six waited. Coy slid out the chair at the head of the table for Jan, then sat on the corner to her right. Claire chose the chair directly opposite Jan, at the other end of the table, and allowed the waiter to seat her. J.D. sat at the first corner seat on her right, so he wouldn't trouble anyone with his left-handed eating. While the other two got situated, J.D. patted his wife's thigh under the table. She flicked a look his way, then flung a bright smile in Jan's direction.

He ordered a rib eye and another Jack Daniel's with water and then sat back, almost relaxed for the first time in a long time. Tonight, instead of worrying about how to hoard all the light Claire cast, he let her glow lift him. From now on, he'd take her with him everywhere he could convince her to go.

Between the salad and arrival of entrees, she edged a boot close and tapped his, touched his leg with hers. Then her hand slid onto his thigh. He leaned toward her and whispered, "If you want a chance to eat that lobster tail you ordered, you'd better keep your hands to yourself."

The warmth on his leg disappeared. She said, "I wouldn't want to miss the seafood. Will you save me some of your steak, too?"

"It'll cost you."

The other committee members chatted, ordered drinks, and took a long time finishing their beef. Then Jan suggested coffee and pie. Claire ordered coffee, said she believed she'd skip dessert for now. When the others' arrived, he noticed Jan pushed hers aside. Not long after—not soon enough to suit J.D.—Jan said, "Anyone need anything else?" No one did. The waiter glided by and silently placed the check, hidden in a leather folder, at Jan's elbow.

She glanced at the folder and said, "Since we're all here, if we get started early tomorrow, I think we can finish our work by five or six. I've ordered continental breakfast for 7:30 in our meeting room, and we can begin work then. Lunch will be brought in, assuming that's okay with everyone."

Trey broke off whatever he was saying to Coy and spoke to Jan. "Thanks for arranging everything. Would it hurt your feelings if I get there at eight?"

She shrugged. "Anyone else prefer eight?" The other two raised a hand, briefly, like bidders at an auction. J.D. followed suit. She said, "Then eight it is. Second floor conference room at Association Headquarters."

Trey stood and went to Jan's side. He sounded like a man in charge when he said, "I know we all appreciate you and everything you do for the association." He lifted the check holder and stepped back. "I'm taking care of this."

J.D. spent maybe a second wondering about that little do-si-do between Trey and Jan. And then another second feeling a little sorry for her. She looked like she lost something and wasn't sure what. But he didn't waste any more time. He said to Claire, "Let's say our goodbyes. I have a surprise for you. Before dessert."

Two blocks west, a bar advertised live music—classic rock and country—and dancing. He'd seen it from the trolley as they passed. Now, early on Friday night, he figured the crowd would still be thin and the band wouldn't have begun. Jukebox music would suit him fine. He intended to twirl his wife around the floor, if only for a couple of tunes. He took her hand and said, "Come with me, ma'am."

An old George Strait song met them at the door. The dance floor accommodated maybe twenty couples, so the three that were two-stepping there had all the room they wanted. At the end of the song, all three men spun their partners and grabbed them up tight when they finished. J.D. ordered beers for them both. He told Claire, "I hate to use their dance floor for free."

Rodney Crowell sang from the jukebox speakers, "Even Cowgirls Get the Blues." J.D. couldn't remember the last time they had been out, much less danced. But as soon as he put his hand on her waist and she drew in close, he had no doubt it was like riding a bicycle, tandem. Before the song stopped, he felt loose and easy and Claire never stopped smiling. Mark Chesnutt's version of "Rainy Day Woman" kept them on the floor, moving together as if they practiced daily. Then the jukebox needed feeding. While they huddled in front of it, searching through the list for the perfect song. Claire said, "Gran was right. These boots are just right for dancing."

"We'll have to do it more often, now that they're yours." He found the song. If things went his way, it would be the last one they heard that night. He scooted his wife away from the jukebox. "You have to move so it'll be a surprise."

He slid a bill into the slot and pushed G12. Seconds later, Randy Travis started singing his heart out, telling some woman he'd love her forever and ever, amen. They moved together to the music like teenagers, so close no light could slip between them. He whispered, "That's what I wanted to remind you. Forever."

He lifted her face from against his chest. He saw tears in her eyes, happy ones, he was certain. When the song stopped, they walked back to their tiny table, and still standing, he drank half his beer. She sipped hers. He said, "Ready to go?"

He waved to the bartender as they left. They held hands all the way to their hotel.

He closed the door to their room and flipped the deadbolt. Claire stood next to him, didn't move except to drop her shawl. He pulled her to him and kissed her. He stepped back and said, "Wait right here." He turned on the bathroom light, closed the door except for a crack. "You need help undressing?"

She said, "We can help each other."

Later, in the dark except for the faint glow from the bathroom, she said, "We nearly waited too long."

He pulled her closer.

The next morning, when he strode into the meeting ten minutes after eight, he arrived with an apology he'd prepared in the elevator. But he never uttered it. He kept his mouth shut about the time. The only other person in the room was Trey, who was heaping a plate with two muffins and fruit. Coffee steamed in the cup waiting at the space he'd claimed at one end of the table.

J.D. said, "Just us this morning?"

"So far." Trey started in on the grapes and took a big bite of his first muffin.

J.D. focused on food. As he filled his plate, he hoped it was his imagination that he wore Claire's scent. No time to shower. As he raised his cup for a first drink of coffee, caught a whiff of vanilla and some other spice, he decided he didn't mind what anyone else thought. If he could be sure everything was okay between them, get rid of that off balance feeling he'd had since last night, then everything would be perfect. Maybe he'd had more to drink at dinner than he realized. He drank half his coffee down and refilled the cup, then sat next to Trey.

Trey said, between bites, "I hope you'll consider getting even more involved in the association, eventually run for office. I can help if you decide you're interested. I think you're level-headed, smart.

Something else I admire about you is you're not in a hurry to make big changes."

J.D. said, "Thank you. I really don't know how involved I can afford to be. I operate lean, do lots of the work myself. Doesn't leave a lot of time for travel."

"How's Willa? You know, she and I go a ways back, from when she was an officer in the association."

"She's moved back to the ranch, just two months ago. Doing real well. I'm glad she's home."

Trey said, "She taught me a lot when I first got involved with the association. Maybe you ought to discuss it with her." Then he edged a little closer and said, "I think we need to kind of steer Jan toward taking things a little slower. I suppose she'd told you about the trouble she's having with her stepdaughter. There's a big fight over the will. Been dragging on for years. She's got plenty on her plate and sure doesn't need to get under a lot of deadlines. Well, you probably know lots more about her business than I do." He stopped talking as Jan and the two other committee members arrived together and all went straight to the coffee urn.

Soon after, she called the meeting to order and drove the group the rest of the day, pushing to finish their report.

J.D. kept quiet unless asked a direct question; mostly because he kept wondering why Trey had a notion he'd know anything about Jan's business. Plus, he preferred watching Jan and Trey jockey for control. In the end, he concluded Trey won. The final report that would come from the committee encouraged further study, collection of data, and lots of other "actions" that would take at least eighteen months before any major rebranding initiative would go to the full membership.

Sitting there, watching the two of them, J.D. couldn't imagine ever having the patience or the interest to let himself get involved in the politics of the organization, couldn't remember why he'd even agreed to be on the committee. Jan took a final vote that the group unanimously endorsed, the "take it slowly" version Trey had herded her into. From her place at the head of the table, she thanked them, as a group, for their work on behalf of the association. Her bright smile never wavered, but when she picked up the three-inch stack of papers in front of her, she jammed them in her deep purse, and strode out of the room without saying another word.

Floyd County Tribune
Thursday, December 12, 2013

Pancho Clos Will Return!

After an absence of 10 years, Pancho Clos, the South Pole cousin of Santa Claus, will return to Jackson's Pond. Accompanied by six motorcycle-driving elves, Señor Clos will arrive at City Park at 6 p.m. Thursday December 19.

City Council member Ray Banks will welcome the sombrero wearing bearer of gifts on behalf of all Jackson's Pond area children.

Each child attending will receive a gift and parents will have the opportunity to take pictures of their children with Pancho Clos.

Banks said, "The City Council is eager to revive Jackson's Pond's holiday traditions. This year decorative lights will also reappear. Citizens will see them on downtown street lamps and the trees in the park. They've been packed away for years, and we think it's time to celebrate the holiday season as a community again. Inviting Pancho Clos is another first step. We hope to add events and activities each year, throughout the year, all focused on reminding us of the importance of supporting our community."

CHAPTER 18
Premonition

Claire stood at the clinic's front door, waving goodbye to the day's last patient. When she turned to go back to her office, Laverne said, "That's the last one. If you have a minute, I need to tell you something." If the eagerness in her voice was any indication, Laverne had something that wouldn't keep. "It won't take long, but I just have to tell you."

"What? Tell it before you burst."

"Oh, honey, I did something I never would have thought I'd do. I went to see a psychic. And you'll never believe what she told me. Did you ever go to a psychic?"

Claire shook her head. "No, I wouldn't even know where to find one."

"I've just had this strongest feeling lately that I'm going to find Wendy, or that she'll come home. But I thought maybe there was something I was supposed to do, you know, to push things along, let her know we aren't upset, just concerned. I've thought all along maybe . . ." She shrugged. "I don't know what I thought. But then I found this ad." She waved a bright red card with the words, ALL IS WELL printed above some other information, phone numbers. Before Claire got a good look, Laverne put it back in her purse.

"I didn't even tell my husband, I just dialed that number and made an appointment. She's in Lubbock. I know you need to leave, but I just want you to know. Wendy is fine and she will come back, not soon, but she will, and meanwhile, I should just think positive thoughts for her. That woman knew lots of things no one would know if she wasn't, you know, tuned in."

"Did she tell you to come back to see her?"

"That's what my husband wanted to know. He was sure she was after more money. But no. I paid her fifty dollars and she just repeated, 'All is well.' I feel so much better knowing that. Don't you think there are people who know things before they happen?"

Her smile said it all. Claire wasn't about to dampen her hope.

"It's possible. I'm glad she helped you."

She touched Laverne's shoulder and said, "I'm so glad."

She wondered if a psychic could tell her all was going to be well for her and her family. She still had dreams—Amy vomiting, J. D. with a blond on his arm. Before she made it to her office, the phone in her pocket vibrated.

Claire lifted her phone, showed it to Laverne, then walked to her office as she answered. It was J.D. She hardly recognized his voice. "Jay Frank's been snake bit."

"When? Where?"

"Just now. Close to the barn."

"No. Where's the bite?"

"On his right ankle. It's swelling."

"I'll be there in ten minutes. Stay on. I'll tell you what to do till I get there." She knew he didn't appreciate taking orders, but he'd have to this time. She snatched up her tote bag and coat, pulled out her keys and hurried to the front desk. "Is he conscious and breathing? . . . Good. Check his pulse. If it's regular. Fast is okay." She slowed only long enough at the desk to write *Emergency, Jay Frank, snakebite* on a note pad she handed to Laverne.

She ran out the back to her Suburban. "You still there? Pulse is regular? Good." She drove one-handed until she could cradle the phone between her ear and shoulder. "We'll have to get him to Calverton. I'll call Emergency there, tell them to expect us. Meanwhile, keep him still. Tell him he'll be fine." She sped out of town, hoping no traffic would slow her.

J.D. said, "Are you there? What now?"

"I'm on the way. Call the sheriff to warn him we'll be speeding. You'll have to drive. My hands are shaking. I'll call you back."

She slowed long enough to hit the Calverton ER on Contacts. After she notified them, she dropped the phone to her lap. Both hands on the wheel, driving eighty, she focused on remembering snakebite care. She called J.D. again. He answered on the first ring. She said, "Get an ace bandage from the kit. Wrap it from his foot to his thigh, just for gentle compression, not like a tourniquet. No ice. Is he in pain?"

"He's tough as a little soldier. Not even crying."

Hearing J.D.'s voice helped her focus. She passed the pond. "I'm nearly there. Hanging up."

She skidded to a stop behind J.D.'s pickup, jumped out, and left her vehicle running. J.D. carried their son toward her and she flung open the SUV's back door. Opening the opposite door, she pulled Jay Frank's shoulders to straighten him on the seat, then placed her coat under his head for a pillow. Moving faster than she thought she could, she ran back to the other side and pulled off his right sneaker and sock. "Edematous, but not enormous. Good." She found the pen in her pocket and drew a line around the edges of the swelling. As J. D. got in the driver's seat, she pulled her door shut and hunched between the back and front seats. As she checked Jay Frank's pulse, then looked again at the puncture wounds, she said, "Okay, go. Wait! Where's Amy?"

J.D. backed out and aimed down the road. He said "She's okay. Great actually. She killed the rattler with a hoe, called me, closed up the goat pen, and ran for the ace bandage. Even took pictures of the snake and Jay Frank's ankle with her phone. She's staying with Willa." As he answered, he accelerated.

Claire brushed her boy's hair out of his eyes and told him he'd be fine, knowing she did it mostly for her own benefit. He said he knew it. Then he closed his eyes and never even whimpered. She couldn't see the speedometer, only fence posts blurring past as J.D. sped toward Calverton.

J.D. ran, carrying their son through the automatic doors. She ran behind, breathing hard. After she'd called from the road, the staff notified Jay Frank's pediatrician. A phlebotomist and a nurse moved efficiently to admit Jay Frank and draw blood for labs. The nurse starting an IV said, "Jay Frank, you certainly are brave."

He looked older than his age, and wise, as he said, "My sister's the brave one. She didn't run away. She chopped that snake's head off."

The doctor arrived, and after assessing Jay Frank's condition and reviewing the lab results, he gave the order to administer antivenom in the IV. Claire knew that even if he tolerated the medication well, Jay Frank would be admitted for twenty-four hours of observation. The doctor pointed to the monitor screen. "I guess you already noticed a sinus tachycardia. We'll observe for any other arrhythmia. I think the rate will settle back down without any meds. We'll keep an eye on it."

After the doctor left, Claire said to J.D., "I'll stay. Laverne can reschedule tomorrow's patients. They'll understand."

J.D. said, "I'm staying. We'll do this together. I'll call Willa and Amy."

She leaned across the chair arm between them and kissed his cheek. "I'll call Mother and Dad and Laverne."

The nurse wheeled Jay Frank and a cart holding his monitor out of ER to a regular room, then trundled a cot in. She said, "I'm sorry only one of these will fit in here."

Jay Frank said, "I can stay by myself."

Looking at her baby, Claire saw him hovering above the bed, tethered only by monitor cables, and an IV, a tiny figure floating in a stark white sky. She caught his hand, shook her head. Stress, she told herself.

J.D. said, "We know you can. But we'll stay. It makes *us* feel better."

After J.D. finished on the phone with Willa, Claire asked to speak to Amy. She told her what had been done for her brother. Then she said, "Jay Frank told us how you took care of him. You were very brave to kill that snake. We're so proud of you."

Amy said, "I couldn't let him hurt my brother again. Did he tell you there were two? I killed them both. Momma, is he going to be okay?"

Claire assured her he would probably be released tomorrow afternoon. She said, "I'm so thankful you weren't hurt, too." After a second's silence, Claire said, "I'm going to hang up now. I'll call in the morning. We love you, Amy."

Accustomed to doing for patients, and with nothing she could do for Jay Frank, Claire stood and paced to the doorway. She looked both ways along the short hall. From what she could see, only two other rooms were occupied. She wondered how long this little rural hospital and others like it would be able to stay in business.

Returning to his bedside, she lifted the cover on Jay Frank's right foot. The edema had spread past the line she'd drawn, but only about ten millimeters, and then below the punctures, not above. "Does this hurt? We can get you something for pain."

"Not much."

She said, "I know you're tough, but a Tylenol might make you more comfortable all over."

"Okay."

Less than thirty minutes after the nurse gave him the pill, he fell asleep and Claire felt herself relax as the steady drop, drop of the IV fluid helped her focus. J.D. whispered, "Need something to eat? I'll go get us a burger if you want. Dairy Queen."

"Yes. You know how I like mine."

"When I come back, after we eat, I'll take the first shift. You can sleep a little."

She said, "My blood pressure's probably back to normal by now. Are you okay?"

He came to where she sat at the bedside and hugged her. "I am. I'll be back real soon."

She startled when he touched her hand. It couldn't have been more than twenty minutes he'd been gone, but somehow, as soon as he walked away, she fell asleep. The aroma of hamburgers and fries sat her up straight. He said, "It's nearly eight. Lunch was a long time ago. Let's take this out to the waiting room."

At a table in the empty waiting area, J. D. opened their food and offered her a foil packet of catsup. She began eating right away, then after several bites, leaned back in the chair. She'd needed food.

J.D. said, "Want to hear a story?"

Her mouth full of another bite of burger, she nodded.

"Middle of the morning, Tag and I were out mending fence up north. You know, where the blow sand is stacked up along the fence line, all those weeds from summer make it look like a hedgerow. Lots of places needed splices. We took the four-wheeler. Tag would go a quarter mile down and we'd work toward each other, then move on. Well, after about a mile, I looked up and saw Tag racing back like he was being chased. I thought he was probably just cutting up. He stirred up a cloud of dust all the way and when he skidded to a stop right in front of me, that cloud caught up with him, nearly choked me. He talked faster than usual, said he'd been paying close attention. I remember he said, 'You can't never tell. December or not, them bastards don't keep a calendar. Three or four warm, sunny days in a row and they'll come out to get a tan.'

"I had to figure out he meant snakes. Then he said to follow him, so I trailed behind in the pickup, and sure enough, down where he'd been mending fence, there lay the carcass of a two and a half foot rattlesnake, head missing. Then he wanted to eat the lunch his wife sent with us, so he retold his narrow escape all the time we were eating. That man can string together some words."

Claire said, "So snakes were already on your mind."

He nodded and stuck two French fries in his mouth. "Good thing we were nearly finished. He'd have kept talking all afternoon. I was driving back to the house, just about a mile away when Amy called. Thinking about it now, she sounded calmer than I probably would have. Just said to get there fast, Jay Frank had been bitten, and she'd killed the snakes. When I got there, she had him lying down with his head on a feed sack, holding his hand and telling him he'd be fine."

Claire had stopped eating while he talked. She said, "So that's how it happened." After two more bites of hamburger, she rewrapped the remaining half. "I hope she tells her classmates. That might back off those bullying girls."

"If they know what's good for them. She's her mother's daughter, fierce."

The next morning, Jay Frank ate the hospital breakfast, and waited without complaint until the doctor came that afternoon at five. As soon as he told him he'd be released in a few minutes, Jay Frank turned back into a ten year-old, asking where his clothes were and could they stop for a milkshake.

The doctor handed Claire a sheet of discharge instructions, pointing to the one about crutches. "He'll need to be on those for at least a week, and I want him to see me in three days. We can decide about return to school after that. The nurse will instruct him about crutch walking before we let him go."

Jay Frank had listened intently to the doctor and as soon as he left, asked to read the instructions. The nurse moved quickly disconnecting him from the IV and monitor. She returned with crutches and made him show her he understood how to use them, not placing his injured foot on the floor at any time. He grumbled at having to ride out in a wheelchair. But once he was at the curb, their son sounded formal when he said to the nurse, "I appreciate everything you did for me. Thank you."

Claire couldn't help smiling, part amusement, part pride. She noticed J.D. giving their boy a nod of approval.

As they left the Dairy Queen drive-through, Jay Frank said, "Dad, how long was that snake, the one that bit me."

"Without his head?"

"No, head and all."

"I didn't stop to measure, but I'd say somewhere between eighteen inches and two feet. Why?"

"Everyone will ask." He went back to nursing the straw in his milkshake.

Claire imagined he was rehearsing his story. After a couple of silent minutes, she turned to look at her boy. His color had changed to chalk white and his eyes widened, unblinking, the milkshake suspended above his lap in his right hand. She said, "J. D.! Stop!" At the same time, she jerked the cup from their son's hand and pulled his left arm off his lap, feeling for his pulse. "Get us back to the E R now, fast."

J. D. never asked why or what, just did as she said. In less than two minutes, they were at the emergency entrance where he scooped Jay Frank up and ran toward the door, Claire running behind. Just as they reached the door, Jay Frank vomited, painting milkshake-colored streaks across his dad's dusty boots. He gasped for breath and yelled, "Momma!"

A nurse met them and pointed to a cubicle, then to a stretcher in that space. Claire said, "His pulse is at least 160. Get a monitor on him."

In seconds, the monitor leads positioned, head of the stretcher raised, Jay Frank's eyes following every movement near him, Claire watched his respiratory rate slow toward normal. She continued holding his hand as the line marching across the monitor screen showed the heart rate rapid at 166, with a sinus rhythm. She said, "Your heart started beating a little too fast, so they'll need to check you again. It'll be okay."

He closed his eyes and said, "I know. Dad, tell her to stop crying."

Ten minutes later, the pediatrician appeared. After examining Jay Frank, he said, "We'll leave that IV in at a keep-open rate in case we need it, but for now, since his heart rate is coming down and he's not in any acute distress, I'd like to just keep him here for observation. If everything stays steady, we'll let you take him home as soon as I'm able to consult a pediatric cardiologist, first thing in the morning."

At 6:30 a.m., the pediatrician did another thorough exam. When he finished, he told them he'd talked with the cardiologist, who had agreed that the combination of the remnants of the antivenom, the excitement of going home, and a belly full of milkshake probably had been too much, too soon.

At nine, they began the drive home. J.D. laughed when Jay Frank said, "I don't think I want another milkshake."

Claire called home when they turned off the highway, so when they stopped out front, Amy and Willa were waiting on the porch. Jay Frank insisted on demonstrating how he handled crutches. Amy pointed to the family room and told them all to go sit and relax, said she'd take care of her brother. Claire shrugged and said, "Looks like we've been relieved of duty."

J.D. said, "Feels good."

A few minutes later, Amy stood in the doorway. She said, "I told Jay Frank he should rest. And surprise, he's doing it. I have an idea, Mom. You can go back to work, and I'll stay home and be his nurse."

Before Claire could say anything, J.D. asked, "What about school?"

"It's all review right now—end of semester. I'll just need a permission note. Please let me. I really want to do it."

J.D. said, "You'd be late if you went today, anyway."

Claire said, "Lots of people, adults, wouldn't have had the presence of mind you did. And you did everything right. I'm very impressed."

Amy shrugged, looked away, toward her shoes. "Thanks. I'm going to check on my patient."

Claire's parents arrived soon after and before long, Jay Frank, accompanied by his sister, crutched into the room. He said, "Amy says I can't stay up long. Want to see my snake bite?"

J.D. whispered to Claire. "Okay with letting Amy take care of him?"

She nodded.

He announced to the family that Amy had not only rescued her brother she also had volunteered to be his home nurse. "She'll be taking care of him so we can get back to work."

Melanie asked, "You don't mind missing school?"

"I *prefer* missing school. I'll take care of my brother, work the goats." She turned toward Willa and said, "And maybe I can talk Gran into a longer ballet class, do some sketching. That's way better than school."

True to her word, Amy then hustled out of the room, toward Jay Frank's bedroom to do private duty nursing. Willa said, "That doesn't surprise me. It's as if she's been changing before my eyes ever since I returned here. From being a slave to her phone and completely self-absorbed, she becoming an increasingly mature and delightful version of that darling child she was before. At first, she barely conversed with me. Now, she fills the air with surprising questions and comments whenever she's not dancing or sketching. And I might add, she's a very good student both in ballet and art. Keeps me on my toes." She paused, then added, "Puberty isn't easy, but I think the worst may be over for her."

Claire's mother said, "I'll keep my fingers crossed. I agree, adolescence is a hard time for all concerned." She checked her watch and said, "Now that we've confirmed that the patient is recovering and in good hands, his granddad and I better get back to town."

Later, after the grandparents left and Willa returned to her house, Amy came looking for Claire in the kitchen. She reported her brother was in bed, his pulse was ninety, and she had checked his ankle, which was no longer red and the swelling had lessened. Claire said, "Those are exactly the things a nurse needs to observe. Good work."

"How many years of school did it take for you to be a nurse practitioner?"

"Four years of undergraduate college, two of graduate school. Why?"

"Just wondering. Maybe I'll want to be a nurse."

"What about your dancing, and art?"

"Gran says a person can do more than one thing in their life."

"You've talked?"

"We talk all the time."

"Whatever you want to learn, I'm sure you can. And you have talent that some don't, in dance and art. You'll have lots of choices."

Claire knew Amy would skitter away if she did what she felt right then—grab her in a tight embrace, hold her close to her heart. Instead, she ruffled her daughter's dark curls, then patted her back, briefly. "I'm leaving you in charge while I take a nap. Clinic will be busy this afternoon."

Note: Information I requested from Dr. Berger—received March, 21, 2013

Willa Jackson

Handbook of the Cerebellum and Cerebellar Disorders
2013, pp 2143-2150

Idiopathic Late Onset Cerebellar Ataxia (ILOCA), and Cerebellar plus Syndrome

- Dr. Shoji Tsuji

Abstract

Spinocerebellar ataxias (SCAs), also called spinocerebellar degenerations, comprise a large group of slowly progressive neurodegenerative diseases characterized by truncal and limb ataxias as the cardinal clinical features.... The clinical presentations of ILOCA (CCA) are characterized by late ages at onset with slow progression and pure cerebellar ataxia with markedly ataxic gait with relative preservation of coordination in the upper limbs...Among these sporadic neurodegenerative ataxias, ILOCA (CCA) is characterized by slow progression rate... Although there are no curative treatments available to prevent disease progression, continuous physiotherapeutic interventions in ataxia patients are encouraged.

CHAPTER 19
Family, Christmas

He and Andrew had only been back in Taos a few days before the faces in Chris' paintings changed; they began appearing as subjects, not as ghosts camouflaged in shadows or underwater in mountain streams. They glared from the focal points of canvases, pointed at the artist, or ran as if pursued. Regardless of whether he recognized the face, he understood they were each haunted by something unnamed. Even though that difference alarmed him even more than the initial changes in his paintings, he followed Gran's and Robert's advice. He worked at his easel each day no matter what emerged, and he saved every canvas.

Although his reason for returning to Jackson's Pond back in September, Claire and J.D.'s troubles, seemed to have quieted, the thought of going back for a family Christmas caused Chris considerable worry. He'd toyed with no small number of changes of plans. Go only for the day, don't go at all, get drunk and sleep through Christmas—he'd considered all of those before Andrew blocked his path one day. He'd said, "Chris! Stop pacing. Say what's on your mind; don't keep acting it out. You're wearing ruts in the floor."

First, Chris said, "Business is slow. We need to attract more tourists into the gallery."

"Someone stole the paintings from the three empty spaces I saw on the wall?" Evasion never worked with Andrew.

Chris sat, shook his head. "No, to tell the truth, business is fine."

Andrew waited.

Chris stood, his shoulders hunched, knowing he looked like a twelve year-old caught in a lie. "I know we've promised, but I literally get sick at my stomach every time I think about going to Jackson's Pond for Christmas."

Andrew gave a gentle push and steered him to the couch. He chose the chair opposite and said, "Talk."

So Chris did—mostly long strings of words, none of which

followed any rule of logic or grammar, punctuated by long pauses.

Andrew listened, and thank God, never told him how childish he sounded.

Later—a long time later—Chris told about the Christmas he was thirteen. He'd fought with his mother, run away from home, hitchhiked to Lubbock, and was returned by the sheriff the following day. As if telling that turned a new key in an old, stubborn lock, bits of several other memories spewed out. In every one of them, some argument, usually with his mother, hurt him or made him angry, and ended with his leaving home. Often he stayed at the ranch with his grandparents, and later when he was in high school, hung out with friends, ignoring curfew.

Then he was all out of words.

After another long silence, Andrew said, "That was then. What's different now?"

Chris said, "Me. Supposedly, I'm a mature man by now." He caught a hint of a smile from Andrew. "And my parents."

Andrew said, "It's three weeks away. No decision has to be made today, or even this week. Give it some time."

"You're not going to tell me what to do?"

"Not my job. You're a mature man."

The next day, Chris told Andrew to send him a bill for the therapy. Then he said, "I'd like to get to Jackson's Pond on the twenty-second or twenty-third. As far as coming back, you decide. We'll do whatever works best with your schedule."

His mother had called several days before they planned to leave. They'd talked about his travel plans and she'd asked him to bring a ristra she could give Gran for a surprise. She said, "About Christmas dinner, is there anything special you'd like? I'm asking everyone their favorite dish and I plan to make them all."

Without hesitating, he answered. "Mincemeat pie."

She laughed and he enjoyed the sound. "No surprise. It always was your favorite. Apparently it's J.D.'s also. Looks like I'll make two. Now, I need to speak to Andrew."

He heard Andrew say, "Green bean casserole." Then a smile changed his face. He said, "If it works for Chris, it works for me. And thank you, Melanie."

Chris didn't have to wonder long about that last exchange. As soon as Andrew handed him the phone, she said, "Your dad and I want you to stay with us while you're here. You have to agree. I've already cleaned the guest room and put your names on the door." She didn't give him time to object. After she hung up, he sat holding the phone, shaking his head.

He said to Andrew, "I didn't know what to say. Don't know now."

"I think they just gave us a gift."

"What does it mean?"

Andrew said, "Motive? Who cares? I plan to say thank you and not assume it obligates me in any way. And I'll enjoy knowing they wanted to give us that gift."

Christmas Eve and Christmas had left him sad. The traditional tree, the holiday decorations his mother had arranged throughout the house, and having the family together had been all anyone could hope for. He knew the emotion came from realizing he'd been at least half to blame for the bad memories the prospect of the holiday had stirred.

Andrew had sensed his mood. Yesterday, he'd said, "Mixed feelings?"

Chris heaved a sigh, then said, "I'm very glad we came. And I'm sorry it took me so long to get here."

Andrew said, "Merry Christmas. I look forward to a happy New Year. Our lives are changing."

Since then Chris had wished he'd explained everything to Andrew. He'd dragged out all that stuff from the past, but hadn't mentioned to him what was troubling from the present, what was happening to his painting. He promised himself he would. But first, he needed to talk with Gran. She'd understand. He trusted Robert's advice, too. Now that they were both here, they'd know what he should do.

Outside Gran's house, Chris parked next to J.D.'s pickup. A stiff northwest wind managed to sweep around the edge of the south facing porch. One of the porch chairs rocked each time a gust pushed past it. He flipped it over so it wouldn't blow, and promised himself he'd put a coat of paint on both of those old rockers next time he came back.

He knocked once on the door, said, "It's me."

J.D. opened the door, wearing his barn coat and holding a gimme cap. "Hey! This is a busy place this morning. I'm just leaving." He pulled on the hat, straightened the brim. "She's planning some remodeling. She'll want your advice." He pointed north, tugging on leather work gloves. "I'm off to check stock tanks. Break ice. See you at the big house later." In three long-legged strides he reached his pickup, then yelled, "If I didn't say so before, I'm sure glad you were able to be here for Christmas. It was the best I can remember in a long time."

Before he stepped inside, Chris waved to his brother-in-law.

The aroma of cinnamon and chocolate welcomed him from the kitchen. Willa said, "You caught us. We've been stuffing ourselves with pan dulce and Mexican cocoa."

Robert Stanley hugged Chris, then retrieved another cup from the kitchen. Willa filled it from a carafe on the coffee table. For a few minutes, they sipped the cocoa and exchanged bits of news from Austin, Taos, and Jackson's Pond. Robert said, "Lots of changes going on. Selfishly, I'm glad Willa's back in Texas, nearer to me."

Robert cleared the cups and carafe away. Willa said, loudly enough for him to hear, "He's very handy to have around."

A voice from the kitchen, Irish brogue and all, said, "I heard that! Should I be offended?"

As soon as Robert returned, Chris sat forward in his chair and tried to make thoughts he'd had for months sound succinct and orderly. In truth, they'd been anything but. "I need advice. You're the two who might understand best. Do you have time?"

Gran said, "Fortunately, we have plenty."

"We do." Robert leaned back in his chair. "And you know how I love to give advice."

Chris told of the disturbing change in his painting, full of darkness and faces that appeared from details, unintended. And he also explained that he'd felt drawn back to photography—mostly animals and landscape detail, not panoramic scenes. He finished by saying, "I don't know what it means, but I can't seem to produce anything else."

Willa said, "And that troubles you?"

He nodded. "The faces. I don't intend to paint them. It's as if they emerge—under rocks, in clouds, in trees—everywhere. It's as if I've lost control of my work." He stood, walked to the window near the front door. He could feel them both watching. "There's not a speck of moisture in those clouds."

She asked, "The technique or the content?"

Chris shook his head. "Technically, the brushwork is competent, design is solid. The palette's changed, though, much darker."

Robert said, "Have you tried painting your way through it?"

Chris nodded, then stared at the rug. "I've painted all day, every day, except for when the light was good for photographs, every day for more than three months. And I've felt pushed to take lots of photographs. Andrew, who never complains about my working, finally asked if I was up against a deadline."

Willa said, "Maybe you are. Do you recognize the faces?"

Chris returned to the couch. "Some I don't recognize. Men, women, children, all different races." He closed his eyes. "And I see Granddad in many of them."

"Who else?"

"You, Claire, Mother, and Dad. J.D. was in one."

Robert asked, "Where are the paintings?"

"At first I painted over them. I stopped that, and now there are at least thirty in the back of the studio. I wouldn't ever put them in the gallery. They're not me."

Neither Willa nor Robert spoke. But both frowned. Then she said, "Not you?"

Robert said, "That statement that they're not you—I'd have to disagree. All good art comes from inside. These are coming from something you may not understand yet, but they are you."

Gran said, "For the past eight years, you've been working hard. Nothing but art—painting and selling. Maybe I'm to blame, for pushing you to focus on art by giving you the money to start the gallery."

"The money gave me freedom, opportunity. I would never

have accomplished half of what I have without that."

His grandmother said, "We'll never know. But if my meddling has caused you misery, I am so sorry."

He reached for her hand. "I'm not miserable. And I have no right to even be concerned. I have everything I ever wanted. I never dreamed, well I hoped, but didn't expect that people would collect my work. But I don't understand what's happening." He put up his hands as if surrendering. "Gran, you've always help me find the right path. And Granddad did, too. That's why I need your advice." He nodded to Robert. "And the gallery would never have ever made money without all you've taught me about the business side."

Gran asked, "When are you leaving?"

"Wednesday. I told Pat Carmichael she'd only have to be there through Wednesday afternoon."

Chris finished his cocoa in silence. He watched Robert take off his glasses, close his eyes, his eyebrows drawn together by a deep wrinkle. That face had appeared in one of his paintings.

Gran said, "Let's think on this overnight and get together tomorrow."

Chris said, "Good. I'm sick of talking about myself." He stood and returned to the window as if he might be expecting a visitor. He turned back to them. "J.D. said something about remodeling. What's up?"

Robert had his glasses on now, his attention focused on Willa. His slight frown hadn't disappeared. Gran said, "The oldest person on the place, yours truly, acting responsibly, is looking toward her future. I intend this house to be my home base the rest of my life. But in its current condition, this is a younger person's house. No accommodation for any disabilities. So now, it's prudent to get this taken care of while I'm still in shape to oversee the work."

Chris said, "What's on your list?"

"Lever type door handles, wider doorways, bathroom grab bars, accessible bathroom fixtures—all relatively small things inside—and outside, porch ramps, front and back."

"Anything I can do to help?"

"I didn't mention that it needs a coat of paint inside and out, and a new roof, a metal one. So any time you're in the mood for manual labor, I can get you work."

He said to Robert, "Have you noticed how slick she is?"

"I remain constantly on guard."

Chris checked his watch. "Andrew and I promised the kids we'd go riding this afternoon. I'll come back in the morning." He turned as he headed for the door. Seeing Robert and Gran, standing side by side, he wished for his camera. "I'll call first."

Close to noon, on Claire's horse, he returned to Gran's porch. He and Andrew and the kids had ridden to the pond and prowled around in the pasture. When the other three turned back toward the big house, he told them he'd meet them there in a bit.

He tied Gus' reins to the front fence. As he dismounted, Gran stepped out on the porch. Robert stood inside behind the screen. Chris said, "As soon as I left this morning, I knew you'd left something out."

Gran raised an eyebrow and said, "You're pretty slick, yourself. Come in."

He followed them to the kitchen table. Slices of apple and orange on a plate told him they'd started preparing lunch. The three of them sat and he leaned forward, elbows on the table. "So, what's the secret?"

"That's the right word. I'm in the process of unburdening myself. No more secrets. You're the first to know this." She cocked her head toward Robert. "Aside from this man."

Robert put his arm on the back of her chair.

"Here's the essence. I've known for a few years now, since 2009 to be exact, that I have a degenerative neurological condition." She held up a hand stopping Chris before he could speak. "Don't look so stricken. It may never kill me. After all, I've made it to eighty-three. For years now I've considered each day a gift without a guarantee."

Doing his best to keep his voice steady, Chris said, "What about a second, or third opinion?"

"I can give you a copy of all the details. It was diagnosed in Denver by the top neurologist. I check in regularly. There's no treatment. If, or when, it progresses, I'll lose my balance, then lower motor muscle function." She shrugged as she said, "And then, who knows?"

"That explains. Wheelchair."

"It's likely. Meanwhile, I take good care of myself and rest more than I used to. So far, so good.

"That's why you came back here?"

"Not entirely." With an elegant shrug of one shoulder, she said, "This is home."

He sat back from the table. Finally, he nodded.

She said, "I plan to tell the others after supper tomorrow evening, together."

"We'll be there."

"One thing more. I thought I was keeping this a secret for the right reason. When a person has a diagnosis, any sort, everyone treats them differently. Lets them win arguments, keeps bad news from them, and worst of all, robs them of their independence. I intended to never tell."

"But you changed your mind?"

"Keeping secrets causes damage too. It's ultimately selfish, prideful."

Chris left his chair and squatted in front of his grandmother, his head on her knees. He'd stopped hiding in her lap a long time ago, but he'd never forgotten the comfort there. She stroked his head.

He took a deep breath and stood. He said, "I'm glad I know." She caught hold of his hand. "But you're wrong; I won't let you win arguments, ever."

She said, "Wait, something occurred to me after you left this morning. I always had other work besides my art—helping with the farming, working the ranch. It never became too much, more as if each part of me fed the other. Think about whether you have the "other part," the not-painting part, feeding your work."

At the big house, after he, J.D., Andrew, Amy, and Jay Frank finished lunch, a make-your-own-leftover turkey-sandwich affair topped off with mincemeat pie from Christmas dinner, the kids trooped off to exercise the goats. J.D. had sent them on, told them he'd take care of the dishes—they'd all used paper plates. As he pushed the last scraps into the trash, he said, "Willa tell you about her remodeling plans?"

Chris nodded.

J.D. said, "She asked me if I knew someone reliable to do the work. Not always easy to find in a town this size."

"Did you?"

"I'd do most of it myself, if I had the time. I'm a pretty fair carpenter. But yeah, I gave her a couple of names." He lifted the plastic trash bag from the container, tied the drawstring. "For some reason, I had the feeling she didn't tell me everything. You get more?"

"I can see it makes sense at her age. And the place has been unoccupied a long time."

J.D. fit an empty bag in the trash can and hoisted the full one. "Sorry to leave good company, but I've got steers to see to. Tell the kids to call if they need me."

As J.D. left, Chris said, "We'll keep an eye on them."

Andrew made a pot of coffee. He said, "I got chilled riding in that wind, and haven't warmed up yet."

Chris said, "Since when do you need an excuse?" Andrew seldom went more than three hours without a cup, no matter what the weather.

Andrew said, "If we had a place to keep horses. I'd ride every day." He filled a mug for each of them. "Dry as it is here, it reminds me a lot of Ozona."

Chris said, "I missed a lot staying away all those years." He surrounded the mug with both hands. "When I told you I was anxious about coming home, I held something back. This morning I talked to Gran and Robert about it. I should have trusted you, and told you first."

"Will I need more coffee?"

Chris explained his concern just as he'd described it to Willa and Robert earlier. The words came more easily this time. Andrew said, "I understand you'll probably want to work this out on your own. I get that. But if there's a point when you think having a listener would help. I'm good at it. Your choice."

For some reason, hearing that took away a bit of Chris' worry, the concern that somehow his confusion, or call it preoccupation, with the change in him and his art might ruin the life he and Andrew had together.

The next morning, around ten, he called ahead, then drove to Gran's house. Yesterday's wind had left traces in the dust in the yard, miniature arroyos running north to south recording its passage. He'd watched the sun rise earlier, orange and angry, a single bleb near bursting, threatening to spew something vile into the blue-gray sky. In minutes, it turned benign, intermittently hiding behind thin clouds, its orange fading to gold. Now he saw it paled to yellow, no longer signaling threat.

Robert opened the door before Chris knocked. "We're in the kitchen. Near the coffee and food."

Chris followed him to the kitchen. He leaned against the cabinet and said, "I promised Amy a drawing lesson this morning, so I won't take too much of your time. Did you come up with any ideas?"

Holding an empanada, Robert said, "Mine's somewhat vague, I'm afraid, a general approach. Do what you feel called to do. Trust yourself. If photography beckons, spend all the time you want to on that. If you paint and find the result continues to trouble you, do only as much as you can tolerate." He took a bite of the pastry. Even eating from his hand, the man looked elegant. "And my final notion is this— save all of the paintings. Perhaps they're weaving a narrative you won't understand until the end."

Chris had listened intently. He chose a pineapple filled empanada and ate it in two bites. "I hadn't thought about a story."

"I could be quite wrong. Your grandmother frequently says I'm full of bull."

Chris saw Willa struggle against a smile. He said, "What about you, Gran?"

"As is often the case, I agree with that Irishman. But if the painting continues to make you uncomfortable, you might also consider working with a counselor."

Chris hesitated, stacking the right words into a sentence before he uttered them. "I live with the best counselor I know. But..." After a second's pause, he said, "But I wouldn't want him to see me weak." He shook his head. "I heard what I just said. It sounded cowardly."

"Wouldn't want to expose your secrets?" She placed a hand on his arm. "It's only a thing to consider. The only other idea you might think about is taking a sabbatical—that's Robert's word. Take time off from the gallery, as long as you need. Couldn't Pat manage it?"

"She could. But I promised you I'd work at painting and developing the gallery for ten years. That was our deal. There are two years left."

"I chose ten as an arbitrary number—time enough to hone your talent, gain commitment to your own value as an artist."

"I honor my agreements."

"As do I. But any contract can be renegotiated by mutual consent. Just bear that in mind."

"Too many choices are as hard to deal with as having none."

That evening, after a dinner his mother brought, Willa said, "I have something I want to tell everyone, all at the same time, over our dessert."

No one said a word, but Chris saw his sister frown and his mother and dad glance at each other, eyebrows raised. Jay Frank surveyed the adults' faces. Amy gnawed at a cuticle. Finally, J.D. said, "I'll make coffee."

Claire followed, saying she'd bring the dessert plates and pie. Chris and Andrew cleared the table and returned to their places. The aroma of coffee preceded J.D. when he returned with the full pot on a tray, wearing a napkin across his forearm like a well-trained waiter.

Willa said, her voice strong and steady, "For most of my life, I have kept much about my personal life secret. Now that I'm older, I believe I often did that out of false pride or as a way of protecting my independence. Don't laugh when I say I'm wiser now."

Chris laughed, others smiled. He watched Gran, amazed at her composure, knowing he would never stop learning from her.

She said, "So now I want you all to know a secret I've kept for too long."

Telling of her diagnosis, explaining its implications took only a few minutes. She handed each one of them, including the children, an information sheet about the diagnosis. "My doctor supplied this."

Chris watched his mother read, then close her eyes briefly, then open them and compose a faint, sad smile on her face. He'd expected something different. His sister's straightening in her chair and lifting her chin, he'd seen from her more times than he could count. She would tackle whatever came.

Willa finished by explaining her plan to remodel her house, preparing for the future. Then she added. "And one other part of remodeling is adding a studio and making the second bedroom larger, more suitable for frequent occupancy." She put a hand on Robert's shoulder. "My best friend and frequent companion, Old Blarney here, will be on the Jackson Ranch a large part of his time. So I want him to have his own space." She pointed to the information sheet in Melanie's hand. "If any of you want to know more about this, we can do it another time. Right now, I'd like to finish my dessert."

Chris concentrated on his pie. Andrew was the one who broke the silence. "I'll bet it's a relief to you for us all to know."

Willa beamed at him. "It is." She ate the last of her pie. Then she said, "Melanie, I think this is even better today than it was on Christmas."

Later, when their parents had left, Chris said to Claire, "Gran's not the only one who feels good tonight. I know now I'm part of a real family."

Amarillo Globe News
Wednesday, January 15, 2014
Panhandle Health Facility Changes

In a press release, St. Mark's Hospital of Amarillo today announced a merger with Texas Integrated Health Systems, effective February 1, 2014.

"As Panhandle Health System, St. Mark's will be the center around which an integrated system of care will revolve. Joining forces with Texas Integrated Health Systems will create opportunities for economies of scale in purchasing and medical information sharing that will enhance patient care.

"The next months will see a gradual series of changes including creation of new primary care facilities, purchase of existing clinics, contractual arrangements with specialists, home health care services, and hospice. Patients will have increased access to all levels of care within the system."

St. Mark's CEO Lloyd Franklin stated, "Current hospital personnel will experience no disruption in employment. They will retain all current salaries and benefits. Under this new arrangement, they will experience the satisfaction of enhanced ability to assure high quality care within a vertically integrated system."

The announcement included a list of physicians and clinics which now become part of the new system. Those are:

We Care Hospice
Amarillo Home Care
Metropolitan Internal Medicine Clinic
Carson and Associates Pediatrics
Amarillo Surgical Associates
Top of Texas Urology Clinic
Pulmonary Associates
Wedgewood Urology
Sports Medicine and Orthopedics
South Amarillo Urgent Care
Express Care
Family Medicine Group

CHAPTER 20
Wins and Prospects

Claire reviewed Nancy Reese's chart before calling her from the waiting room. When Nancy had been in clinic back in September, Claire had discussed in detail the importance of losing weight and had given her a handout for a 2000 calorie diet. Today, she planned to deal with whatever her current problem might be and set her up for lab work. Over age fifty, with 285 pounds on her five-foot-five inch frame and a family history of heart disease and diabetes, Nancy was trouble waiting to happen. Claire had asked Laverne to schedule her at 10:30, for a thirty minute slot. That would only give her time to make a dent in the wall of objections Nancy would hide behind. But hell or high water, Claire had to be in Calverton no later than twelve forty-five.

Moving the weights on the scale bar, she kept her expression neutral, a chore because the beam didn't balance until it hit 292. Nancy's blood pressure registered one hundred fifty-eight over ninety. Claire had a hunch she should do a spot glucose before taking her to the exam room. When the rapid test finished, she turned the glucometer where Nancy could see for herself—220 mg./dl.

As Claire interviewed her, it became apparent that Nancy not only had *not* changed her diet nor added any exercise, but in fact, she spent almost all of her time seated—at the dining table, or at her computer, or in front of the television. She reeled off a list of body parts that ached every day, and said that in the past few weeks, she'd had several spells of general weakness and had frequent urination.

After she listened to Nancy's heart and lungs, checked her joints for swelling and tenderness, and palpated her obese abdomen, Claire asked her to get a urine specimen and then dress and come to her office.

Claire did a dipstick test on the urine—no leukocytes, 1+ glucose. No surprise. Now came the part she disliked the most. Patients who could remember her as a child often resisted accepting her instructions. She hurried to her desk and faced her patient. She started with the bad news first. "Mrs. Reese, you know you must lose weight. Your blood glucose shows me it's likely you now have Type II diabetes, and you have high blood pressure that must be treated." She chose her words carefully—people understood *high blood pressure* better than hypertension; *must be treated* was stronger than should. "Your urine doesn't show any infection, but there is glucose in it. Further lab test are required to confirm the diabetes. And we must start medication for your blood pressure." The look on Nancy's face suggested she wasn't so certain about *must*.

"You sound just the way Junior does. Not a day goes by he doesn't tell me I'm too fat. I tried cooking like that diet said, but he demands I fry everything, says he'll find somewhere else to eat if I don't."

Claire waited. If her patient needed to talk, she'd listen. After a long silence, she said, "Please be here at eight tomorrow morning for the lab work. Eat nothing after midnight and drink only water."

Claire disliked being so directive, but she knew that some patients only responded to specific orders delivered with confidence and authority. She'd practiced imitating a drill sergeant for just that reason. "I'm writing a prescription for blood pressure medicine." She wrote the prescription and handed it to Mrs. Reese. "Fill it right away and take the first dose today."

The woman rose forward in her chair and said, "I'll come back for the tests." She pushed the prescription toward Claire. "But I'm not taking that. Write one for diet pills instead. I've asked you before. I know my blood pressure and sugar will get back to normal when I lose some weight."

Claire leaned her elbows on the desk. "Mrs. Reese, this is serious. I don't prescribe diet pills and no one else should. They can be dangerous. I don't want you to have a stroke or a heart attack. And now there's diabetes."

Nancy shook her head. "I'll go to that weight loss doctor in Lubbock."

"I can't make you do anything you don't want to. All I can tell you is I'll work with you to regain your health. It'll take time and won't be easy for you. It's your choice."

Claire followed as her patient headed toward the waiting room. She doubted she'd see Nancy Reese tomorrow or anytime soon. Not until the next time she needed someone to listen to her troubles with Junior. Claire stood at the front desk, after handing Nancy a reminder sheet for the lab work. She watched the woman trudge to her Cadillac, shoulders slumped forward, head down, her slow, clumsy gait making her appear old and tentative. Laverne said, "She was a cheerleader when we were in high school. I feel bad now for being jealous."

Claire returned to her office, where she charted the visit and completed a lab request she doubted would be used. After rereading her notes, she added an EKG to the lab list. Moving quickly, she carried the chart and request to the front. Laverne said, "Your dad called, said not to bother you. Asked me to put him on your schedule for tomorrow." She shrugged. "He didn't say why. Said he'd see you at the stock show."

Claire stopped long enough to make a reminder to herself to search again for a certified diabetes educator in the area. Mrs. Reese and several other patients needed far more than she had time to provide to learn to properly manage their diabetes. To the reminder she added, "Spanish/ English bilingual preferred." She shook her head at her next thought, and lectured herself. *No, you will not take the certification course. You have a more-than-full-time job already.*

On the way to Calverton, Nancy Reese and her dad's puzzling appointment competed for her attention, along with images of Jay Frank and Amy—her boy in his new, inch longer, Wranglers and Amy, wearing her favorite Levi's and ruffled, long-sleeved shirt—as they left early with J.D. for the stock show. They'd be the best looking exhibitors in the goat show, for sure.

Before she left clinic, she'd peeled out of her white lab coat, and changed into Levi's and a red sweater over a black shirt. Black boots and a black down jacket completed her outfit. Scouting for a parking space at the Floyd County Community Events Center, she saw Mother, Dad, and Gran making their way toward the building. She pulled in next to a horse trailer occupied by a bored looking gray gelding and trotted toward the building.

Holding the door open for the Jackson's Pond delegation, she said, "Jay Frank and Amy will be thrilled the whole family's here."

J.D. and the kids had trailered the four goats to the exhibit barn yesterday evening for the weigh-in. At breakfast this morning, Jay Frank talked faster than usual and ate like he might be heading off to hibernate. Between bites, he asked, "Dad, are you sure the night watchman stayed awake?"

"Pretty sure. He's watched animals for the livestock show every January for a long time. He had my phone number if they needed us."

Inside, Claire and the others found the goats and Jay Frank, along with Amy and J.D., among the pens back of the show ring. The goat owner said, "Dad was right. 'Cause of their weights, my goats are in two classes. For all four to show, Amy has to help. I'll take Zeppo and Groucho. They lead and set up best. Amy'll show Harpo and Chico."

J.D, one hand on Jay Frank's shoulder and the other on Amy's, said, "They'll do great."

Tag hustled toward them from the back of the pen area. "Thought I better stop by and see Goat Whisperer and Snake Killer strut their stuff." He squatted in front of Jay Frank, beckoned Amy to stand close. "Now I know your dad gave you both lots of good advice. So you two get out there and let that judge see what winners from Jackson Ranch look like. I'll be cheering for you."

The announcer's voice over the loudspeaker said, "First call for Junior goats, Class 2. Junior Goats, Class 2."

Jay Frank alerted fast as a prodded calf. Claire said, "Let's all have a kiss for good luck." The kids actually stood still while she planted kisses on their cheeks. Then she laid a big one on J.D.'s mouth. She said, "We'll be in the stands. You'll hear us."

The four of them found front row seats in the stands, across the show ring from where J.D. stood behind the entry gate. When the Superintendent gave the signal, the Havlicek kids and eight others led the ten goats from their pens into the show ring. The judge waved them forward, and they all marched their animals single file around the ring. She doubted anyone could tell that neither Jay Frank nor Amy had ever made that trip before. She'd heard J.D. coaching them about keeping the goats' heads up and remembering to keep an eye on the judge at all times. They both performed like pros.

The judge instructed the young exhibitors to form a single line in front of the pens. Jay Frank set up the goat the way he'd practiced each day, showing its form to the best advantage. He lifted Zeppo's head, raised its front shoulders and supported them with his right knee until the animal tiptoed slightly in front. The muscles of its hindquarters tightened. When the judge approached Chico, Amy's smile widened. Gran nudged Claire. "Your daughter takes after you."

The judge ranked all ten goats, offering positive comments and suggestions about each animal. Zeppo placed third and Chico fourth. The Jackson clan cheered and applauded. Watching the pride on J.D.'s face as he hugged the kids, Claire had trouble staying in the bleachers.

Minutes later, Jay Frank's two heavier goats and seven other Junior goats, Class 1, went through the same routine. When Groucho took Reserve Champion and Harpo came in third, Claire jumped to her feet and shouted, "Yes!"

After she and her dad traded high fives, she said, "Don't anyone leave. Jay Frank and Groucho will be in Junior Showmanship next."

She hurried to the pens and returned with Amy, all smiles. The announcement blared, "First call, Junior goat showmanship. All exhibitors in Junior goats competing in showmanship, move to the ring now." Amy leaned toward her and said, "If I had my own animal, I bet I could win showmanship. Maybe I'll raise a lamb or goat next year."

"You could have passed for someone who showed goats all her life. If you bought a good quality animal, I'm sure you could win." Claire watched her daughter as she chattered with her grandparents about the goats and her brother. In the past month, she'd seemed more like the happy girl she'd been before her hormones struck.

As businesslike as Jay Frank had been showing his goats— focused on the judge, responding to every cue—the ten-year-old in him showed up briefly. When the judge called his number and handed him the first place showmanship award, a big belt buckle, he waved to them in the stands. Then he was all business again, marching Groucho from the ring.

The family and Tag ate lunch from the 4-H concession stand, seated together at a picnic table in a corner. All of them asked lots of questions of both kids, who answered and smiled full time, even while consuming Frito chili pie. Claire polished off a burrito and leaned lightly against J.D.

Now that the excitement of Jay Frank's first stock show competition settled a bit, Claire breathed in the scents mingled in the arena—straw, manure, dust, tinged with sweat—the smell that clung to J.D. when he came in after a day's work, that always brought a faint memory of Granddad Frank. He'd have loved being here with them. She looked toward Gran, who wore the inward glance of a woman remembering.

Her parents and Gran gathered their coats, saying they'd go on, now that the important part was over. Claire intended to stop by the Calverton clinic to review charts. Her dad leaned toward her and said, "I put myself on your schedule for tomorrow. I have to go to Lubbock now, but there are some things you need to know."

Before she could ask any questions, he held the door open for Gran and the three of them left.

J.D. told Amy she could take the rest of the afternoon off, if she wanted to. He and Jay Frank planned to stay for the lamb and swine competitions. Claire said to her, "I have to go to the clinic here for about an hour. You can come with me or stay here with them. Your choice."

Amy asked, "Can we stop at Bartlett's? I need something there."

After she breezed through reviewing thirty-five charts, finding no errors or billing problems, Claire said, "Now, to Bartlett's. What do you need there?"

"New bras."

"Same size?"

"Bigger."

A month ago, Amy would have been upset, but her voice gave no clue. Claire held her breath for a few second; she knew Amy had a menstrual period a week earlier. She remembered the counselor's words about physical changes of puberty and disordered eating. Until this minute, she'd been able to convince herself Amy was better; she'd checked her room twice and found no laxatives, and she hadn't heard her up in the bathroom at night.

She put on what she hoped was a "let's get into a little mischief" smile. "Mother always shopped for pretty ones for me every time I had to have a new size. Maybe they'll have bright red. Do you want that for a change?"

"Really?"

Claire shrugged. "Up to you, as long as you have a white or pink one, too, for when red or purple won't do."

They left Bartlett's with three bras in size 34 A, two inches and one cup size larger. Amy had chosen white, red, and a multicolored, floral-patterned one. As far as Claire was concerned, as long as her growing daughter hadn't broken into tears or slammed a door, price was no object, and they'd had a good afternoon.

Amy stuck in her earbuds and plugged into her iPad, then closed her eyes. Her subtle upper body movements, rhythmic and smooth, suggested music occupied her. Claire kept her eyes on the road and thought about her Dad's making an appointment with her. Surely he'd see his primary doc in Lubbock if he had a health concern.

Near the turn from the county road onto Jackson land, Amy unplugged. She said, "Have you ever heard of Misty Copeland?"

Claire shook her head. Amy said, "Gran told me to look her up. She's a ballerina with American Ballet Theater in New York City, very famous." She turned her iPad so Claire could see it.

The photograph showed a tall, beautiful woman, voluptuous for a ballerina.

"She never had a lesson until she was thirteen. Then after she matured, they said she was too muscular, her feet were too big, and other stuff. Now she's the main soloist. I've seen videos. She's amazing."

Claire nodded. Better to let Amy make her point. She usually had one.

Just before they turned into the drive, Amy said, "One of the articles I read about her said she had a binge eating disorder for a while.

She got over it."

"If you'd give me the link, I'd like to read that."

Amy said she would, then plugged into her iPad again, closed her eyes.

The next day, Claire found her dad sitting in her office when she finished with the final morning patient. A Subway bag sat in the middle of her desk along with two large Styrofoam cups of iced tea. He said, "Let's eat, first."

He bit into his sandwich. She opened hers and pulled out the sliced onions, then began eating. Neither of them spoke until she said, "The kids are still excited from yesterday. Already talking about next year."

"What are you going to do with the goats? Barbecue?"

"Tag already tried to talk Jay Frank into that. He said no way. He has plans to start a goat herd. Visions of a new business."

She wrapped the last quarter of her sandwich and returned it to the bag. Her dad finished his, wiped his hands on a napkin. He sat back in his chair. "Well, here's the good news first. Remember Richard Jesko? That computer wizard a year ahead of you in school?"

She nodded. "I heard he's in Dallas. Some big technology business."

"Big business is right. And he wants to help Jackson's Pond. He made a presentation at the last City Council meeting, in Executive Session. Impressive. If it all works out, he intends to buy a major portion of the wind-generated electricity from here and start a facility dedicated mainly to data storage. It could mean as many as fifty jobs. It would be a real shot in the arm for Jackson's Pond."

"You had something to do with that, I'll bet."

He let a smile escape. "Maybe just a bit. All those years in Austin, I made some contacts. This is confidential until he makes his announcement next week. Besides the construction jobs, some of the permanent jobs will bring new people in, the tech folks. But he wants to train area people for other jobs and later, to connect with Texas Tech and one of the community colleges for a training program based out here. That was a big factor in his presentation—keeping young people in the area."

"Do you think it's real or so much smoke?"

"He's already nailed down the financing. Showed us the contracts."

"New people means more patients. We might be able to add two nurse practitioners, not just replace Sandra, not that I've had any success with that."

Her dad nodded, busied himself making a neat package of their trash.

She said, "That was the good news. So…"

"Maybe this other isn't bad news. It'll depend on you."

She waited as he laid two file folders on the desk. He pushed one toward her. "Your copy."

She left it closed, waiting for an explanation. He said, "The short version is that St. Mark's in Amarillo merged with a big company that plans next to buy up as many rural primary care practices in the Panhandle as they can." He pointed to the folders. "One of their cast of VPs called, and I met him in Lubbock yesterday. These are from him. I didn't mention it to you because without you present, I could truthfully tell that VP I'm only the manager and the owner has never mentioned an interest in selling."

"How did you know what he wanted?"

"Searched the Internet, called some people in Amarillo, talked to the clinic manager in Hale Center, a friend of mine—you know, checked all my traps."

"If you said I wasn't interested in selling, didn't that settle it?"

"I'm afraid not. After a lot of talk, it came clear. If you don't sell, they'll put up competing clinics and force you out."

She sat back, listening to her heart beat in her ears. "Isn't that illegal?"

"They can open a clinic anywhere they want. They've already bought property in Hale Center since the doctor there said he wouldn't sell."

She pushed back her chair and stood, walked to the windows and back. "Damn it all. We've provided service when no one else wanted to. Now they want to take over. I won't work for some big company only interested in money."

"You couldn't even if you wanted to." He pointed to the folder again. "When you read that, check the back page. There's a non-compete clause."

She said, "We need a lawyer, someone specialized in health care facilities."

"I agree. And a consulting accountant to determine a value for the clinics. Worst case, if you have to sell, you should make them pay."

She shook her head. "I'm not selling."

"Regardless, it's always good business to have contingency plans. I'll get recommendations and make preliminary contacts. You'll want to read that file. They wanted to meet with you this week, but I slow-played them, said I'd have to check with you. Let's keep this on our timetable."

Claire sat down again. "Have you told Mother?"

"I won't until you say it's okay."

"Go ahead and tell her." She flipped open the folder, then closed it. "Dad, I can't do this without your help."

"That's why you hired me."

That afternoon, Claire strained to stay focused on each patient's problem. Otherwise, she'd have buried her nose in that file immediately. As it was, images of a faceless gang invading Jackson's Pond, holding her hostage, nipped at her thoughts until closing time.

On the way home, she quickly discarded the first plan that came to mind—the one in which she'd take care of the problem without telling J.D. Besides, there would be no way she could keep this a secret, even if she hadn't already learned that lesson.

After supper, the kids in the family room watching a Tech basketball game, she asked J.D. to sit with her in the kitchen. "Something's come up. I want you to know what I'm dealing with. I'll need your advice."

"There's something I need to show you, too."

Then she told him what her dad had said, all of it. And before he asked, she also told him how angry it made her thinking someone might destroy all she'd worked so hard to build. She said, "Just imagine if someone could make you sell your herd if you didn't want to, after working all these years to build it up."

He reached for her hand and held it. "I'd be mad and I'd want to fight. And then…" He frowned and his voice trailed off. "Well, I don't have any idea what I'd do." He shook his head. "Just when things were settled down." He pointed to the folder. "Have you read this yet?"

"No. I'm waiting until the kids are in bed. They don't need to see me break that rule."

She overcame an urge to clean out the cabinets or scrub the oven, told herself to be still. Then she said, "You had something you wanted me to see?"

J.D. stood, reaching into his hip pocket. He handed her a single printed sheet. "I got this email today. It's the first I've heard from Jan since we were in Ft. Worth."

Claire scanned the note—planning to have a meeting by conference call; wanted his advice on date; you're the first, most important one; another meeting later in spring, probably in Abilene; please phone right away. "Why did you want me to see this?"

"I'm going to call like she asks. I wanted you to know."

She'd be lying if she said she hadn't had some doubts since Ft. Worth, times she wanted to pull away from him, make him understand how it felt to be empty and betrayed. After studying his face for a long minute, she said, "I think there'll probably always be opportunities when we might each be tempted. Predictions are guesses. Promises are all we can rely on. All I can tell you is I plan to trust you and trust us both to keep our promises. No secrets."

He touched her face. "Thank you for that. You're right—no secrets. We'll be fine."

Floyd County Tribune
Thursday, January 29, 2014
Public Meeting in Jackson's Pond

All interested area citizens are invited to attend a public meeting at the Jackson's Pond City Council chambers Wednesday, February 5, 2014 at 7:30 p.m.

The meeting is to receive public input on the planned development of a digital data storage facility near Jackson's Pond.

Richard Jesko, CEO of JTB Data Solutions, will address his company's plans for business development in the area. Jesko said, "We see financial opportunity for our business as well as important prospects for economic diversification in the region as outcomes of locating our campus in this area."

A former resident of Jackson's Pond, with family in the area, Jesko mentioned a personal reason for choosing the location. He said, "I've long been concerned that so many rural towns are losing their young people to the metropolitan areas. I am convinced that complementary industrial diversity can help stabilize this rural area. Agriculture must continue to predominate. Adding non-competing career opportunities which will retain young people and recruit some older workers to this area can benefit both types of business. Perhaps our project will serve as a model for development in other similar rural areas.

"I want Jackson's Pond to thrive. I plan to make my home here again someday."

The meeting will include a presentation on JTB Data Solutions' history and other current operations and on the facility planned for a site near Jackson's Pond, including a projected timetable. Time is set aside for comments and questions from the audience.

CHAPTER 21
Losses and Gains

As soon as Laverne left for lunch, Claire locked the clinic door behind her and walked as fast as she could without looking as if she were being chased, even though that's how she felt. Lunch could wait. She'd either exercise or have a screaming fit. She clipped past the empty store fronts and crossed over to the park. Once around and she turned toward her mother's school.

She kept moving fast for three blocks, and then slowed to a normal pace until she reached the school's sidewalk. Opening the front door, she called, "Mother?"

"I'm in the break room."

Melanie Banks, whose weight hadn't changed in thirty years, who still spent thirty minutes a day on her elliptical trainer, stood leaning over the sink, a piece of chocolate cake, iced pink, in her right hand. "Caught me." She straightened up and dusted cake crumbs from her hands. A spot of icing clung to her chin. "It's good school's over at twelve. I thought about cake, not yogurt and carrot sticks, all morning. I'm not through yet. There's ice cream."

Claire managed a laugh. "When you fall off the wagon, you go all the way."

Her mother nodded. "Join me."

"Why not? Maybe it'll get me through the afternoon."

Melanie cut a slice of cake, then opened the refrigerator's freezer compartment. "Ben and Jerry's Cherry Garcia. Want a bowl?"

"A spoon will do, if you share."

They both stood at the sink to eat, passing the pint carton back and forth. When she'd finished her cake, Claire licked her spoon. "That ought to do it."

After her mother disposed of the evidence, she pointed to the chairs at the small table. "Let's sit."

Claire scanned the room. Neat and tidy like her mother, the small space felt homey, the faux window with the outdoor scene painted in, framed by blue gingham kitchen curtains. The blue-topped, two-person dinette table and chrome chairs added to the effect.

Potpourri in an open apothecary jar lent a clove and apple scent, a welcome contrast to the disinfectant aroma of her clinic. She wished she could stay here all afternoon.

"Your dad hasn't said much about the clinic buy-out threat. But he's spent a lot of time poring over legal papers and talking on the telephone. Any new developments?"

"We meet with Panhandle Health Systems people Monday. I've stayed in the background, as Dad suggested, so he can negotiate as manager. The lawyer's strategy is to get them to expose their best offer before I ever make a move."

"Have you decided?"

Claire shrugged, her palms open and upward. "I'm confused."

"You're in a tough position."

"That's putting it mildly." She picked at a hangnail on her ring finger. "J.D. listens, but hasn't said what he thinks. He told me he'd support whatever I decide."

Her mother said, "We all will."

"That ought to make it easier. But I'm not sure it does." She shook her head and stood. "I'd better go. If I don't move now, that ice cream will put me to sleep." A long nap might make up for the past two restless nights. "Back to clinic."

"Let me know if there's anything I can do to help."

"You just did. A sugar fix helped a lot."

The one o'clock patient was a no-show. Fifteen minutes gave Claire time to make a list. Maybe moving the mass of factors swirling in her head to an orderly form would show her an answer to the main question. Would she sell the clinics or wait to see if Panhandle Health actually could or would force her out of business? Trouble was, the blank paper jeered at her and stayed empty.

After several minutes of waiting, she admitted to herself it would be nice to spend her days on the ranch, taking care of the kids, working alongside J. D., enjoying life for a few years. But she'd prefer to choose that freely, not because she was forced.

Her dad had told her she had to think like a businesswoman, not take it personally. He'd said, "You're up against people whose goal is winning, sticking to their strategy, taking a broad view. Their aim is to make money by dominating health care in the Texas Panhandle. Your clinics are one small step. They'll do whatever it takes."

Trying to assume that same business perspective, she focused on the paper. She wrote:

Current Status

- Providing important service. Paying overhead, including all salaries and benefits. No clinic cash reserve—only personal funds.
- No luck recruiting another NP yet. (Salary competition, location) Four months without means I have no time to do anything other than see patients— no planning, no quality improvement.
- Accountant values clinics, together, at $215,000, including Jackson's Pond building, owned by the clinic. Some equity, some loan balance. Check amounts.
- Clinic work often interferes with family life.
- I love taking care of patients. Most people trust me.
- Scope of care we provide does not address all needs I hoped for. (e.g. diabetes management)
- Fighting Panhandle Health requires money— accountant, attorney
- I don't like being forced

If Panhandle Health Competes and We Stay Open

- Some patients will change providers
- Panhandle Health likely to offer "bargains" (athletic physicals, immunizations, etc.) to acquire patients
- We lose revenue
- They have money to wait us out and to supply seven-day coverage of providers
- Will drain our resources and we'd eventually have to close

At 1:15, she was still writing when Laverne came to the door and said, "Your next patient's here. And your 1:30's early."

One patient followed another all afternoon, until she ushered the last one out at 4:45.

Laverne looked up as Claire dropped the final chart on the desk. "Honey, you look worn out. You get on out the back door and I'll lock up."

Claire stowed the lists she'd started in her tote bag. Worn out. Laverne was exactly right. She knew her well, read her moods. Loyal as she was, Laverne deserved to know what was happening.

Claire went up front and, after telling Laverne what she was going to say was confidential, in as few words as possible explained their "up in the air" situation. She finished by saying, "Whatever happens, I'll take care of you. Either a guaranteed job or a payout bonus."

Laverne shook her head. "I'm so sorry you have to deal with this. Life hasn't been easy on you lately." She put her arm around Claire. "Honey, you don't have to worry about me. I wasn't looking for a job when you called me to work here. But if you want to fight them, I'll stick with you. I'd work for free. You're like a daughter to me."

When Claire neared home, the sun, which spent all day behind a curtain of haze, had already sunk below a wide ledge of dark clouds. Winter days, with their skimpy ten hours of sunlight, always gave her a sense they arrived with something missing. Not real days, but excuses for days, insufficient for anything more than passing through, not lingering. And when one was as gray as today, it didn't even deserve a space on the calendar.

She let herself in the back door and met faint music. Gran and Amy often finished ballet about this time. She climbed the stairs to the ballroom as quietly as she could. So far, Amy hadn't let her watch anything more than her barre exercises. Tuesday and Thursday each week, Gran provided formal lessons for her one pupil.

Mozart, she didn't recall which sonata, filled the room. From beside the door, she watched as Amy performed a combination, then repeated it twice. She heard Gran say, "Very good. Each lesson shows improvement. You'll need a better teacher before long." Amy rushed to hug her great-grandmother, running in the classic ballerina way, demi-pointe, graceful ballet hands trailing slightly, as if blown by a gentle breeze. Claire caught her breath and stepped quietly back down the stairs.

Minutes later, as she sat at the kitchen table, Jay Frank clomped in, then shut the back door. Claire watched him open and close it a second time. He said, "What happened to this door? It's easy to close now and it wasn't before."

She said, "The house shifted. Smoothed it out. It comes and goes."

To hear him tell it—he said all this while staring in the refrigerator—school was okay and the goats were fine and he'd finished his homework. Just a normal ten-year-old. Before he left the room, a glass of milk in one hand and a banana in his shirt pocket, he stopped at the table to polish his prize buckle with a dish towel. "How was your day, Mom?" She told him she had cake and ice cream for lunch. As he left the room, he said, "Sweet!"

Amy twirled into the kitchen, followed by Gran. "Mom! Gran says I'm improving."

Standing in the doorway, Gran said, "It's true. All that barre time is paying off. Your daughter's going to need a better teacher before long. I'll go home now. I'm eager to see if they've finished the work inside. Next is the studio."

After she left, Amy perched on a kitchen stool. "I have a new friend. Can she spend the night on Friday?"

"What happened to Chelsea and Tiffany?"

Amy shrugged. "They're bullies." She hopped down and stood beside Claire. She said, "I blocked their numbers."

Claire waited for more. But Amy began peeling a banana. After a bite, she said, "Her name's Elisa Montoya."

"She moved to Calverton recently?"

Amy said, "She was home schooled until this semester. She wanted to try public school and her parents let her."

"And you're making her welcome. Are other people nice to her?"

"She's really smart and funny, too. Chelsea hates her. Can she come? You'd have to call her mom."

Claire then recalled Mrs. Montoya's name from the Home School Co-op. Amy handed her a scrap of paper. "That's her mother's number. Elisa doesn't have a cell phone. If she makes honor roll, she gets one in ninth grade."

Without even knowing Elisa, Claire liked her mother already. "I'll call her right now."

If she were in Mrs. Montoya's place, she'd want to meet the parents before letting Amy sleep over. Claire had known, at least by sight, the mothers of Amy's classmates in elementary school. Now that Amy and the rest of the handful of Jackson's Pond middle schoolers went to Calverton, Claire hadn't met any of the parents whose kids now populated Amy's classes. A better mother wouldn't use her work as an excuse for not getting to know the other parents. She told herself she'd have made the effort if Amy had asked to visit any of their homes.

When Mrs. Montoya answered, Claire introduced herself and explained why she called. She said, "Would you like to meet me before you decide? I know I would if I were you."

Mrs. Montoya immediately agreed, said she'd stop by clinic at noon tomorrow. "Elisa has mentioned Amy. We've heard so many negative things about the school, I'm happy to help her have a nice friend."

When Claire told Amy, she answered with a huge smile and a plie. Then she placed her phone in the kitchen basket atop her brother's. Claire added hers to the stack.

J.D. came in covered in dust, after plowing all day. The tiny shoots of wheat that struggled to emerge after he planted in September had given up. After three months with no rain, a week of steady twenty mile per hour wind with temperatures below freezing finished them off last week, shriveled flat. He said, "Chiseling's mighty slow work. Dusty, too."

After he cleaned up and they ate, J.D. helped Claire clear the table. He said, "Sorry I didn't have much to say at supper. I was out of steam, didn't stop for lunch because I wanted to get finished. Those tacos revived me. Hear anything from your dad?"

She shook her head no. "I have to decide whether to sell, but only after you and I discuss it."

Later, when the house was quiet and bedroom lights went out, she and J.D. sat at the kitchen table, on the same side, so they could both look at the lists she'd started earlier. She said, "The missing part is the list of what happens if we sell out."

"When?"

"We'll know after we meet with them on Monday, I guess."

"Is there any way to delay selling, if that's what you choose?"

She consulted the lists. Waiting for decisions from her husband often made her edgy. But she knew farmers and ranchers learned patience or didn't succeed. They tended to hold out hope for something good to happen. She said, "I was seeing it as yes or no. That's probably just the way they want us to see it."

She wrote two headings on the empty space following the other lists

Sell Out Now   *Sell Out As Late as Possible*

Both would require she and her dad decide on a price and on stipulations about keeping Laverne and the three staff at Calverton. She stopped writing, stared at the sheet. Then she wrote under each heading.

Positive Outcomes   *Positive Outcomes*
More time with family   *More time with family*
Can take time thinking re: later work   *Can take time thinking re: later work*

After another pause, she added two more items under Sell Out Late as Possible.

                                  Better sale price ?
                                  More Time for Transition.

The truth was, she didn't want to have to decide because every choice seemed to result in a loss. She would no longer have the clinics she'd worked so hard first to be qualified to develop and then eventually to build. If she could make herself think as a business person, not as a person whose work represented more than an enterprise for making money, to look only at the logic of the situation, at her lists, it would be easy. Maybe not easy, but deciding probably wouldn't be so painful.

She sighed, then said, "I think that's my answer." She pointed at the Sell Out As Late as Possible column. "Much as I hate to admit it, there's no sense spending my time and our money fighting a losing battle, but there's also no sense in making it easy for them, giving up too soon."

His smile showed her he agreed. But she needed to hear him say it. "If you had to decide, which would you choose?"

"Same as you did." He tipped back his chair. "Pretty soon we need to have another talk about business. About what we're going to do if it doesn't rain. Me, you, and Willa."

"Maybe it will rain. But I'm glad to be included."

She called her dad the next morning and together they agreed he'd tell the Panhandle Health representatives they'd meet in Jackson's Pond. He said, "Better to have them on our turf." He mentioned he'd heard in town that someone from Panhandle Health had scouted properties in Jackson's Pond last week, and had confirmed an option on a lot near the convenience store on the edge of town. "I believe they want us to think they'll move fast." He said they'd done the same in Hale Center, but after two months, hadn't begun construction. "Maybe they had trouble getting city permits to build. I imagine they might have some trouble in Jackson's Pond, too."

He sounded surprised when she told him her decision. "I thought I was going to have to convince you not to take them on directly."

Together they agreed on her response for Monday's meeting. She repeated her lines. "I hadn't ever thought of selling. But I'm open to considering your offer, once you provide it on paper." She added, "Don't worry, Dad. I'll be polite."

Then they discussed the rock bottom price she'd be willing to accept, $205,000, and her stipulations. He said, "There's one other thing. You should be prepared for the non-compete clause."

She sat silent for a few seconds. Then, her voice calm and controlled, she said, "They're going to have to pay." She watched the pulse at her wrist, rapid. "I *will* fight about that. I worked hard to become a nurse practitioner. Selling the clinics is one thing, not practicing at all is another. Meanwhile, I'm prepared to wait and see."

When Claire and Mrs. Montoya finished eating lunch the next day, she'd agreed to bring Elisa out to the ranch late that afternoon. Claire's time with the tall African-American woman, who seemed friendly, articulate, and determined to make her daughter's first public school experience positive, made Claire eager to meet Elisa. After Mrs. Montoya left, Claire thought of another possible positive outcome for selling out—time available to make friends.

The moment Elisa arrived, excitement showed in Amy's eyes. The two stayed in constant motion as Amy introduced Elisa to the goats, the horses, her little brother, and the ballroom. Giggles from Amy's bedroom tripped their way down the hall until after midnight.

The next morning Amy said, "Elisa wants to ask Gran if she'll let her come for ballet lessons, too. Is it all right to ask?"

"You're willing to share?"

"She's my friend."

After she left the girls poring over a recipe book, planning to make cookies, Claire went back to help Gran clear her house of dust and debris from the carpenters' work. Gran told her she'd be pleased to have another pupil.

Saturday afternoon, Claire invited Dolores Montoya in when she arrived to pick up Elisa. "I know the girls are going to ask you if Elisa can join Amy's ballet class. Let me give you some background before they spring that on you."

She led Dolores up to the ballroom and explained about her grandmother teaching her when she was a child and now Amy. She explained about the mirrors and the barre, installed when Gran lived in the house. "For years, she danced for exercise and her own enjoyment. After my grandfather died, I think it helped her even more. And I know beginning ballet again has helped Amy through a rough time with the start of puberty. Gran said she'd welcome Elisa if you agree."

Claire stood on the porch with Amy as she waved goodbye to her new friend. "Her mother said yes, I heard her." The hug Amy gave her lasted only a couple of seconds, but Claire could feel it long after.

Sunday, a day full of sunshine, with only moderate winds, she and J.D. rode to the pond. When they stopped and dismounted to let Gus and Dobie drink and amble a bit, they talked about Amy and Elisa. He said, "New friend to match her new attitude. I hope it lasts."

Gus nosed at Claire, as if he had a train to meet. She pushed him away. She said, "I think she's coming out of a phase. We were lucky her first twelve years. Remember how loveable she was all that time?"

Dobie apparently had a schedule to keep, too. He nudged at J.D. He said, "It's not supper time. You two just relax." He opened his pocket knife and squatted to push the long blade into the ground, twisting it to core out a small hole. "See that? Dry all the way down. I checked with a rod up on the north pastures—dry up there down nearly to the hard pan." He stood, wiped the blade before closing it, then returned the knife to his pocket.

Monday morning, before Claire left for work, J.D. kissed her gently. "That's for luck, even though you won't need it. You're ready."

Claire took her time sending away her final morning patient, an elderly woman accompanied by her two daughters, while the two Panhandle Health men and her dad watched from the waiting room. She led the men to her office, where she'd arranged two chairs in front of her desk and one for her dad next to hers on the other side.

After introductions, one of the men complimented the physical facilities of the two clinics. The other mentioned the clinics' good reputation. Claire wondered how he had any idea about their reputation. She offered a smile, not caring that she felt its lack of warmth. "I understand you have big plans for health care in the Panhandle. Tell me how that will affect us."

The two reeled off the company line, all the things her dad had told her. They finally got through their corporation's plans for improving care in the part of West Texas they had staked claim to and spoke of specifics. She listened without interrupting through their plans for acquiring and/or building primary care practices so that "no citizen will be more than thirty miles from health care."

Her smile hadn't wavered. She said, "That's precisely why we started our clinics. Access."

If there had been a clock on the wall in her office, she'd have been watching it, but as it was, she estimated it took another twelve minutes of corporate-speak before one of the men got around to saying they hoped to reach agreement today on a purchase contract for the two clinics.

She said, "Until you contacted Mr. Banks, I'd never thought of selling. Now that we've gotten through our start-up phase, I'm thrilled with our current operation."

Her last sentence was barely out of her mouth when the gloves came off. The younger of the two men took charge. "If you choose not to sell, our alternate plan is to open a clinic near each of yours."

Proud that she controlled her voice, she said, "So I understand. How long do you project it would take to put those competing facilities in operation?"

Neither of them answered. She said, "Maybe that's a corporate secret." Her smile began to feel genuine; it was hard not to laugh. "That's okay, don't bother to answer. Perhaps I wasn't clear. I said I hadn't *previously* thought of selling. I've now seen the standard contract you left with Mr. Banks. If you're prepared with a specific contract today, I'm open to considering it."

The quieter of the two men produced a folder, surrendered it to the man in charge. He held it while he made a short speech that sounded as if he were awarding her a prize. When she finally had it in her hand, she opened the folder and scanned the three pages inside. She looked up from the papers and said, "I'm sure you understand proper consideration will take some time. Our attorney and accountants will need copies."

She waited, but no more folders appeared. She let them see her check her watch. "If you will send those to my attention at this address, I'll get them on board and we'll give this full consideration."

The man who'd become the mouthpiece said, "Do you have questions about the contract?"

"Not at this time."

"Any immediate reactions?"

"No." She moved the folder aside and pushed her chair back from the desk. "Do you have any for me?"

For a few seconds, neither of them responded. Then the talkative one said, "We need to schedule another appointment. Next Monday?"

Claire flipped open the desk calendar she'd received as a gift and never yet used. "I'm afraid I'm booked until Friday afternoon, the fourteenth of February. I have some open times that following week, also."

They dickered about a time and date for a couple of minutes and eventually everyone settled on the seventeenth. She said, "Let's tentatively set it for eleven that morning. Depending on when our attorney and accountant receive the material."

She stood. Apparently they got the message.

After they left, her dad said, "You didn't need me at all."

That's when she let herself relax.

Together they reviewed the contract's key provisions, all the same as in the material he'd given her last week. Panhandle Health had inserted a purchase price of $205,000; they would take possession within six weeks from date of acceptance of terms, no employee guarantees. There at the bottom was the non-compete clause, her name filled in and the term—owner, Claire Havlicek, DBA Jackson's Pond Wellness, agrees not to operate a competing practice within a sixty-mile radius of either clinic, or to work as a primary care provider in any competing clinic within those boundaries for a period of two years.

Her dad said, "You'd be a threat one way or another, whether you worked for them or somewhere else."

"It's odd thinking of myself as a threat."

She shrugged, then said, "How long can we avoid giving them an answer?"

"Newman's a good, thorough attorney. Never moves in a hurry. We'll put it in his hands. You know, that "Our lawyer will talk to your lawyer" tactic. It'll take a while to bargain and see if they come up any on the sale price. And your stipulations about staff. Plus they'll need to entice you to accept the non-compete."

"I'd expect at least $50,000 for each year. That's half of what salary plus benefits would be if I worked in Lubbock. If they don't want to pay, then the clause goes." She tossed the folder in her tote bag. "Actually, a two-year vacation sounds pretty good to me right now. I haven't asked—what about you? Do you want to stay, work with them?"

"I'm considering a career in local politics. Mayor, king, whichever."

"Then we're good." For the first time since she'd heard of Panhandle Health, she let herself laugh. "That would make me Princess."

Floyd County Tribune
Thursday, March 20, 2014

JTB Data Solutions Progress

Richard Jesko, CEO of JTB Data Solutions provided an update recently on progress for his company's planned operation in Jackson's Pond.

"The first timeline target in development of our Jackson's Pond operation was completed March 13, 2014 when a contract was signed with Texas Turbines, electricity supplier from the wind farm north of Jackson's Pond. The generating facility will supply all electricity required for our data storage operation.

"Our facility design includes solar roof panels that will meet some of our other energy needs. Any excess power generated, will be made available to the grid for distributed use.

"Next comes a final decision on site purchase, which we aim to complete by April 1. A primary consideration in determining location is access to water, preferably via the Jackson's Pond water department, as fees our facility pays for water use will produce additional city revenue beyond the taxes generated by our business.

"We are on target with other aspects of development and looking forward to full operation at what promises to be a long-term collaboration between a rural community and a 21st century non-polluting industry."

County Burn Ban Extended

Floyd County Commissioners recently extended the ban on all outdoor fires through the end of May for the entire county. Citing continuing dry conditions, with no precipitation since January 15, 2014, when a meager 1 inch of snow fell, the Commissioners urged residents to cooperate to prevent wildfires.

CHAPTER 22
Top Hand

Her copy of *Harrison's Principles of Internal Medicine* fit on top of two other equally heavy textbooks in the packing box. As Claire taped it closed, she remembered how proud she'd been to buy those books. That act convinced her she was serious about becoming a nurse practitioner. Their pages now wore yellow highlighter marks and penciled comments throughout. Graduate school challenged her, the first time she'd ever actually had to study in order to do well. And she'd loved every minute.

Laverne came to the office doorway. "Do you need any help, honey?"

"No, there's not much more to do. I've already emptied my desk." She tipped her head toward one remaining shelf of books. "And these are all I lack."

"There's a patient up front. She heard you were leaving and wanted to see you one more time, said it wouldn't take long."

Claire flipped through the chart before she entered the room. It was Deborah, her patient from Idalou. After the initial six weeks of treatment, the exam at her last visit showed the genital warts completely cleared. And at least as importantly, she'd held her head up, no tears, no slumping when she left. Glad to focus on something other than locking the clinic door for the last time, Claire knocked before she walked in.

After they finished, the woman said, "You made such a difference for me by listening and not judging. I won't forget you." After the patient left—no charge for the visit—Claire attacked the packing, intent on finishing before five o'clock.

Her watch showed 4:30. Nothing left to pack, she made herself sit at her desk, perfectly still. Looking at the empty bookshelves took her back to the day she'd signed the contract with Panhandle Health. That day her books stood witness to a dream changing from intangible aspiration to hard cash.

That day, she and her dad; Newman, her attorney; the in-charge Panhandle Health man, whose name she'd chosen to forget;

and the attorney who trailed in behind him crowded her office. Negotiations completed, that little ceremony formally acknowledged the result.

Before she signed, the Panhandle Health attorney insisted on reviewing the key points. He cleared his throat and said, "Sale price $210,000 which compensates for the building in Jackson's Pond, all fixtures and furniture in both locations, and pending receivable business accounts free of any unpaid debts; written offers of immediate employment at current salary and benefits to four personnel from the Jackson's Pond and Calverton clinics; and a non-competition guarantee by Claire Havlicek for one year, area limited to a thirty-mile radius from each clinic compensated by a one-time payment of $40,000." Then, with a flourish, he handed her a pen and pointed to the line on the contract next to an orange "sign here" sticker.

She had taken her own pen from the pocket of her white lab coat, the Cross ballpoint her parents had given her as a graduation present when she completed her Master's degree, and inked in her name. Mr. Panhandle Health, managing not to smirk, handed her two checks, one purchasing the clinics from her corporation, the other for $40,000 made to her personally, for promising not to compete. The rational, logical part of her agreed with Newman—she had come out a winner.

The only thing left to do was load the boxes and lock the doors. But she didn't move. In seconds, the vague sadness she'd been pushing against all week crept from somewhere just below her heart up her throat and pushed tears from her eyes. She didn't wipe them away, just let them flow until they stopped. After that, toting boxes occupied her until closing time.

Then she walked to the front and asked Laverne if she was all right. "I'm more than all right. My husband's taking me to Padre Island. He said if I wanted to, from now on, we'd be on permanent vacation. Being married to a retired man may have some benefits."

"Thank you for everything. I would have been lost without you." Claire handed Laverne an envelope. The check inside was for $5,000. She said, "Take this and don't argue."

Laverne frowned and opened the envelope. "You didn't have

to do this. You should keep it, you know, for the next thing you do."
She tried to put it back in Claire's hand.

"Since you won't take Panhandle's job offer. This will let you
have some time off work before you start somewhere else. Or if you
decide not to, then save it for retirement. I want you to have it."

Laverne's husband honked as he pulled into the parking space
out front. She turned to Claire and said, "Okay. Then this'll be our
secret, yours and mine. I'm leaving before I cry. You take care of
yourself, honey. And if you ever need anything, you let me know."

Claire locked the front door, then walked slowly through every
space in the clinic, seeing images of patients who had been there, who
had trusted her, people she had helped. She smelled the mixture of
disinfectant and lemon-scented soap and heard children crying with
ear pain, then laughing as she tickled them to distract their interest in
her otoscope. She locked the back door, and as she left, drove around
the block to see the sign on the front window. Farther on, toward the
blinking light, she nodded to a yard sign, lettered in black, bordered in
red, that said "Vote for Ray Banks for City Council."

Neither of the kids was in the kitchen when she opened the
back door. She hadn't told them the clinics were closing, not because
it was secret, only because, well, if she admitted it to herself, she hadn't
been ready to speak calmly about it. J.D. opened the door, came in only
far enough to ask, "Want me to unload those boxes?"

She shook her head. "I don't know where I want them. Let's
wait till tomorrow."

He came the rest of the way in. "Did you tell the kids yet?"

"Let's tell them at supper. I can hardly wait to hear what they'll
line up to keep me busy."

Halfway out the door again, J.D. said, "I've already made a list
of things, myself. You just became top hand on the Jackson Ranch,
like it or not."

Later, Claire called everyone to supper and as soon as they were
seated, she said, "Before we start, Dad and I have something we want
to tell you. Now that everything's final, there will be some changes."

The smile that started when Jay Frank saw her set a pan of
green chile enchiladas on the table disappeared. His eyes widened,

giving him the appearance of a small rabbit pursued by a coyote.

Amy's fork fell from her hand, landing with a clatter against her empty dinner plate. "No! Don't do it!"

J.D. said, "Whoa, what's wrong with you two?"

Jay Frank, slumped forward, his plate pushed away, said to Amy, "See, I told you."

Amy shook her head, curls bouncing like loose springs. "Please, everything's perfect. I've been good, we both have. Please don't get a divorce."

J.D. said, "Come over here, both of you." Amy and Jay Frank did as they were told. "Listen here, we're not getting a divorce, never would consider that."

Claire reached around Jay Frank to hold him and Amy both. J.D's arm met hers. She knew the four of them in a row, parents seated, arms around the children, looked posed for a family portrait. She said, "You're right. A while back, we argued a lot. It upset you. It upset us, too. We'd both made mistakes. But we worked it out. Okay?"

Both kids went back to their chairs. Jay Frank sighed and leaned his elbows on the table. "I was scared."

Amy didn't raise her eyes, stared toward her empty plate. In a near whisper, she said, "I was mad. At both of you." Then she looked up. "Scared, too."

J.D. said, "Let's all take a deep breath and start over." He winked at Claire. "Now your mom's going to tell you our news."

Claire explained that she wouldn't be going to clinic for at least a year, and why, and that she'd be helping on the ranch and working at home. "At first I was upset and then I felt really sad. But now I'm happy I'll have more time to do lots of things I couldn't before." She scanned their faces waiting for questions, but none came. "That's probably enough for now. Anyone hungry?"

As she and J.D. sat in the family room, after the kids were in bed, she said, "I forgot to tell you Chris is going to call you tonight. I didn't get to talk but a minute when he called today. Dad had filled him in about the clinics. He said he called to remind me of all the benefits of free time. He didn't say what he needed to talk to you about."

Pushing back in his recliner, footrest extended, J.D. said, "He'd better hurry. I'm about out of steam. I'll be down for the count before long."

"Now that you have a new hand, maybe you won't have to work so hard."

"Why do you think I hired her?"

After he said that, he flipped the footrest down and stood, as if he'd been ejected. "I nearly forgot. I got this e-mail." He read from a paper he pulled from his shirt pocket. "Jan's scheduled that meeting in Abilene. Saturday, April twelfth. Starts at nine and ends at five. Want to go with me?"

"Abilene's not Ft. Worth. Plus I have a lot to do here with my new job."

"We could stay over, see the sights and come back Sunday afternoon"

She knew he was watching her face, waiting for a sign. "Thanks. But I really do have some projects here, things I've put off for about three years."

"If you say so. Well, I'll leave here early Saturday and come back right after the meeting."

Before she could respond, his phone rang. He turned it to show her CHRIS on the screen, and said, "Hey bud, what's up?"

For what seemed like a long time, J.D. listened without saying anything. Then he said, "Well sure, from my point of view it'd be great. You should check with Claire, though. Yeah, she's your competition. Here she is. Talk to me again after you finish with her."

She took the phone and said, "Sounds like a plot from what little I heard. Tell me."

Her brother explained. On the way to Taos, after being home in Jackson's Pond at Christmas—that alerted her, *Jackson's Pond, home*—and many times since, he and Andrew had concluded they were ready for some changes. "When we heard about your clinic sale, we agreed we envy you. You've succeeded. Now you can do something else if you want to."

She didn't know what to say, so she kept quiet.

Then, in a rush of words that told her he was excited, he said, "Andrew's quit his job, effective May first. Gran and Robert had suggested I might need to take a sabbatical from the gallery and focus on my painting and photography. She said I need to find balance. I won't bore you now with the reasons. So the bottom line is, I applied for a job on the Jackson Ranch."

She still didn't say anything. He said, "So, what do you think?"

"Where will you live? What will Andrew do?"

"You don't want me there?"

"No. I mean yes, I do. It's just such a surprise. Are you sure?"

"I have to run some more things by Gran. Mainly, I need to see if she's okay with us getting a ready-built house moved in next to hers, or maybe a trailer for a while."

"When?"

"I'm calling her next. I wanted to check with you and J.D. first."

"I mean when are you moving?"

"By summer for sure. Depends on details."

"You know how many times I've wished you were here. I can't quite believe you'll actually do it. I won't till I see you and hear it all. There's one thing you need to know, though. I've already been hired. So you'll have to take orders from me."

Handing the phone to her husband, she said, "He wants to complain about my being top hand. Tough!"

The next morning, even though she wasn't expected anywhere, no patients waited, Claire was up before anyone in the house. After J.D. and the kids left, about 7:45, she put on her sweat suit and running shoes, the first time she'd had them on in months, and trotted the three miles to Gran's house.

Robert's car sat in the drive. He opened the front door before she had a chance to knock. "I watched you running this way. Willa's in the bedroom. She's already begun working on our mission for the day. Myself, I prefer easing into serious labor. Prolonging my coffee. Could I offer you some?"

"What's the mission?"

"Now that the remodeling is complete and the studio ready for occupancy, all her painting supplies must be put in the proper places. Only she knows what's proper, but I will be allowed to lift and tote."

Gran said from the bedroom, "I heard that. Every woman needs a beast of burden. I claim you."

Claire said, "Gran! You really should treat your workforce better. Amy can come help if you want."

Robert said, "Definitely. I need all the support I can muster." He continued toward the studio, then turned around and, using a stage whisper said, "You heard her. She called me a beast. She doesn't feed me well, either."

He waved and went on to the studio, which now attached to the house on the north, connected by a doorway into the utility room. Claire found her grandmother sitting on her bed, surrounded by easels, sketchpads, paints, brushes, and boxes of other supplies.

"I don't want to interrupt your moving. Just one question. Did Chris call you last night?"

"He did. The three of us talked for nearly an hour."

"What do you think?"

"Coming here will be an opportunity for Chris and Andrew both. I hope they'll stay a very long time. I've already chosen a spot they could place their house if they choose to do that."

"One more question. Do you know if he also told Mother and Dad?"

"He said they were next on his list to call, right after us." She rose from the bed in a graceful motion, and walked to the east-facing window.

Claire watched her grandmother's posture and gait—erect and steady. She said, "I'll go now. Don't overdo."

Still at the window, Willa said, "I saw the sunrise from here this morning. It called to me to get back to painting. Spring always urges me. I believe it's the sunlight—more hours each day—and the position of the sun as it moves across the sky. In the morning and again in the evening, the angle creates unique colors."

"Only an artist sees that. All the rest of us have to try to learn it from you."

Saturday morning, J.D. left for Abilene at 5:30, well before sunrise. He said he should make it there in three hours or less. "I'm going the shortest route, south from Paducah. It's mostly two lane, but seldom any traffic. I'll be back near dark."

Claire kissed him, a lingering, I'll-have-a-surprise-for-you-when-you-get-home, kind of kiss. "Drive carefully. We'll be waiting for you."

After the morning routine of caring for animals, eating breakfast, and looking toward the sky hoping for rain, Claire spent most of the afternoon cleaning out her closet. Amy helped, or at least entertained herself and her mother with a stream of chatter. The pile of things destined for the Methodist Church's Clothing for the Homeless barrel grew as Claire systematically eliminated every item in any muted color and anything she hadn't worn in the past three years. A long-sleeved blouse of made of shiny brown polyester, to which Amy had said, "YUK!" landed on the stack. Claire said, "That's the last one. And that's all the work I'm doing today. Let's call Gran and Robert, and see if they want to come up and sit on the porch."

Rocking in the porch chairs, the kids perched nearby on the steps, the three adults took turns describing the changing colors of the sky as the sun sank. Their game required accurately identifying as many of the different hues of red and yellow as they could without repeating. Jay Frank said he preferred to watch for aircraft. He ran inside and came back with J.D.'s binoculars. Situated on the steps again, field glasses properly positioned, he scanned from west to south. As if air raids were imminent, he peered silently as the sky gradually darkened.

Gran and Robert left soon. They had something cooking in the crock pot. Jay Frank changed position and focused toward the west. Just after twilight turned to night, He sprang up, shouting, pointing southwest. "See those lights. That's a helicopter. It's coming this way."

He followed the movement of the dot he reckoned was a helicopter. "I think it came from Lubbock. It's moving fast."

As the lights disappeared, Claire said, "It was probably a medical helicopter from the emergency center. There must have been an accident somewhere."

Jay Frank let the glasses dangle from their strap around his neck. "I thought it might be a black helicopter, like in those spy movies."

Amy said, "I'm hungry. Do we have to wait for Dad?"

"I will, but you can go ahead. I'd hate for either one of you to starve." Claire ushered them toward the house, promising pizza, pronto. After turning on the oven to preheat and setting the table, she returned to the porch. A few minutes later she heard rotor noise. The helicopter passed, flying low this time, headed toward Lubbock.

Floyd County Tribune
May 15, 2014

County Election Results

Jackson's Pond held the only local election in the county last week, as all candidates in Calverton ran uncontested. In the Jackson's Pond election Ray Banks was elected to a full term on the City Council. He garnered 78% of the votes, with 391. His opponent Jerry McClendon received 119.

Talks Underway between RBJ Data Solutions and Texas Tech

Representatives of RBJ Data Solutions, the company currently constructing the facilities for its new data storage and service operation in Jackson's Pond, have begun discussion with Texas Tech on the topic of a cooperative program to prepare graduates in computer science and engineering for careers in data management positions.

Richard Jesko announced the activity in a press release on Tuesday. "Our facility can serve as a model laboratory for selected students planning to enter this field. We hope these discussions with educational institutions will result in learning opportunities in our site being an integral part of our operations. When RBJ contributes to students' education with work experiences and mentorship by key personnel, our company will benefit, as will the students. We also anticipate funding a scholarship program to support one or more students studying in this field at Texas Tech."

CHAPTER 23

Memorable

When the arguing ended and the meeting was finally over, just after 6:00, Jan said to him, "J.D., if you have a couple of minutes, I need to ask you something, as soon as the others leave."

J.D. thought, but didn't say it, that he only had a couple to spare. Things had already dragged on an extra hour. He'd promised to be home by dark. He hung back, waved goodbye to Trey and the others, then checked his watch. Ten minutes, maximum, was as long as he'd stay. If he didn't stop anywhere on the way, he'd make it in time.

Jan sauntered over to where he stood near the picked-clean refreshment table. She said, "I need your help. It's about my husband's will, his stepdaughter's legal actions against me."

"I don't know how I can help. Don't you have lawyers?"

"That's the problem. I don't trust the one I have. I think she's gotten to him."

"You should be talking to Trey. He knows people."

She made a shooing motion, flashing bright red fingernails. "Not him. I recently found out from a reliable source that Trey never wanted Paul to marry me in the first place." She moved closer. "Finding another lawyer's not the problem. I need a plan, how to approach this. You can help me figure out what to do next." She reached across him and picked up a bottle of water. "I think you probably understand how it is marrying into money. People like us have to be cautious."

He stepped back. "*No*, I don't understand." Checking his watch again, he said, "I have to get on the road."

In the hotel parking lot, he slammed the pickup door and jammed a key in the ignition. It wouldn't turn. That comment about him marrying into money ate at him like a coyote gnawing the neck of a downed calf. It edged out all other thoughts. Another try and the key still didn't work. He jerked it out, glared at it, saw it fit the Suburban.

The one next to it, his key, did its job, and he didn't care that his tires announced his exit. In what seemed like a minute, he passed the "reduced speed" sign outside Anson twenty miles up the road. He slowed and turned on the radio, said, "Hell no" to no one and nothing in particular, everything in general.

He made good time, and a little more than an hour later, gave himself permission for a pit stop and a Dr Pepper in Guthrie. He thought about calling Claire, but she'd be able to tell from his voice he was pissed. She never missed a thing. He didn't want to try to explain. The rest of the miles would help him settle down. So he drove on. Thirty minutes later he turned left in Paducah and started up onto the Caprock. West of Matador, passing through the curves, he cussed again when his phone rang. Jan's number. Paying close attention to the twisting road, he turned off the phone. It slid to the floor. He caught himself short of reaching for it.

Headlights on high beam, truck height, coming directly at him, on his side of the two lane road, bore down fast and swerved slightly farther into his lane. He braked, steering to the shoulder at the same time, hoping not to roll the pickup. The headlights veered sharply to his right, seeming to track him. Then they swerved to the left, and the cattle truck's trailer jackknifed. He saw it in slow motion, coming directly at him, knew he'd be crushed. Wondered how many cattle would be killed. Then the airbag slammed into his chest.

Lying on the road, not knowing how he ended up there, he moved his head to locate the sirens that pierced his brain, and saw something burst into flames across the road. Diesel fumes urged him to cough, but getting one big breath was all the work he could accomplish, even though he should run, or crawl away. He closed his eyes.

Sometime later, the screams of panicked cattle and people shouting words he couldn't make out pried his eyes open. Then the whomp, whomp of helicopter blades and bright lights made him close them again. He felt himself rising. Someone needed to call Claire. He was late.

A man standing over him asked his name, what day it was, the year, where he was, and the name of the President. Then the man said,

"Unconscious six hours." All that time he wanted to tell someone to call Claire, but couldn't make a full sentence, much less answer questions.

Next thing he knew, Claire was calling his name, crying. "J.D., you're in the hospital in Lubbock. Wake up! They told me you'd been conscious. Please open your eyes."

He tried, but all he saw was dark.

She had hold of his left hand. "I need to know you're okay. If you can't open your eyes, squeeze my hand."

He thought he did, then heard a groan that must have come from him. Giving in seemed like the best thing to do. Probably wasn't any choice.

Claire had hold of his hand, and his head hurt worse than any of the several other spots that gouged back at him if he even twitched. She said, "I know you're awake now. It's a concussion giving you that headache. They said the airbag probably saved your life. Don't try to talk. I'll be right here."

He tried opening his eyes. "What day?"

"Monday morning, April fourteenth. You lost a day."

Her voice a pillow, he let himself sleep in its comfort. Claire would answer those questions about President and all the rest.

A nurse told him it was Wednesday when he next asked. Before he said anything else, she told him Claire had gone for coffee and would be right back. Couldn't have been long and there she was. He managed to focus on her and listen as she ticked off his injuries. Pelvic fracture, collapsed right lung, three broken ribs, bruised liver, fractured left wrist, fractured right tibia, concussion. She finished by saying, "The good news is there's no bleeding on your brain, no skull fracture, no other internal injury."

"All these tubes?"

"They're necessary for now. Just do what they tell you and focus on getting well." She brushed his hair away back from his brow, her touch like soft suede. "I was so worried I'd lost you."

He smiled and his face hurt. Before sleep could overtake him again, he asked, "What about that truck driver?"

"The doctor told me he's in better condition than you. But he won't be driving truck anytime soon. When he hit you he was talking on his cell phone and his blood alcohol was way over the limit."

Eight days after the accident, out of Intensive Care and well enough to complain and worry, J.D. said to Claire, "How long are they going to keep me? We'll never be able to pay."

"They'll hold you for ransom if we don't."

It took him a bit to realize she was joking. Then she said, "I put our attorney on it. The trucking company agreed to pay all medical bills, plus a new pickup. They were liable for it. I told him to feel free to threaten to sue if they didn't."

May fifth, three weeks and a day after the helicopter took him there, J.D. left the hospital, free of chest tubes, urinary catheter, and IV lines. Still, he had to be loaded like an invalid onto the flattened back seats of the Suburban. An external rig on his broken leg, a cast on an arm, and orders not to put his full weight on that good foot, left him barely mobile. When Claire parked at the big house, she told him all the equipment needed for his home rehab, including a newly installed ramp to the porch was ready. Tag had figured out they'd need that ramp and built it one afternoon. The kids had the wheelchair waiting and Tag and Robert stood by to hoist him out of the Suburban.

As soon as they got him situated in the chair and up the ramp, he caught hold of Claire's hand. He said, "First thing in the morning, we have to talk, Willa, too. There's a lot to be done and decisions to make."

She nodded. "I'll let Gran know."

He let her roll the wheelchair to the bedroom, even though he hated to admit he needed to rest. When he saw the hospital bed, he said, "Wait. I don't want to be in here without you."

"You won't be. Not for a minute." She pointed toward the bed. "I had a twin bed moved in on the other side. The hospital bed will lower to the same level. You know I sleep better when I can touch you."

The next morning, after his first full night's sleep in weeks, he, Claire, and Willa met at the dining room table. He laid out the papers Claire picked up from his office, three sets of two sheets. He'd gotten them ready before the accident. They'd talked about this in bits and pieces, but never all of it at once and not all three of them together.

After Claire and Willa scanned the pages, he said, "That first sheet lists the cow-calf pairs, 320; cows without calves, 75; the heifers, 120; steers, 150; and the two older bulls and five younger ones we kept. If you wonder about those numbers, in the past two years, I've sold off the two-year-olds, some each time the market was up. So that took off some pressure on the grass. And last year, I held back some of the older cows from breeding, so we're seventy-five calves short from our usual.

"That date there at the bottom shows how long I think our current grass and the hay we have left will hold them. June fifteenth. All except the seven bulls. I think we can graze them together in the pond pasture for a good while."

Willa said, "Before we go further, I must say one thing." She looked away, as if listening to a distant voice, then turned back and said, "In my lifetime, there have been lots of dry years out here, often several in a row. The only real decision I've ever felt was important was whether to stick it out. After that one, everything else has direction. Choices become easier."

J. D. wasn't sure whether the weight in his chest was from broken ribs or gratefulness. Whichever it was, just then he had to duck his head so Willa wouldn't see his eyes and right on into his heart. No one had ever done so much for him, from the time he was a kid, and all for no reason. Except maybe he reminded her of someone. He shuffled his papers around and stared at them until he could make sense out loud again. He saw Claire flip to the second page.

He drew a breath that eased the weight some. "I never thought of that, because I'd never even think of not sticking it out. Would either of you?"

Claire had glanced up from the paper when he spoke. Now she shook her head. "No way. I know how to let go, but not of this place."

Willa said, "You know my answer."

He said, "Well then, I guess the rest ought to be easy."

Returning to the papers, Claire said, "Am I correct, it's either spend the reserve, plus more, to buy hay, *or* sell off some of the herd?"

Willa said, "Or a combination—sell off a few now, hold back some to sell later, if needed."

He shifted in the wheelchair so he could ease the pain and see both of them at the same time. "I hate the idea of selling off any that aren't at their best weight. Prices are down because everyone out here's selling. They're all in the same shape without rain."

J.D. had already checked on loan rates. The local bank was at around seven percent and currently paying interest on their reserve account at only one percent. Ag Credit Corporation rates were close to the same. He said, "You'll see on the second page that the reserve account has only $4000 in it—ought to be ten times that. And the operating account's not in much better shape." He didn't mention he hadn't paid himself a salary since the first of the year. "I'd hate to have to lay Tag off, even if Chris is going to be here."

Claire said, "I don't see the money from the bull sale on here."

Apparently she'd been paying more attention to the ranch business than he'd thought. He said, "Spent. The commission on the sale, vet bills for performance testing on the bulls, a couple of other bills I'd delayed—fuel, seed, and paying off the new planter." He thought a few seconds, then added, "The good thing is we're paid up to date everywhere."

The more he talked, the more he knew they should have had this discussion sooner, but he'd kept hoping it would rain. He could have handled things on his own. Claire was staring at the second sheet. She said, "So, other than rain, operating money and reserve are the main issues. Have you considered other sources of money besides the bank or Ag Credit?"

Now he wished he'd kept her up to speed. Explaining took energy and patience, and pain left him little of either to spare these days. He said, "We have plenty of collateral to get a loan—cattle, equipment. But that's gambling even more than we already are."

Willa shook her head, just slightly. She said, "There's something about the bank holding the cattle hostage that always irritated me."

He felt the same way. It's one thing to gamble, but it's another to let someone else hold your cards. "Don't forget we're going to have to deepen that north well another thirty to sixty feet. Several thousand dollars for that. It's at 245 feet now. And it's had to run so much sand through, it'll take a new pump, too. What I didn't put on here is how much we'd expect to spend for hay to get through the summer, if I can even find a source of organic hay."

Willa eyed him over the sheaf of papers. "What's your guess?"

"Including delivery, probably fifteen thousand a month, maybe more."

Claire sat back in her chair, her eyes closed. Willa poured more coffee for them. He felt himself slump. He straightened. They didn't need to see how close he felt to a failure. And he knew that desperation, not wanting to fail them, was the only reason he even entertained for a second what he'd been ready to say, but didn't, that he'd convert his retirement account to cash to take them through the summer. If he did, Willa would say she would do the same. He knew her that well. Her money should stay where it was. At her age, anything could happen. She might need it, and more. And Claire had used the clinic money, what was left, to make up for retirement she'd gone without the last four years. So he kept his mouth shut.

Claire opened her eyes, looked directly at him. "You may not like this idea, but it seems sensible to me. We should use that thirty-five thousand left of the non-competition money from Panhandle Health."

He shook his head. "That's your wages for next year. Top hand pay at Jackson Ranch."

Willa smiled at him over her coffee cup, then spoke to Claire. "Perhaps you could make it a loan at a rate better than the bank."

Another half hour passed before they'd talked enough about that idea for him to agree it made more sense than anything else. He didn't know how long it would take for him to feel okay about it.

The next morning, the kids already outside after breakfast, Claire putting away clean dishes from the dishwasher, he told her he'd thought about the loan idea overnight. He would call their accountant on Tuesday to get a proper loan document. He said, "It ought to be set up on a business basis." Then he tried to make light of it. "I knew you could do anything you set out to, but I never thought about you turning into a loan shark."

She rolled her eyes. "You can call me Mrs. Shylock."

He beckoned her to his side and whispered, "I'll call you the best wife a man could have."

The kiss that followed was interrupted by honking outside. The kids ran from the corral as he and Claire reached the front door. Andrew kept honking the horn of the Chevy pickup he'd driven, pulling a thirty-two foot travel trailer. Chris parked his SUV behind the trailer, and they both hurried to the porch.

J.D. reached up and hugged them both and said, "It's about time you got here."

Andrew said, "We made it as fast as we could."

J.D. said, "The hookup for your trailer's ready down at Willa's place. You have water; the sewage diverts into the septic system; and the electrical outlet works. If you have an air card for your computer, you'll have all the comforts." He peered toward the trailer and shook his head. "Well, maybe not *all* the comforts."

"It'll do fine until we decide about the house."

Tag wheeled his pickup in beside Chris' vehicle, making the driveway look like a used car lot. He skirted around the trailer and walked to the porch. "Chris Banks! I heard you were coming, but I still don't believe it. Sorry I missed you at Christmas."

They shook hands and Tag never batted an eye when Chris introduced Andrew as "my partner." In fact, Tag started in on a long story about how Chris had been one of his heroes in high school. He finished by saying, "I wanted to play trumpet and he had the guts to be in the band instead of playing football. Why, I'd a never passed geometry without him. And back then I might as well a had a target on my back. Weighed ninety-five pounds soppin' wet. Easy pickins for every bully in school. I wouldn't a lived through ninth grade if he hadn't taught me how to fight."

After he ran out of high school escapades to recall, Tag said, "I guess you noticed it's dryer than a popcorn fart out here." He shook his head, "Well, guess I better get back to work. Cattle to check." He stepped off the porch, then turned around. "Good to meet you, Andrew. Glad you're back, Chris."

Later, when Tag had gone, Chris said, "I wondered if you'd told him."

J.D. said, "He knows you'll be here. But, Claire said he never stopped talking long enough to hear all the details. It'll be fine. There's plenty of work to go around and his pay is in the budget." He looked directly at Chris, trying hard not to smile. "Nothing there for you, though. Anyway, as long as we don't disturb Tag's routine, he'll be happy to have you working on the place. Someone else to talk to."

After they left for Willa's, J.D. said, "Let's get this rehab business underway. I've got to get able to work. With all this help around here, I could lose my job."

The next two and a half weeks passed in a blur of physical therapy, deep sleep, and pain. Claire told him each day how much he had improved, very precisely in medical terms. Each morning, she forced him to set some new therapy goal, then left him to the professional and the kids, who checked with him hourly. In the evening, she reported on the day's ranch work she and Tag and the two new hands, Andrew and Chris, had accomplished. Chris drove the tractor up to the front of the house, just to prove he now remembered how. Thanks to Andrew's grooming, the horses sported shiny coats, trimmed hooves, and new shoes. Claire found a source for hay and arranged for delivery of the first load.

His follow-up trip to the orthopedist in Lubbock on May twenty-third liberated him from the arm cast and the fixator on his leg. Even though pain often reminded him of the pelvic fracture, his first moments of new freedom left him aching to drive on the trip home. He kept quiet on that score. As they parked back at the big house where Jay Frank waited with the wheelchair, he said, "This'll be my last ride in that. Soon as I get inside, I'll start practicing with those crutches."

When the family met at the Jackson's Pond cemetery the next afternoon, he rode upright in the front seat. And when they stopped to unload the tools and wreaths they'd need to prepare the graves for Memorial Day, he crutch-walked like a pro from his passenger-side door to the Jackson plot.

Claire had brought the artificial flower wreaths, ten in all, which took up half of the cargo area of the Suburban. She sent Jay Frank and Amy to a faucet several plots away to fill three two-gallon plastic containers with water. The easels on the wreaths wouldn't stick in the dry ground far enough to tolerate the wind. If they didn't make mud, they'd never get them dug in. Two hoes, a shovel, and a spading fork filled the rest of the space. Out here perpetual care meant families tended the gravesites and the cemetery association hauled off trash.

Jackson's Pond Cemetery sat on the east side of town, down the highway a half mile from the blinking light, and a quarter mile south on a dirt road. Populated by graves from as far back as 1889, it was the resting place for many who had served in the military. Each year, the local chapter of the Veterans of Foreign Wars made certain each of those graves was marked by a small American flag.

As soon as she delivered the water, Amy ran toward the VFW group. Her friend Elisa, along with her parents and two brothers, each carrying an armload of flags, apparently were the troops assigned this year.

Claire said, "I'll introduce you to my friend." Her claiming someone as a friend surprised him. She knew a lot of women but never spent time doing the things with them he thought women friends did—shop, trade recipes, share secrets. Then she added, "Let's invite them to the picnic on Monday."

He shrugged and said, "Sure."

After chatting briefly, promising to come to the house Memorial Day, the Montoyas proceeded with the flag-planting. J.D. doled out wreaths and tools, and they all set to work on the ten graves they'd come to care for.

The others arrived, and Willa's family, that's how he thought of the clan he was part of, moved among the headstones, digging weeds, edging around concrete lot markers, picking up remnants of flags and wreaths from prior years. As the nine others began, working silently, J.D. leaned against the Suburban and called himself lucky.

Then as they moved along, stories of the people in those graves came from one, then another, as if there'd been eulogies planned. Willa stayed behind near Frank's and Baby George's graves when the others continued to the Lofland plot. Melanie stood by her mother, touching her arm, her own head bowed.

It took him a while to get to his parents' graves, and when he got there, J. D. leaned forward on his crutches, resting. He thought about his father and Frank Jackson, and hoped they were both proud of him for sticking it out, doing his best. He knew they both had. Jay Frank, wielding a hoe, staying beside him since they started, said, "Does it make you sad to come here?"

"Not sad, just serious."

His son hacked away a batch of mustard weed near the single headstone marked Havlicek above both his grandparents' names. He stopped and asked, "Do people who are dead watch us?"

J.D. took his time coming up with an answer. "I can't say for sure, but I think they do, now and then, when they're not busy with chores."

"Can they make things happen for people who're alive?"

J.D. smiled at his old-beyond-his-years son and said, "Like make it rain? If they could, I know both your granddad Jacob and great-granddad Frank would do that." He watched to see if the boy was listening. "I'm pretty sure they did all they could here on earth when they were alive, tried to teach us and show us how to do the right things. Now that they're gone, it's up to us."

Just then, he sensed a movement in dry grass in the plot next to them. A snake, reddish brown, about two feet long, essed his way toward them, making a thin trail in the dust. Then, as if it had just noticed them, it stopped and coiled. Jay Frank froze, holding the hoe with both hands. He said, "It's okay, Dad. I won't kill it. He's a bull snake, not a rattler. I can tell the difference."

Seconds later, the snake flicked its tail as it traveled away.

By noon on Monday, Claire had fried enough chicken for an army. The refrigerator shelves bulged with coleslaw, potato salad, the chicken, plus dip and raw vegetables. Soft drinks and beer were iced in a cooler in the utility room. J.D. directed the kids where to set up tables and chairs for fifteen out on the front porch.

He found Claire in the kitchen, staring out the window. He said, "I'll get the kids to take out some extra chairs. Anything else?"

She said, "Do you have a Plan B?"

"Always. Several. Which one you interested in?"

"The one in case of rain."

He'd always known optimism kept her from ever giving up. "I haven't needed that kind of plan in so long, I don't even remember it.

Besides, it's mostly clear right now."

She said, "I have a feeling we'll get rain this afternoon or evening."

"Nothing in the forecast this morning." He looked over her shoulder and out the window. Corralled by him, his crutches, and the kitchen sink, she turned and kissed him. If he'd put his arms around her the way he wanted to, the crutches would clatter and bring in the kids. He said, "Tell you what; if it rains, not a shower, a real rain, I'll personally move all the chairs and tables anywhere you want them, in a ten mile radius. That's right after I fling away the crutches and walk unassisted. I'll give thanks for miracles."

"Fine, make jokes. I'll remind you of what you said. I have a feeling you better practice that unassisted walking thing."

Close to two, Melanie and Ray arrived, bringing loads of food hidden under foil. One dish that passed by smelled to J.D. like the chocolate-pecan sheet cake his mother used to make. A little bit later, Willa, Chris, Andrew, and Robert rolled up.

When the Montoyas arrived at three, J.D. took care of introducing them, and before long, conversation and beer occupied the adults. Jay Frank led the Montoya boys off to see his goats, and Amy and Elisa disappeared upstairs to their dance studio.

Being a good host meant J.D. should talk to every person on the porch, make sure they had all the beer they wanted. So, he made the rounds, joining in, making an effort to smile even though the ache in his hip and leg seemed to be permanent. He got Montoya started telling about his retirement job at the prison outside Plainview and left him explaining his military career to Andrew and Ray. Robert, who never met a stranger, had Willa, Claire, her mother, and Mrs. Montoya all involved listening to a tale of some sort about lecturing on a cruise ship. And there was Chris, a camera around his neck and another in a pocket of his gear vest, moving among the groups, stopping briefly, pretending to listen, occupying himself with the cameras, hiding behind the lenses.

J.D. hoped Claire's prediction panned out. More than his usual sort of vague-desperation hope, this felt like there might actually be a possibility. But even if it did rain and rained on for days, one good rain won't break a drought. And for that matter, nothing else he could recall ever worked out immediately. At least nothing good.

While the others visited, J.D. crutched to the porch edge far enough to get a good look at the sky all the way around, although the southwest was the likeliest source for a good cloud this time of year. Sure enough, down low, a dark gray-blue line had formed, blurring the horizon's edge, off to the southwest. But he didn't smell any rain in the faint breeze.

Claire sent Amy and Elisa to the goat pens to bring the boys in to wash up. Then she and her mother and Dolores Montoya went in to bring food out to the table. Just then a gust rose and pushed dust across the yard. J.D. opened the screen and yelled inside, "Maybe we ought to wait a few minutes, see if the wind lays."

The women reversed direction and came back out with two bowls of chips and some dip that made the rounds from hand to hand. Minutes later, the wind steadied at a stiff breeze, and soon after, the first drops of rain fell. Big, fat drops that made rhythmic sounds on the roof. Its tune then quickly muffled to the silence of a dusting of snow similar to the hush that came with the last moisture they'd had, back in January. He warned himself not to expect anything more than a fast-moving shower today, lasting only a few minutes, accomplishing nothing more than settling a little dust.

The wind died as quickly as it had gusted. Rain continued, falling steadily, straight down, as if a gentle hand were pouring endless gallons through a fine sieve. The water sounds came together to form a melody, volume increasing. As Chris and Andrew moved the tables nearer to the house, away from the porch edges, but not indoors, J.D. couldn't help smiling.

No one seemed to mind waiting. J.D. roved among them again. To tell the truth, he eavesdropped. He picked up bits of conversation—Chris saying to Robert he thought he'd figured out what the story was; Andrew telling Willa he had a line on a job in Matador as a veterinary assistant; Claire agreeing to teach the home school students first aid; the Montoya boys telling their father they wanted some goats, they'd take care of them. And laughter, often. He looked across the porch and saw Amy and Elisa, heads close together, arms linked, practicing a combination of dance steps.

Claire eased up beside him as he stood near the porch steps. She said, "You'll recall, I had a feeling."

An hour later, rain still falling, the food filled the center of the large table they'd made of the two pushed together. J.D. sat in the center on one side, Claire next to him on his right, her mother on her other side. Amy and Elisa bookended Willa. Jay Frank squeezed in beside J.D. on his left, and the others filled in.

Claire touched his hand and pointed toward the western sky. Through the curtain of raindrops, he saw the descending sun send a single broad oblique ray to pierce the lower edge of the dark clouds, as if binding together sky and earth. Then a second beam emerged under the heavy gray clouds, suggesting contrast between times past and the promise of the future, glowing golden.

Chris moved across the porch firing a flurry of shots of the horizon's changing light, snapping from different angles. J. D. knew that somewhere among his brother-in-law's images, there would be one that captured that moment, a brief time where all his doubts were suspended.

When they had all mounded their plates, before anyone began eating, Willa lifted a hand. "I'd like to say grace."

As they bowed their heads, Claire reached for J.D.'s hand, held it tight. Willa prayed, "Almighty Creator, we give thanks for all our blessings, particularly for this day set aside to remember those no longer with us. And we rejoice thankfully for this gift of rain. Bless us all, family and friends. Amen."

Echoes of "Amen" rippled among them, a melody that complimented the rain. From Robert's strong bass, through the soprano and tenor chimes of the kids, every voice at the table joined.

J.D. had never heard Willa pray before. He looked up and saw her watching him. Then he nodded to her, and clutching Claire's hand, added his "Amen."

CONNECT WITH THE AUTHOR

For more information about the author or to contact her about presentations and book signing events, please visit www.tjoneswrites.net http://facebook.com/slantedlight .